The
Nightingale

Signed Edition

The
Nightingale

Also by Kristin Hannah

Fly Away

Home Front

Night Road

Winter Garden

True Colors

Firefly Lane

Magic Hour

Comfort & Joy

The Things We Do for Love

Between Sisters

Distant Shores

Summer Island

Angel Falls

On Mystic Lake

Home Again

Waiting for the Moon

When Lightning Strikes

If You Believe

Once in Every Life

The Enchantment

A Handful of Heaven

The Nightingale

Kristin Hannah

ST. MARTIN'S PRESS
New York

THE NIGHTINGALE. Copyright © 2015 by Kristin Hannah. All rights reserved.
Printed in the United States of America.
For information, address St. Martin's Press,
175 Fifth Avenue, New York, N.Y. 10010.

www.stmartins.com

Designed by Kathryn Parise
Endpaper photograph copyright © Jim Barber

The Library of Congress Cataloging-in-Publication Data is available upon request.

ISBN 978-0-312-57722-3 (hardcover)
ISBN 978-1-4668-5060-6 (e-book)

St. Martin's Press books may be purchased for educational, business, or promotional use. For information on bulk purchases,
please contact the Macmillan Corporate and Premium Sales Department at 1-800-221-7945, extension 5442, or write to special
markets@macmillan.com.

First Edition: February 2015

10 9 8 7 6 5 4 3 2 1

To Matthew Shear. Friend. Mentor. Champion. You are missed.
And to Kaylee Nova Hannah, the newest star in our world:
Welcome, baby girl.

The
Nightingale

ONE

April 9, 1995
The Oregon Coast

*I*f I have learned anything in this long life of mine, it is this: In love we find out who we want to be; in war we find out who we are. Today's young people want to know everything about everyone. They think talking about a problem will solve it. I come from a quieter generation. We understand the value of forgetting, the lure of reinvention.

Lately, though, I find myself thinking about the war and my past, about the people I lost.

Lost.

It makes it sound as if I misplaced my loved ones; perhaps I left them where they don't belong and then turned away, too confused to retrace my steps.

They are not lost. Nor are they in a better place. They are gone. As I approach the end of my years, I know that grief, like regret, settles into our DNA and remains forever a part of us.

I have aged in the months since my husband's death and my diagnosis. My skin has the crinkled appearance of wax paper that someone has tried to flatten and reuse. My eyes fail me often—in the darkness, when headlights flash, when rain falls. It is unnerving, this new unreliability in my vision. Perhaps that's why I find myself looking backward. The past has a clarity I can no longer see in the present.

I want to imagine there will be peace when I am gone, that I will see all of the people I have loved and lost. At least that I will be forgiven.

I know better, though, don't I?

⌘

My house, named The Peaks by the lumber baron who built it more than a hundred years ago, is for sale, and I am preparing to move because my son thinks I should.

He is trying to take care of me, to show how much he loves me in this most difficult of times, and so I put up with his controlling ways. What do I care where I die? That is the point, really. It no longer matters where I live. I am boxing up the Oregon beachside life I settled into nearly fifty years ago. There is not much I want to take with me. But there is one thing.

I reach for the hanging handle that controls the attic steps. The stairs unfold from the ceiling like a gentleman extending his hand.

The flimsy stairs wobble beneath my feet as I climb into the attic, which smells of must and mold. A single, hanging lightbulb swings overhead. I pull the cord.

It is like being in the hold of an old steamship. Wide wooden planks panel the walls; cobwebs turn the creases silver and hang in skeins from the indentations between the planks. The ceiling is so steeply pitched that I can stand upright only in the center of the room.

I see the rocking chair I used when my grandchildren were young, then an old crib and a ratty-looking rocking horse set on rusty springs, and the chair my daughter was refinishing when she got sick. Boxes are tucked along the wall, marked "Xmas," "Thanksgiving," "Easter," "Halloween," "Serveware," "Sports." In those boxes are the things I don't use much anymore but can't bear to part with. For me, admitting that I won't decorate a tree for Christmas is giving up, and I've never been good at letting go. Tucked in the corner is what I am looking for: an ancient steamer trunk covered in travel stickers.

With effort, I drag the heavy trunk to the center of the attic, directly beneath the hanging light. I kneel beside it, but the pain in my knees is piercing, so I slide onto my backside.

For the first time in thirty years, I lift the trunk's lid. The top tray is full of baby memorabilia. Tiny shoes, ceramic hand molds, crayon drawings populated by stick figures and smiling suns, report cards, dance recital pictures.

I lift the tray from the trunk and set it aside.

The mementos in the bottom of the trunk are in a messy pile: several faded leather-bound journals; a packet of aged postcards tied together with a blue satin ribbon; a cardboard box bent in one corner; a set of slim books of poetry by Julien Rossignol; and a shoebox that holds hundreds of black-and-white photographs.

On top is a yellowed, faded piece of paper.

My hands are shaking as I pick it up. It is a *carte d'identité*, an identity card, from the war. I see the small, passport-sized photo of a young woman. *Juliette Gervaise.*

"Mom?"

I hear my son on the creaking wooden steps, footsteps that match my heartbeats. Has he called out to me before?

"Mom? You shouldn't be up here. Shit. The steps are unsteady." He comes to stand beside me. "One fall and—"

I touch his pant leg, shake my head softly. I can't look up. "Don't" is all I can say.

He kneels, then sits. I can smell his aftershave, something subtle and spicy, and also a hint of smoke. He has sneaked a cigarette outside, a habit he gave up decades ago and took up again at my recent diagnosis. There is no reason to voice my disapproval: He is a doctor. He knows better.

My instinct is to toss the card into the trunk and slam the lid down, hiding it again. It's what I have done all my life.

Now I am dying. Not quickly, perhaps, but not slowly, either, and I feel compelled to look back on my life.

"Mom, you're crying."

"Am I?"

I want to tell him the truth, but I can't. It embarrasses and shames me, this failure. At my age, I should not be afraid of anything—certainly not my own past.

I say only, "I want to take this trunk."

"It's too big. I'll repack the things you want into a smaller box."

I smile at his attempt to control me. "I love you and I am sick again. For these reasons, I have let you push me around, but I am not dead yet. I want this trunk with me."

"What can you possibly need in it? It's just our artwork and other junk."

If I had told him the truth long ago, or had danced and drunk and sung more, maybe he would have seen *me* instead of a dependable, ordinary mother. He loves a version of me that is incomplete. I always thought it was what I wanted: to be loved and admired. Now I think perhaps I'd like to be known.

"Think of this as my last request."

I can see that he wants to tell me not to talk that way, but he's afraid his voice will catch. He clears his throat. "You've beaten it twice before. You'll beat it again."

We both know this isn't true. I am unsteady and weak. I can neither sleep nor eat without the help of medical science. "Of course I will."

"I just want to keep you safe."

I smile. Americans can be so naïve.

Once I shared his optimism. I thought the world was safe. But that was a long time ago.

"Who is Juliette Gervaise?" Julien says and it shocks me a little to hear that name from him.

I close my eyes and in the darkness that smells of mildew and bygone lives, my mind casts back, a line thrown across years and continents. Against my will—or maybe in tandem with it, who knows anymore?—I remember.

TWO

The lights are going out all over Europe;
We shall not see them lit again in our lifetime.
—Sir Edward Grey, on World War I

August 1939
France

Vianne Mauriac left the cool, stucco-walled kitchen and stepped out into her front yard. On this beautiful summer morning in the Loire Valley, everything was in bloom. White sheets flapped in the breeze and roses tumbled like laughter along the ancient stone wall that hid her property from the road. A pair of industrious bees buzzed among the blooms; from far away, she heard the chugging purr of a train and then the sweet sound of a little girl's laughter.

Sophie.

Vianne smiled. Her eight-year-old daughter was probably running through the house, making her father dance attendance on her as they readied for their Saturday picnic.

"Your daughter is a tyrant," Antoine said, appearing in the doorway.

He walked toward her, his pomaded hair glinting black in the sunlight. He'd been working on his furniture this morning—sanding a chair that was already as soft as satin—and a fine layer of wood dust peppered his face and shoulders. He was a big man, tall and broad shouldered, with a rough face and a dark stubble that took constant effort to keep from becoming a beard.

He slipped an arm around her and pulled her close. "I love you, V."

"I love you, too."

It was the truest fact of her world. She loved everything about this man, his smile, the way he mumbled in his sleep and laughed after a sneeze and sang opera in the shower.

She'd fallen in love with him fifteen years ago, on the school play yard, before she'd even known what love was. He was her first everything—first kiss, first love, first lover. Before him, she'd been a skinny, awkward, anxious girl given to stuttering when she got scared, which was often.

A motherless girl.

You will be the adult now, her father had said to Vianne as they walked up to this very house for the first time. She'd been fourteen years old, her eyes swollen from crying, her grief unbearable. In an instant, this house had gone from being the family's summer house to a prison of sorts. Maman had been dead less than two weeks when Papa gave up on being a father. Upon their arrival here, he'd not held her hand or rested a hand on her shoulder or even offered her a handkerchief to dry her tears.

B-but I'm just a girl, she'd said.

Not anymore.

She'd looked down at her younger sister, Isabelle, who still sucked her thumb at four and had no idea what was going on. Isabelle kept asking when Maman was coming home.

When the door opened, a tall, thin woman with a nose like a water spigot and eyes as small and dark as raisins appeared.

These are the girls? the woman had said.

Papa nodded.

They will be no trouble.

It had happened so fast. Vianne hadn't really understood. Papa dropped off his daughters like soiled laundry and left them with a stranger. The girls were so far apart in age it was as if they were from different families. Vianne had wanted to comfort Isabelle—meant to—but Vianne had been in so much pain it was impossible to think of anyone else, especially a child as willful and impatient and loud as Isabelle. Vianne still remembered those first days here: Isabelle shrieking and Madame spanking her. Vianne had pleaded with her sister, saying, again and again, *Mon Dieu, Isabelle, quit screeching. Just do as she bids,* but even at four, Isabelle had been unmanageable.

Vianne had been undone by all of it—the grief for her dead mother, the pain of her father's abandonment, the sudden change in their circumstances, and Isabelle's cloying, needy loneliness.

It was Antoine who'd saved Vianne. That first summer after Maman's death, the two of them had become inseparable. With him, Vianne had found an escape. By the time she was sixteen, she was pregnant; at seventeen, she was married and the mistress of Le Jardin. Two months later, she had a miscarriage and she lost herself for a while. There was no other way to put it. She'd crawled into her grief and cocooned it around her, unable to care about anyone or anything—certainly not a needy, wailing four-year-old sister.

But that was old news. Not the sort of memory she wanted on a beautiful day like today.

She leaned against her husband as their daughter ran up to them, announcing, "I'm ready. Let's go."

"Well," Antoine said, grinning. "The princess is ready and so we must move."

Vianne smiled as she went back into the house and retrieved her hat from the hook by the door. A strawberry blonde, with porcelain-thin skin and sea-blue eyes, she always protected herself from the sun. By the time she'd settled the wide-brimmed straw hat in place and collected her lacy gloves and picnic basket, Sophie and Antoine were already outside the gate.

Vianne joined them on the dirt road in front of their home. It was barely wide enough for an automobile. Beyond it stretched acres of hayfields, the green here and there studded with red poppies and blue cornflowers. Forests grew in patches. In this corner of the Loire Valley, fields were more likely to be growing hay than grapes. Although less than two hours from Paris by train, it felt like a different world altogether. Few tourists visited, even in the summer.

Now and then an automobile rumbled past, or a bicyclist, or an ox-driven cart, but for the most part, they were alone on the road. They lived nearly a mile from Carriveau, a town of less than a thousand souls that was known mostly as a stopping point on the pilgrimage of Ste. Jeanne d'Arc. There was no industry in town and few jobs—except for those at the air-field that was the pride of Carriveau. The only one of its kind for miles.

In town, narrow cobblestoned streets wound through ancient limestone buildings that leaned clumsily against one another. Mortar crumbled from stone walls, ivy hid the decay that lay beneath, unseen but always felt. The village had been cobbled together piecemeal—crooked streets, uneven steps, blind alleys—over hundreds of years. Colors enlivened the stone buildings: red awnings ribbed in black metal, ironwork balconies decorated with geraniums in terra-cotta planters. Everywhere there was something to tempt the eye: a display case of pastel macarons, rough willow baskets filled with cheese and ham and *saucisson*, crates of colorful tomatoes and aubergines and cucumbers. The cafés were full on this sunny day. Men sat around metal tables, drinking coffee and smoking hand-rolled brown cigarettes and arguing loudly.

A typical day in Carriveau. Monsieur LaChoa was sweeping the street in front of his *saladerie*, and Madame Clonet was washing the window of her hat shop, and a pack of adolescent boys was strolling through town, shoulder to shoulder, kicking bits of trash and passing a cigarette back and forth.

At the end of town, they turned toward the river. At a flat, grassy spot along the shore, Vianne set down her basket and spread out a blanket in the shade of a chestnut tree. From the picnic basket, she withdrew a crusty baguette, a wedge of rich, double-cream cheese, two apples, some slices of paper-thin Bayonne ham, and a bottle of Bollinger '36. She poured her husband a glass of champagne and sat down beside him as Sophie ran toward the riverbank.

The day passed in a haze of sunshine-warmed contentment. They talked and laughed and shared their picnic. It wasn't until late in the day, when Sophie was off with her fishing pole and Antoine was making their daughter a crown of daisies, that he said, "Hitler will suck us all into his war soon."

War.

It was all anyone could talk about these days, and Vianne didn't want to hear it. Especially not on this lovely summer day.

She tented a hand across her eyes and stared at her daughter. Beyond the river, the green Loire Valley lay cultivated with care and precision. There were no fences, no boundaries, just miles of rolling green fields and patches of trees and the occasional stone house or barn. Tiny white blossoms floated like bits of cotton in the air.

She got to her feet and clapped her hands. "Come, Sophie. It's time to go home."

"You can't ignore this, Vianne."

"Should I look for trouble? Why? You are here to protect us."

Smiling (too brightly, perhaps), she packed up the picnic and gathered her family and led them back to the dirt road.

In less than thirty minutes, they were at the sturdy wooden gate of Le Jardin, the stone country house that had been in her family for three hundred years. Aged to a dozen shades of gray, it was a two-story house with blue-shuttered windows that overlooked the orchard. Ivy climbed up the two chimneys and covered the bricks beneath. Only seven acres of the original parcel were left. The other two hundred had been sold off over the course of two centuries as her family's fortune dwindled. Seven acres was plenty for Vianne. She couldn't imagine needing more.

Vianne closed the door behind them. In the kitchen, copper and cast-iron pots and pans hung from an iron rack above the stove. Lavender and rosemary and thyme hung in drying bunches from the exposed timber beams of the ceiling. A copper sink, green with age, was big enough to bathe a small dog in.

The plaster on the interior walls was peeling here and there to reveal paint from years gone by. The living room was an eclectic mix of furniture and fabrics—tapestried settee, Aubusson rugs, antique Chinese porcelain, chintz and toile. Some of the paintings on the wall were excellent—perhaps important—and some were amateurish. It had the jumbled, cobbled-together look of lost money and bygone taste—a little shabby, but comfortable.

She paused in the salon, glancing through the glass-paned doors that led to the backyard, where Antoine was pushing Sophie on the swing he'd made for her.

Vianne hung her hat gently on the hook by the door and retrieved her apron, tying it in place. While Sophie and Antoine played outside, Vianne cooked supper. She wrapped a pink pork tenderloin in thick-cut bacon, tied it in twine, and browned it in hot oil. While the pork roasted in the oven, she made the rest of the meal. At eight o'clock—right on time—she called everyone to supper and couldn't help smiling at the thundering of feet and the chatter of conversation and the squealing of chair legs scraping across the floor as they sat down.

Sophie sat at the head of the table, wearing the crown of daisies Antoine had made for her at the riverbank.

Vianne set down the platter. A delicious fragrance wafted upward— roasted pork and crispy bacon and apples glazed in a rich wine sauce, resting on a bed of browned potatoes. Beside it was a bowl of fresh peas, swimming in butter seasoned with tarragon from the garden. And of course there was the baguette Vianne had made yesterday morning.

As always, Sophie talked all through supper. She was like her Tante Isabelle in that way—a girl who couldn't hold her tongue.

When at last they came to dessert—*ile flottante,* islands of toasted meringue floating in a rich crème anglaise—there was a satisfied silence around the table.

"Well," Vianne said at last, pushing her half-empty dessert plate away, "it's time to do the dishes."

"Ahh, Maman," Sophie whined.

"No whining," Antoine said. "Not at your age."

Vianne and Sophie went into the kitchen, as they did each night, to their stations—Vianne at the deep copper sink, Sophie at the stone counter—and began washing and drying the dishes. Vianne could smell the sweet, sharp scent of Antoine's after-supper cigarette wafting through the house.

"Papa didn't laugh at a single one of my stories today," Sophie said as Vianne placed the dishes back in the rough wooden rack that hung on the wall. "Something is wrong with him."

"No laughter? Well, certainly that *is* cause for alarm."

"He's worried about the war."

The war. Again.

Vianne shooed her daughter out of the kitchen. Upstairs, in Sophie's bedroom, Vianne sat on the double bed, listening to her daughter chatter as she put on her pajamas and brushed her teeth and got into bed.

Vianne leaned down to kiss her good night.

"I'm scared," Sophie said. "Is war coming?"

"Don't be afraid," Vianne said. "Papa will protect us." But even as she said it, she remembered another time, when her maman had said to her, *Don't be afraid.*

It was when her own father had gone off to war.

Sophie looked unconvinced. "But—"

"But nothing. There is nothing to worry about. Now go to sleep."

She kissed her daughter again, letting her lips linger on the little girl's cheek.

Vianne went down the stairs and headed for the backyard. Outside, the night was sultry; the air smelled of jasmine. She found Antoine sitting in one of the iron café chairs out on the grass, his legs stretched out, his body slumped uncomfortably to one side.

She came up beside him, put a hand on his shoulder. He exhaled smoke and took another long drag on the cigarette. Then he looked up at her. In the moonlight, his face appeared pale and shadowed. Almost unfamiliar. He reached into the pocket of his vest and pulled out a piece of paper. "I have been mobilized, Vianne. Along with most men between eighteen and thirty-five."

"Mobilized? But . . . we are not at war. I don't—"

"I am to report for duty on Tuesday."

"But . . . but . . . you're a postman."

He held her gaze and suddenly she couldn't breathe. "I am a soldier now, it seems."

THREE

Vianne knew something of war. Not its clash and clatter and smoke and blood, perhaps, but the aftermath. Though she had been born in peacetime, her earliest memories were of the war. She remembered watching her maman cry as she said good-bye to Papa. She remembered being hungry and always being cold. But most of all, she remembered how different her father was when he came home, how he limped and sighed and was silent. That was when he began drinking and keeping to himself and ignoring his family. After that, she remembered doors slamming shut, arguments erupting and disappearing into clumsy silences, and her parents sleeping in different rooms.

The father who went off to war was not the one who came home. She had tried to be loved by him; more important, she had tried to keep loving him, but in the end, one was as impossible as the other. In the years since he'd shipped her off to Carriveau, Vianne had made her own life. She sent her father Christmas and birthday cards, but she'd never received one in return, and they rarely spoke. What was there left to say? Unlike Isabelle, who seemed incapable of letting go, Vianne understood—and accepted—that when Maman had died, their family had been irreparably broken. He was a man who simply refused to be a father to his children.

"I know how war scares you," Antoine said.

"The Maginot Line will hold," she said, trying to sound convincing. "You'll be home by Christmas." The Maginot Line was miles and miles of concrete walls and obstacles and weapons that had been constructed along the German border after the Great War to protect France. The Germans couldn't breach it.

Antoine took her in his arms. The scent of jasmine was intoxicating, and she knew suddenly, certainly, that from now on, whenever she smelled jasmine, she would remember this good-bye.

"I love you, Antoine Mauriac, and I expect you to come home to me."

Later, she couldn't remember them moving into the house, climbing the stairs, lying down in bed, undressing each other. She remembered only being naked in his arms, lying beneath him as he made love to her in a way he never had before, with frantic, searching kisses and hands that seemed to want to tear her apart even as they held her together.

"You're stronger than you think you are, V," he said afterward, when they lay quietly in each other's arms.

"I'm not," she whispered too quietly for him to hear.

The next morning, Vianne wanted to keep Antoine in bed all day, maybe even convince him that they should pack their bags and run like thieves in the night.

But where would they go? War hung over all of Europe.

By the time she finished making breakfast and doing the dishes, a headache throbbed at the base of her skull.

"You seem sad, Maman," Sophie said.

"How can I be sad on a gorgeous summer's day when we are going to visit our best friends?" Vianne smiled a bit too brightly.

It wasn't until she was out the front door and standing beneath one of the apple trees in the front yard that she realized she was barefoot.

"Maman," Sophie said impatiently.

"I'm coming," she said, as she followed Sophie through the front yard, past the old dovecote (now a gardening shed) and the empty barn. Sophie opened the back gate and ran into the well-tended neighboring yard, toward a small stone cottage with blue shutters.

Sophie knocked once, got no answer, and went inside.

"Sophie!" Vianne said sharply, but her admonishment fell on deaf ears. Manners were unnecessary at one's best friend's house, and Rachel de Champlain had been Vianne's best friend for fifteen years. They'd met only a month after Papa had so ignominiously dropped his children off at Le Jardin.

They'd been a pair back then: Vianne, slight and pale and nervous, and Rachel, as tall as the boys, with eyebrows that grew faster than a lie and a voice like a foghorn. Outsiders, both of them, until they met. They'd become inseparable in school and stayed friends in all the years since. They'd gone to university together and both had become schoolteachers. They'd even been pregnant at the same time. Now they taught in side-by-side classrooms at the local school.

Rachel appeared in the open doorway, holding her newborn son, Ariel.

A look passed between the women. In it was everything they felt and feared.

Vianne followed her friend into a small, brightly lit interior that was as neat as a pin. A vase full of wildflowers graced the rough wooden trestle table flanked by mismatched chairs. In the corner of the dining room was a leather valise, and sitting on top of it was the brown felt fedora that Rachel's husband, Marc, favored. Rachel went into the kitchen for a small crockery plate full of *canelés*. Then the women headed outside.

In the small backyard, roses grew along a privet hedge. A table and four chairs sat unevenly on a stone patio. Antique lanterns hung from the branches of a chestnut tree.

Vianne picked up a *canelé* and took a bite, savoring the vanilla-rich cream center and crispy, slightly burned-tasting exterior. She sat down.

Rachel sat down across from her, with the baby asleep in her arms. Silence seemed to expand between them and fill with their fears and misgivings.

"I wonder if he'll know his father," Rachel said as she looked down at her baby.

"They'll be changed," Vianne said, remembering. Her father had been in the Battle of the Somme, in which more than three-quarters of a million men had lost their lives. Rumors of German atrocities had come home with the few who survived.

Rachel moved the infant to her shoulder, patted his back soothingly. "Marc is no good at changing diapers. And Ari loves to sleep in our bed. I guess that'll be all right now."

Vianne felt a smile start. It was a little thing, this joke, but it helped. "Antoine's snoring is a pain in the backside. I should get some good sleep."

"And we can have poached eggs for supper."

"Only half the laundry," she said, but then her voice broke. "I'm not strong enough for this, Rachel."

"Of course you are. We'll get through it together."

"Before I met Antoine . . ."

Rachel waved a hand dismissively. "I know. I know. You were as skinny as a branch, you stuttered when you got nervous, and you were allergic to everything. I know. I was there. But that's all over now. You'll be strong. You know why?"

"Why?"

Rachel's smile faded. "I know I'm big—statuesque, as they like to say when they're selling me brassieres and stockings—but I feel . . . undone by this, V. I am going to need to lean on you sometimes, too. Not with *all* my weight, of course."

"So we can't both fall apart at the same time."

"*Voilà,*" Rachel said. "Our plan. Should we open a bottle of cognac now, or gin?"

"It's ten o'clock in the morning."

"You're right. Of course. A French 75."

On Tuesday morning when Vianne awoke, sunlight poured through the window, glazing the exposed timbers.

Antoine sat in the chair by the window, a walnut rocker he'd made during Vianne's second pregnancy. For years that empty rocker had mocked them. The miscarriage years, as she thought of them now. Desolation in a land of plenty. Three lost lives in four years; tiny thready heartbeats, blue hands. And then, miraculously: a baby who survived. Sophie. There were sad little ghosts caught in the wood grain of that chair, but there were good memories, too.

"Maybe you should take Sophie to Paris," he said as she sat up. "Julien would look out for you."

"My father has made his opinion on living with his daughters quite clear. I cannot expect a welcome from him." Vianne pushed the matelasse coverlet aside and rose, putting her bare feet on the worn rug.

"Will you be all right?"

"Sophie and I will be fine. You'll be home in no time anyway. The Maginot Line will hold. And Lord knows the Germans are no match for us."

"Too bad their weapons are. I took all of our money out of the bank. There are sixty-five thousand francs in the mattress. Use it wisely, Vianne. Along with your teaching salary, it should last you a good long time."

She felt a flutter of panic. She knew too little about their finances. Antoine handled them.

He stood up slowly and took her in his arms. She wanted to bottle how safe she felt in this moment, so she could drink of it later when loneliness and fear left her parched.

Remember this, she thought. The way the light caught in his unruly hair, the love in his brown eyes, the chapped lips that had kissed her only an hour ago, in the darkness.

Through the open window behind them, she heard the slow, even clop-clop-clop of a horse moving up the road and the clattering of the wagon being pulled along behind.

That would be Monsieur Quillian on his way to market with his flowers. If she were in the yard, he would stop and give her one and say it couldn't match her beauty, and she would smile and say *merci* and offer him something to drink.

Vianne pulled away reluctantly. She went over to the wooden dresser and poured tepid water from the blue crockery pitcher into the bowl and washed her face. In the alcove that served as their wardrobe, behind a pair of gold and white toile curtains, she put on her brassiere and stepped into her lace-trimmed drawers and garter. She smoothed the silk stockings up her legs, fastened them to her garters, and then slipped into a belted cotton frock with a squared yoke collar. When she closed the curtains and turned around, Antoine was gone.

She retrieved her handbag and went down the hallway to Sophie's room. Like theirs, it was small, with a steeply pitched, timbered ceiling, wide plank wooden floors, and a window that overlooked the orchard. An ironwork bed, a nightstand with a hand-me-down lamp, and a blue-painted armoire filled the space. Sophie's drawings decorated the walls.

Vianne opened the shutters and let light flood the room.

As usual in the hot summer months, Sophie had kicked the coverlet to the floor sometime in the night. Her pink stuffed teddy bear, Bébé, slept against her cheek.

Vianne picked up the bear, staring down at its matted, much petted face. Last year, Bébé had been forgotten on a shelf by the window as Sophie moved on to newer toys.

Now Bébé was back.

Vianne leaned down to kiss her daughter's cheek.

Sophie rolled over and blinked awake.

"I don't want Papa to go, Maman," she whispered. She reached out for Bébé, practically snatched the bear from Vianne's hands.

"I know." Vianne sighed. "I know."

Vianne went to the armoire, where she picked out the sailor dress that was Sophie's favorite.

"Can I wear the daisy crown Papa made me?"

The daisy "crown" lay crumpled on the nightstand, the little flowers wilted. Vianne picked it up gently and placed it on Sophie's head.

Vianne thought she was doing all right until she stepped into the living room and saw Antoine.

"Papa?" Sophie touched the wilted daisy crown uncertainly. "Don't go."

Antoine knelt down and drew Sophie into his embrace. "I have to be a soldier to keep you and Maman safe. But I'll be back before you know it."

Vianne heard the crack in his voice.

Sophie drew back. The daisy crown was sagging down the side of her head. "You promise you'll come home?"

Antoine looked past his daughter's earnest face to Vianne's worried gaze. "*Oui,*" he said at last.

Sophie nodded.

The three of them were silent as they left the house. They walked hand in hand up the hillside to the gray wooden barn. Knee-high golden grass covered the knoll, and lilac bushes as big as hay wagons grew along the perimeter of the property. Three small white crosses were all that remained in this world to mark the babies Vianne had lost. Today, she didn't let her gaze linger there at all. Her emotions were heavy enough right now; she couldn't add the weight of those memories, too.

Inside the barn sat their old, green Renault. When they were all in the automobile, Antoine started up the engine, backed out of the barn, and drove on browning ribbons of dead grass to the road. Vianne stared out the small, dusty window, watching the green valley pass in a blur of familiar images—red tile roofs, stone cottages, fields of hay and grapes, spindly-treed forests.

All too quickly they arrived at the train station near Tours.

The platform was filled with young men carrying suitcases and women kissing them good-bye and children crying.

A generation of men were going off to war. Again.

Don't think about it, Vianne told herself. *Don't remember what it was like last time when the men limped home, faces burned, missing arms and legs . . .*

Vianne clung to her husband's hand as Antoine bought their tickets and led them onto the train. In the third-class carriage—stiflingly hot, people packed in like marsh reeds—she sat stiffly upright, still holding her husband's hand, with her handbag on her lap.

At their destination, a dozen or so men disembarked. Vianne and Sophie and Antoine followed the others down a cobblestoned street and into a charming village that looked like most small communes in Touraine. How was it possible that war was coming and that this quaint town with its tumbling flowers and crumbling walls was amassing soldiers to fight?

Antoine tugged at her hand, got her moving again. When had she stopped?

Up ahead a set of tall, recently erected iron gates had been bolted into stone walls. Behind them were rows of temporary housing.

The gates swung open. A soldier on horseback rode out to greet the new arrivals, his leather saddle creaking at the horse's steps, his face dusty and flushed from heat. He pulled on the reins and the horse halted, throwing its head and snorting. An aeroplane droned overhead.

"You, men," the soldier said. "Bring your papers to the lieutenant over there by the gate. Now. Move."

Antoine kissed Vianne with a gentleness that made her want to cry.

"I love you," he said against her lips.

"I love you, too," she said but the words that always seemed so big felt small now. What was love when put up against war?

"Me, too, Papa. Me, too!" Sophie cried, flinging herself into his arms. They embraced as a family, one last time, until Antoine pulled back.

"Good-bye," he said.

Vianne couldn't say it in return. She watched him walk away, watched him merge into the crowd of laughing, talking young men, becoming indistinguishable. The big iron gates slammed shut, the clang of metal reverberating in the hot, dusty air, and Vianne and Sophie stood alone in the middle of the street.

FOUR

June 1940
France

he medieval villa dominated a deeply green, forested hillside. It looked like something in a confectioner's shopwindow; a castle sculpted of caramel, with spun-sugar windows and shutters the color of candied apples. Far below, a deep blue lake absorbed the reflection of the clouds. Manicured gardens allowed the villa's occupants—and, more important, their guests—to stroll about the grounds, where only acceptable topics were to be discussed.

In the formal dining room, Isabelle Rossignol sat stiffly erect at the white-clothed table that easily accommodated twenty-four diners. Everything in this room was pale. Walls and floor and ceiling were all crafted of oyster-hued stone. The ceiling arched into a peak nearly twenty feet overhead. Sound was amplified in this cold room, as trapped as the occupants.

Madame Dufour stood at the head of the table, dressed in a severe black dress that revealed the soup spoon–sized hollow at the base of her long neck. A single diamond brooch was her only adornment (one good piece, ladies, and choose it well; everything makes a statement, nothing speaks quite so loudly as cheapness). Her narrow face ended in a blunt chin and was framed by curls so obviously peroxided the desired impression of youth was quite undone. "The trick," she was saying in a cultivated voice, clipped and cut, "is to be completely quiet and unremarkable in your task."

Each of the girls at the table wore the fitted blue woolen jacket and skirt that was the school uniform. It wasn't so bad in the winter, but on this hot June afternoon, the ensemble was unbearable. Isabelle could feel herself beginning to sweat, and no amount of lavender in her soap could mask the sharp scent of her perspiration.

She stared down at the unpeeled orange placed in the center of her Limoges china plate. Flatware lay in precise formation on either side of the plate. Salad fork, dinner fork, knife, spoon, butter knife, fish fork. It went on and on.

"Now," Madame Dufour said. "Pick up the correct utensils—quietly, *s'il vous plaît*, quietly, and peel your orange."

Isabelle picked up her fork and tried to ease the sharp prongs into the heavy peel, but the orange rolled away from her and bumped over the gilt edge of the plate, clattering the china.

"*Merde*," she muttered, grabbing the orange before it fell to the floor.

"*Merde?*" Madame Dufour was beside her.

Isabelle jumped in her seat. *Mon Dieu,* the woman moved like a viper in the reeds. "Pardon, Madame," Isabelle said, returning the orange to its place.

"Mademoiselle Rossignol," Madame said. "How is it that you have graced our halls for two years and learned so little?"

Isabelle again stabbed the orange with her fork. A graceless—but effective—move. Then she smiled up at Madame. "Generally, Madame, the failing of a student to learn is the failing of the teacher to teach."

Breaths were indrawn all down the table.

"Ah," Madame said. "So we are the reason you still cannot manage to eat an orange properly."

Isabelle tried to slice through the peel—too hard, too fast. The silver blade slipped off the puckered peel and clanged on the china plate.

Madame Dufour's hand snaked out; her fingers coiled around Isabelle's wrist.

All up and down the table, the girls watched.

"Polite conversation, girls," Madame said, smiling thinly. "No one wants a statue for a dinner partner."

On cue, the girls began speaking quietly to one another about things that did not interest Isabelle. Gardening, weather, fashion. Acceptable topics for women. Isabelle heard the girl next to her say quietly, "I am so very fond of Alençon lace, aren't you?" and really, it was all she could do to keep from screaming.

"Mademoiselle Rossignol," Madame said. "You will go see Madame Allard and tell her that our experiment has come to an end."

"What does that mean?"

"She will know. Go."

Isabelle scooted back from the table quickly, lest Madame change her mind.

Madame's face scrunched in displeasure at the loud screech the chair legs made on the stone floor.

Isabelle smiled. "I really do not like oranges, you know."

"Really?" Madame said sarcastically.

Isabelle wanted to run from this stifling room, but she was already in enough trouble, so she forced herself to walk slowly, her shoulders back, her chin up. At the stairs (which she could navigate with three books on her head if required), she glanced sideways, saw that she was alone, and rushed down.

In the hallway below, she slowed and straightened. By the time she reached the headmistress's office, she wasn't even breathing hard.

She knocked.

At Madame's flat "Come in," Isabelle opened the door.

Madame Allard sat behind a gilt-trimmed mahogany writing desk. Medieval tapestries hung from the stone walls of the room and an arched, leaded-glass window overlooked gardens so sculpted they were more art than nature. Even birds rarely landed here; no doubt they sensed the stifling atmosphere and flew on.

Isabelle sat down—remembering an instant too late that she hadn't been offered a seat. She popped back up. "Pardon, Madame."

"Sit down, Isabelle."

She did, carefully crossing her ankles as a lady should, clasping her hands together. "Madame Dufour asked me to tell you that the experiment is over."

Madame reached for one of the Murano fountain pens on her desk and picked it up, tapping it on the desk. "Why are you here, Isabelle?"

"I hate oranges."

"Pardon?"

"And if I *were* to eat an orange—which, honestly, Madame, why would I when I don't like them—I would use my hands like the Americans do. Like everyone does, really. A fork and knife to eat an orange?"

"I mean, why are you at the school?"

"Oh. That. Well, the Convent of the Sacred Heart in Avignon expelled me. For nothing, I might add."

"And the Sisters of St. Francis?"

"Ah. They had reason to expel me."

"And the school before that?"

Isabelle didn't know what to say.

Madame put down her fountain pen. "You are almost nineteen."

"*Oui*, Madame."

"I think it's time for you to leave."

Isabelle got to her feet. "Shall I return to the orange lesson?"

"You misunderstand. I mean you should leave the school, Isabelle. It is clear that you are not interested in learning what we have to teach you."

"How to eat an orange and when you can spread cheese and who is more important—the second son of a duke or a daughter who won't inherit or an ambassador to an unimportant country? Madame, do you not know what is going on in the world?"

Isabelle might have been secreted deep in the countryside, but still she knew. Even here, barricaded behind hedges and bludgeoned by politeness, she knew what was happening in France. At night in her monastic cell, while her classmates were in bed, she sat up, long into the night, listening to the BBC on her contraband radio. France had joined Britain in declaring war on Germany, and Hitler was on the move. All across France people had stockpiled food and put up blackout shades and learned to live like moles in the dark.

They had prepared and worried and then . . . nothing.

Month after month, nothing happened.

At first all anyone could talk about was the Great War and the losses that had touched so many families, but as the months went on, and there was only *talk* of war, Isabelle heard her teachers calling it the *drôle de guerre,* the phony war. The real horror was happening elsewhere in Europe; in Belgium and Holland and Poland.

"Will manners not matter in war, Isabelle?"

"They don't matter *now*," Isabelle said impulsively, wishing a moment later that she'd said nothing.

Madame stood. "We were never the right place for you, but . . ."

"My father would put me anywhere to be rid of me," she said. Isabelle would rather blurt out the truth than hear another lie. She had learned many lessons in the parade of schools and convents that had housed her for more than a decade—most of all, she'd learned that she had to rely on herself. Certainly her father and her sister couldn't be counted on.

Madame looked at Isabelle. Her nose flared ever so slightly, an indication of polite but pained disapproval. "It is hard for a man to lose his wife."

"It is hard for a girl to lose her mother." She smiled defiantly. "I lost both parents though, didn't I? One died, and the other turned his back on me. I can't say which hurt more."

"*Mon Dieu*, Isabelle, must you always speak whatever is on your mind?"

Isabelle had heard this criticism all her life, but why should she hold her tongue? No one listened to her either way.

"So you will leave today. I will telegram your father. Tómas will take you to the train."

"Tonight?" Isabelle blinked. "But . . . Papa won't want me."

"Ah. Consequences," Madame said. "Perhaps now you will see that they should be considered."

❧

Isabelle was alone on a train again, heading toward an unknown reception.

She stared out the dirty, mottled window at the flashing green landscape: fields of hay, red roofs, stone cottages, gray bridges, horses.

Everything looked exactly as it always had and that surprised her. War was coming, and she'd imagined it would leave a mark on the countryside somehow, changing the grass color or killing the trees or scaring away the birds, but now, as she sat on this train chugging into Paris, she saw that everything looked completely ordinary.

At the sprawling Gare de Lyon, the train came to a wheezing, belching stop. Isabelle reached down for the small valise at her feet and pulled it onto her lap. As she watched the passengers shuffle past her, exiting the train carriage, the question she'd avoided came back to her.

Papa.

She wanted to believe he would welcome her home, that finally, he would hold out his hands and say her name in a loving way, the way he had Before, when Maman had been the glue that held them together.

She stared down at her scuffed suitcase.

So small.

Most of the girls in the schools she'd attended had arrived with a collection of trunks bound in leather straps and studded with brass tacks. They had pictures on their desks and mementos on their nightstands and photograph albums in their drawers.

Isabelle had a single framed photograph of a woman she wanted to remember and couldn't. When she tried, all that came to her were blurry images of people crying and the physician shaking his head and her mother saying something about holding tightly to her sister's hand.

As if that would help. Vianne had been as quick to abandon Isabelle as Papa had been.

She realized that she was the only one left in the carriage. Clasping her suitcase in her gloved hand, she sidled out of the seat and exited the carriage.

The platforms were full of people. Trains stood in shuddering rows; smoke filled the air, puffed up toward the high, arched ceiling. Somewhere a whistle blared. Great iron wheels began to churn. The platform trembled beneath her feet.

Her father stood out, even in the crowd.

When he spotted her, she saw the irritation that transformed his features, reshaped his expression into one of grim determination.

He was a tall man, at least six foot two, but he had been bent by the Great War. Or at least that was what Isabelle remembered hearing once. His broad shoulders sloped downward, as if posture were too much to think about with all that was on his mind. His thinning hair was gray and unkempt. He had a broad, flattened nose, like a spatula, and lips as thin as an afterthought. On this hot summer day, he wore a wrinkled white shirt, with sleeves rolled up; a tie hung loosely tied around his fraying collar, and his corduroy pants were in need of laundering.

She tried to look . . . mature. Perhaps that was what he wanted of her. "Isabelle."

She clutched her suitcase handle in both hands. "Papa."

"Kicked out of another one."

She nodded, swallowing hard.

"How will we find another school in these times?"

That was her opening. "I want to live with you, Papa."

"With me?" He seemed irritated and surprised. But wasn't it normal for a girl to want to live with her father?

She took a step toward him. "I could work in the bookstore. I won't get in your way."

She drew in a sharp breath, waiting. Sound amplified suddenly. She heard people walking, the platforms groaning beneath them, pigeons flapping their wings overhead, a baby crying.

Of course, Isabelle.

Come home.

Her father sighed in disgust and walked away.

"Well," he said, looking back. "Are you coming?"

❧

Isabelle lay on a blanket in the sweet-smelling grass, a book open in front of her. Somewhere nearby a bee buzzed at a blossom; it sounded like a tiny motorcycle amid all this quiet. It was a blisteringly hot day, a week after she'd come home to Paris. Well, not *home*. She knew her father was still plotting to be rid of her, but she didn't want to think about that on such a gorgeous day, in the air that smelled of cherries and sweet, green grass.

"You read too much," Christophe said, chewing on a stalk of hay. "What is that, a romantic novel?"

She rolled toward him, snapping the book shut. It was about Edith Cavell, a nurse in the Great War. A hero. "I could be a war hero, Christophe."

He laughed. "A girl? A hero? Absurd."

Isabelle got to her feet quickly, yanking up her hat and white kid gloves.

"Don't be mad," he said, grinning up at her. "I'm just tired of the war talk. And it's a fact that women are useless in war. Your job is to wait for our return."

He propped his cheek in one hand and peered up at her through the mop of blond hair that fell across his eyes. In his yachting-style blazer and wide-legged white pants, he looked exactly like what he was—a privileged university student who was unused to work of any kind. Many students his age had volunteered to leave university and join the army. Not Christophe.

Isabelle hiked up the hill and through the orchard, out to the grassy knoll where his open-topped Panhard was parked.

She was already behind the wheel, with the engine running, when Christophe appeared, a sheen of sweat on his conventionally handsome face, the empty picnic basket hanging from his arm.

"Just throw that stuff in the back," she said with a bright smile.

"You're not driving."

"It appears that I am. Now get in."

"It's my automobile, Isabelle."

"Well, to be precise—and I know how important the facts are to you, Christophe—it's your mother's automobile. And I believe a woman should drive a woman's automobile."

Isabelle tried not to smile when he rolled his eyes and muttered "fine" and leaned over to place the basket behind Isabelle's seat. Then, moving slowly enough to make his point, he walked around the front of the automobile and took his place in the seat beside her.

He had no sooner clicked the door shut than she put the automobile in gear and stomped on the gas. The automobile hesitated for a second, then lurched forward, spewing dust and smoke as it gathered speed.

"*Mon Dieu*, Isabelle. Slow down!"

She held on to her flapping straw hat with one hand and clutched the steering wheel with the other. She barely slowed as she passed other motorists.

"*Mon Dieu*, slow down," he said again.

Certainly he must know that she had no intention of complying.

"A woman can go to war these days," Isabelle said when the Paris traffic finally forced her to slow down. "I could be an ambulance driver, maybe. Or I could work on breaking secret codes. Or charming the enemy into telling me a secret location or plan. Remember that game—"

"War is not a game, Isabelle."

"I believe I know that, Christophe. But if it *does* come, I can help. That's all I'm saying."

On the rue de l'Amiral de Coligny, she had to slam on the brakes to avoid hitting a lorry. A convoy from the Comédie Française was pulling out of the Louvre museum. In fact, there were lorries everywhere and uniformed gendarmes directing traffic. Sandbags were piled up around several buildings and monuments to protect from attack—of which there had been none since France joined the war.

Why were there so many French policemen out here?

"Odd," Isabelle mumbled, frowning.

Christophe craned his neck to see what was going on. "They're moving treasures out of the Louvre," he said.

Isabelle saw a break in traffic and sped up. In no time, she had pulled up in front of her father's bookshop and parked.

She waved good-bye to Christophe and ducked into the shop. It was long and narrow, lined from floor to ceiling with books. Over the years, her father had tried to increase his inventory by building freestanding bookcases. The result of his "improvements" was the creation of a labyrinth. The stacks led one this way and that, deeper and deeper within. At the very back were the books for tourists. Some stacks were well lit, some in shadows. There weren't enough outlets to illuminate every nook and cranny. But her father knew every title on every shelf.

"You're late," he said, looking up from his desk in the back. He was doing something with the printing press, probably making one of his books of poetry, which no one ever purchased. His blunt-tipped fingers were stained blue. "I suppose boys are more important to you than employment."

She slid onto the stool behind the cash register. In the week she'd lived with her father she'd made it a point not to argue back, although acquiescing gnawed at her. She tapped her foot impatiently. Words, phrases—excuses—clamored to be spoken aloud. It was hard not to tell him how she felt, but she knew how badly he wanted her gone, so she held her tongue.

"Do you hear that?" he said sometime later.

Had she fallen asleep?

Isabelle sat up. She hadn't heard her father approach, but he was beside her now, frowning.

There was a strange sound in the bookshop, to be sure. Dust fell from the ceiling; the bookcases clattered slightly, making a sound like chattering teeth. Shadows passed in front of the leaded-glass display windows at the entrance. Hundreds of them.

People? So many of them?

Papa went to the door. Isabelle slid off her stool and followed him. As he opened the door, she saw a crowd running down the street, filling the sidewalks.

"What in the world?" Papa muttered.

Isabelle pushed past Papa, elbowed her way into the crowd.

A man bumped into her so hard she stumbled, and he didn't even apologize. More people rushed past them.

"What is it? What's happened?" she asked a florid, wheezing man who was trying to break free of the crowd.

"The Germans are coming into Paris," he said. "We must leave. I was in the Great War. I know . . ."

Isabelle scoffed. "Germans in Paris? Impossible."

He ran away, bobbing from side to side, weaving, his hands fisting and unfisting at his sides.

"We must get home," Papa said, locking the bookshop door.

"It can't be true," she said.

"The worst can always be true," Papa said grimly. "Stay close to me," he added, moving into the crowd.

Isabelle had never seen such panic. All up and down the street, lights were coming on, automobiles were starting, doors were slamming shut. People screamed to one another and reached out, trying to stay connected in the melee.

Isabelle stayed close to her father. The pandemonium in the streets slowed them down. The Métro tunnels were too crowded to navigate, so they had to walk all the way. It was nearing nightfall when they finally made it home. At their apartment building, it took her father two tries to open the main door, his hands were shaking so badly. Once in, they ignored the rickety cage elevator and hurried up five flights of stairs to their apartment.

"Don't turn on the lights," her father said harshly as he opened the door.

Isabelle followed him into the living room and went past him to the window, where she lifted the blackout shade, peering out.

From far away came a droning sound. As it grew louder, the window rattled, sounding like ice in a glass.

She heard a high whistling sound only seconds before she saw the black flotilla in the sky, like birds flying in formation.

Aeroplanes.

"Boches," her father whispered.

Germans.

German aeroplanes, flying over Paris. The whistling sound increased, became like a woman's scream, and then somewhere—maybe in the second arrondissement, she thought—a bomb exploded in a flash of eerie bright light, and something caught fire.

The air raid siren sounded. Her father wrenched the curtains shut and led her out of the apartment and down the stairs. Their neighbors were all doing the same thing, carrying coats and babies and pets down the stairs to the lobby and then down the narrow, twisting stone stairs that led to the cellar. In the dark, they sat together, crowded in close. The air stank of mildew and body odor and fear—that was the sharpest scent of all. The bombing went on and on and on, screeching and droning, the cellar walls vibrating around them; dust fell from the ceiling. A baby started crying and couldn't be soothed.

"Shut that child up, *please*," someone snapped.

"I am trying, M'sieur. He is scared."

"So are we all."

After what felt like an eternity, silence fell. It was almost worse than the noise. What of Paris was left?

By the time the all clear sounded, Isabelle felt numb.

"Isabelle?"

She wanted her father to reach out for her, to take her hand and comfort her, even if it was just for a moment, but he turned away from her and headed up the dark, twisting basement stairs. In their apartment, Isabelle went immediately to the window, peering past the shade to look for the Eiffel Tower. It was still there, rising above a wall of thick black smoke.

"Don't stand by the windows," he said.

She turned slowly. The only light in the room was from his torch, a sickly yellow thread in the dark. "Paris won't fall," she said.

He said nothing. Frowned. She wondered if he was thinking of the Great War and what he'd seen in the trenches. Perhaps his injury was hurting again, aching in sympathy with the sound of falling bombs and hissing flames.

"Go to bed, Isabelle."

"How can I possibly sleep at a time like this?"

He sighed. "You will learn that a lot of things are possible."

FIVE

They had been lied to by their government. They'd been assured, time and time again, that the Maginot Line would keep the Germans out of France.

Lies.

Neither concrete and steel nor French soldiers could stop Hitler's march, and the government had run from Paris like thieves in the night. It was said they were in Tours, strategizing, but what good did strategy do when Paris was to be overrun by the enemy?

"Are you ready?"

"I am not going, Papa. I have told you this." She had dressed for travel—as he'd asked—in a red polka-dot summer dress and low heels.

"We will not have this conversation again, Isabelle. The Humberts will be here soon to pick you up. They will take you as far as Tours. From there, I leave it to your ingenuity to get to your sister's house. Lord knows you have always been adept at running away."

"So you throw me out. Again."

"Enough of this, Isabelle. Your sister's husband is at the front. She is alone with her daughter. You will do as I say. You will leave Paris."

Did he know how this hurt her? Did he care?

"You've never cared about Vianne or me. And she doesn't want me any more than you do."

"You're going," he said.

"I want to stay and fight, Papa. To be like Edith Cavell."

He rolled his eyes. "You remember how she died? Executed by the Germans."

"Papa, please."

"Enough. I have seen what they can do, Isabelle. You have not."

"If it's that bad, you should come with me."

"And leave the apartment and bookshop to them?" He grabbed her by the hand and dragged her out of the apartment and down the stairs, her straw hat and valise banging into the wall, her breath coming in gasps.

At last he opened the door and pulled her out onto the Avenue de La Bourdonnais.

Chaos. Dust. Crowds. The street was a living, breathing dragon of humanity, inching forward, wheezing dirt, honking horns; people yelling for help, babies crying, and the smell of sweat heavy in the air.

Automobiles clogged the area, each burdened beneath boxes and bags. People had taken whatever they could find—carts and bicycles and even children's wagons.

Those who couldn't find or afford the petrol or an automobile or a bicycle walked. Hundreds—thousands—of women and children held hands, shuffled forward, carrying as much as they could hold. Suitcases, picnic baskets, pets.

Already the very old and very young were falling behind.

Isabelle didn't want to join this hopeless, helpless crowd of women and children and old people. While the young men were away—dying for them at the front—their families were leaving, heading south or west, although, really, what made any of them think it would be safer there? Hitler's troops had already invaded Poland and Belgium and Czechoslovakia.

The crowd engulfed them.

A woman ran into Isabelle, mumbled pardon, and kept walking.

Isabelle followed her father. "I can be useful. Please. I'll be a nurse or drive an ambulance. I can roll bandages or even stitch up a wound."

Beside them, a horn *aah-ooh-gahed.*

Her father looked past her, and she saw the relief that lifted his counte-
nance. Isabelle recognized that look: it meant he was getting rid of her.
Again. "They are here," he said.

"Don't send me away," she said. "Please."

He maneuvered her through the crowd to where a dusty black automobile was parked. It had a saggy, stained mattress strapped to its roof,
along with a set of fishing poles and a rabbit cage with the rabbit still inside. The boot was open but also strapped down; inside she saw a jumble
of baskets and suitcases and lamps.

Inside the automobile, Monsieur Humbert's pale, plump fingers
clutched the steering wheel as if the automobile were a horse that might
bolt at any second. He was a pudgy man who spent his days in the butcher
shop near Papa's bookstore. His wife, Patricia, was a sturdy woman who
had the heavy-jowled-peasant look one saw so often in the country. She
was smoking a cigarette and staring out the window as if she couldn't believe what she was seeing.

Monsieur Humbert rolled down his window and poked his face into
the opening. "Hello, Julien. She is ready?"

Papa nodded. "She is ready. *Merci,* Edouard."

Patricia leaned over to talk to Papa through the open window. "We are
only going as far as Orléans. And she has to pay her share of petrol."

"Of course."

Isabelle couldn't leave. It was cowardly. Wrong. "Papa—"

"*Au revoir,*" he said firmly enough to remind her that she had no choice.
He nodded toward the car and she moved numbly toward it.

She opened the back door and saw three small, dirty girls lying together, eating crackers and drinking from bottles and playing with dolls.
The last thing she wanted was to join them, but she pushed her way in,
made a space for herself among these strangers that smelled vaguely of
cheese and sausage, and closed the door.

Twisting around in her seat, she stared at her father through the back
window. His face held her gaze; she saw his mouth bend ever so slightly
downward; it was the only hint that he saw her. The crowd surged around

him like water around a rock, until all she could see was the wall of be-
draggled strangers coming up behind the car.

Isabelle faced forward in her seat again. Out her window, a young
woman stared back at her, wild eyes, hair a bird's nest, an infant suckling on
her breast. The car moved slowly, sometimes inching forward, sometimes
stopped for long periods of time. Isabelle watched her countrymen—
country*women*—shuffle past her, looking dazed and terrified and confused.
Every now and then one of them would pound on the car bonnet or boot,
begging for something. They kept the windows rolled up even though the
heat in the car was stifling.

At first, she was sad to be leaving, and then her anger bloomed, growing hotter even than the air in the back of this stinking car. She was so tired
of being considered disposable. First, her papa had abandoned her, and
then Vianne had pushed her aside. She closed her eyes to hide tears she
couldn't suppress. In the darkness that smelled of sausage and sweat and
smoke, with the children arguing beside her, she remembered the first
time she'd been sent away.

The long train ride . . . Isabelle stuffed in beside Vianne, who did nothing but sniff and cry and pretend to sleep.

And then Madame looking down her copper pipe of a nose saying,
They will be no trouble.

Although she'd been young—only four—Isabelle thought she'd
learned what alone meant, but she'd been wrong. In the three years she'd
lived at Le Jardin, she'd at least *had* a sister, even if Vianne was never
around. Isabelle remembered peering down from the upstairs window,
watching Vianne and her friends from a distance, praying to be remembered, to be invited, and then when Vianne had married Antoine and fired
Madame Doom (not her real name, of course, but certainly the truth), Isabelle had believed she was a part of the family. But not for long. When
Vianne had her miscarriage, it was instantly *good-bye, Isabelle.* Three weeks
later—at seven—she'd been in her first boarding school. That was when
she really learned about alone.

"You. Isabelle. Did you bring food?" Patricia asked. She was turned
around in her seat, peering at Isabelle.

"No."

"Wine?"

"I brought money and clothes and books."

"Books," Patricia said dismissively, and turned back around. "That should help."

Isabelle looked out the window again. What other mistakes had she already made?

❧

Hours passed. The automobile made its slow, agonizing way south. Isabelle was grateful for the dust. It coated the window and obscured the terrible, depressing scene.

People. Everywhere. In front of them, behind them, beside them; so thick was the crowd that the automobile could only inch forward in fits and starts. It was like driving through a swarm of bees that pulled apart for a second and then swarmed again. The sun was punishingly hot. It turned the smelly automobile interior into an oven and beat down on the women outside who were shuffling toward . . . what? No one knew what exactly was happening behind them or where safety lay ahead.

The car lurched forward and stopped hard. Isabelle hit the seat in front of her. The children immediately started to cry for their mother.

"*Merde*," Monsieur Humbert muttered.

"M'sieur Humbert," Patricia said primly. "The children."

An old woman pounded on the car's bonnet as she shuffled past.

"That's it, then, Madame Humbert," he said. "We are out of petrol."

Patricia looked like a landed fish. "What?"

"I stopped at every chance along the way. You know I did. We have no more petrol and there's none to be had."

"But . . . well . . . what are we to do?"

"We'll find a place to stay. Perhaps I can convince my brother to come fetch us." Humbert opened his automobile door, being careful not to hit anyone ambling past, and stepped out onto the dusty, dirt road. "See. There. Étampes is not far ahead. We'll get a room and a meal and it will all look better in the morning."

Isabelle sat upright. Surely she had fallen asleep and missed something.

Were they going to simply abandon the automobile? "You think we can walk to Tours?"

Patricia turned around in her seat. She looked as drained and hot as Isabelle felt. "Perhaps one of your books can help you. Certainly they were a smarter choice than bread or water. Come, girls. Out of the automobile."

Isabelle reached down for the valise at her feet. It was wedged in tightly and required some effort to extricate. With a growl of determination, she finally yanked it free and opened the car door and stepped out.

She was immediately surrounded by people, pushed and shoved and cursed at.

Someone tried to yank her suitcase out of her grasp. She fought for it, hung on. As she clutched it to her body, a woman walked past her, pushing a bicycle laden with possessions. The woman stared at Isabelle hopelessly, her dark eyes revealing exhaustion.

Someone else bumped into Isabelle; she stumbled forward and almost fell. Only the thicket of bodies in front of her saved her from going to her knees in the dust and dirt. She heard the person beside her apologize, and Isabelle was about to respond when she remembered the Humberts.

She shoved her way around to the other side of the car, crying out, "M'sieur Humbert!"

There was no answer, just the ceaseless pounding of feet on the road.

She called out Patricia's name, but her cry was lost in the thud of so many feet, so many tires crunching on the dirt. People bumped her, pushed past her. If she fell to her knees, she'd be trampled and die here, alone in the throng of her countrymen.

Clutching the smooth leather handle of her valise, she joined the march toward Étampes.

She was still walking hours later when night fell. Her feet ached; a blister burned with every step. Hunger walked beside her, poking her insistently with its sharp little elbow, but what could she do about it? She'd packed for a visit with her sister, not an endless exodus. She had her favorite copy of *Madame Bovary* and the book everyone was reading—*Autant en emporte le vent*—and some clothes; no food or water. She'd expected that this whole journey would last a few hours. Certainly not that she would be *walking* to Carriveau.

At the top of a small rise, she came to a stop. Moonlight revealed thousands of people walking beside her, in front of her, behind her; jostling her, bumping into her, shoving her forward until she had no choice but to stumble along with them. Hundreds more had chosen this hillside as a resting place. Women and children were camped along the side of the road, in fields and gutters and gullies.

The dirt road was littered with broken-down automobiles and belongings; forgotten, discarded, stepped on, too heavy to carry. Women and children lay entangled in the grass or beneath trees or alongside ditches, asleep, their arms coiled around each other.

Isabelle came to an exhausted halt on the outskirts of Étampes. The crowd spilled out in front of her, stumbling onto the road to town.

And she knew.

There would be nowhere to stay in Étampes and nothing to eat. The refugees who had arrived before her would have moved through the town like locusts, buying every foodstuff on the shelves. There wouldn't be a room available. Her money would do her no good.

So what should she do?

Head southwest, toward Tours and Carriveau. What else? As a girl, she'd studied maps of this region in her quest to return to Paris. She knew this landscape, if only she could *think*.

She peeled away from the crowd headed toward the collection of moonlit gray stone buildings in the distance and picked her way carefully through the valley. All around her people were seated in the grass or sleeping beneath blankets. She could hear them moving, whispering. Hundreds of them. Thousands. On the far side of the field, she found a trail that ran south along a low stone wall. Turning onto it, she found herself alone. She paused, letting the feel of that settle through her, calm her. Then she began walking again. After a mile or so the trail led her into a copse of spindly trees.

She was deep in the woods—trying not to focus on the pain in her toe, the ache in her stomach, the dryness in her throat—when she smelled smoke.

And roasting meat. Hunger stripped her resolve and made her careless. She saw the orange glow of the fire and moved toward it. At the last minute, she realized her danger and stopped. A twig snapped beneath her foot.

"You may as well come over," said a male voice. "You move like an elephant through the woods."

Isabelle froze. She knew she'd been stupid. There could be danger here for a girl alone.

"If I wanted you dead, you'd be dead."

That was certainly true. He could have come upon her in the dark and slit her throat. She'd been paying attention to nothing except the gnawing in her empty stomach and the aroma of roasting meat.

"You can trust me."

She stared into the darkness, trying to make him out. Couldn't. "You would say that if the opposite were true, too."

A laugh. "*Oui.* And now, come here. I have a rabbit on the fire."

She followed the glow of firelight over a rocky gully and uphill. The tree trunks around her looked silver in the moonlight. She moved lightly, ready to run in an instant. At the last tree between her and the fire she stopped.

A young man sat by the fire, leaning back against a rough trunk, one leg thrust forward, one bent at the knee. He was probably only a few years older than Isabelle.

It was hard to see him well in the orange glow. He had longish, stringy black hair that looked unfamiliar with a comb or soap and clothes so tattered and patched she was reminded of the war refugees who'd so recently shuffled through Paris, hoarding cigarettes and bits of paper and empty bottles, begging for change or help. He had the pale, unwholesome look of someone who never knew where his next meal was coming from.

And yet he was offering her food.

"I hope you are a gentleman," she said from her place in the darkness.

He laughed. "I'm sure you do."

She stepped into the light cast by the fire.

"Sit," he said.

She sat across from him in the grass. He leaned around the fire and handed her the bottle of wine. She took a long drink, so long he laughed as she handed him back the bottle and wiped wine from her chin.

"What a pretty drunkard you are."

She had no idea how to answer that.

He smiled.

"Gaëtan Dubois. My friends call me Gaët."

"Isabelle Rossignol."

"Ah, a nightingale."

She shrugged. It was hardly a new observation. Her surname meant "nightingale." Maman had called Vianne and Isabelle her nightingales as she kissed them good night. It was one of Isabelle's few memories of her. "Why are you leaving Paris? A man like you should stay and fight."

"They opened the prison. Apparently it is better to have us fight for France than sit behind bars when the Germans storm through."

"You were in prison?"

"Does that scare you?"

"No. It's just . . . unexpected."

"You should be scared," he said, pushing the stringy hair out of his eyes. "Anyway, you are safe enough with me. I have other things on my mind. I am going to check on my maman and sister and then find a regiment to join. I'll kill as many of those bastards as I can."

"You're lucky," she said with a sigh. Why was it so easy for men in the world to do as they wanted and so difficult for women?

"Come with me."

Isabelle knew better than to believe him. "You only ask because I'm pretty and you think I'll end up in your bed if I stay," she said.

He stared across the fire at her. It cracked and hissed as fat dripped onto the flames. He took a long drink of wine and handed the bottle back to her. Near the flames, their hands touched, the barest brushing of skin on skin. "I could have you in my bed right now if that's what I wanted."

"Not willingly," she said, swallowing hard, unable to look away.

"Willingly," he said in a way that made her skin prickle and made breathing difficult. "But that's not what I meant. Or what I said. I asked you to come with me to fight."

Isabelle felt something so new she couldn't quite grasp it. She knew she was beautiful. It was simply a fact to her. People said it whenever they met her. She saw how men gazed at her with unabashed desire, remarking on her hair or green eyes or plump lips; how they looked at her breasts. She saw her beauty reflected in women's eyes, too, girls at school who didn't want her to stand too near the boys they liked and judged her to be arrogant before she'd even spoken a word.

Beauty was just another way to discount her, to not see her. She had grown used to getting attention in other ways. And she wasn't a complete innocent when it came to passion, either. Hadn't the good Sisters of St. Francis expelled her for kissing a boy during mass?

But this felt different.

He saw her beauty, even in the half-light, she could tell, but he looked past it. Either that, or he was smart enough to see that she wanted to offer more to the world than a pretty face.

"I could do something that matters," she said quietly.

"Of course you could. I could teach you to use a gun and a knife."

"I need to go to Carriveau and make sure my sister is well. Her husband is at the front."

He gazed at her across the fire, his expression intent. "We will see your sister in Carriveau and my mother in Poitiers, and then we will be off to join the war."

He made it sound like such an adventure, no different from running off to join the circus, as if they would see men who swallowed swords and fat women with beards along the way.

It was what she'd been looking for all of her life. "A plan, then," she said, unable to hide her smile.

SIX

The next morning Isabelle blinked awake to see sunlight gilding the leaves rustling overhead.

She sat up, resmoothing the skirt that had hiked up in her sleep, revealing lacy white garters and ruined silk stockings.

"Don't do that on my account."

Isabelle glanced to her left and saw Gaëtan coming toward her. For the first time, she saw him clearly. He was lanky, wiry as an apostrophe mark, and dressed in clothes that appeared to have come from a beggar's bin. Beneath a fraying cap, his face was scruffy and sharp, unshaven. He had a wide brow and a pronounced chin and deep-set gray eyes that were heavily lashed. The look in those eyes was as sharp as the point of his chin, and revealed a kind of clarified hunger. Last night she'd thought it was how he'd looked at her. Now she saw that it was how he looked at the world.

He didn't scare her, not at all. Isabelle was not like her sister, Vianne, who was given to fear and anxiety. But neither was Isabelle a fool. If she was going to travel with this man, she had better get a few things straight.

"So," she said. "Prison."

He stared at her, raised a black eyebrow, as if to say, *Scared yet?* "A girl like you wouldn't know anything about it. I could tell you it was a Jean Valjean sort of stay and you would think it was romantic."

It was the kind of thing she heard all the time. It circled back to her looks, as most snide comments did. Surely a pretty blond girl had to be shallow and dim-witted. "Were you stealing food to feed your family?"

He grinned crookedly. It gave him a lopsided look, with one side of his smile hiking up farther than the other. "No."

"Are you dangerous?"

"It depends. What do you think of communists?"

"Ah. So you were a political prisoner."

"Something like that. But like I said, a nice girl like you wouldn't know anything about survival."

"You'd be surprised the things I know, Gaëtan. There is more than one kind of prison."

"Is there, pretty girl? What do you know about it?"

"What was your crime?"

"I took things that didn't belong to me. Is that enough of an answer?"

Thief.

"And you got caught."

"Obviously."

"That isn't exactly comforting, Gaëtan. Were you careless?"

"Gaët," he said, moving toward her.

"I haven't decided if we're friends yet."

He touched her hair, let a few strands coil around his dirty finger. "We're friends. Bank on it. Now let's go."

When he reached for her hand, it occurred to her to refuse him, but she didn't. They walked out of the forest and back onto the road, merging once again into the crowd, which opened just enough to let them in and then closed around them. Isabelle hung on to Gaëtan with one hand and held her suitcase in the other.

They walked for miles.

Automobiles died around them. Cartwheels broke. Horses stopped and couldn't be made to move again. Isabelle felt herself becoming listless and dull, exhausted by heat and dust and thirst. A woman limped along beside her, crying, her tears black with dirt and grit, and then that woman was replaced by an older woman in a fur coat who was sweating profusely and seemed to be wearing every piece of jewelry she owned.

The sun grew stronger, became stiflingly, staggeringly hot. Children whined, women whimpered. The acrid, stuffy scent of body odor and sweat filled the air, but Isabelle had grown so used to it that she barely noticed other people's smell or her own.

It was almost three o'clock, the hottest part of the day, when they saw a regiment of French soldiers walking alongside them, dragging their rifles. The soldiers moved in a disorganized way, not in formation, not smartly. A tank rumbled beside them, crunching over belongings left in the road; on it several whey-faced French soldiers sat slumped, their heads hung low.

Isabelle pulled free of Gaëtan and stumbled through the crowd, elbowing her way to the regiment. "You're going the wrong way!" she screamed, surprised to hear how hoarse her voice was.

Gaëtan pounced on a soldier, shoved him back so hard he stumbled and crashed into a slow-moving tank. "Who is fighting for France?"

The bleary-eyed soldier shook his head. "No one." In a glint of silver, Isabelle saw the knife Gaëtan held to the man's throat. The soldier's gaze narrowed. "Go ahead. Do it. Kill me."

Isabelle pulled Gaëtan away. In his eyes, she saw a rage so deep it scared her. He could do it; he could kill this man by slitting his throat. And she thought: *They opened the prisons.* Was he worse than a thief?

"Gaët?" she said.

Her voice got through to him. He shook his head as if to clear it and lowered his knife. "Who is fighting for us?" he said bitterly, coughing at the dust.

"We will be," she said. "Soon."

Behind her, an automobile honked its horn. *Aah-ooh-gah.* Isabelle ignored it. Automobiles were no better than walking anymore—the few that were still running were moving only at the whim of the people around them; like flotsam in the reeds of a muddy river. "Come on." She pulled him away from the demoralized regiment.

They walked on, still holding hands, but as the hours passed, Isabelle noticed a change in Gaëtan. He rarely spoke and didn't smile.

At each town, the crowd thinned. People stumbled into Artenay, Saran, and Orléans, their eyes alight with desperation as they reached into handbags and pockets and wallets for money they hoped to be able to spend.

Still, Isabelle and Gaëtan kept going. They walked all day and fell into exhausted sleep in the dark and woke again to walk the next day. By their third day, Isabelle was numb with exhaustion. Oozing red blisters had formed between most of her toes and on the balls of her feet and every step was painful. Dehydration gave her a terrible, pounding headache and hunger gnawed at her empty stomach. Dust clogged her throat and eyes and made her cough constantly.

She stumbled past a freshly dug grave on the side of the road, marked by a crudely hammered-together wooden cross. Her shoe caught on something—a dead cat—and she staggered forward, almost falling to her knees. Gaëtan steadied her.

She clung to his hand, remained stubbornly upright.

How much later was it that she heard something?

An hour? A day?

Bees. They buzzed around her head; she batted them away. She licked her dried lips and thought of pleasant days in the garden, with bees buzzing about.

No.

Not bees.

She knew that sound.

She stopped, frowning. Her thoughts were addled. What had she been trying to remember?

The droning grew louder, filling the air, and then the aeroplanes appeared, six or seven of them, looking like small crucifixes against the blue and cloudless sky.

Isabelle tented a hand over her eyes, watching the aeroplanes fly closer, lower . . .

Someone yelled, "It's the Boches!"

In the distance, a stone bridge exploded in a spray of fire and stone and smoke.

The aeroplanes dropped lower over the crowd.

Gaëtan threw Isabelle to the ground and covered her body with his. The world became pure sound: the roar of the aeroplane engines, the *rat-ta-ta-tat* of machine-gun fire, the beat of her heart, people screaming. Bullets ate up the grass in rows, people screamed and cried out. Isabelle saw a woman fly into the air like a rag doll and hit the ground in a heap.

Trees snapped in half and fell over, people yelled. Flames burst into existence. Smoke filled the air.

And then . . . quiet.

Gaëtan rolled off her.

"Are you all right?" he asked.

She pushed the hair from her eyes and sat up.

There were mangled bodies everywhere, and fires, and billowing black smoke. People were screaming, crying, dying.

An old man moaned, "Help me."

Isabelle crawled to him on her hands and knees, realizing as she got close that the ground was marshy with his blood. A stomach wound gaped through his ripped shirt; entrails bulged out of the torn flesh.

"Maybe there's a doctor" was all she could think of to say. And then she heard it again. The droning.

"They're coming back." Gaëtan pulled her to her feet. She almost slipped in the blood-soaked grass. Not far away a bomb hit, exploding into fire. Isabelle saw a toddler in soiled nappies standing by a dead woman, crying.

She stumbled toward the toddler. Gaëtan yanked her sideways.

"I have to help—"

"Your dying won't help that kid," he growled, pulling her so hard it hurt. She stumbled along beside him in a daze. They dodged discarded automobiles and bodies, most of which were ripped beyond repair, bleeding, bones sticking out through clothes.

At the edge of town, Gaëtan pulled Isabelle into a small stone church. Others were already there, crouching in corners, hiding amid the pews, hugging their loved ones close.

Aeroplanes roared overhead, accompanied by the stuttering shriek of machine guns. The stained-glass window shattered; bits of colored glass clattered to the floor, slicing through skin on the way down. Timbers cracked, dust and stones fell. Bullets ran across the church, nailing arms and legs to the floor. The altar exploded.

Gaëtan said something to her, and she answered, or she thought she did, but she wasn't sure, and before she could figure it out, another bomb whistled, fell, and the roof over her head exploded.

SEVEN

The *école élementaire* was not a big school by city standards, but it was spacious and well laid out, plenty large enough for the children of the commune of Carriveau. Before its life as a school, the building had been stables for a rich landowner, and thus its U-shape design; the central courtyard had been a gathering place for carriages and tradesmen. It boasted gray stone walls, bright blue shutters, and wooden floors. The manor house, to which it had once been aligned, had been bombed in the Great War and never rebuilt. Like so many schools in the small towns in France, it stood on the far edge of town.

Vianne was in her classroom, behind her desk, staring out at the shining children's faces in front of her, dabbing her upper lip with her wrinkled handkerchief. On the floor by each child's desk was the obligatory gas mask. Children now carried them everywhere.

The open windows and thick stone walls helped to keep the sun at bay, but still the heat was stifling. Lord knew, it was hard enough to concentrate without the added burden of the heat. The news from Paris was terrible, terrifying. All anyone could talk about was the gloomy future and the shocking present: Germans in Paris. The Maginot Line broken. French soldiers dead in trenches and running from the front. For the last three nights—since the telephone call from her father—she hadn't slept. Isabelle was God-knew-where between Paris and Carriveau, and there had been no word from Antoine.

"Who wants to conjugate the verb *courir* for me?" she asked tiredly.

"Shouldn't we be learning German?"

Vianne realized what she'd just been asked. The students were interested now, sitting upright, their eyes bright.

"Pardon?" she said, clearing her throat, buying time.

"We should be learning German, not French."

It was young Gilles Fournier, the butcher's son. His father and all three of his older brothers had gone off to the war, leaving only him and his mother to run the family's butcher shop.

"And shooting," François agreed, nodding his head. "My maman says we will need to know how to shoot Germans, too."

"My grandmère says we should all just leave," said Claire. "She remembers the last war and she says we are fools for staying."

"The Germans won't cross the Loire, will they, Madame Mauriac?"

In the front row, center, Sophie sat forward in her seat, her hands clasped atop the wooden desk, her eyes wide. She had been as upset by the rumors as Vianne. The child had cried herself to sleep two nights in a row, worrying over her father. Now Bébé came to school with her. Sarah sat in the desk beside her best friend, looking equally fearful.

"It is all right to be afraid," Vianne said, moving toward them. It was what she'd said to Sophie last night and to herself, but the words rang hollow.

"I'm not afraid," Gilles said. "I got a knife. I'll kill any dirty Boches who show up in Carriveau."

Sarah's eyes widened. "They're coming here?"

"No," Vianne said. The denial didn't come easily; her own fear caught at the word, stretched it out. "The French soldiers—your fathers and uncles and brothers—are the bravest men in the world. I'm sure they are fighting for Paris and Tours and Orléans even as we speak."

"But Paris is overrun," Gilles said. "What happened to the French soldiers at the front?"

"In wars, there are battles and skirmishes. Losses along the way. But our men will never let the Germans win. We will never give up." She moved closer to her students. "But we have a part to play, too; those of us left behind. We have to be brave and strong, too, and not believe the worst. We have to keep on with our lives so our fathers and brothers and . . . husbands have lives to come home to, *oui?*"

"But what about Tante Isabelle?" Sophie asked. "Grandpère said she should have been here by now."

"My cousin ran from Paris, too," François said. "He is not arrived here, either."

"My uncle says it is bad on the roads."

The bell rang and students popped from their seats like springs. In an instant the war, the aeroplanes, the fear were forgotten. They were eight- and nine-year-olds freed at the end of a summer school day, and they acted like it. Yelling, laughing, talking all at once, pushing one another aside, running for the door.

Vianne was thankful for the bell. She was a teacher, for God's sake. What did she know to say about dangers such as these? How could she assuage a child's fear when her own was straining at the leash? She busied herself with ordinary tasks—gathering up the detritus that sixteen children left behind, banging chalk from the soft erasers, putting books away. When everything was as it should be, she put her papers and pencils into her own leather satchel and took her handbag out of the desk's bottom drawer. Then she put on her straw hat, pinned it in place, and left her classroom.

She walked down the quiet hallways, waving to colleagues who were still in their classrooms. Several of the rooms were closed up now that the male teachers had been mobilized.

At Rachel's classroom, she paused, watching as Rachel put her son in his pram and wheeled it toward the door. Rachel had been planning to take this term off from teaching to stay home with Ari, but the war had changed all of that. Now, she had no choice but to bring her baby to work with her.

"You look like I feel," Vianne said as her friend neared. Rachel's dark hair had responded to the humidity and doubled in size.

"That can't be a compliment but I'm desperate, so I am taking it as one. You have chalk on your cheek, by the way."

Vianne wiped her cheek absently and leaned over the pram. The baby was sleeping soundly. "How's he doing?"

"For a ten-month-old who is supposed to be at home with his maman and is instead gallivanting around town beneath enemy aeroplanes and listening to ten-year-old students shriek all day? Fine." She smiled and pushed a damp ringlet from her face as they headed down the corridor. "Do I sound bitter?"

"No more than the rest of us."

"Ha! Bitterness would do you good. All that smiling and pretending of yours would give me hives."

Rachel bumped the pram down the three stone steps and onto the walkway that led to the grassy play area that had once been an exercise arena for horses and a delivery area for tradesmen. A four-hundred-year-old stone fountain gurgled and dripped water in the center of the yard.

"Come on, girls!" Rachel called out to Sophie and Sarah, who were sitting together on a park bench. The girls responded immediately and fell into step ahead of the women, chattering constantly, their heads cocked together, their hands clasped. A second generation of best friends.

They turned into an alleyway and came out on rue Victor Hugo, right in front of a bistro where old men sat on ironwork chairs, drinking coffee and smoking cigarettes and talking politics. Ahead of them, Vianne saw a haggard trio of women limping along, their clothes tattered, their faces yellow with dust.

"Poor women," Rachel said with a sigh. "Hélène Ruelle told me this morning that at least a dozen refugees came to town late last night. The stories they bring are not good. But no one embellishes a story like Hélène."

Ordinarily Vianne would make a comment about what a gossip Hélène was, but she couldn't be glib. According to Papa, Isabelle had left Paris days ago. She still hadn't arrived at Le Jardin. "I'm worried about Isabelle," she said.

Rachel linked her arm through Vianne's. "Do you remember the first time your sister ran away from that boarding school in Lyon?"

"She was seven years old."

"She made it all the way to Amboise. Alone. With no money. She spent two nights in the woods and talked her way onto the train."

Vianne barely remembered anything of that time except for her own grief. When she'd lost the first baby, she'd fallen into despair. The lost year, Antoine called it. That was how she thought of it, too. When Antoine told her he was taking Isabelle to Paris, and to Papa, Vianne had been—God help her—relieved.

Was it any surprise that Isabelle had run away from the boarding school to which she'd been sent? To this day, Vianne felt an abiding shame at how she had treated her baby sister.

"She was nine the first time she made it to Paris," Vianne said, trying to find comfort in the familiar story. Isabelle was tough and driven and determined; she always had been.

"If I'm not mistaken, she was expelled two years later for running away from school to see a traveling circus. Or was that when she climbed out of the second-floor dormitory window using a bedsheet?" Rachel smiled. "The point is, Isabelle will make it here if that's what she wants."

"God help anyone who tries to stop her."

"She will arrive any day. I promise. Unless she has met an exiled prince and fallen desperately in love."

"That is the kind of thing that could happen to her."

"You see?" Rachel teased. "You feel better already. Now come to my house for lemonade. It's just the thing on a day this hot."

After supper, Vianne got Sophie settled into bed and went downstairs. She was too worried to relax. The silence in her house kept reminding her that no one had come to her door. She could not remain still. Regardless of her conversation with Rachel, she couldn't dispel her worry—and a terrible sense of foreboding—about Isabelle.

Vianne stood up, sat down, then stood again and walked to the front door, opening it.

Outside, the fields lay beneath a purple and pink evening sky. Her yard was a series of familiar shapes—well-tended apple trees stood protectively between the front door and the rose-and-vine-covered stone wall, beyond which lay the road to town and acres and acres of fields, studded here and there with thickets of narrow-trunked trees. Off to the right was the deeper woods where she and Antoine had often sneaked off to be alone when they were younger.

Antoine.

Isabelle.

Where were they? Was he at the front? Was she walking from Paris? *Don't think about it.*

She needed to do something. Gardening. Keep her mind on something else.

After retrieving her worn gardening gloves and stepping into the boots by the door, she made her way to the garden positioned on a flat patch of land between the shed and the barn. Potatoes, onions, carrots, broccoli, peas, beans, cucumbers, tomatoes, and radishes grew in its carefully tended beds. On the hillside between the garden and the barn were the berries— raspberries and blackberries in carefully contained rows. She knelt down in the rich, black dirt and began pulling weeds.

Early summer was usually a time of promise. Certainly, things could go wrong in this most ardent season, but if one remained steady and calm and didn't shirk the all-important duties of weeding and thinning, the plants could be guided and tamed. Vianne always made sure that the beds were precisely organized and tended with a firm yet gentle hand. Even more important than what she gave her garden was what it gave her. In it, she found a sense of calm.

She became aware of something wrong slowly, in pieces. First, there was a sound that didn't belong, a vibration, a thudding, and then a murmur. The odors came next: something wholly at odds with her sweet garden smell, something acrid and sharp that made her think of decay.

Vianne wiped her forehead, aware that she was smearing black dirt across her skin, and stood up. Tucking her dirty gloves in the gaping hip pockets of her pants, she rose to her feet and moved toward her gate. Before she reached it, a trio of women appeared, as if sculpted out of the shadows. They stood clumped together in the road just behind her gate. An old woman, dressed in rags, held the others close to her—a young woman with a babe-in-arms and a teenaged girl who held an empty birdcage in one hand and a shovel in the other. Each looked glassy-eyed and feverish; the young mother was clearly trembling. Their faces were dripping with sweat, their eyes were filled with defeat. The old woman held out dirty, empty hands. "Can you spare some water?" she asked, but even as she asked her the question, she looked unconvinced. Beaten.

Vianne opened the gate. "Of course. Would you like to come in? Sit down, perhaps?"

The old woman shook her head. "We are ahead of them. There's nothing for those in the back."

Vianne didn't know what the woman meant, but it didn't matter. She could see that the women were suffering from exhaustion and hunger. "Just a moment." She went into the house and packed them some bread and raw carrots and a small bit of cheese. All that she had to spare. She filled a wine bottle with water and returned, offering them the provisions. "It's not much," she said.

"It is more than we've had since Tours," the young woman said in a toneless voice.

"You were in Tours?" Vianne asked.

"Drink, Sabine," the old woman said, holding the water to the girl's lips.

Vianne was about to ask about Isabelle when the old woman said sharply, "They're here."

The young mother made a moaning sound and tightened her hold on the baby, who was so quiet—and his tiny fist so blue—that Vianne gasped.

The baby was dead.

Vianne knew about the kind of talon grief that wouldn't let go; she had fallen into the fathomless gray that warped a mind and made a mother keep holding on long after hope was gone.

"Go inside," the old woman said to Vianne. "Lock your doors."

"But . . ."

The ragged trio backed away—lurched, really—as if Vianne's breath had become noxious.

And then she saw the mass of black shapes moving across the field and coming up the road.

The smell preceded them. Human sweat and filth and body odor. As they neared, the miasma of black separated, peeled into forms. She saw people on the road and in the fields; walking, limping, coming toward her. Some were pushing bicycles or prams or dragging wagons. Dogs barked, babies cried. There was coughing, throat clearing, whining. They came forward, through the field and up the road, relentlessly moving closer, pushing one another aside, their voices rising.

Vianne couldn't help so many. She rushed into her house and locked the door behind her. Inside, she went from room to room, locking doors and closing shutters. When she was finished, she stood in the living room, uncertain, her heart pounding.

The house began to shake, just a little. The windows rattled, the shutters thumped against the stone exterior. Dust rained down from the exposed timbers of the ceiling.

Someone pounded on the front door. It went on and on and on, fists landing on the front door in hammer blows that made Vianne flinch.

Sophie came running down the stairs, clutching Bébé to her chest. "Maman!"

Vianne opened her arms and Sophie ran into her embrace. Vianne held her daughter close as the onslaught increased. Someone pounded on the side door. The copper pots and pans hanging in the kitchen clanged together, made a sound like church bells. She heard the high squealing of the outdoor pump. They were getting water.

Vianne said to Sophie, "Wait here one moment. Sit on the divan."

"Don't leave me!"

Vianne peeled her daughter away and forced her to sit down. Taking an iron poker from the side of the fireplace, she crept cautiously up the stairs. From the safety of her bedroom, she peered out the window, careful to remain hidden.

There were dozens of people in her yard; mostly women and children, moving like a pack of hungry wolves. Their voices melded into a single desperate growl.

Vianne backed away. What if the doors didn't hold? So many people could break down doors and windows, even walls.

Terrified, she went back downstairs, not breathing until she saw Sophie still safe on the divan. Vianne sat down beside her daughter and took her in her arms, letting Sophie curl up as if she were a much littler girl. She stroked her daughter's curly hair. A better mother, a stronger mother, would have had a story to tell right now, but Vianne was so afraid that her voice had gone completely. All she could think was an endless, beginningless prayer. *Please.*

She pulled Sophie closer and said, "Go to sleep, Sophie. I'm here."

"Maman," Sophie said, her voice almost lost in the pounding on the door. "What if Tante Isabelle is out there?"

Vianne stared down at Sophie's small, earnest face, covered now in a sheen of sweat and dust. "God help her" was all she could think of to say.

❧

At the sight of the gray stone house, Isabelle felt awash in exhaustion. Her shoulders sagged. The blisters on her feet became unbearable. In front of her, Gaëtan opened the gate. She heard it clatter brokenly and tilt sideways.

Leaning into him, she stumbled up to the front door. She knocked twice, wincing each time her bloodied knuckles hit the wood.

No one answered.

She pounded with both of her fists, trying to call out her sister's name, but her voice was too hoarse to find any volume.

She staggered back, almost sinking to her knees in defeat.

"Where can you sleep?" Gaëtan said, holding her upright with his hand on her waist.

"In the back. The pergola."

He led her around the house to the backyard. In the lush, jasmine-perfumed shadows of the arbor, she collapsed to her knees. She hardly noticed that he was gone, and then he was back with some tepid water, which she gulped from his cupped hands. It wasn't enough. Her stomach gnarled with hunger, sent an ache deep, deep inside of her. Still, when he started to leave again, she reached out for him, mumbled something, a plea not to be left alone, and he sank down beside her, putting out his arm for her to rest her head upon. They lay side by side in the warm dirt, staring up through the black thicket of vines that looped around the timbers and cascaded to the ground. The heady aromas of jasmine and blooming roses and rich earth created a beautiful bower. And yet, even here, in this quiet, it was impossible to forget what they'd just been through . . . and the changes that were close on their heels.

She had seen a change in Gaëtan, watched anger and impotent rage erase the compassion in his eyes and the smile from his lips. He had hardly spoken since the bombing, and when he did his voice was clipped and curt. They both knew more about war now, about what was coming.

"You could be safe here, with your sister," he said.

"I don't want to be safe. And my sister will not want me."

She twisted around to look at him. Moonlight came through in lacy patterns, illuminating his eyes, his mouth, leaving his nose and chin in darkness. He looked different again, older already, in just these few days; careworn, angry. He smelled of sweat and blood and mud and death, but she knew she smelled the same.

"Have you heard of Edith Cavell?" she asked.

"Do I strike you as an educated man?"

She thought about that for a moment and then said, "Yes."

He was quiet long enough that she knew she'd surprised him. "I know who she is. She saved the lives of hundreds of Allied airmen in the Great War. She is famous for saying that 'patriotism is not enough.' And this is your hero, a woman executed by the enemy."

"A woman who made a difference," Isabelle said, studying him. "I am relying on you—a criminal and a communist—to help me make a difference. Perhaps I am as mad and impetuous as they say."

"Who are 'they'?"

"Everyone." She paused, felt her expectation gather close. She had made a point of never trusting anyone, and yet she believed Gaëtan. He looked at her as if she mattered. "You will take me. As you promised."

"You know how such bargains are sealed?"

"How?"

"With a kiss."

"Quit teasing. This is serious."

"What's more serious than a kiss on the brink of war?" He was smiling, but not quite. That banked anger was in his eyes again, and it frightened her, reminded her that she really didn't know him at all.

"I would kiss a man who was brave enough to take me into battle with him."

"I think you know nothing of kissing," he said with a sigh.

"Shows what you know." She rolled away from him and immediately missed his touch. Trying to be nonchalant, she rolled back to face him and felt his breath on her eyelashes. "You may kiss me then. To seal our deal."

He reached out slowly, put a hand around the back of her neck, and pulled her toward him.

"Are you sure?" he asked, his lips almost touching hers. She didn't know if he was asking about going off to war or granting permission for a kiss, but right now, in this moment, it didn't matter. Isabelle had traded kisses with boys as if they were pennies to be left on park benches and lost in chair cushions—meaningless. Never before, not once, had she really yearned for a kiss.

"*Oui*," she whispered, leaning toward him.

At his kiss, something opened up inside the scraped, empty interior of her heart, unfurled. For the first time, her romantic novels made sense; she realized that the landscape of a woman's soul could change as quickly as a world at war.

"I love you," she whispered. She hadn't said these words since she was four years old; then, it had been to her mother. At her declaration, Gaëtan's expression changed, hardened. The smile he gave her was so tight and false she couldn't make sense of it. "What? Did I do something wrong?"

"No. Of course not," he said.

"We are lucky to have found each other," she said.

"We are not lucky, Isabelle. Trust me on this." As he said it, he drew her in for another kiss.

She gave herself over to the sensations of the kiss, let it become the whole of her universe, and knew finally how it felt to be enough for someone.

❧

When Vianne awoke, she noticed the quiet first. Somewhere a bird sang. She lay perfectly still in bed, listening. Beside her Sophie snored and grumbled in her sleep.

Vianne went to the window, lifting the blackout shade.

In her yard, apple branches hung like broken arms from the trees; the gate hung sideways, two of its three hinges ripped out. Across the road, the hay-field was flattened, the flowers crushed. The refugees who'd come through had left belongings and refuse in their wake—suitcases, buggies, coats too heavy to carry and too hot to wear, pillowcases, and wagons.

Vianne went downstairs and cautiously opened the front door. Listening for noise—hearing none—she unlatched the lock and turned the knob.

They had destroyed her garden, ripping up anything that looked edible, leaving broken stalks and mounds of dirt.

Everything was ruined, gone. Feeling defeated, she walked around the house to the backyard, which had also been ravaged.

She was about to go back inside when she heard a sound. A mewling. Maybe a baby crying.

There it was again. Had someone left an infant behind?

She moved cautiously across the yard to the wooden pergola draped in roses and jasmine.

Isabelle lay curled up on the ground, her dress ripped to shreds, her face cut up and bruised, her left eye swollen nearly shut, a piece of paper pinned to her bodice.

"Isabelle!"

Her sister's chin tilted upward slightly; she opened one bloodshot eye. "V," she said in a cracked, hoarse voice. "Thanks for locking me out."

Vianne went to her sister and knelt beside her. "Isabelle, you are covered in blood and bruised. Were you . . ."

Isabelle seemed not to understand for a moment. "Oh. It is not my blood. Most of it isn't, anyway." She looked around. "Where's Gaët?"

"What?"

Isabelle staggered to her feet, almost toppling over. "Did he leave me? He did." She started to cry. "He left me."

"Come on," Vianne said gently. She guided her sister into the cool interior of the house, where Isabelle kicked off her blood-splattered shoes, let them crack into the wall and clatter to the floor. Bloody footprints followed them to the bathroom tucked beneath the stairs.

While Vianne heated water and filled the bath, Isabelle sat on the floor, her legs splayed out, her feet discolored by blood, muttering to herself and wiping tears from her eyes, which turned to mud on her cheeks.

When the bath was ready, Vianne returned to Isabelle, gently undressing her. Isabelle was like a child, pliable, whimpering in pain.

Vianne unbuttoned the back of Isabelle's once-red dress and peeled it away, afraid that the slightest breath might topple her sister over. Isabelle's lacy undergarments were stained in places with blood. Vianne unlaced the corseted midsection of the foundation and eased it off.

Isabelle gritted her teeth and stepped into the tub.

"Lean back."

Isabelle did as she was told, and Vianne poured hot water over her sister's head, keeping the water from her sister's eyes. All the while, as she washed Isabelle's dirty hair and bruised body, she kept up a steady, soothing croon of meaningless words, meant to comfort.

She helped Isabelle out of the tub and dried her body with a soft, white towel. Isabelle stared at her, slack-jawed, blank-eyed.

"How about some sleep?" Vianne said.

"Sleep," Isabelle mumbled, her head lolling to one side.

Vianne brought Isabelle a nightdress that smelled of lavender and rose water and helped her into it. Isabelle could hardly keep her eyes open as Vianne guided her to the upstairs bedroom and settled her beneath a light blanket. Isabelle was asleep before her head hit the pillow.

❧

Isabelle woke to darkness. She remembered daylight.

Where was she?

She sat up so quickly her head spun. She took a few shallow breaths and then looked around.

The upstairs bedroom at Le Jardin. Her old room. It did not give her a warm feeling. How often had Madame Doom locked her in the bedroom "for her own good"?

"Don't think about that," she said aloud.

An even worse memory followed: Gaëtan. He had abandoned her after all; it filled her with the kind of bone-deep disappointment she knew so well.

Had she learned *nothing* in life? People left. She knew that. They especially left her.

She dressed in the shapeless blue housedress Vianne had left draped across the foot of the bed. Then she went down the narrow, shallow-stepped stairs, holding on to the iron banister. Every pain-filled step felt like a triumph.

Downstairs, the house was quiet except for the crackling, staticky sound of a radio on at a low volume. She was pretty sure Maurice Chevalier was singing a love song. *Perfect.*

Vianne was in the kitchen, wearing a gingham apron over a pale yellow housedress. A floral scarf covered her hair. She was peeling potatoes with a paring knife. Behind her, a cast-iron pot made a cheery little bubbling sound.

The aromas made Isabelle's mouth water.

Vianne rushed forward to pull out a chair at the small table in the kitchen's corner. "Here, sit."

Isabelle fell onto the seat. Vianne brought her a plate that was already prepared. A hunk of still-warm bread, a triangle of cheese, a smear of quince paste, and a few slices of ham.

Isabelle took the bread in her red, scraped-up hands, lifting it to her face, breathing in the yeasty smell. Her hands were shaking as she picked up a knife and slathered the bread with fruit and cheese. When she set down the knife it clattered. She picked up the bread and bit into it; the single best bite of food of her life. The hard crust of the bread, its pillow-soft interior, the buttery cheese, and the fruit all combined to make her practically swoon. She ate the rest of it like a madwoman, barely noticing the cup of *café noir* her sister had set down beside her.

"Where's Sophie?" Isabelle asked, her cheeks bulging with food. It was difficult to stop eating, even to be polite. She reached for a peach, felt its fuzzy ripeness in her hand, and bit into it. Juice dribbled down her chin.

"She's next door, playing with Sarah. You remember my friend, Rachel?"

"I remember her," Isabelle said.

Vianne poured herself a tiny cup of espresso and brought it to the table, where she sat down.

Isabelle burped and covered her mouth. "Pardon."

"I think a lapse in manners can be overlooked," Vianne said with a smile.

"You haven't met Madame Dufour. No doubt she would hit me with a brick for that transgression." Isabelle sighed. Her stomach hurt now; she felt like she might vomit. She wiped her moist chin with her sleeve. "What is the news from Paris?"

"The swastika flag flies from the Eiffel Tower."

"And Papa?"

"Fine, he says."

"Worried about me, I'll bet," Isabelle said bitterly. "He shouldn't have sent me away. But when has he ever done anything else?"

A look passed between them. It was one of the few memories they shared, that abandonment, but clearly Vianne didn't want to remember it. "We hear there were more than ten million of you on the roads."

"The crowds weren't the worst of it," Isabelle said. "We were mostly women and children, V, and old men and boys. And they just . . . obliterated us."

"It's over now, thank God," Vianne said. "It's best to focus on the good. Who is Gaëtan? You spoke of him in your delirium."

Isabelle picked at one of the scrapes on the back of her hand, realizing an instant too late that she should have let it alone. The scab ripped away and blood bubbled up.

"Maybe he has to do with this," Vianne said when the silence elongated. She pulled a crumpled piece of paper out of her apron pocket. It was the note that had been pinned to Isabelle's bodice. Dirty, bloody fingerprints ran across the paper. On it was written: *You are not ready.*

Isabelle felt the world drop out from under her. It was a ridiculous, girlish reaction, overblown, and she knew it, but still it hit her hard, wounded deep. He had wanted to take her with him until the kiss. Somehow he'd tasted the lack in her. "He's no one," she said grimly, taking the note, crumpling it. "Just a boy with black hair and a sharp face who tells lies. He's nothing." Then she looked at Vianne. "I'm going off to the war. I don't care what anyone thinks. I'll drive an ambulance or roll bandages. Anything."

"Oh, for heaven's sake, Isabelle. Paris is overrun. The Nazis control the city. What is an eighteen-year-old girl to do about all of that?"

"I am not hiding out in the country while the Nazis destroy France. And let's face it, you have never exactly felt sisterly toward me." Her aching face tightened. "I'll be leaving as soon as I can walk."

"You will be safe here, Isabelle. That's what matters. You must stay."

"Safe?" Isabelle spat. "You think that is what matters now, Vianne? Let me tell you what I saw out there. French troops running from the enemy. Nazis murdering innocents. Maybe you can ignore that, but I won't."

"You will stay here and be safe. We will speak of it no more."

"When have I ever been safe with you, Vianne?" Isabelle said, seeing hurt blossom in her sister's eyes.

"I was young, Isabelle. I tried to be a mother to you."

"Oh, please. Let's not start with a lie."

"After I lost the baby—"

Isabelle turned her back on her sister and limped away before she said something unforgiveable. She clasped her hands to still their trembling. *This* was why she hadn't wanted to return to this house and see her sister, why she'd stayed away for years. There was too much pain between them. She turned up the radio to drown out her thoughts.

A voice crackled over the airwaves. ". . . Maréchal Pétain speaking to you . . ."

Isabelle frowned. Pétain was a hero of the Great War, a beloved leader of France. She turned up the volume further.

Vianne appeared beside her.

". . . I assumed the direction of the government of France . . ."

Static overtook his deep voice, crackled through it.

Isabelle thumped the radio impatiently.

". . . our admirable army, which is fighting with a heroism worthy of its long military traditions against an enemy superior in numbers and arms . . ."

Static. Isabelle hit the radio again, whispering, "*Zut.*"

". . . in these painful hours I think of the unhappy refugees who, in extreme misery, clog our roads. I express to them my compassion and my solicitude. It is with a broken heart that I tell you today it is necessary to stop fighting."

"We've won?" Vianne said.

"Shhh," Isabelle said sharply.

". . . addressed myself last night to the adversary to ask him if he is ready to speak with me, as soldier to soldier, after the actual fighting is over, and with honor, the means of putting an end to hostilities."

The old man's words droned on, saying things like "trying days" and "control their anguish" and, worst of all, "destiny of the fatherland." Then he said the word Isabelle never thought she'd hear in France.

Surrender.

Isabelle hobbled out of the room on her bloody feet and went into the backyard, needing air suddenly, unable to draw a decent breath.

Surrender. France. To Hitler.

"It must be for the best," her sister said calmly.

When had Vianne come out here?

"You've heard about Maréchal Pétain. He is a hero unparalleled. If he says we must quit fighting, we must. I'm sure he'll reason with Hitler." Vianne reached out.

Isabelle yanked away. The thought of Vianne's comforting touch made her feel sick. She limped around to face her sister. "You don't *reason* with men like Hitler."

"So you know more than our heroes now?"

"I know we shouldn't give up."

Vianne made a tsking sound, a little scuff of disappointment. "If Maréchal Pétain thinks surrender is best for France, it is. Period. At least the war will be over and our men will come home."

"You are a fool."

Vianne said, "Fine," and went back into the house.

Isabelle tented a hand over her eyes and stared up into the bright and cloudless sky. How long would it be before all this blue was filled with German aeroplanes?

She didn't know how long she stood there, imagining the worst— remembering how the Nazis had opened fire on innocent women and children in Tours, obliterating them, turning the grass red with their blood.

"Tante Isabelle?"

Isabelle heard the small, tentative voice as if from far away. She turned slowly.

A beautiful girl stood at Le Jardin's back door. She had skin like her mother's, as pale as fine porcelain, and expressive eyes that appeared coal black from this distance, as dark as her father's. She could have stepped from the pages of a fairy tale—Snow White or Sleeping Beauty.

"You can't be Sophie," Isabelle said. "The last time I saw you . . . you were sucking your thumb."

"I still do sometimes," Sophie said with a conspiratorial smile. "You won't tell?"

"Me? I am the best of secret keepers." Isabelle moved toward her, thinking, *my niece*. Family. "Shall I tell you a secret about me, just so that we are fair?"

Sophie nodded earnestly, her eyes widening.

"I can make myself invisible."

"No, you can't."

Isabelle saw Vianne appear at the back door. "Ask your maman. I have sneaked onto trains and climbed out of windows and run away from convent dungeons. All of this because I can disappear."

"Isabelle," Vianne said sternly.

Sophie stared up at Isabelle, enraptured. "Really?"

Isabelle glanced at Vianne. "It is easy to disappear when no one is looking at you."

"I am looking at you," Sophie said. "Will you make yourself invisible now?"

Isabelle laughed. "Of course not. Magic, to be its best, must be unexpected. Don't you agree? And now, shall we play a game of checkers?"

EIGHT

The surrender was a bitter pill to swallow, but Maréchal Pétain was an honorable man. A hero of the last war with Germany. Yes, he was old, but Vianne shared the belief that this only gave him a better perspective from which to judge their circumstances. He had fashioned a way for their men to come home, so it wouldn't be like the Great War.

Vianne understood what Isabelle could not: Pétain had surrendered on behalf of France to save lives and preserve their nation and their way of life. It was true that the terms of this surrender were difficult: France had been divided into two zones. The Occupied Zone—the northern half of the country and the coastal regions (including Carriveau)—was to be taken over and governed by the Nazis. The great middle of the country, the land that lay below Paris and above the sea, would be the Free Zone, governed by a new French government in Vichy, led by Maréchal Pétain himself, in collaboration with the Nazis.

Immediately upon France's surrender, food became scarce. Laundry soap: unobtainable. Ration cards could not be counted upon. Phone service became unreliable, as did the mail. The Nazis effectively cut off communication between cities and towns. The only mail allowed was on official German postcards. But for Vianne, these were not the worst of the changes.

Isabelle became impossible to live with. Several times since the surrender, while Vianne toiled to reconstruct and replant her garden and repair her damaged fruit trees, she had paused in her work and seen Isabelle standing at the gate staring up at the sky as if some dark and horrible thing were headed this way.

All Isabelle could talk about was the monstrosity of the Nazis and their determination to kill the French. She had no ability—of course—to hold her tongue, and since Vianne refused to listen, Sophie became Isabelle's audience, her acolyte. She filled poor Sophie's head with terrible images of what would happen, so much so that the child had nightmares. Vianne dared not leave the two of them alone, and so today, like each of the previous days, she made them both come to town with her to see what their ration cards would get them.

They had been standing in a food queue at the butcher's shop for two hours already. Isabelle had been complaining nearly that whole time. Apparently it made no sense to her that she should have to shop for food.

"Vianne, look," Isabelle said.

More dramatics.

"Vianne. *Look.*"

She turned—just to silence her sister—and saw them.

Germans.

Up and down the street, windows and doors slammed shut. People disappeared so quickly Vianne found herself suddenly standing alone on the sidewalk with her sister and daughter. She grabbed Sophie and pulled her against the butcher shop's closed door.

Isabelle stepped defiantly into the street.

"Isabelle," Vianne hissed, but Isabelle stood her ground, her green eyes bright with hatred, her pale, fine-boned beautiful face marred by scratches and bruises.

The green lorry in the lead came to a halt in front of Isabelle. In the back, soldiers sat on benches, facing one another, rifles laid casually across their laps. They looked young and clean shaven and eager in brand-new helmets, with medals glinting on their gray-green uniforms. Young most of all. Not monsters; just boys, really. They craned their necks to see what had stopped traffic. At the sight of Isabelle standing there, the soldiers started to smile and wave.

Vianne grabbed Isabelle's hand and yanked her out of the way.

The military entourage rumbled past them, a string of vehicles and motorcycles and lorries covered in camouflaged netting. Armored tanks rolled thunderously on the cobblestoned street. And then came the soldiers.

Two long lines of them, marching into town.

Isabelle walked boldly alongside them, up rue Victor Hugo. The Germans waved to her, looking more like tourists than conquerors.

"Maman, you can't let her go off by herself," Sophie said.

"Merde." Vianne clutched Sophie's hand and ran after Isabelle. They caught up with her in the next block.

The town square, usually full of people, had practically emptied. Only a few townspeople dared to remain as the German vehicles pulled up in front of the town hall and parked.

An officer appeared—or Vianne assumed he was an officer because of the way he began barking orders.

Soldiers marched around the large cobblestoned square, claiming it with their overwhelming presence. They ripped down the flag of France and replaced it with their Nazi flag: a huge black swastika against a red and black background. When it was in place, the troops stopped as one, extended their right arms, and yelled, *"Heil Hitler."*

"If I had a gun," Isabelle said, "I'd show them not all of us wanted to surrender."

"Shhh," Vianne said. "You'll get us all killed with that mouth of yours. Let's go."

"No. I want—"

Vianne spun to face Isabelle. "Enough. You will *not* draw attention to us. Is that understood?"

Isabelle gave one last hate-filled glance at the marching soldiers and then let Vianne lead her away.

They slipped from the main street and entered a dark cleft in the walls that led to a back alley behind the milliner's shop. They could hear the soldiers singing. Then a shot rang out. And another. Someone screamed.

Isabelle stopped.

"Don't you dare," Vianne said. *"Move."*

They kept to the dark alleys, ducking into doorways when they heard voices coming their way. It took longer than usual to get through town, but eventually they made it to the dirt road. They walked silently past the cemetery and all the way home. Once inside, Vianne slammed the door behind her and locked it.

"You see?" Isabelle said instantly. She had obviously been waiting to throw out the question.

"Go to your room," Vianne said to Sophie. Whatever Isabelle was going to say, she didn't want Sophie to hear. Vianne eased the hat from her head and set down her empty basket. Her hands were shaking.

"They're here because of the airfield," Isabelle said. She began pacing. "I didn't think it would happen so fast, even with the surrender. I didn't believe . . . I thought our soldiers would fight anyway. I thought . . ."

"Quit biting at your nails. You'll make them bleed, you know."

Isabelle looked a madwoman, with her waist-length blond hair falling loose from its braid and her bruised face twisted with fury. "The Nazis are *here*, Vianne. In Carriveau. Their flag flies from the *hôtel de ville* as it flies from the Arc du Triomphe and the Eiffel Tower. They weren't in town five minutes and a shot was fired."

"The war is over, Isabelle. Maréchal Pétain said so."

"The war is over? The war is *over*? Did you *see* them back there, with their guns and their flags and their arrogance? We need to get out of here, V. We'll take Sophie and leave Carriveau."

"And go where?"

"Anywhere. Lyon, maybe. Provence. What was that town in the Dordogne where Maman was born? Brantôme. We could find her friend, that Basque woman, what was her name? She might help us."

"You are giving me a headache."

"A headache is the least of your problems," Isabelle said, pacing again.

Vianne approached her. "You are not going to do anything crazy or stupid. Am I understood?"

Isabelle growled in frustration and marched upstairs, slamming the door behind her.

Surrender.

The word stuck in Isabelle's thoughts. That night, as she lay in the downstairs guest bedroom, staring up at the ceiling, she felt frustration lodge in her so deeply she could hardly think straight.

Was she supposed to spend the war in this house like some helpless girl, doing laundry and standing in food lines and sweeping the floor? Was she to stand by and watch the enemy take everything from France?

She had always felt lonely and frustrated—or at least she had felt it for as long as she could remember—but never as sharply as now. She was stuck here in the country with no friends and nothing to do.

No.

There must be something she could do. Even here, even now.

Hide the valuables.

It was all that came to her. The Germans would loot the houses in town; of that she had no doubt, and when they did they would take everything of value. Her own government—cowards that they were—had known that. It was why they had emptied much of the Louvre and put fake paintings on the museum walls.

"Not much of a plan," she muttered. But it was better than nothing.

The next day, as soon as Vianne and Sophie left for school, Isabelle began. She ignored Vianne's request that she go to town for food. She couldn't stand to see the Nazis, and one day without meat would hardly matter. Instead, she searched the house, opening closets and rummaging through drawers and looking under the beds. She took every item of value and set it on the trestle table in the dining room. There were lots of valuable heirlooms. Lacework tatted by her great-grandmother, a set of sterling silver salt and pepper shakers, a gilt-edged Limoges platter that had been their aunt's, several small impressionist paintings, a tablecloth made of fine ivory Alençon lace, several photograph albums, a silver-framed photograph of Vianne and Antoine and baby Sophie, her mother's pearls, Vianne's wedding dress and more. Isabelle boxed up everything that would fit in a wooden-trimmed leather trunk, which she dragged through the trampled grass, wincing every time it scraped on a stone or thudded into something. By the time she reached the barn, she was breathing hard and sweating.

The barn was smaller than she remembered. The hayloft—once the only place in the world where she was happy—was really just a small tier on the second floor, a bit of floor perched at the top of a rickety ladder and beneath the roof, through which slats of sky could be seen. How many hours had she spent up there alone with her picture books, pretending that someone cared enough to come looking for her? Waiting for her sister, who was always out with Rachel or Antoine.

She pushed that memory aside.

The center of the barn was no more than thirty feet wide. It had been built by her great-grandfather to hold buggies—back when the family had money. Now there was only an old Renault parked in the center. The stalls were filled with tractor parts and web-draped wooden ladders and rusted farm implements.

She closed the barn door and went to the automobile. The driver's side door opened with a squeaking, clattering reluctance. She climbed in, started the engine, drove forward about eight feet, and then parked.

The trapdoor was revealed now. About five feet long and four feet wide and made of planks connected by leather straps, the cellar door was nearly impossible to see, especially as it was now, covered in dust and old hay. She pulled the trapdoor open, letting it rest against the automobile's dinged-up bumper, and peered down into the musty darkness.

Holding the trunk by its strap, she turned on her torchlight and clamped it under her other armpit and climbed down the ladder slowly, clanking the trunk down, rung by rung, until she was at the bottom. The trunk clattered onto the dirt floor beside her.

Like the loft, this hidey-hole had seemed bigger to her as a child. It was about eight feet wide and ten feet long, with shelving along one side and an old mattress on the floor. The shelves used to hold barrels for winemaking, but a lantern was the only thing left on the shelves.

She tucked the trunk into the back corner and then went back to the house, where she gathered up some preserved food, blankets, some medical supplies, her father's hunting shotgun, and a bottle of wine, all of which she put out on the shelves.

When she climbed back up the ladder, she found Vianne in the barn.

"What in the world are you doing out here?"

Isabelle wiped her dusty hands on the worn cotton of her skirt. "Hiding your valuables and putting supplies down here—in case we need to hide from the Nazis. Come down and look. I did a good job, I think." She backed down the ladder and Vianne followed her into the darkness. Lighting a lantern, Isabelle proudly showed off Papa's shotgun and the foodstuffs and medical supplies.

Vianne went straight to their mother's jewelry box, opening it.

Inside lay brooches and earrings and necklaces, mostly costume pieces. But at the bottom, lying on blue velvet, were the pearls that Grandmère had worn on her wedding day and given to Maman to wear on her wedding day.

"You may need to sell them someday," Isabelle said.

Vianne clamped the box shut. "They are heirlooms, Isabelle. For Sophie's wedding day—and yours. I would never sell them." She sighed impatiently and turned to Isabelle. "What food were you able to get in town?"

"I did this instead."

"Of course you did. It's more important to hide Maman's pearls than to feed your niece supper. Honestly, Isabelle." Vianne climbed up the ladder, her displeasure revealed in tiny, disgusted huffs.

Isabelle left the cellar and drove the Renault back into place over the door. Then she hid the keys behind a broken board in one of the stalls. At the last moment, she disabled the automobile by removing the distributor cap. She hid it with the keys.

When she finally returned to the house, Vianne was in the kitchen, frying potatoes in a cast-iron skillet. "I hope you aren't hungry."

"I'm not." She moved past Vianne, barely making eye contact. "Oh, and I hid the keys and distributor cap in the first stall, behind a broken board." In the living room, she turned on the radio and scooted close, hoping for news from the BBC.

There was a staticky crackle and then an unfamiliar voice said, "This is the BBC. Général de Gaulle is speaking to you."

"Vianne!" Isabelle yelled toward the kitchen. "Who is Général de Gaulle?"

Vianne came into the living room, drying her hands on her apron. "What is—"

"Shush," Isabelle snapped.

". . . the leaders who have been at the head of the French army for many years have formed a government. On the pretext that our army has been defeated, this government has approached the enemy with a view to ceasing hostilities."

Isabelle stared at the small wooden radio, transfixed. This man they'd never heard of spoke directly to the people of France, not at them as Pétain had done, but to them in an impassioned voice. "Pretext of defeat. I *knew* it!"

". . . we certainly have been, and still are, submerged by the mechanical strength of the enemy, both on land and in the air. The tanks, the aeroplanes, the tactics of the Germans astounded our generals to such an extent that they have been brought to the pain which they are in today. But has the last word been said? Has all hope disappeared? Is the defeat final?"

"*Mon Dieu*," Isabelle said. This was what she'd been waiting to hear. There *was* something to be done, a fight to engage in. The surrender wasn't final.

"Whatever happens," de Gaulle's voice went on, "the flame of French resistance must not and shall not die."

Isabelle hardly noticed that she was crying. The French hadn't given up. Now all Isabelle had to do was figure out how to answer this call.

⁂

Two days after the Nazis occupied Carriveau, they called a meeting for the late afternoon. Everyone was to attend. No exceptions. Even so, Vianne had had to fight with Isabelle to get her to come. As usual, Isabelle did not think ordinary rules pertained to her and she wanted to use defiance to show her displeasure. As if the Nazis cared what one impetuous eighteen-year-old girl thought of their occupation of her country.

"Wait here," Vianne said impatiently when she'd finally gotten Isabelle and Sophie out of the house. She gently closed the broken gate behind them. It gave a little click of closure.

Moments later, Rachel appeared in the road, coming toward them, with the baby in her arms and Sarah at her side.

"That's my best friend, Sarah," Sophie said, gazing up at Isabelle.

"Isabelle," Rachel said with a smile. "It is good to see you again."

"Is it?" Isabelle said.

Rachel moved closer to Isabelle. "That was a long time ago," Rachel said gently. "We were young and stupid and selfish. I'm sorry we treated you badly. Ignored you. That must have been very painful."

Isabelle's mouth opened, closed. For once, she had nothing to say.

"Let's go," Vianne said, irritated that Rachel had said to Isabelle what Vianne had not been able to. "We shouldn't be late."

Even this late in the day, the weather was unseasonably warm, and in no time, Vianne felt herself beginning to sweat. In town, they joined the grumbling crowd that filled the narrow cobblestoned street from storefront to storefront. The shops were closed and the windows were shuttered, even though the heat would be unbearable when they got home. Most of the display cases were empty, which was hardly surprising. The Germans ate so much; even worse, they left food on their plates in the cafés. Careless and cruel, it was, with so many mothers beginning to count the jars in their cellars so that they could dole out every precious bite to their children. Nazi propaganda was everywhere, on windows and shop walls; posters that showed smiling German soldiers surrounded by French children with captions designed to encourage the French to accept their conquerors and become good citizens of the Reich.

As the crowd approached the town hall, the grumbling stopped. Up close, it felt even worse, this following of instructions, walking blindly into a place with guarded doors and locked windows.

"We shouldn't go in," Isabelle said.

Rachel, who stood between the sisters, towering over both of them, made a tsking sound. She resettled the baby in her arms, patting his back in a comforting rhythm. "We have been summoned."

"All the more reason to hide," Isabelle said.

"Sophie and I are going in," Vianne said, although she had to admit that she felt a prickly sense of foreboding.

"I have a bad feeling about it," Isabelle muttered.

Like a thousand-legged centipede, the crowd moved forward into the great hall. Tapestries had once hung from these walls, leftover treasure from the time of kings, when the Loire Valley had been the royal hunting ground, but all that was gone now. Instead there were swastikas and propagandist posters on the walls—*Trust in the Reich!*—and a huge painting of Hitler.

Beneath the painting stood a man wearing a black field tunic decorated with medals and iron crosses, knee breeches, and spit-shined boots. A red swastika armband circled his right bicep.

When the hall was full, the soldiers closed the oak doors, which creaked in protest. The officer at the front of the hall faced them, shot his right arm out, and said, *"Heil Hitler."*

The crowd murmured softly among themselves. What should they do? *"Heil Hitler,"* a few said grudgingly. The room began to smell of sweat and leather polish and cigarette smoke.

"I am Sturmbannführer Weldt of the Geheime Staatspolizei. The Gestapo," the man in the black uniform said in heavily accented French. "I am here to carry out the terms of the armistice on behalf of the fatherland and the Führer. It will be of little hardship on those of you who obey the rules." He cleared his throat.

"The rules: All radios are to be turned in to us at the town hall, immediately, as are all guns, explosives, and ammunition. All operational vehicles will be impounded. All windows will be equipped with material for blackout, and you shall use it. A nine P.M. curfew is instantly in effect. No lights shall be on after dusk. We will control all food, whether grown or imported." He paused, looked out over the mass of people standing in front of him. "Not so bad, see? We will live together in harmony, yes? But know this. Any act of sabotage or espionage or resistance will be dealt with swiftly and without mercy. The punishment for such behavior is death by execution." He pulled a pack of cigarettes from his breast pocket and extracted a single cigarette. Lighting it, he stared out at the people so intently it seemed he was memorizing each face. "Also, although many of your ragged, cowardly soldiers are returning, we must inform you that the men taken prisoner by us shall remain in Germany."

Vianne felt confusion ripple through the audience. She looked at Rachel, whose square face was blotchy in places—a sign of anxiety. "Marc and Antoine will come home," Rachel said stubbornly.

The Sturmbannführer went on. "You may leave now, as I am sure we understand each other. I will have officers here until eight forty-five tonight. They will receive your contraband. Do not be late. And . . ." He smiled good-naturedly. "Do not risk your lives to keep a radio. Whatever you keep—or hide—we will find, and if we find it . . . death." He said it so casually, and wearing such a fine smile, that for a moment, it didn't sink in.

The crowd stood there a moment longer, uncertain whether it was safe to move. No one wanted to be seen as taking the first step, and then suddenly they were moving, pack-like, toward the open doors that led them outside.

"Bastards," Isabelle said as they moved into an alley.

"And I was so sure they'd let us keep our guns," Rachel said, lighting up a cigarette, inhaling deeply and exhaling in a rush.

"I'm keeping our gun, I can tell you," Isabelle said in a loud voice. "And our radio."

"Shhh," Vianne said.

"Général de Gaulle thinks—"

"I don't want to hear that foolishness. We have to keep our heads down until our men come home," Vianne said.

"*Mon Dieu*," Isabelle said sharply. "You think your husband can fix this?"

"No," Vianne said. "I believe *you* will fix it, you and your Général de Gaulle, of whom no one has ever heard. Now, come. While you are hatching a plan to save France, I need to tend to my garden. Come on, Rachel, let us dullards be away."

Vianne held tightly to Sophie's hand and walked briskly ahead. She did not bother to glance back to see if Isabelle was following. She knew her sister was back there, hobbling forward on her damaged feet. Ordinarily Vianne would keep pace with her sister, out of politeness, but just now she was too mad to care.

"Your sister may not be so wrong," Rachel said as they passed the Norman church on the edge of town.

"If you take her side in this, I may be forced to hurt you, Rachel."

"That being said, your sister may not be entirely wrong."

Vianne sighed. "Don't tell her that. She's unbearable already."

"She will have to learn propriety."

"*You* teach her. She has proven singularly resistant to improving herself or listening to reason. She's been to two finishing schools and still can't hold her tongue or make polite conversation. Two days ago, instead of going to town for meat, she hid the valuables and created a hiding place for us. Just in case."

"I should probably hide mine, too. Not that we have much."

Vianne pursed her lips. There was no point in talking further about this. Soon, Antoine would be home and he would help keep Isabelle in line.

At the gate to Le Jardin, Vianne said good-bye to Rachel and her children, who kept walking.

"Why do we have to give them our radio, Maman?" Sophie asked. "It belongs to Papa."

"We don't," Isabelle said, coming up beside them. "We will hide it."

"We will not hide it," Vianne said sharply. "We will do as we are told and keep quiet and soon Antoine will be home and he will know what to do."

"Welcome to the Middle Ages, Sophie," Isabelle said.

Vianne yanked her gate open, forgetting a second too late that the refugees had broken it. The poor thing clattered on its single hinge. It took all of Vianne's fortitude to act as if it hadn't happened. She marched up to the house, opened the door, and immediately turned on the kitchen light. "Sophie," she said, unpinning her hat. "Would you please set the table?"

Vianne ignored her daughter's grumbling—it was to be expected. In only a few days, Isabelle had taught her niece to challenge authority.

Vianne lit the stove and started cooking. When a creamy potato and lardon soup was simmering, she began to clean up. Of course Isabelle was nowhere around to help. Sighing, she filled the sink with water to wash dishes. She was so intent on her task that it took her a moment to notice that someone was knocking on the front door. Patting her hair, she walked into the living room, where she found Isabelle rising from the divan, a book in her hands. Reading while Vianne cooked and cleaned. Naturally.

"Are you expecting anyone?" Isabelle asked.

Vianne shook her head.

"Maybe we shouldn't answer," Isabelle said. "Pretend we're not here."

"It's most likely Rachel."

There was another knock at the door.

Slowly, the doorknob turned, and the door creaked open.

Yes. Of course it was Rachel. Who else would—

A German soldier stepped into her home.

"Oh, my pardons," the man said in terrible French. He removed his military hat, tucked it in his armpit, and smiled. He was a good-looking man—tall and broad-shouldered and narrow-hipped, with pale skin and light gray eyes. Vianne guessed he was roughly her age. His field uniform was precisely pressed and looked brand new. An iron cross decorated his stand-up collar. Binoculars hung from a strap around his neck and a chunky leather utility belt cinched his waist. Behind him, through the branches of the orchard, she saw his motorcycle parked on the side of the road. A sidecar was attached to it, mounted with machine guns.

"Mademoiselle," he said to Vianne, giving her a swift nod as he clicked his boots together.

"Madame," she corrected him, wishing she sounded haughty and in control, but even to her own ears she sounded scared. "Madame Mauriac."

"I am Hauptmann—Captain—Wolfgang Beck." He handed her a piece of paper. "My French is not so good. You will excuse my ineptitude, please." When he smiled, deep dimples formed in his cheeks.

She took the paper and frowned down at it. "I don't read German."

"What do you want?" Isabelle demanded, coming to stand by Vianne.

"Your home is most beautiful and very close to the airfield. I noticed it upon our arrival. How many bedrooms have you?"

"Why?" Isabelle said at the same time Vianne said, "Three."

"I will billet here," the captain said in his bad French.

"Billet?" Vianne said. "You mean . . . to stay?"

"*Oui,* Madame."

"Billet? You? A man? A *Nazi?* No. No." Isabelle shook her head. "*No.*"

The captain's smile neither faded nor fell. "You were to town," he said, looking at Isabelle. "I saw you when we arrived."

"You noticed me?"

He smiled. "I am sure every red-blooded man in my regiment noticed you."

"Funny you would mention blood," Isabelle said.

Vianne elbowed her sister. "I am sorry, Captain. My young sister is obstinate on occasion. But I am married, you see, and my husband is at the front, and there is my sister and my daughter here, so you must see how inappropriate it would be to have you here."

"Ah, so you would rather leave the house to me. How difficult that must be for you."

"Leave?" Vianne said.

"I believe you aren't understanding the captain," Isabelle said, not taking her gaze from him. "He's moving into your home, taking it over, really, and that piece of paper is a requisition order that makes it possible. And Pétain's armistice, of course. We can either make room for him or abandon a home that has been in our family for generations."

He looked uncomfortable. "This, I'm afraid, is the situation. Many of your fellow villagers are facing the same dilemma, I fear."

"If we leave, will we get our home back?" Isabelle asked.

"I would not think so, Madame."

Vianne dared to take a step toward him. Perhaps she could reason with him. "My husband will be home any day now, I imagine. Perhaps you could wait until he is here?"

"I am not the general, alas. I am simply a captain in the Wehrmacht. I follow orders, Madame, I do not give them. And I am ordered to billet here. But I assure you that I am a gentleman."

"We will leave," Isabelle said.

"Leave?" Vianne said to her sister in disbelief. "This is my home." To the captain she said, "I can count on you to be a gentleman?"

"Of course."

Vianne looked at Isabelle, who shook her head slowly.

Vianne knew there was no real choice. She had to keep Sophie safe until Antoine came home, and then he would handle this unpleasantness. Surely he would be home soon, now that the armistice had been signed. "There is a small bedroom downstairs. You'll be comfortable there."

The captain nodded. "*Merci*, Madame. I will get my things."

❦

As soon as the door closed behind the captain, Isabelle said, "Are you mad? We can't live with a Nazi."

"He said he's in the Wehrmacht. Is that the same thing?"

"I'm hardly interested in their chain of command. You haven't seen what they're willing to do to us, Vianne. I have. We'll leave. Go next door, to Rachel's. We could live with her."

"Rachel's house is too small for all of us, and I am not going to abandon my home to the Germans."

To that, Isabelle had no answer.

Vianne felt anxiety turn to an itch along her throat. An old nervous habit returned. "You go if you must, but I am waiting for Antoine. We have surrendered, so he'll be home soon."

"Vianne, please—"

The front door rattled hard. Another knock.

Vianne walked dully forward. With a shaking hand, she reached for the knob and opened the door.

Captain Beck stood there, holding his military hat in one hand and a small leather valise in the other. He said, "Hello again, Madame," as if he'd been gone for some time.

Vianne scratched at her neck, feeling acutely vulnerable beneath this man's gaze. She backed away quickly, saying, "This way, Herr Captain."

As she turned, she saw the living room that had been decorated by three generations of her family's women. Golden stucco walls, the color of freshly baked brioche, gray stone floors covered by ancient Aubusson rugs, heavily carved wooden furniture upholstered in mohair and tapestry fabric, lamps made of porcelain, curtains of gold and red toile, antiques and treasures left over from the years when the Rossignols had been wealthy tradesmen. Until recently there had been artwork on the walls. Now only the unimportant pieces remained. Isabelle had hidden the good ones.

Vianne walked past all of it to the small guest bedroom tucked beneath the stairs. At the closed door, to the left of the bathroom that had been added in the early twenties, she paused. She could hear him breathing behind her.

She opened the door to reveal a narrow room with a large window, bracketed by blue-gray curtains that pooled on the wooden floor. A painted chest of drawers supported a blue pitcher and ewer. In the corner was an aged oak armoire with mirrored doors. By the double bed sat a nightstand; on it, an antique ormolu clock. Isabelle's clothes lay everywhere, as if she were packing for an extended holiday. Vianne picked them up quickly, and the valise, too. When she finished, she turned.

His suitcase plunked to the floor. She looked at him, compelled by simple politeness to offer a tense smile.

"You needn't worry, Madame," he said. "We have been admonished to act as gentlemen. My mother would demand the same, and, in truth, she scares me more than my general." It was such an ordinary remark that Vianne was taken aback.

She had no idea how to respond to this stranger who dressed like the enemy and looked like a young man she might have met at church. And what was the price for saying the wrong thing?

He remained where he was, a respectful distance from her. "I apologize for any inconvenience, Madame."

"My husband will be home soon."

"We all hope to be home soon."

Another unnerving comment. Vianne nodded politely and left him alone in the room, closing the door behind her.

"Tell me he's not staying," Isabelle said, rushing at her.

"He says he is," Vianne said tiredly, pushing back the hair from her eyes. She realized just now that she was trembling. "I know how you feel about these Nazis. Just make sure he doesn't know it. I won't let you put Sophie at risk with your childish rebellion."

"Childish rebellion! Are you—"

The guest room door opened, silencing Isabelle.

Captain Beck strode confidently toward them, smiling broadly. Then he saw the radio in the room and he paused. "Do not worry, ladies. I am most pleased to deliver your radio to the Kommandant."

"Really?" Isabelle said. "You consider this a kindness?"

Vianne felt a tightening in her chest. There was a storm brewing in Isabelle. Her sister's cheeks had gone pale, her lips were drawn in a thin, colorless line, her eyes were narrowed. She was glaring at the German as if she could kill him with a look.

"Of course." He smiled, looking a little confused. The sudden silence seemed to unnerve him. Suddenly he said, "You have beautiful hair, M'mselle." At Isabelle's frown, he said, "This is an appropriate compliment, yes?"

"Do you think so?" Isabelle said, her voice low.

"Quite lovely." Beck smiled.

Isabelle walked into the kitchen and came back with a pair of boning shears.

His smile faded. "Am I misunderstood?"

Vianne said, "Isabelle, don't," just as Isabelle gathered up her thick blond hair and fisted it. Staring grimly at Captain Beck's handsome face, she hacked off her hair and handed the long blond tail to him. "It must be *verboten* for us to have anything beautiful, is it not, Captain Beck?"

Vianne gasped. "Please, sir. Ignore her. Isabelle is a silly, prideful girl."

"No," Beck said. "She is angry. And angry people make mistakes in war and die."

"So do conquering soldiers," Isabelle snapped.

Beck laughed at her.

Isabelle made a sound that was practically a snarl and pivoted on her heel. She marched up the stairs and slammed the door shut so hard the house shook.

"You will want to speak to her now, I warrant," Beck said. He looked at Vianne in a way that made it seem as if they understood each other. "Such . . . theatrics in the wrong place could be most dangerous."

Vianne left him standing in her living room and went upstairs. She found Isabelle sitting on Sophie's bed, so angry she was shaking.

Scratches marred her cheeks and throat; a reminder of what she'd seen and survived. And now her hair was hacked off, the ends uneven.

Vianne tossed Isabelle's belongings onto the unmade bed and closed the door behind her. "What in the name of all that's holy were you thinking?"

"I could kill him in his sleep, just slit his throat."

"And do you think they would not come looking for a captain who had orders to billet here? *Mon Dieu*, Isabelle." She took a deep breath to calm her racing nerves. "I know there are problems between us, Isabelle. I know I treated you badly as a child—I was too young and scared to help you— and Papa treated you worse. But this is not about us now, and you can't be the girl who acts impetuously anymore. It is about my daughter now. Your niece. We must protect her."

"But—"

"France has surrendered, Isabelle. Certainly this fact has not escaped you."

"Didn't you hear Général de Gaulle? He said—"

"And who is this Général de Gaulle? Why should we listen to him? Maréchal Pétain is a war hero and our leader. We have to trust our government."

"Are you joking, Vianne? The government in Vichy is collaborating with Hitler. How can you not understand this danger? Pétain is wrong. Does one follow a leader blindly?"

Vianne moved toward Isabelle slowly, half afraid of her now. "You don't remember the last war," she said, clasping her hands to still them. "I do. I remember the fathers and brothers and uncles who didn't come home. I remember hearing children in my class cry quietly when bad news came by telegram. I remember the men who came home on crutches, their pant legs empty and flapping, or an arm gone, or a face ruined. I remember how Papa was before the war—and how different he was when he came home, how he drank and slammed doors and screamed at us, and then when he stopped. I remember the stories about Verdun and Somme and a million Frenchmen dying in trenches that ran red with blood. And the German atrocities, don't forget that part of it. They were *cruel*, Isabelle."

"That's my point exactly. We must—"

"They were cruel because we were at war with them, Isabelle. Pétain has saved us from going through that again. He has kept us safe. He has stopped the war. Now Antoine and all our men will come home."

"To a *Heil Hitler* world?" Isabelle said with a sneer. "'The flame of French resistance must not and shall not die.' That's what de Gaulle said. We have to fight however we can. For France, V. So it stays France."

"Enough," Vianne said. She moved close enough that she could have whispered to Isabelle, or kissed her, but Vianne did neither. In a steady, even voice, she said, "You will take Sophie's room upstairs and she will move in with me. And remember this, Isabelle, he could shoot us. *Shoot us*, and no one would care. You will not provoke this soldier in my home."

She saw the words hit home. Isabelle stiffened. "I will try to hold my tongue."

"Do more than try."

NINE

Vianne closed the bedroom door and leaned against it, trying to calm her nerves. She could hear Isabelle pacing in the room behind her, moving with an anger that made the floorboards tremble. How long did Vianne stand there alone, trembling, trying to get her nerves under control? It felt like hours passed while she struggled with her fear.

In ordinary times, she would have found the strength to talk rationally with her sister, to say some of the things that had long been unspoken. Vianne would have told Isabelle how sorry she was for the way she'd treated her as a little girl. Maybe she could have made Isabelle understand.

Vianne had been so helpless after Maman's death. When Papa had sent them away, to live in this small town, beneath the cold, stern eyes of a woman who had shown the girls no love, Vianne had . . . wilted.

In another time, she might have shared with Isabelle what they had in common, how undone she'd been by Maman's death, how Papa's rejection had broken her heart. Or how he treated her at sixteen when she'd come to him, pregnant and in love . . . and been slapped across the face and called a disgrace. How Antoine had pushed Papa back, hard, and said, *I'm going to marry her.*

And Papa's answer: *Fine, she's all yours. You can have the house. But you'll take her squalling sister, too.*

Vianne closed her eyes. She hated to think about all of that; for years, she'd practically forgotten it. Now, how could she push it aside? She had done to Isabelle exactly what their father had done to them. It was the greatest regret of Vianne's life.

But this was not the time to repair that damage.

Now she had to do everything in her power to keep Sophie safe until Antoine came home. Isabelle would simply have to be made to understand that.

With a sigh, she went downstairs to check on supper.

In the kitchen, she found her potato soup simmering a bit too briskly, so she uncovered it and lowered the heat.

"Madame? Are you sanguine?"

She flinched at the sound of his voice. When had he come in here? She took a deep breath and patted her hair. It was not the word he meant. Really, his French was terrible.

"That smells delicious," he said, coming up behind her.

She set the wooden spoon down on the rest beside the stove.

"May I see what you are making?"

"Of course," she said, both of them pretending her wishes mattered. "It's just potato soup."

"My wife, alas, is not much of a cook."

He was right beside her now, taking Antoine's place, a hungry man peering down at a cooking dinner.

"You are married," she said, reassured by it, although she couldn't say why.

"And a baby soon to be born. We are planning to call him Wilhelm, although I will not be there when he is born, and of course, such decisions must inevitably be his mother's."

It was such a . . . human thing to say. She found herself turning slightly to look at him. He was her height, almost exactly, and it unnerved her; looking directly into his eyes made her feel vulnerable.

"God willing, we will all be home soon," he said.

He wants this over, too, she thought with relief.

"It's suppertime, Herr Captain. Will you be joining us?"

"It would be an honor, Madame. Although you will be pleased to hear that most evenings I will be working late and enjoying my supper with the officers. I shall also often be out on campaigns. You shall sometimes hardly notice my presence."

Vianne left him in the kitchen and carried silverware into the dining room, where she almost ran into Isabelle.

"You shouldn't be alone with him," Isabelle hissed.

The captain came into the room. "You cannot think I would accept your hospitality and then do harm? Consider this night. I have brought you wine. A lovely Sancerre."

"You brought us wine," Isabelle said.

"As any good guest would," he answered.

Vianne thought, *oh, no*, but there was nothing she could do to stop Isabelle from speaking.

"You know about Tours, Herr Captain?" Isabelle asked. "How your Stukas fired on innocent women and children who were fleeing for their lives and dropped bombs on us?"

"Us?" he said, his expression turning thoughtful.

"I was there. You see the marks on my face."

"Ah," he said. "That must have been most unpleasant."

Isabelle went very still. The green of her eyes seemed to blaze against the red marks and bruises on her pale skin. "Unpleasant."

"Think about Sophie," Vianne reminded her evenly.

Isabelle gritted her teeth and then turned it into a fake smile. "Here, Captain Beck, let me show you to your seat."

Vianne took her first decent breath in at least an hour. Then, slowly, she headed into the kitchen to dish up supper.

❧

Vianne served supper in silence. The atmosphere at the table was as heavy as coal soot, settling on all of them. It frayed Vianne's nerves to the breaking point. Outside, the sun began to set; pink light filled the windows.

"Would you care for wine, Mademoiselle?" Beck said to Isabelle, pouring himself a large glass of the Sancerre he had brought to the table.

"If ordinary French families can't afford to drink it, Herr Captain, how can I enjoy it?"

"A sip perhaps would not be—"

Isabelle finished her soup and got to her feet. "Excuse me. I am feeling sick to my stomach."

"Me, too," Sophie said. She got to her feet and followed her aunt out of the room like a puppy follows the lead dog, with her head down.

Vianne sat perfectly still, her soup spoon held above her bowl. They were leaving her alone with him.

Her breathing was a flutter in her chest. She carefully set down her spoon and dabbed at her mouth with her serviette. "Forgive my sister, Herr Captain. She is impetuous and willful."

"My oldest daughter is such a girl. We expect nothing but trouble when she gets a little older."

That surprised Vianne so much that she turned. "You have a daughter?"

"Gisela," he said, his mouth curving into a smile. "She is six and already her mother is unable to get her to reliably do the simplest of tasks—like brush her teeth. Our Gisela would rather build a fort than read a book." He sighed, smiling.

It flustered her, knowing this about him. She tried to think of a response, but her nerves were too overwrought. She picked up her spoon and began eating again.

The meal seemed to go on forever, in a silence that was her undoing. The moment he finished, saying, "A lovely meal. My thanks," she got to her feet and began clearing the table.

Thankfully, he didn't follow her into the kitchen. He remained in the dining room, at the table by himself, drinking the wine he'd brought, which she knew would have tasted of autumn—pears and apples.

By the time she'd washed and dried the dishes, and put them away, night had fallen. She left the house, stepping into the starlit front yard for a moment's peace. On the stone garden wall, a shadow moved; it was a cat perhaps.

Behind her, she heard a footfall, then a match strike and the smell of sulfur.

She took a quiet step backward, wanting to melt into the shadows. If she could move quietly enough, perhaps she could return by the side door without alerting him to her presence. She stepped on a twig, heard it snap beneath her heel, and she froze.

He stepped out from the orchard.

"Madame," he said. "So you love the starlight also. I am sorry to intrude upon you."

She was afraid to move.

He closed the distance between them, taking up a place beside her as if he belonged there, looking out across her orchard.

"You would never know there is a war on out here," he said.

Vianne thought he sounded sad and it reminded her that they were alike in a way, both of them far away from the people they loved. "Your . . . superior . . . he said that all prisoners of war will remain in Germany. What does this mean? What of our soldiers? Surely you did not capture *all* of them."

"I do not know, Madame. Some will return. Many will not."

"Well. Isn't this a lovely little moment between new friends," Isabelle said.

Vianne flinched, horrified that she had been caught standing out here with a German, the enemy, a man.

Isabelle stood in the moonlight, wearing a caramel-colored suit; she held her valise in one hand and Vianne's best Deauville in the other.

"You have my hat," Vianne said.

"I may have to wait for a train. My face is still tender from the Nazi attack." She was smiling at Beck as she said this. It wasn't really a smile.

Beck inclined his head in a curt nod. "You have sisterly things to discuss, obviously. I will take my leave." With a brisk, polite nod, he returned to the house, closing the door behind him.

"I can't stay here," Isabelle said.

"Of course you can."

"I have no interest in making friends with the enemy, V."

"Damn it, Isabelle. Don't you dare—"

Isabelle stepped closer. "I'll put you and Sophie at risk. Sooner or later. You know I will. You told me I needed to protect Sophie. This is the only way I can do it. I feel like I'll explode if I stay, V."

Vianne's anger dissolved; without it, she felt inexpressibly tired. This essential difference had always been between them. Vianne the rule follower and Isabelle the rebel. Even in girlhood, in grief, they had expressed their emotions differently. Vianne had gone silent after Maman's death, tried to pretend that Papa's abandonment didn't wound her, while Isabelle had thrown tantrums and run away and demanded attention. Maman had sworn that one day they would be the best of friends. Never had this prediction seemed less likely.

In this, right now, Isabelle was right. Vianne would be constantly afraid of what her sister would say or do around the captain, and truthfully, Vianne hadn't the strength for it.

"How will you go? And where?"

"Train. To Paris. I'll telegram you when I arrive safely."

"Be careful. Don't do anything foolish."

"Me? You know better than that."

Vianne pulled Isabelle into a fierce embrace and then let her go.

❧

The road to town was so dark Isabelle couldn't see her own feet. It was preternaturally quiet, as suspenseful as a held breath, until she came to the airfield. There, she heard boots marching on hard-packed dirt, motorcycles and trucks rolling alongside the skein of barbed wire that now protected the ammunitions dump.

A lorry appeared out of nowhere, its headlamps off, thundering up the road; she lurched out of its way, stumbling into the ditch.

In town, it was no easier to navigate with the shops closed and the streetlamps off and the windows blacked out. The silence was eerie and unnerving. Her footsteps seemed too loud. With every step, she was aware that a curfew was in effect and she was violating it.

She ducked into one of the alleys, feeling her way along the rough sidewalk, her fingertips trailing along the storefronts for guidance. Whenever she heard voices, she froze, shrinking into the shadows until silence returned. It seemed to take forever to reach her destination: the train station on the edge of town.

"Halt!"

Isabelle heard the word at the same time a floodlight sprayed white light over her. She was a shadow hunched beneath it.

A German sentry approached her, his rifle held in his arms. "You are just a girl," he said, drawing close. "You know about the curfew, *ja?*" he demanded.

She rose slowly, facing him with a courage she didn't feel. "I know we aren't allowed to be out this late. It is an emergency, though. I must go to Paris. My father is ill."

"Where is your *Ausweis?*"

"I don't have one."

He eased the rifle off his shoulder and into his hands. "No travel without an *Ausweis.*"

"But—"

"Go home, girl, before you get hurt."

"But—"

"*Now*, before I decide not to ignore you."

Inside, Isabelle was screaming in frustration. It took considerable effort to walk away from the sentry without saying anything.

On the way home, she didn't even keep to the shadows. She flaunted her disregard of the curfew, daring them to stop her again. A part of her wanted to get caught so she could let loose the string of invectives screaming inside her head.

This could not be her life. Trapped in a house with a Nazi in a town that had given up without a whimper of protest. Vianne was not alone in her desire to pretend that France had neither surrendered nor been conquered. In town, the shopkeepers and bistro owners smiled at the Germans and poured them champagne and sold them the best cuts of meat. The villagers, peasants mostly, shrugged and went on with life; oh, they muttered disapprovingly and shook their heads and gave out wrong directions when asked, but beyond those small rebellions, there was nothing. No wonder the German soldiers were swollen with arrogance. They had taken over this town without a fight. Hell, they had done the same thing to all of France.

But Isabelle could never forget what she'd seen in the field near Tours.

At home, when she was upstairs again, in the bedroom that had been hers as a child, she slammed the door shut behind her. A few moments later, she smelled cigarette smoke and it made her so angry she wanted to scream.

He was down there, smoking a cigarette. Captain Beck, with his cut-stone face and fake smile, could toss them all out of this house at will. For any reason or no reason at all. Her frustration curdled into an anger that was like nothing she'd ever known. She felt as if her insides were a bomb that needed to go off. One wrong move—or word—and she might explode.

She marched over to Vianne's bedroom and opened the door. "You need a pass to leave town," she said, her anger expanding. "The bastards won't let us take a train to see family."

From the darkness, Vianne said, "So that's that."

Isabelle didn't know if it was relief or disappointment she heard in her sister's voice.

"Tomorrow morning you will go to town for me. You will stand in the queues while I am at school and get what you can."

"But—"

"No buts, Isabelle. You are here now and staying. It's time you pulled your weight. I need to be able to count on you."

⁂

For the next week, Isabelle tried to be on her best behavior, but it was impossible with that man living under the same roof. Night after night she didn't sleep. She lay in her bed, alone in the dark, imagining the worst.

This morning, well before dawn, she gave up the pretense and got out of bed. She washed her face and dressed in a plain cotton day dress, wrapping a scarf around her butchered hair as she went downstairs.

Vianne sat on the divan, knitting, an oil lamp lit beside her. In the ring of lamplight that separated her from the darkness, Vianne looked pale and sickly; she obviously hadn't slept much this week, either. She looked up at Isabelle in surprise. "You're up early."

"I have a long day of standing in lines ahead of me. Might as well get started," Isabelle said. "The first in line get the best food."

Vianne put her knitting aside and stood. Smoothing her dress (another reminder that *he* was in the house: neither of them came downstairs in nightdresses), she went into the kitchen and then returned with ration cards. "It's meat today."

Isabelle grabbed the ration cards from Vianne and left the house, plunging into the darkness of a blacked-out world.

Dawn rose as she walked, illuminating a world within a world—one that looked like Carriveau but felt entirely foreign. As she passed the airfield, a small green car with the letters POL on the rear roared past her.

Gestapo.

The airfield was already a hive of activity. She saw four guards out front—two at the newly constructed gated entrance and two at the building's double doors. Nazi flags snapped in the early-morning breeze. Several aeroplanes stood ready for takeoff—to drop bombs on England and across Europe. Guards marched in front of red signs that read: VERBOTEN. KEEP OUT UNDER PENALTY OF DEATH.

She kept walking.

There were already four women queued up in front of the butcher's shop when she arrived. She took her place at the back of the line.

That was when she saw a piece of chalk lying in the road, tucked in against the curb. She knew instantly how she could use it.

She glanced around, but no one was looking at her. Why would they be when there were German soldiers everywhere? Men in uniforms strode through town like peacocks, buying whatever caught their eye. Rambunctious and loud and quick to laugh. They were unfailingly polite, opening doors for women and tipping their hats, but Isabelle wasn't fooled.

She bent down and palmed the bit of chalk, hiding it in her pocket. It felt dangerous and wonderful just having it. She tapped her foot impatiently after that, waiting for her turn.

"Good morning," she said, offering her ration card to the butcher's wife, a tired-looking woman with thinning hair and even thinner lips.

"Ham hocks, two pounds. That's what is left."

"Bones?"

"The Germans take all the good meat, M'mselle. You're lucky, in fact. Pork is *verboten* for the French, don't you know, but they don't want the hocks. Do you want them or *non?*"

"I'll take them," someone said behind her.

"So will I!" yelled another woman.

"I'll take them," Isabelle said. She took the small packet, wrapped up in wrinkled paper and tied with twine.

Across the street, she heard the sound of jackboots marching on cobblestone, the rattling of sabers in scabbards, the sound of male laughter and the purring voices of the French women who warmed their beds. A trio of German soldiers sat at a bistro table not far away.

"Mademoiselle?" one of them said, waving to her. "Come have coffee with us."

She clutched her willow basket with its paper-wrapped treasures, small and insufficient as they were, and ignored the soldiers. She slipped around the corner and into an alley that was narrow and crooked, like all such passageways in town. Entrances were slim, and from the street, they appeared to be dead ends. Locals knew how to navigate them as easily as a boatman knows a boggy river. She walked forward, unobserved. The shops in the alley had all been shut down.

A poster in the abandoned milliner's shopwindow showed a crooked old man with a huge, hooked nose, looking greedy and evil, holding a bag of money and trailing blood and bodies behind him. She saw the word— *Juif*—Jew—and stopped.

She knew she should keep walking. It was just propaganda, after all, the enemy's heavy-handed attempt to blame the Jewish people for the ills of the world, and this war.

And yet.

She glanced to her left. Not fifty feet away was rue La Grande, a main street through town; to her right was an elbow bend in the alleyway.

She reached into her pocket and pulled out her piece of chalk. When she was sure the coast was clear, she drew a huge *V* for victory on the poster, obliterating as much of the image as she could.

Someone grabbed her wrist so hard she gasped. Her piece of chalk fell, clattered to the cobblestones, and rolled into one of the cracks.

"Mademoiselle," a man said, shoving her against the poster she'd just defaced, pressing her cheek into the paper so that she couldn't see him, "do you know it is *verboten* to do that? And punishable by death?"

TEN

Vianne closed her eyes and thought, *Hurry home, Antoine.*

It was all she allowed herself, just that one small plea. How could she handle all of this—war, and Captain Beck, and Isabelle—alone?

She wanted to daydream, pretend that her world was upright instead of fallen on its side; that the closed guest room door meant nothing, that Sophie had slept with Vianne last night because they'd fallen asleep reading, that Antoine was outside on this dewy dawn morning, chopping wood for a winter that was still months away. Soon he would come in and say, *Well, I am off to a day of delivering mail.* Perhaps he would tell her of his latest postmark—a letter in from Africa or America—and he would spin her a romantically imagined tale to go along with it.

Instead, she returned her knitting to the basket by the divan, put on her boots, and went outside to chop wood. It would be autumn again in no time, and then winter, and the devastation of her garden by the refugees had reminded her how perilously balanced her survival was. She lifted the axe and brought it down, hard.

Grasp. Raise. Steady. Chop.

Every chop reverberated up her arms and lodged painfully in the muscles of her shoulders. Sweat squeezed from her pores, dampened her hair.

"Allow me please to do this for you."

She froze, the axe in midair.

Beck stood nearby, dressed in his breeches and boots, with only a thin white T-shirt covering his chest. His pale cheeks were reddened from a morning shave and his blond hair was wet. Droplets fell onto his T-shirt, making a pattern of small gray sunbursts.

She felt acutely uncomfortable in her robe and work boots, with her hair pinned in curls. She lowered the axe.

"There are some things a man does around the house. You are much too fragile to chop wood."

"I can do it."

"Of course you can, but why should you? Go, Madame. See to your daughter. I can do this small thing for you. Otherwise my mother will beat me with a switch."

She meant to move, but somehow she didn't, and then he was there, pulling the axe gently out of her hand. She held on instinctively for a moment.

Their gazes met, held.

She released her hold and stepped back so quickly she stumbled. He caught her by the wrist, steadied her. Mumbling a thank-you, she turned and walked away from him, keeping her spine as straight as she could. It took all of her limited courage not to speed up. Even so, by the time she reached her door, she felt as if she'd run from Paris. She kicked free of the oversized gardening boots, saw them hit the house with a thunk and fall in a heap. The last thing she wanted was kindness from this man who had invaded her home.

She slammed the door shut behind her and went to the kitchen, where she lit the stove and put a pot of water on to boil. Then she went to the bottom of the stairs and called her daughter down to breakfast.

She had to call two more times—and then threaten—before Sophie came trudging down the stairs, her hair a mess, the look in her eyes sullen. She was wearing her sailor dress—again. In the ten months Antoine had been gone, she'd outgrown it, but she refused to stop wearing it. "I'm up," she said, shuffling to the table, taking her seat.

Vianne placed a bowl of cornmeal mush in front of her daughter. She had splurged this morning and added a tablespoon of preserved peaches on top.

"Maman? Can't you hear that? There's someone knocking at the door."

Vianne shook her head (all she'd heard was the *thunk-thunk-thunk* of the axe) and went to the door, opening it.

Rachel stood there, with the baby in her arms and Sarah tucked in close to her side. "You are teaching today with your hair pinned?"

"Oh!" Vianne felt like a fool. What was wrong with her? Today was the last day of school before the summer break. "Let's go, Sophie. We are late." She rushed back inside and cleared the table. Sophie had licked her plate clean, so Vianne laid it in the copper sink to wash later. She covered the leftover pot of mush and put the preserved peaches away. Then she ran upstairs to get ready.

In no time, she had removed her hairpins and combed her hair into smooth waves. She grabbed her hat, gloves, and handbag and left the house to find Rachel and the children waiting in the orchard.

Captain Beck was there, too, standing by the shed. His white T-shirt was soaked in places and clung to his chest, revealing the whorls of hair beneath. He had the axe slung casually against one shoulder.

"Ah, greetings," he said.

Vianne could feel Rachel's scrutiny.

Beck lowered the axe. "This is a friend of yours, Madame?"

"Rachel," Vianne said tightly. "My neighbor. This is Herr Captain Beck. He is . . . the one billeting with us."

"Greetings," Beck said again, nodding politely.

Vianne put a hand on Sophie's back and gave her daughter a little shove, and they were off, trudging through the tall grass of the orchard and out onto the dusty road.

"He's handsome," Rachel said as they came to the airfield, which was abuzz with activity behind the coils of barbed wire. "You didn't tell me that."

"Is he?"

"I'm pretty sure you know he is, so your question is interesting. What's he like?"

"German."

"The soldiers billeted with Claire Moreau look like sausages with legs. I hear they drink enough wine to kill a judge and snore like rooting hogs. You're lucky, I guess."

"You're the lucky one, Rachel. No one has moved into your house."

"Poverty has its reward at last." She linked her arm through Vianne's. "Don't look so stricken, Vianne. I hear they have orders to be 'correct.'"

Vianne looked at her best friend. "Last week, Isabelle chopped off her hair in front of the captain and said beauty must be *verboten.*"

Rachel couldn't stifle her smile completely. "Oh."

"It's hardly funny. She could get us killed with her temper."

Rachel's smile faded. "Can you talk to her?"

"Oh, I can talk. When has she ever listened to anyone?"

⌾

"You are hurting me," Isabelle said.

The man yanked her away from the wall and dragged her down the street, moving so fast she had to run along beside him; she bumped into the stone alley wall with every step. When she tripped on a cobblestone and almost fell, he tightened his hold and held her upright.

Think, Isabelle. He wasn't in uniform, so he must be Gestapo. That was bad. And he'd seen her defacing the poster. Did it count as an act of sabotage or espionage or resistance to the German occupation?

It wasn't like blowing up a bridge or selling secrets to Britain.

I was making art . . . it was going to be a vase full of flowers . . . Not a *V* for *victory,* a vase. No resistance, just a silly girl drawing on the only paper she could find. I have never even heard of Général de Gaulle.

And what if they didn't believe her?

The man stopped in front of an oak door with a black lion's head knocker at its center.

He rapped four times on the door.

"W-where are you taking me?" Was this a back door to the Gestapo headquarters? There were rumors about these Gestapo interrogators. Supposedly they were ruthless and sadistic, but no one knew for sure.

The door opened slowly, revealing an old man in a beret. A hand-rolled cigarette hung from his fleshy, liver-spotted lips. He saw Isabelle and frowned.

"Open up," the man beside Isabelle growled and the old man stepped aside.

Isabelle was pulled into a room full of smoke. Her eyes stung as she looked around. It was an abandoned novelty store that had once sold bonnets and notions and sewing supplies. In the smoky light, she saw empty display cases that had been shoved up against the walls, empty metal hat racks were piled in the corner. The window out front had been bricked up and the back door that faced rue La Grande was padlocked from the inside.

There were four men in the room: a tall, graying man, dressed in rags, standing in the corner; a boy seated beside the old man who had opened the door, and a handsome young man in a tattered sweater and worn pants with scuffed boots who sat at a café table.

"Who is this, Didier?" asked the old man who had opened the door.

Isabelle got the first good look at her captor—he was big and brawny, with the puffed-up look of a circus strong man and a heavily jowled, oversized face.

She stood as tall as possible, with her shoulders pressed back and her chin lifted. She knew she looked ridiculously young in her plaid skirt and fitted blouse, but she refused to give them the satisfaction of knowing she was afraid.

"I found her chalking V's on the German posters," said the swarthy man who'd caught her. Didier.

Isabelle fisted her right hand, trying to rub the orange chalk away without them noticing.

"Have you nothing to say?" said the old man standing in the corner. He was the boss, obviously.

"I have no chalk."

"I saw her doing it."

Isabelle took a chance. "You're not German," she said to the strong man. "You're French. I'd bet money on it. And you," she said to the old man who was seated by the boy, "you're the pork butcher." The boy she dismissed altogether, but to the handsome young man in the tattered clothes, she said, "You look hungry, and I think you're wearing your brother's clothes, or something you found hanging on a line somewhere. Communist."

He grinned at her, and it changed his whole demeanor.

But it was the man standing in the corner she cared about. The one in charge. She took a step toward him. "You could be Aryan. Maybe you're forcing the others to be here."

"I've known him all my life, M'mselle," the pork butcher said. "I fought beside his father—and yours—at Somme. You're Isabelle Rossignol, *oui?*"

She didn't answer. Was it a trap?

"No answer," said the Bolshevik. He rose from his seat, came toward her. "Good for you. Why were you chalking a *V* on the poster?"

Again, Isabelle remained silent.

"I am Henri Navarre," he said, close enough now to touch her. "We are not Germans, nor do we work with them, M'mselle." He gave her a meaningful look. "Not all of us are passive. Now why were you marking up their posters?"

"It was all I could think of," she said.

"Meaning?"

She exhaled evenly. "I heard de Gaulle's speech on the radio."

Henri turned to the back of the room, sent a glance to the old man. She watched the two men have an entire conversation without speaking a word. At the end of it, she knew who the boss was: the handsome communist. Henri.

At last, Henri said, turning to her again, "If you could do something more, would you?"

"What do you mean?" she asked.

"There is a man in Paris—"

"A group, actually, from the Musée de l'Homme—" the burly man corrected him.

Henri held up a hand. "We don't say more than we must, Didier. Anyway, there is a man, a printer, risking his life to make tracts that we can distribute. Maybe if we can get the French to wake up to what is happening, we have a chance." Henri reached into a leather bag that hung on his chair and pulled out a sheaf of papers. A headline jumped out at her: "Vive le Général de Gaulle."

The text was an open letter to Maréchal Pétain that expressed criticism of the surrender. At the end it read, *"Nous sommes pour le général de Gaulle."* We support Général de Gaulle.

"Well?" Henri said quietly, and in that single word, Isabelle heard the call to arms she'd been waiting for. "Will you distribute them?"

"Me?"

"We are communists and radicals," Henri said. "They are already watching us. You are a girl. And a pretty one at that. No one would suspect you."

Isabelle didn't hesitate. "I'll do it."

The men started to thank her; Henri silenced them. "The printer is risking his life by writing these tracts, and someone is risking his or her life by typing them. We are risking our lives by bringing them here. But you, Isabelle, you are the one who will be caught distributing them—if you are caught. Make no mistake. This is not chalking a *V* on a poster. This is punishable by death."

"I won't get caught," she said.

Henri smiled at that. "How old are you?"

"Almost nineteen."

"Ah," he said. "And how can one so young hide this from her family?"

"My family's not the problem," Isabelle said. "They pay no attention to me. But . . . there's a German soldier billeted at my house. And I would have to break curfew."

"It will not be easy. I understand if you are afraid." Henri began to turn away.

Isabelle snatched the papers back from him. "I said I'd do it."

*

Isabelle was elated. For the first time since the armistice, she wasn't completely alone in her need to do something for France. The men told her about dozens of groups like theirs throughout the country, mounting a resistance to follow de Gaulle. The more they talked, the more excited she became at the prospect of joining them. Oh, she knew she should be afraid. (They told her often enough.)

But it was ridiculous—the Germans threatening death for handing out a few pieces of paper. She could talk her way out of it if she were caught; she was sure of it. Not that she would get caught. How many times had she sneaked out of a locked school or boarded a train without a ticket or talked her way out of trouble? Her beauty had always made it easy for her to break rules without reprisal.

"When we have more, how will we contact you?" Henri asked as he opened the door to let her leave.

She glanced down the street. "The apartment above Madame La Foy's hat shop. Is it still vacant?"

Henri nodded.

"Open the curtains when you have papers. I'll come by as soon as I can."

"Knock four times. If we don't answer, walk away," he said. After a pause, he added, "Be careful, Isabelle."

He shut the door between them.

Alone again, she looked down at her basket. Settled under a red-and-white-checked linen cloth were the tracts. On top lay the butcher-paper-wrapped ham hocks. It wasn't much of a camouflage. She would need to figure out something better.

She walked down the alley and turned onto a busy street. The sky was darkening. She'd been with the men all day. The shops were closing up; the only people milling about were German soldiers and the few women who'd chosen to keep them company. The café tables out on the street were full of uniformed men eating the best food, drinking the best wines.

It took every ounce of nerve she had to walk slowly. The minute she was out of town, she started to run. As she neared the airfield, she was sweating and out of breath, but she didn't slow. She ran all the way into her yard. With the gate clattering shut behind her, she bent forward, gasping hard, holding the stitch in her side, trying to catch her breath.

"M'mselle Rossignol, are you unwell?"

Isabelle snapped upright.

Captain Beck appeared beside her. Had he been there before her?

"Captain," she said, working hard to still the racing of her heart. "A convoy went past . . . I . . . uh, rushed to get out of their way."

"A convoy? I didn't see that."

"It was a while back. And I am . . . silly sometimes. I lost track of time, talking to a friend, and, well . . ." She gave him her prettiest smile and patted her butchered hair as if it mattered to her that she looked nice for him.

"How were the queues today?"

"Interminable."

"Please, allow me to carry your basket inside."

She looked down at her basket, saw the tiniest white paper corner visible under the linen cloth. "No, I—"

"Ah, I insist. We are gentlemen, you know."

His long, well-manicured fingers closed around the willow handle. As he turned toward the house, she remained at his side. "I saw a large group gathering at the town hall this afternoon. What are the Vichy police doing here?"

"Ah. Nothing to concern you." He waited at the front door for her to open it. She fumbled nervously with the center-mounted knob, turned it, and opened the door. Although he had every right to go in at will, he waited to be invited in, as if he were a guest.

"Isabelle, is that you? Where have you been?" Vianne rose from the divan.

"The queues were awful today."

Sophie popped up from the floor by the fireplace, where she'd been playing with Bébé. "What did you get today?"

"Ham hocks," Isabelle said, glancing worriedly at the basket in Beck's hand.

"That's all?" Vianne said. "What about the cooking oil?"

Sophie sank back to the rug on the floor, clearly disappointed.

"I will put the hocks in the pantry," Isabelle said, reaching for the basket.

"Please, allow me," Beck said. He was staring at Isabelle, watching her closely. Or maybe it only felt like that.

Vianne lit a candle and handed it to Isabelle. "Don't waste it. Hurry."

Beck was very gallant as he walked through the shadowy kitchen and opened the door to the cellar.

Isabelle went down first, lighting the way. The wooden steps creaked beneath her feet until she stepped down onto the hard-packed dirt floor and into the subterranean chill. The wooden shelves seemed to close in around them as Beck came up beside her. The candle flame sent light gamboling in front of them.

She tried to still the trembling in her hand as she reached for the paper-wrapped ham hocks. She placed them on the shelf beside their dwindling supplies.

"Bring up three potatoes and a turnip," Vianne called down. Isabelle jumped a little at the sound.

"You seem nervous," Beck said. "Is that the right word, M'mselle?"

The candle sputtered between them. "There were a lot of dogs in town today."

"The Gestapo. They love their shepherds. There is no reason for this to concern you."

"I am afraid . . . of big dogs. I was bitten once. As a child."

Beck gave her a smile that was stretched out of shape by the light.

Don't look at the basket. But it was too late. She saw a little more of the hidden papers sticking out.

She forced a smile. "You know us girls. Scared of everything."

"That is not how I would describe you, M'mselle."

She reached carefully for the basket and tugged it from his grasp. Without breaking eye contact, she set the basket on the shelf, beyond the candle's light. When it was there, in the dark, she finally released her breath.

They stared at each other in uncomfortable silence.

Beck nodded. "And now I must away. I have only come here to pick up some papers for a meeting tonight." He turned back for the steps and began climbing them.

Isabelle followed the captain up the narrow stairs. When she emerged into the kitchen, Vianne was standing there with her arms crossed, frowning.

"Where are the potatoes and a turnip?" Vianne asked.

"I forgot."

Vianne sighed. "Go," she said. "Get them."

Isabelle turned and went back into the cellar. After she'd gathered up the potatoes and turnip, she went to the basket, lifted the candle to expose the basket to light. There it was: the tiny white triangle of paper, peeking out. She quickly withdrew the papers from the basket and shoved them into her panty girdle. Feeling the papers against her skin, she went upstairs, smiling.

❧

At supper, Isabelle sat with her sister and niece, eating watery soup and day-old bread, trying to think of something to say, but nothing came to her. Sophie, who seemed not to notice, rambled on, telling one story after another. Isabelle tapped her foot nervously, listening for the sound of a motorcycle approaching the house, for the clatter of German jackboots on the walkway out front, for a sharp, impersonal knock on the door. Her gaze kept cutting to the kitchen and the cellar door.

"You are acting strangely tonight," Vianne said.

Isabelle ignored her sister's observation. When the meal was finally over, Isabelle popped out of her seat and said, "I'll do the dishes, V. Why don't you and Sophie finish your game of checkers?"

"You'll do dishes?" Vianne said, giving Isabelle a suspicious look.

"Come on, I've offered before," Isabelle said.

"Not in my memory."

Isabelle gathered the empty soup bowls and utensils. She had offered only to keep busy, to do something with her hands.

Afterward, Isabelle could find nothing to do. The night dragged on. Vianne and Sophie and Isabelle played Belote, but Isabelle couldn't concentrate, she was so nervous and excited. She made some lame excuse and quit the game early, pretending to be tired. In her upstairs bedroom, she lay atop the blankets, fully dressed. Waiting.

It was past midnight when she heard Beck return. She heard him enter the yard; then she smelled the smoke from his cigarette drift up. Later, he came into the house—clomping around in his boots—but by one o'clock everything was quiet again. Still she waited. At four A.M., she got out of bed and dressed in a heavy worsted knit black sweater and plaid tweed skirt. She ripped a seam open in her summer-weight coat and slid the papers inside, then she put the coat on, tying the belt at her waist. She slipped the ration cards in her front pocket.

On the way downstairs, she winced at every creak of sound. It seemed to take forever to get to the front door, more than forever, but finally she was there, opening it quietly, closing it behind her.

· The early morning was cold and black. Somewhere a bird called out, his slumber probably disturbed by the opening of the door. She breathed in the scent of roses and was overcome by how ordinary it seemed in this moment.

From here there would be no turning back.

She walked to the still-broken gate, glancing back often at the blacked-out house, expecting Beck to be there, arms crossed, booted feet in a warrior's stance, watching her.

But she was alone.

Her first stop was Rachel's house. There were almost no mail deliveries these days, but women like Rachel, whose men were gone, checked their letter boxes each day, hoping against hope that the mail would bring them news.

Isabelle reached inside her coat, felt for the slit in the silk lining, and pulled out a single piece of paper. In one movement, she opened the letterbox and slid the paper inside and quietly shut the lid.

Out on the road again, she looked around and saw no one.

She had done it!

Her second stop was old man Rivet's farm. He was a communist through and through, a man of the revolution, and he'd lost a son at the front.

By the time she gave away her last tract, she felt invincible. It was just past dawn; pale sunlight gilded the limestone buildings in town.

She was the first woman to queue up outside the shop this morning, and because of that, she got her full ration of butter. One hundred fifty grams for the month. Two-thirds of a cup.

A treasure.

ELEVEN

*E*very day that long, hot summer, Vianne woke to a list of chores. She (along with Sophie and Isabelle) replanted and expanded the garden and converted a pair of old bookcases into rabbit hutches. She used chicken wire to enclose the pergola. Now the most romantic place on the property stank of manure—manure they collected for their garden. She took in wash from the farmer down the road—old man Rivet—in exchange for feed. The only time she really relaxed, and felt like herself, was on Sunday mornings, when she took Sophie to church (Isabelle refused to attend Mass) and then had coffee with Rachel, sitting in the shade of her backyard, just two best friends talking, laughing, joking. Sometimes Isabelle joined them, but she was more likely to play with the children than talk with the women—which was fine with Vianne.

Her chores were necessary, of course—a new way of preparing for a winter that seemed far away but would arrive like an unwanted guest on the worst possible day. More important, it kept Vianne's mind occupied. When she was working in her garden or boiling strawberries for preserves or pickling cucumbers, she wasn't thinking of Antoine and how long it had been since she'd heard from him. It was the uncertainty that gnawed at her: Was he a prisoner of war? Was he wounded somewhere? Dead? Or would she look up one day and see him walking up this road, smiling?

Missing him. Longing for him. Worrying about him. Those were her nighttime journeys.

In a world now laden with bad news and silence, the one bit of good news was that Captain Beck had spent much of the summer away on one campaign or another. In his absence, the household settled into a routine of sorts. Isabelle did all that was asked of her without complaint.

It was October now, and chilly. Vianne found herself distracted as she walked home from school with Sophie. She could feel that one of her heels was coming loose; it made her slightly unsteady. Her black kidskin oxfords weren't made for the kind of everyday use to which they'd been put in the past few months. The sole was beginning to pull away at the toe, which often caused her to trip. The worry about replacing things like shoes was never far away. A ration card did not mean there were shoes—or food—to be bought.

Vianne kept one hand on Sophie's shoulder, both to steady her gait and to keep her daughter close. There were Nazi soldiers everywhere; riding in lorries and on motorcycles with machine-gun-mounted sidecars. They marched in the square, their voices raised in triumphant song.

A military lorry honked at them and they moved farther onto the sidewalk as a convoy rumbled past. More Nazis.

"Is that Tante Isabelle?" Sophie asked.

Vianne glanced in the direction of Sophie's finger. Sure enough, Isabelle was coming out of an alley, clutching her basket. She looked . . . "furtive" was the only word that came to mind.

Furtive. At that, a dozen little pieces clicked into place. Tiny incongruities became a pattern. Isabelle had often left Le Jardin in the wee hours of the morning, much earlier than necessary. She had dozens of long-winded excuses for absences that Vianne had barely cared about. Heels that broke, hats that flew off in the wind and had to be chased down, a dog that frightened her and blocked her way.

Was she sneaking out to be with a boy?

"Tante Isabelle!" Sophie cried out.

Without waiting for a reply—or permission—Sophie darted into the street. She dodged a trio of German soldiers who were tossing a ball back and forth.

"*Merde*," Vianne muttered. "Pardon," she said, ducking around the soldiers and striding across the cobblestoned street.

"What did you get today?" she heard Sophie ask Isabelle as her daughter reached into the willow basket.

Isabelle slapped Sophie's hand. Hard.

Sophie yelped and drew her hand back.

"Isabelle!" Vianne said harshly. "What's wrong with you?"

Isabelle had the good grace to blush. "I am sorry. It's just that I'm tired. I have been in queues all day. And for what? A veal jelly bone with barely any meat on it and a tin of milk. It's disheartening. Still, I shouldn't be rude. I'm sorry, Soph."

"Perhaps if you didn't sneak out so early in the morning you wouldn't be tired," Vianne said.

"I'm not sneaking out," Isabelle said. "I'm going to the shops for food. I thought you wanted that of me. And by the way, we need a bicycle. These walks to town on bad shoes are killing me."

Vianne wished she knew her sister well enough to read the look in her eyes. Was it guilt? Or worry or defiance? If she didn't know better, she'd say it was pride.

Sophie linked arms with Isabelle as the three of them set off for home.

Vianne studiously ignored the changes to Carriveau—the Nazis taking up so much space, the posters on the limestone walls (the new anti-Jewish tracts were sickening), and the red and black swastika flags hanging above doorways and from balconies. People had begun to leave Carriveau, abandoning their homes to the Germans. The rumor was that they were going to the Free Zone, but no one knew for sure. Shops closed and didn't reopen.

She heard footsteps coming up behind her and said evenly, "Let's walk faster."

"Madame Mauriac, if I may interrupt."

"Good Lord, is he *following* you?" Isabelle muttered.

Vianne slowly turned around. "Herr Captain," she said. People in the street watched Vianne closely, eyes narrowed in disapproval.

"I wanted to say that I will be late tonight and will, sorrowfully, not be there for supper," Beck said.

"How terrible," Isabelle said in a voice as sweet and bitter as burned caramel.

Vianne tried to smile, but really, she didn't know why he'd stopped her. "I will save you something—"

"*Nein. Nein.* You are most kind." He fell silent.

Vianne did the same.

Finally Isabelle sighed heavily. "We are on our way home, Herr Captain."

"Is there something I can do for you, Herr Captain?" said Vianne.

Beck moved closer. "I know how worried you have been about your husband, so I did some checking."

"Oh."

"It is not fine news, I am sorrowful to report. Your husband, Antoine Mauriac, has been captured along with many of your town's men. He is in a prisoner of war camp." He handed her a list of names and a stack of official postcards. "He will not be coming home."

Vianne barely remembered leaving town. She knew Isabelle was beside her, holding her upright, urging her to put one foot in front of the other, and that Sophie was beside her, chirping out questions as sharp as fish hooks. *What is a prisoner of war? What did Herr Captain mean that Papa would not be coming home? Never?*

Vianne knew when they'd arrived home because the scents of her garden greeted her, welcomed her. She blinked, feeling a little like someone who had just wakened from a coma to find the world impossibly changed.

"Sophie," Isabelle said firmly. "Go make your mother a cup of coffee. Open a tin of milk."

"But—"

"Go," Isabelle said.

When Sophie was gone, Isabelle turned to Vianne, cupped her face with cold hands. "He'll be all right."

Vianne felt as if she were breaking apart bit by bit, losing blood and bone as she stood here, contemplating something she had studiously avoided thinking about: a life without him. She started to shiver; her teeth chattered.

"Come inside for coffee," Isabelle said.

Into the house? *Their* house? His ghost would be everywhere in there—a dent in the divan where he sat to read, the hook that held his coat. And the bed.

She shook her head, wishing she could cry, but there were no tears in her. This news had emptied her. She couldn't even breathe.

Suddenly all she could think about was the sweater of his that she was wearing. She started to strip out of her clothes, tearing off the coat and the vest—ignoring Isabelle's shouted *NO!*—as she yanked the sweater over her head and buried her face in the soft wool, trying to smell him in the yarn—his favorite soap, *him*.

But there was nothing but her own smell. She lowered the bunched-up sweater from her face and stared down at it, trying to remember the last time he'd worn it. She picked at a loose thread and it unraveled in her hand, became a squiggly coil of wine-colored yarn. She bit it off and tied a knot to save the rest of the sleeve. Yarn was precious these days.

These days.

When the world was at war and everything was scarce and your husband was gone. "I don't know how to be on my own."

"What do you mean? We were on our own for years. From the moment Maman died."

Vianne blinked. Her sister's words sounded a little jumbled, as if they were running on the wrong speed. "You were alone," she said. "I never was. I met Antoine when I was fourteen and got pregnant at sixteen and married him when I was barely seventeen. Papa gave me this house to get rid of me. So, you see, I've *never* been on my own. That's why you're so strong and I'm not."

"You will have to be," Isabelle said. "For Sophie."

Vianne drew in a breath. And there it was. The reason she couldn't eat a bowl of arsenic or throw herself in front of a train. She took the short coil of crooked yarn and tied it to an apple tree branch. The burgundy color stood out against the green and brown. Now, each day in her garden and when she walked to her gate and when she picked apples, she would pass this branch and see this bit of yarn and think of Antoine. Each time she would pray—to him and to God—*Come home.*

"Come," Isabelle said, putting an arm around Vianne, pulling her close. Inside, the house echoed the voice of a man who wasn't there.

❧

Vianne stood outside Rachel's stone cottage; overhead the sky was the color of smoke on this cold, late afternoon. The leaves of the trees, marigold and tangerine and scarlet, were just beginning to darken around the edges. Soon they would drop to the ground.

Vianne stared at the door, wishing she didn't need to be here, but she had read the names Beck had given her. Marc de Champlain was also listed.

When she finally found the courage to knock, Rachel answered almost instantly, wearing an old housedress and sagging woolen stockings. A cardigan sweater hung askew, buttoned incorrectly. It gave her an odd, tilted look.

"Vianne! Come in. Sarah and I were just making a rice pudding—it's mostly water and gelatin, of course, but I used a bit of milk."

Vianne managed a smile. She let her friend sweep her into the kitchen and pour her a cup of the bitter, ersatz coffee that was all they could get. Vianne was remarking on the rice pudding—what she even said she didn't know—when Rachel turned and asked, "What's wrong?"

Vianne stared at her friend. She wanted to be the strong one—for once—but she couldn't stop the tears that filled her eyes.

"Stay in the kitchen," Rachel said to Sarah. "If you hear your brother wake up, get him. You," she said to Vianne, "come with me." She took Vianne by the arm and guided her through the small salon and into Rachel's bedroom.

Vianne sat on the bed and looked up at her friend. Silently, she held out the list of names she'd gotten from Beck. "They're prisoners of war, Rachel. Antoine and Marc and all the others. They won't be coming home."

❧

Three days later, on a frosty Saturday morning, Vianne stood in her classroom and stared out at the group of women seated in desks that were too small for them. They looked tired and a little wary. No one felt comfortable gathering these days. It was never clear exactly how far *verboten* extended into conversations about the war, and besides that, the women of

Carriveau were exhausted. They spent their days standing in line for insufficient quantities of foods, and when they weren't in line, they were foraging the countryside or trying to sell their dancing shoes or a silk scarf for enough money to buy a loaf of good bread. In the back of the room, tucked into the corner, Sophie and Sarah were leaning against each other, knees drawn up, reading books.

Rachel moved her sleeping son from one shoulder to the other and closed the door of the classroom. "Thank you all for coming. I know how difficult it is these days to do anything more than the absolutely necessary." There was a murmuring of agreement among the women.

"Why are we here?" Madame Fournier asked tiredly.

Vianne stepped forward. She had never felt completely comfortable around some of the women, many of whom had disliked Vianne when she moved here at fourteen. When Vianne had "caught" Antoine—the best-looking young man in town—they'd liked her even less. Those days were long past, of course, and now Vianne was friendly with these women and taught their children and frequented their shops, but even so, the pains of adolescence left a residue of discomfort. "I have received a list of French prisoners of war from Carriveau. I am sorry—terribly sorry—to tell you that your husbands—and mine, and Rachel's—are on the list. I am told they will not be coming home."

She paused, allowing the women to react. Grief and loss transformed the faces around her. Vianne knew the pain mirrored her own. Even so, it was difficult to watch, and she found her eyes misting again. Rachel stepped close, took her hand.

"I got us postcards," Vianne said. "Official ones. So we can write to our men."

"How did you get so many postcards?" Madame Fournier asked, wiping her eyes.

"She asked her German for a favor," said Hélène Ruelle, the baker's wife.

"I did not! And he's not my German," Vianne said. "He is a soldier who has requisitioned my home. Should I just let the Germans have Le Jardin? Just walk away and have nothing? Every house or hotel in town with a spare room has been taken by them. I am not special in this."

More tsking and murmurs. Some women nodded; others shook their heads.

"I would have killed myself before I let one of them move into my house," Hélène said.

"Would you, Hélène? Would you really?" Vianne said. "And would you kill your children first or throw them out into the street to survive on their own?"

Hélène looked away.

"They have taken over my hotel," a woman said. "And they are gentlemen, for the most part. A bit crude, perhaps. Wasteful."

"*Gentlemen*." Hélène spat the word. "We are pigs to slaughter. You will see. Pigs who put up no fight at all."

"I haven't seen you at my butcher shop recently," Madame Fournier said to Vianne in a judgmental voice.

"My sister goes for me," Vianne said. She knew this was the point of their disapproval; they were afraid that Vianne would get—and take—special privileges that they would be denied. "I would not take food—or anything—from the enemy." She felt suddenly as if she were back in school, being bullied by the popular girls.

"Vianne is trying to help," Rachel said sternly enough to shut them up. She took the postcards from Vianne and began handing them out.

Vianne took a seat and stared down at her own blank postcard.

She heard the chicken-scratching of other pencils on other postcards and slowly, she began to write.

> *My beloved Antoine,*
>   *We are well. Sophie is thriving, and even with*
> *so many chores, we found some time*
> *this summer to spend by the river. We—I—think*
> *of you with every breath and pray*
> *you are well. Do not worry about us,*
> *and come home.*
> *Je t'aime, Antoine.*

Her lettering was so small she wondered if he would even be able to read it.

Or if he would get it.

Or if he was alive.

For God's sake, she was *crying*.

Rachel moved in beside her, laid a hand on her shoulder. "We all feel it," she said quietly.

Moments later, the women rose one by one. Wordlessly, they shuffled forward and gave Vianne their postcards.

"Don't let them hurt your feelings," Rachel said. "They're just scared."

"I'm scared, too," Vianne said.

Rachel pressed her postcard to her chest, her fingers splayed across the small square of paper as if she needed to touch each corner. "How can we not be?"

⸙

Afterward, when they returned to Le Jardin, Beck's motorcycle with the machine-gun-mounted sidecar was parked in the grass outside the gate.

Rachel turned to her. "Do you want us to come in with you?"

Vianne appreciated the worry in Rachel's gaze, and she knew that if she asked for help she would get it, but how was she to be helped?

"No, *merci*. We are fine. He has probably forgotten something and will soon leave again. He is rarely here these days."

"Where is Isabelle?"

"A good question. She sneaks out every Friday morning before the sunrise." She leaned closer, whispered, "I think she is meeting a boy."

"Good for her."

To that, Vianne had no answer.

"Will he mail the postcards for us?" Rachel asked.

"I hope so." Vianne stared at her friend a moment longer. Then she said, "Well, we will know soon enough," and led Sophie into the house. Once inside, she instructed Sophie to go upstairs to read. Her daughter was used to such directives, and she didn't mind. Vianne tried to keep her daughter and Beck separated as much as possible.

He was seated at the dining room table with papers spread out in front of him. At her entrance, he looked up. A drop of ink fell from the tip of his fountain pen, landed in a blue starburst on the white sheet of paper in front of him. "Madame. Most excellent. I am pleased you are returned."

She moved forward cautiously, holding the packet of postcards tightly. They'd been tied up with a scrap of twine. "I . . . have some postcards here . . . written by friends in town . . . to our husbands . . . but we don't know where to send them. I hoped . . . perhaps you could help us."

She shifted uncomfortably from one foot to the other, feeling acutely vulnerable.

"Of course, Madame. I would be pleased to do this favor for you. Although it will take much time and research to accomplish." He rose politely. "As it happens, I am now concocting a list for my superiors at the Kommandantur. They need to know the names of some of the teachers at your school."

"Oh," she said, uncertain as to why he would tell her this. He never spoke of his work. Of course, they didn't speak often about anything.

"Jews. Communists. Homosexuals. Freemasons. Jehovah's Witnesses. Do you know these people?"

"I am Catholic, Herr Captain, as you know. We do not speak of such things at school. I hardly know who are homosexuals and Freemasons, at any rate."

"Ah. So you know the others."

"I don't understand . . ."

"I am unclear. My pardons. I would appreciate it most sternly if you would let me know the names of the teachers in your school who are Jewish or communist."

"Why do you need their names?"

"It is clerical, merely. You know us Germans: we are list makers." He smiled and pulled out a chair for her.

Vianne stared down at the blank paper on the table; then at the postcards in her hand. If Antoine received one, he might write back. She might know at last if he was alive. "This is not secret information, Herr Captain. Anyone can give you these names."

He moved in close to her. "With some effort, Madame, I believe I can find your husband's address and mail a package for you, also. Would this be sanguine?"

"'Sanguine' is not the right word, Herr Captain. You mean to ask me if it would be all right." She was stalling and she knew it. Worse, she was pretty sure that he knew it.

"Ah. Thank you so much for tutoring me in your beautiful language. My apologies." He offered her a pen. "Do not worry, Madame. It is clerical, merely."

Vianne wanted to say that she wouldn't write down any names, but what would be the point? It was easy enough for him to get this information in town. Everyone knew whose names belonged on the list. And Beck could throw her out of her own house for such a defiance—and what would she do then?

She sat down and picked up the pen and began to write down names. It wasn't until the end of the list that she paused and lifted the pen tip from the paper. "I'm done," she said in a soft voice.

"You have forgotten your friend."

"Did I?"

"Surely you meant to be accurate."

She bit her lip nervously and looked down at the list of names. She was certain suddenly that she shouldn't have done this. But what choice did she have? He was in control of her home. What would happen if she defied him? Slowly, feeling sick to her stomach, she wrote the last name on the list.

Rachel de Champlain.

TWELVE

On a particularly cold morning in late November, Vianne woke with tears on her cheeks. She had been dreaming about Antoine again.

With a sigh, she eased out of bed, taking care not to waken Sophie. Vianne had slept fully dressed, wearing a woolen vest, a long-sleeved sweater, woolen stockings, a pair of flannel pants (Antoine's, cut down to fit her), and a knit cap and mittens. It wasn't even Christmas and already layering had become de rigueur. She added a cardigan and still she was cold.

She burrowed her mittened hands into the slit at the foot of the mattress and withdrew the leather pouch Antoine had left for her. Not much money remained in it. Soon, they would have to live on her teaching salary alone.

She returned the money (counting it had become an obsession since the weather turned cold) and went downstairs.

There was never enough of anything anymore. The pipes froze at night and so there was no water until midday. Vianne had taken to leaving buckets full of water positioned near the stove and fireplaces for washing. Gas and electricity were scarce, as was money to pay for them, so she was miserly with both. The flames on her stove were so low it barely boiled water. They rarely turned on the lights.

She made a fire and then wrapped herself in a heavy eiderdown and sat on the divan. Beside her was a bag of yarn that she'd collected by pulling apart one of her old sweaters. She was making Sophie a scarf for Christmas, and these early-morning hours were the only time she could find.

With only the creaking of the house for company, she focused on the pale blue yarn and the way the knitting needles dove in and out of the soft strands, creating every moment something that hadn't existed before. It calmed her nerves, this once-ordinary morning ritual. If she loosed her thoughts, she might remember her mother sitting beside her, teaching her, saying, "Knit one, purl two, that's right . . . beautiful . . ."

Or Antoine, coming down the stairs in his stockinged feet, smiling, asking her what she was making for him . . .

Antoine.

The front door opened slowly, bringing a burst of ice-cold air and a flurry of leaves. Isabelle came in, wearing Antoine's old wool coat and knee-high boots and a scarf that coiled around her head and neck, obscuring all but her eyes. She saw Vianne and came to a sudden stop. "Oh. You're up." She unwound the scarf and hung up her coat. There was no mistaking the guilty look on her face. "I was out checking on the chickens."

Vianne's hands stilled; the needles paused. "You might as well tell me who he is, this boy you keep sneaking out to meet."

"Who would meet a boy in this cold?" Isabelle went to Vianne, pulling her to her feet, leading her to the fire.

At the sudden warmth, Vianne shivered. She hadn't realized how cold she'd been. "You," she said, surprised that it made her smile. "You would sneak out in the cold to meet a boy."

"He would have to be some boy. Clark Gable, maybe."

Sophie rushed into the room, snuggling up to Vianne. "This feels good," she said, holding out her hands.

For a beautiful, tender moment, Vianne forgot her worries, and then Isabelle said, "Well, I'd best go. I need to be first in the butcher's queue."

"You need to eat something before you go," Vianne said.

"Give mine to Sophie," Isabelle answered, pulling the coat back on and rewinding the scarf around her head.

Vianne walked her sister to the door, watched her slip out into the darkness, then returned to the kitchen and lit an oil lamp and went down to the cellar pantry, where rows of shelving ran along the stone wall. Two years ago this pantry had been full to overflowing with hams smoked in ash and jars full of duck fat set beside coils of sausage. Bottles of aged champagne vinegar, tins of sardines, jars of jam.

Now, they were nearly to the end of the chicory coffee. The last of the sugar was a sparkly white residue in the glass container, and the flour was more precious than gold. Thank God the garden had produced a good crop of vegetables in spite of the war refugees' rampage. She had canned and preserved every single fruit and vegetable, no matter how undersized.

She reached for a piece of wholemeal bread that was about to go bad. As breakfast for growing girls went, a boiled egg and a piece of toast wasn't much, but it could be worse.

"I want more," Sophie said when she'd finished.

"I can't," Vianne said.

"The Germans are taking all of our food," Sophie said just as Beck emerged from his room, dressed in his gray-green uniform.

"Sophie," Vianne said sharply.

"Well, it is true, young lady, that we German soldiers are taking much of the food France produces, but men who are fighting need to eat, do they not?"

Sophie frowned up at him. "Doesn't everyone need to eat?"

"*Oui*, M'mselle. And we Germans do not only take, we give back to our friends." He reached into the pocket of his uniform and drew out a chocolate bar.

"Chocolate!"

"Sophie, no," Vianne said, but Beck was charming her daughter, teasing her as he made the chocolate bar disappear and reappear by sleight of hand. At last, he gave it to Sophie, who squealed and ripped off the paper.

Beck approached Vianne. "You look . . . sad this morning," he said quietly.

Vianne didn't know how to respond.

He smiled and left. Outside, she heard his motorcycle start up and putter away.

"Tha' was good cho'clate," Sophie said, smacking her lips.

"You know, it would have been a good idea to have a small piece each night rather than to gobble it all up at once. And I shouldn't have to mention the virtues of sharing."

"Tante Isabelle says it's better to be bold than meek. She says if you jump off a cliff at least you'll fly before you fall."

"Ah, yes. That sounds like Isabelle. Perhaps you should ask her about the time she broke her wrist jumping from a tree she shouldn't have been climbing in the first place. Come on, let's go to school."

Outside, they waited at the side of the muddy, icy road for Rachel and the children. Together, they set off on the long, cold walk to school.

"I ran out of coffee four days ago," Rachel said. "In case you've been wondering why I have been such a witch."

"I'm the one who has been short-tempered lately," Vianne said. She waited for Rachel to disagree, but Rachel knew her well enough to know when a simple statement wasn't so simple. "It's that . . . I've had some things on my mind."

The list. She'd written down the names weeks ago, and nothing had come of it. Still, worry lingered.

"Antoine? Starvation? Freezing to death?" Rachel smiled. "What small worry has obsessed you this week?"

The school bell pealed.

"Hurry, Maman, we are late," Sophie said, grabbing her by the arm, dragging her forward.

Vianne let herself be led up the stone steps. She and Sophie and Sarah turned into Vianne's classroom, which was already filled with students.

"You're late, Madame Mauriac," Gilles said with a smile. "That's one demerit for you."

Everyone laughed.

Vianne took off her coat and hung it up. "You are very humorous, Gilles, as usual. Let's see if you're still smiling after our spelling test."

This time they groaned and Vianne couldn't help smiling at their crestfallen faces. They all looked so disheartened; it was difficult, honestly, to feel otherwise in this cold, blacked-out room that didn't have enough light to dispel the shadows.

"Oh, what the heck, it is a cold morning. Maybe a game of tag is what we need to get our blood running."

A roar of approval filled the room. Vianne barely had time to grab her coat before she was swept out of the classroom on a tide of laughing children.

They had been outside only a few moments when Vianne heard the grumble of automobiles coming toward the school.

The children didn't notice—they only noticed aeroplanes these days, it seemed—and went on with their play.

Vianne walked down to the end of the building and peered around the corner.

A black Mercedes-Benz roared up the dirt driveway, its fenders decorated with small swastika flags that flapped in the cold. Behind it was a French police car.

"Children," Vianne said, rushing back to the courtyard, "come here. Stand by me."

Two men rounded the corner and came into view. One she had never seen before—he was a tall, elegant, almost effete blond man wearing a long black leather coat and spit-shined boots. An iron cross decorated his stand-up collar. The other man she knew; he had been a policeman in Carriveau for years. Paul Jeauelere. Antoine had often remarked that he had a mean and cowardly streak.

"Madame Mauriac," the French police officer said with an officious nod.

She didn't like the look in his eyes. It reminded her of how boys sometimes looked at one another when they were about to bully a weaker child. "*Bonjour,* Paul."

"We are here for some of your colleagues. There is nothing to concern you, Madame. You are not on our list."

List.

"What do you want with my colleagues?" she heard herself asking, but her voice was almost inaudible, even though the children were silent.

"Some teachers will be dismissed today."

"Dismissed? Why?"

The Nazi agent flicked his pale hand as if he were batting at a fly. "Jews and communists and Freemasons. Others," he sneered, "who are no longer permitted to teach school or work in civil service or in the judiciary."

"But—"

The Nazi nodded at the French policeman and the two turned as one and marched into the school.

"Madame Mauriac?" someone said, tugging on her sleeve.

"Maman?" Sophie said, whining. "They can't do that, can they?"

"'Course they can," Gilles said. "Damn Nazi bastards."

Vianne should have disciplined him for his language, but she couldn't think of anything except the list of names she'd given to Beck.

Vianne wrestled with her conscience for hours. She'd continued teaching for much of the day, although she couldn't remember how. All that stuck in her mind was the look Rachel had given her as she walked out of the school with the other dismissed teachers. Finally, at noon, although they were already shorthanded at school, Vianne had asked another teacher to take over her classroom.

Now, she stood at the edge of the town square.

All the way here, she had planned what she would say, but when she saw the Nazi flag flying above the *hôtel de ville*, her resolve faltered. Everywhere she looked there were German soldiers, walking in pairs, or riding gorgeous, well-fed horses, or darting up the streets in shiny black Citröens. Across the square, a Nazi blew his whistle and used his rifle to force an old man to his knees.

Go, Vianne.

She walked up the stone steps to the closed oak doors, where a fresh-faced young guard stopped her and demanded to know her business.

"I am here to see Captain Beck," she said.

"Ah." The guard opened the door for her and pointed up the wide stone staircase, making the number two with his fingers.

Vianne stepped into the main room of the town hall. It was crowded with men in uniforms. She tried not to make eye contact with anyone as she hurried across the lobby to the stairs, which she ascended under the watchful eyes of the Führer, whose portrait took up much of the wall.

On the second floor, she found a man in uniform and she said to him, "Captain Beck, *s'il vous plaît?*"

"*Oui,* Madame." He showed her to a door at the end of the hall and rapped smartly upon it. At a response from within, he opened the door for her.

Beck was seated behind an ornate black and gold desk—obviously taken from one of the grand homes in the area. Behind him a portrait of Hitler and a collection of maps were affixed to the walls. On his desk was a typewriter and a roneo machine. In the corner stood a pile of confiscated radios, but worst of all was the food. There were boxes and boxes of food, heaps of cured meats and wheels of cheese stacked against the back wall.

"Madame Mauriac," he said, rising quickly. "What a most pleasant surprise." He came toward her. "What may I do for you?"

"It's about the teachers you fired at the school."

"Not I, Madame."

Vianne glanced at the open door behind them and took a step toward him, lowering her voice to say, "You told me the list of names was clerical in nature."

"I am sorry. Truly. This is what I was told."

"We need them at the school."

"You being here, it is . . . dangerous perhaps." He closed the small distance between them. "You do not want to draw attention to yourself, Madame Mauriac. Not here. There is a man . . ." He glanced at the door and stopped speaking. "Go, Madame."

"I wish you hadn't asked me."

"As do I, Madame." He gave her an understanding look. "Now, go. Please. You should not be here."

Vianne turned away from Captain Beck—and all that food and the picture of the Führer—and left his office. On her way down the stairs, she saw how the soldiers observed her, smiling to one another, no doubt joking about another Frenchwoman courting a dashing German soldier who had just broken her heart. But it wasn't until she stepped back out into the sunshine that she realized fully her mistake.

Several women were in the square, or near it, and they saw her step out of the Nazis' lair.

One of the women was Isabelle.

Vianne hurried down the steps, toward Hélène Ruelle, the baker's wife, who was delivering bread to the Kommandantur.

"Socializing, Madame Mauriac?" Hélène said archly as Vianne rushed past her.

Isabelle was practically running across the square toward her. With a defeated sigh, Vianne came to a standstill, waiting for her sister to reach her.

"What were you doing in there?" Isabelle demanded, her voice too loud, or maybe that was only to Vianne's ears.

"They fired the teachers today. No. Not all of them, just the Jews and the Freemasons and the communists." The memory welled up in her, made her feel sick. She remembered the quiet hallway and the confusion among the teachers who remained. No one knew what to do, how to defy the Nazis.

"*Just* them, huh?" Isabelle said, her face tightening.

"I didn't mean it to sound that way. I meant to clarify. They didn't fire all the teachers." Even to her own ears it sounded a feeble excuse, so she shut up.

"And this says nothing to explain your presence at their headquarters."

"I . . . thought Captain Beck could help us. Help Rachel."

"You went to Beck for a favor?"

"I had to."

"Frenchwomen do not ask Nazis for help, Vianne. *Mon Dieu*, you must know this."

"I know," Vianne said defiantly. "But . . ."

"But what?"

Vianne couldn't hold it in anymore. "I gave him a list of names."

Isabelle went very still. For an instant she seemed not to be breathing. The look she gave Vianne stung more than a slap across the face. "How could you do that? Did you give him Rachel's name?"

"I d-didn't know," Vianne stammered. "How could I know? He said it was clerical." She grabbed Isabelle's hand. "Forgive me, Isabelle. Truly. I didn't know."

"It is not my forgiveness you need to seek, Vianne."

Vianne felt a stinging, profound shame. How could she have been so foolish, and how in God's name could she make amends? She glanced at her wristwatch. Classes would be ending soon. "Go to the school," Vianne said. "Get Sophie, Sarah, and take them home. There's something I need to do."

"Whatever it is, I hope you've thought it through."

"Go," Vianne said tiredly.

❧

The chapel of St. Jeanne was a small stone Norman church at the edge of town. Behind it, and within its medieval walls, lay the convent of the Sisters of St. Joseph, nuns who ran both an orphanage and a school.

Vianne went into the church, her footsteps echoing on the cold stone floor; her breath plumed in front of her. She took off her mittens just long enough to touch her fingertips to the frozen holy water. She made the sign of the cross and went to an empty pew; she genuflected and then knelt. Closing her eyes, she bent her head in prayer.

She needed guidance—and forgiveness—but for the first time in her life she could find no words for her prayer. How could she be forgiven for such a foolish, thoughtless act?

God would see her guilt and fear, and He would judge her. She lowered her clasped hands and climbed back up to sit on the wooden pew.

"Vianne Mauriac, is that you?"

Mother Superior Marie-Therese moved in beside Vianne and sat down. She waited for Vianne to speak. It had always been this way between them. The first time Vianne had come to Mother for advice, Vianne had been sixteen years old and pregnant. It had been Mother who comforted Vianne after Papa called her a disgrace; Mother who had planned for a rushed wedding and talked Papa into letting Vianne and Antoine have Le Jardin; Mother who'd promised Vianne that a child was always a miracle and that young love could endure.

"You know there is a German billeted at my house," Vianne said finally.

"They are at all of the big homes and in every hotel."

"He asked me which of the teachers at school were Jewish or communist or Freemasons."

"Ah. And you answered him."

"That makes me the fool Isabelle calls me, doesn't it?"

"You are no fool, Vianne." She gazed at Vianne. "And your sister is quick to judge. That much I remember about her."

"I ask myself if they would have found these names without my help."

"They have dismissed Jews from positions all over town. Do you not know this? M'sieur Penoir is not the postmaster anymore, and Judge Braias has been replaced. I have had news from Paris that the headmistress of Collège Sévigné was forced to resign, as have all of the Jewish singers at the Paris Opera. Perhaps they needed your help, perhaps they did not. Certainly they would have found the names without your help," Mother said in a voice that was both gentle and stern. "But that is not what matters."

"What do you mean?"

"I think, as this war goes on, we will all have to look more deeply. These questions are not about them, but about *us*."

Vianne felt tears sting her eyes. "I don't know what to do anymore. Antoine always took care of everything. The Wehrmacht and the Gestapo are more than I can handle."

"Don't think about who they are. Think about who *you* are and what sacrifices you can live with and what will break you."

"It's *all* breaking me. I need to be more like Isabelle. She is so certain of everything. This war is black and white for her. Nothing seems to scare her."

"Isabelle will have her crisis of faith in this, too. As will we all. I have been here before, in the Great War. I know the hardships are just beginning. You must stay strong."

"By believing in God."

"Yes, of course, but not *only* by believing in God. Prayers and faith will not be enough, I'm afraid. The path of righteousness is often dangerous. Get ready, Vianne. This is only your first test. Learn from it." Mother leaned forward and hugged Vianne again. Vianne held on tightly, her face pressed to the scratchy wool habit.

When she pulled back, she felt a little better.

Mother Superior stood, took Vianne's hand, and drew her to a stand. "Perhaps you could find the time to visit the children this week and give them a lesson? They loved it when you taught them painting. As you can imagine, there's a lot of grumbling about empty bellies these days. Praise the Lord the sisters have an excellent garden, and the goats' milk and cheese is a Godsend. Still . . ."

"Yes," Vianne said. Everyone knew about how the belt-tightening felt, especially to children.

"You're not alone, and you're not the one in charge," Mother said gently. "Ask for help when you need it, and give help when you can. I think that is how we serve God—and each other and ourselves—in times as dark as these."

You're not the one in charge.

Vianne contemplated Mother's words all the way home.

She had always taken great comfort in her faith. When Maman had first begun to cough, and then when that coughing deepened into a hacking shudder that left sprays of blood on handkerchiefs, Vianne had prayed to God for all that she needed. Help. Guidance. A way to cheat the death that had come to call. At fourteen she'd promised God anything—everything—if He would just spare her maman's life. With her prayers unanswered, she returned to God and prayed for the strength to deal with the aftermath—her loneliness, Papa's bleak, angry silences and drunken rages, Isabelle's wailing neediness.

Time and again, she had returned to God, pleading for help, promising her faith. She wanted to believe that she was neither alone nor in charge, but rather that her life was unfolding according to His plan, even if she couldn't see it.

Now, though, such hope felt as slight and bendable as tin.

She *was* alone and there was no one else in charge, no one but the Nazis.

She had made a terrible, grievous mistake. She couldn't take it back, however much she might hope for such a chance; she couldn't undo it, but a good woman would accept responsibility—and blame—and apologize. Whatever else she was or wasn't, whatever her failings, she intended to be a good woman.

And so she knew what she needed to do.

She knew it, and still when she came to the gate at Rachel's cottage, she found herself unable to move. Her feet felt heavy, her heart even more so.

She took a deep breath and knocked on the door. There was a shuffling of feet within and then the door opened. Rachel held her sleeping son in one arm and had a pair of dungarees slung over the other. "Vianne," she said, smiling. "Come in."

Vianne almost gave in to cowardice. *Oh, Rachel, I just stopped by to say hello.* Instead, she took a deep breath and followed her friend into the house. She took her usual place in the comfortable upholstered chair tucked in close to the blazing fire.

"Take Ari, I'll make us coffee."

Vianne reached for the sleeping baby and took him in her arms. He snuggled close and she stroked his back and kissed the back of his head.

"We heard that some care packages were being delivered to prisoner of war camps by the Red Cross," Rachel said a moment later, coming into the room carrying two cups of coffee. She set one down on the table next to Vianne. "Where are the girls?"

"At my house, with Isabelle. Probably learning how to shoot a gun."

Rachel laughed. "There are worse skills to have." She pulled the dungarees from her shoulder and tossed them onto a straw basket with the rest of her sewing. Then she sat down across from Vianne.

Vianne breathed in deeply of the sweet scent that was pure baby. When she looked up, Rachel was staring at her.

"Is it one of those days?" she asked quietly.

Vianne gave an unsteady smile. Rachel knew how much Vianne sometimes mourned her lost babies and how deeply she'd prayed for more children. It had been difficult between them—not a lot, but a little—when Rachel had gotten pregnant with Ari. There was joy for Rachel . . . and a thread of envy. "No," she said. She lifted her chin slowly, looked her best friend in the eyes. "I have something to tell you."

"What?"

Vianne drew in a breath. "Do you remember the day we wrote the postcards? And Captain Beck was waiting for me when we got home?"

"*Oui.* I offered to come in with you."

"I wish you had, although I don't suppose it would have made a difference. He just would have waited until you left."

Rachel started to rise. "Did he—"

"No, no," she said quickly. "Not that. He was working at the dining room table that day, writing something when I returned. He . . . asked me for a list of names. He wanted to know which of the teachers at the school were Jewish or communists." She paused. "He asked about homosexuals and Freemasons, too, as if people talk about such things."

"You told him you didn't know."

Shame made Vianne look away, but only for a second. She forced herself to say, "I gave him your name, Rachel. Along with the others."

Rachel went very still; the color drained from her face, making her dark eyes stand out. "And they fired us."

Vianne swallowed hard, nodded.

Rachel got to her feet and walked past Vianne without stopping, ignoring her pleading *please, Rachel,* pulling away so she couldn't be touched. She went into her bedroom and slammed the door shut.

Time passed slowly, in indrawn breaths and captured prayers and creaks of the chair. Vianne watched the tiny black hands on the mantel clock click forward. She patted the baby's back in rhythm with the passing minutes.

Finally, the door opened. Rachel walked back into the room. Her hair was a mess, as if she'd been shoving her hands through it; her cheeks were blotchy, from either anxiety or anger. Maybe both. Her eyes were red from crying.

"I'm so sorry," Vianne said, rising. "Forgive me."

Rachel came to a stop in front of her, looking down at her. Anger flashed in her eyes, then faded and was replaced by resignation. "Everyone in town knows I'm a Jew, Vianne. I've always been proud of it."

"I know that. It's what I told myself. Still, I shouldn't have helped him. I am sorry. I wouldn't hurt you for the world. I hope you know that."

"Of course I know it," Rachel said quietly. "But V, you need to be more careful. I know Beck is young and handsome and friendly and polite, but he's a Nazi, and they are dangerous."

❧

The winter of 1940 was the coldest anyone could remember. Snow fell day after day, blanketing the trees and fields; icicles glittered on drooping tree branches.

And still, Isabelle woke every Friday morning, hours before dawn, and distributed her "terrorist papers," as the Nazis now called them. Last week's tract followed the military operations in North Africa and alerted the French people to the fact that the winter's food shortages were not a result of the British blockades—as Nazi propaganda insisted—but rather were caused by the Germans looting everything France produced.

Isabelle had been distributing these tracts for months now, and truthfully, she couldn't see that they were having much impact on the people of Carriveau. Many of the villagers still supported Pétain. Even more didn't care. A disturbing number of her neighbors looked upon the Germans and thought *so young, just boys,* and went on trudging through life with their heads down, just trying to stay out of danger.

The Nazis had noticed the flyers, of course. Some French men and women would use any excuse to curry favor—and giving the Nazis the flyers they found in their letter boxes was a start.

Isabelle knew that the Germans were looking for whoever printed and distributed the tracts, but they weren't looking too hard. Especially not on these snowy days when the Blitz of London was all anyone could talk about. Perhaps the Germans knew that words on a piece of paper were not enough to turn the tide of a war.

Today, Isabelle lay in bed, with Sophie curled like a tiny sword fern beside her, and Vianne sleeping heavily on the girl's other side. The three of them now slept together in Vianne's bed. Over the past month they'd added every quilt and blanket they could find to the bed. Isabelle lay watching her breath gather and disappear in thin white clouds.

She knew how cold the floor would be even through the woolen stockings she wore to bed. She knew this was the last time all day she would be warm. She steeled herself and eased out from underneath the pile of quilts. Beside her, Sophie made a moaning sound and rolled over to her mother's body for heat.

When Isabelle's feet hit the floor, pain shot into her shins. She winced and hobbled out of the room.

The stairs took forever; her feet hurt so badly. The damn chilblains. Everyone was suffering from them this winter. Supposedly it was from a lack of butter and fat, but Isabelle knew it was caused by cold weather and socks full of holes and shoes that were coming apart at the seams.

She wanted to start a fire—ached for even a moment's warmth, really—but they were on their last bit of wood. In late January they'd started ripping out barn wood and burning it, along with tool boxes and old chairs and whatever else they could find. She made herself a cup of boiling water and drank it down, letting the heat and weight trick her stomach into thinking it wasn't empty. She ate a small bit of stale bread, wrapped her body in a layer of newsprint, and then put on Antoine's coat and her own mittens and boots. A woolen scarf she wrapped around her head and neck, and even so, when she stepped outside the cold took her breath away. She closed the door behind her and trudged out into the snow, her chilblained toes throbbing with every step, her fingers going cold instantly, even inside the mittens.

It was eerily quiet out here. She hiked through the knee-deep snow and opened the broken gate and stepped out onto the white-packed road.

Because of the cold and snow, it took her three hours to deliver her papers (this week's content was about the Blitz—the Boches had dropped 32,000 bombs on London in one night alone). Dawn, when it came, was as weak as meatless broth. She was the first in line at the butcher's shop, but others soon followed. At seven A.M., the butcher's wife rolled open the window gate and unlocked the door.

"Octopus," the woman said.

Isabelle felt a pang of disappointment. "No meat?"

"Not for the French, M'mselle."

She heard grumbling behind her from the women who wanted meat, and farther back, from the women who knew they wouldn't even be lucky enough to get octopus.

Isabelle took the paper-wrapped octopus and left the shop. At least she'd gotten something. There was no tinned milk to be had anymore, not with ration cards or even on the black market. She was fortunate enough to get a little Camembert after two more hours in line. She covered her precious items with the heavy towel in her basket and hobbled down rue Victor Hugo.

As she passed a café filled with German soldiers and French policemen, she smelled brewed coffee and freshly baked croissants and her stomach grumbled.

"M'mselle."

A French policeman nodded crisply and indicated a need to step around her. She moved aside and watched him put up a poster in an abandoned storefront's window. The first poster read:

NOTICE

SHOT FOR SPYING. THE JEW JAKOB MANSARD, THE COMMUNIST VIKTOR YABLONSKY, AND THE JEW LOUIS DEVRY.

And the second:

NOTICE

HENCEFORTH, ALL FRENCH PEOPLE ARRESTED FOR ANY
CRIME OR INFRACTION WILL BE CONSIDERED HOSTAGES.
WHEN A HOSTILE ACT AGAINST GERMANY OCCURS IN
FRANCE, HOSTAGES WILL BE SHOT.

"They're shooting ordinary French people for nothing?" she said.

"Don't look so pale, Mademoiselle. These warnings are not for beautiful women such as yourself."

Isabelle glared at the man. He was worse than the Germans, a Frenchman doing this to his own people. This was why she hated the Vichy government. What good was self-rule for half of France if it turned them into Nazi puppets?

"Are you unwell, Mademoiselle?"

So solicitous. So caring. What would he do if she called him a traitor and spat in his face? "I am fine, *merci*."

She watched him cross the street confidently, his back straight, his hat positioned just so on his cropped brown hair. The German soldiers in the café welcomed him warmly, clapped him on the back and pulled him into their midst.

Isabelle turned away in disgust.

That was when she saw it: a bright silver bicycle leaning against the side wall of the café. At the sight of it, she thought how much it would change her life, ease her pain, to ride to town and back each day.

Normally a bicycle would be guarded by the soldiers in the café, but on this snow-dusted morning, no one was outside at a table.

Don't do it.

Her heart started beating quickly, her palms turned damp and hot within her mittens. She glanced around. The women queued up at the butcher's made it a point to see nothing and make eye contact with no one. The windows of the café across the street were fogged; inside, the men were olive-hued silhouettes.

So certain of themselves.

Of us, she thought bitterly.

At that, whatever sliver of restraint she possessed disappeared. She held the basket close to her side and limped out onto the ice-slicked cobblestoned street. From that second, that one step forward, the world seemed to blur around her and time slowed down. She heard her breath, saw the plumes of it in front of her face. The buildings blurred or faded into white hulks, the snow dazzled, until all she could see was the glint of the silver handlebars and the two black tires.

She knew there was only one way to do this. Fast. Without a glance sideways or a pause in her step.

Somewhere a dog barked. A door banged shut.

Isabelle kept walking; five steps separated her from the bicycle.

Four.

Three.

Two.

She stepped up onto the sidewalk and took hold of the bicycle and jumped onto it. She rode down the cobblestoned street, the chassis clanging at bumps in the road. She skidded around the corner, almost fell, and righted herself, pedaling hard toward rue La Grande.

There, she turned into the alley and jumped off the bicycle to knock on the door. Four hard clacks.

The door opened slowly. Henri saw her and frowned.

She pushed her way inside.

The small meeting room was barely lit. A single oil lamp sat on a scarred wooden table. Henri was the only one here. He was making sausage from a tray of meat and fat. Skeins of it hung from hooks on the wall. The room smelled of meat and blood and cigarette smoke. She yanked the bicycle in with her and slammed the door shut.

"Well, hello," he said, wiping his hands on a towel. "Have we called a meeting I don't know about?"

"No."

He glanced at her side. "That's not your bicycle."

"I stole it," she said. "From right under their noses."

"It is—or was—Alain Deschamp's bicycle. He left everything and fled to Lyon with his family when the occupation began." Henri moved toward her. "Lately, I have been seeing an SS soldier riding it around town."

"SS?" Isabelle's elation faded. There were ugly rumors swirling about the SS and their cruelty. Perhaps she should have thought this through . . .

He moved closer, so close she could feel the warmth of his body.

She had never been alone with him before, nor so near him. She saw for the first time that his eyes were neither brown nor green but rather a hazel gray that made her think of fog in a deep forest. She saw a small scar at his brow that had either been a terrible gash at one time or poorly stitched and it made her wonder all at once what kind of life he'd led that had brought him here, and to communism. He was older than she by at least a decade, although to be honest, he seemed even older sometimes, as if perhaps he'd suffered a great loss.

"You'll need to paint it," he said.

"I don't have any paint."

"I do."

"Would you—"

"A kiss," he said.

"A kiss?" She repeated it to stall for time. This was the sort of thing that she'd taken for granted before the war. Men desired her; they always had. She wanted that back, wanted to flirt with Henri and be flirted with, and yet the very idea of it felt sad and a little lost, as if perhaps kisses didn't mean much anymore and flirtation even less.

"One kiss and I'll paint your bicycle tonight and you can pick it up tomorrow."

She stepped toward him and tilted her face up to his.

They came together easily, even with all the coats and layers of news-print and wool between them. He took her in his arms and kissed her. For a beautiful second, she was Isabelle Rossignol again, the passionate girl whom men desired.

When it ended and he drew back, she felt . . . deflated. Sad.

She should say something, make a joke, or perhaps pretend that she felt more than she did. That's what she would have done before, when kisses had meant more, or maybe less.

"There's someone else," Henri said, studying her intently.

"No there isn't."

Henri touched her cheek gently. "You're lying."

Isabelle thought of all that Henri had given her. He was the one who'd brought her into the Free French network and given her a chance; he was the one who believed in her. And yet when he kissed her, she thought of Gaëtan. "He didn't want me," she said. It was the first time she'd told any-one the truth. The admission surprised her.

"If things were different, I'd make you forget him."

"And I'd let you try."

She saw the way he smiled at that, saw the sorrow in it. "Blue," he said after a pause.

"Blue?"

"It's the paint color I have."

Isabelle smiled. "How fitting."

Later that day, as she stood in one line after another for too little food, and then as she gathered wood from the forest and carried it home, she thought about that kiss.

What she thought, over and over again, was *if only*.

THIRTEEN

On a beautiful day in late April 1941, Isabelle lay stretched out on a woolen blanket in the field across from the house. The sweet smell of ripening hay filled her nostrils. When she closed her eyes, she could almost forget that the engines in the distance were German lorries taking soldiers—and France's produce—to the train station at Tours. After the disastrous winter, she appreciated how sunshine on her face lulled her into a drowsy state.

"There you are."

Isabelle sighed and sat up.

Vianne wore a faded blue gingham day dress that had been grayed by harsh homemade soap. Hunger had whittled her down over the winter, sharpened her cheekbones and deepened the hollow at the base of her throat. An old scarf turbaned her head, hiding hair that had lost its shine and curl.

"This came for you." Vianne held out a piece of paper. "It was delivered. By a man. For you," she said, as if that fact bore repeating.

Isabelle clambered awkwardly to her feet and snatched the paper from Vianne's grasp. On it, in scrawled handwriting, was: *The curtains are open.* She reached down for her blanket and began folding it up. What did it mean? They'd never summoned her before. Something important must be happening.

"Isabelle? Would you care to explain?"

"No."

"It was Henri Navarre. The innkeeper's son. I didn't think you knew him."

Isabelle ripped the note into tiny pieces and let it fall away.

"He is a communist, you know," Vianne said in a whisper.

"I need to go."

Vianne grabbed her wrist. "You cannot have been sneaking out all winter to see a communist. You know what the Nazis think of them. It's dangerous to even be seen with this man."

"You think I care what the Nazis think?" Isabelle said, wrenching free. She ran barefooted across the field. At home, she grabbed some shoes and climbed aboard her bicycle. With an *au revoir!* to a stunned-looking Vianne, Isabelle was off, pedaling down the dirt road.

In town, she coasted past the abandoned hat shop—sure enough, the curtains were open—and veered into the cobblestoned alley and came to a stop.

She leaned her bicycle against the rough limestone wall beside her and rapped four times. It didn't occur to her until the final knock that it might be a trap. The idea, when it came, made her draw in a sharp breath and glance left and right, but it was too late now.

Henri opened the door.

Isabelle ducked inside. The room was hazy with cigarette smoke and reeked of burned chicory coffee. There was about the place a lingering scent of blood—sausage making. The burly man who had first grabbed her—Didier—was seated on an old hickory-backed chair. He was leaning back so far the two front chair legs were off the floor and his back grazed the wall behind him.

"You shouldn't have brought a notice to my house, Henri. My sister is asking questions."

"It was important we talk to you immediately."

Isabelle felt a little bump of excitement. Would they finally ask her to do something more than dropping papers in letter boxes? "I am here."

Henri lit up a cigarette. She could feel him watching her as he exhaled the gray smoke and put down his match. "Have you heard of a prefect in Chartres who was arrested and tortured for being a communist?"

Isabelle frowned. "No."

"He cut his own throat with a piece of glass rather than name anyone or confess." Henri snubbed his cigarette out on the bottom of his shoe and saved the rest for later in his coat pocket. "He is putting a group together, of people like us who want to heed de Gaulle's call. He—the one who cut his own throat—is trying to get to London to speak to de Gaulle himself. He seeks to organize a Free French movement."

"He didn't die?" Isabelle asked. "Or cut his vocal cords?"

"No. They're calling it a miracle," Didier said.

Henri studied Isabelle. "I have a letter—very important—that needs to be delivered to our contact in Paris. Unfortunately, I am being watched closely these days. As is Didier."

"Oh," Isabelle said.

"I thought of you," Didier said.

"Me?"

Henri reached into his pocket and withdrew a crumpled envelope. "Will you deliver this to our man in Paris? He is expecting it a week from today."

"But . . . I don't have an *Ausweis.*"

"*Oui,*" Henri said quietly. "And if you were caught . . ." He let that threat dangle. "Certainly no one would think badly of you if you declined. This is dangerous."

Dangerous was an understatement. There were signs posted through-out Carriveau about executions that were taking place all over the Occu-pied Zone. The Nazis were killing French citizens for the smallest of infractions. Aiding this Free French movement could get her imprisoned at the very least. Still, she believed in a free France the way her sister be-lieved in God. "So you want me to get a pass, go to Paris, deliver a letter, and come home." It didn't sound so perilous when put that way.

"No," Henri said. "We need you to stay in Paris and be our . . . letter box, as it were. In the coming months there will be many such deliveries. Your father has an apartment there, *oui?*"

Paris.

It was what she'd longed for from the moment her father had exiled her. To leave Carriveau and return to Paris and be part of a network of people who resisted this war. "My father will not offer me a place to stay."

"Convince him otherwise," Didier said evenly, watching her. Judging her.

"He is not a man who is easily convinced," she said.

"So you can't do it. *Voilà.* We have our answer."

"Wait," Isabelle said.

Henri approached her. She saw reluctance in his eyes and knew that he wanted her to turn down this assignment. No doubt he was worried about her. She lifted her chin and looked him in the eyes. "I will do this."

"You will have to lie to everyone you love, and always be afraid. Can you live that way? You'll not feel safe anywhere."

Isabelle laughed grimly. It was not so different from the life she'd lived since she was a little girl. "Will you watch over my sister?" she asked Henri. "Make sure she's safe?"

"There is a price for all our work," Henri said. He gave her a sad look. In it was the truth they had all learned. There was no safety. "I hope you see that."

All Isabelle saw was her chance to do something that mattered. "When do I leave?"

"As soon as you get an *Ausweis*, which will not be easy."

❧

What in heaven's name is that girl thinking?

Really, a school-yard-style note from a man? A communist?

Vianne unwrapped the stringy piece of mutton that had been this week's ration and set it on the kitchen counter.

Isabelle had always been impetuous, a force of nature, really, a girl who liked to break rules. Countless nuns and teachers had learned that she could be neither controlled nor contained.

But this. This was not kissing a boy on the dance floor or running away to see the circus or refusing to wear a girdle and stockings.

This was wartime in an occupied country. How could Isabelle still believe that her choices had no consequences?

Vianne began finely chopping the mutton. She added a precious egg to the mix, and stale bread, then seasoned it with salt and pepper. She was forming the mixture into patties when she heard a motorcycle *putt-puttering* toward the house. She went to the front door and opened it just enough to peer out.

Captain Beck's head and shoulders could be seen above the stone wall as he dismounted his motorcycle. Moments later, a green military lorry pulled up behind him and parked. Three other German soldiers appeared in her yard. The men talked among themselves and then gathered at the rose-covered stone wall her great-great-grandfather had built. One of the soldiers lifted a sledgehammer and brought it down hard on the wall, which shattered. Stones broke into pieces, a skein of roses fell, their pink petals scattering across the grass.

Vianne rushed out into her yard. "Herr Captain!"

The sledgehammer came down again. *Craaaack.*

"Madame," Beck said, looking unhappy. It bothered Vianne that she knew him well enough to notice his state of mind. "We have orders to tear down all the walls along this road."

As one soldier demolished the wall, two others came toward the front door, laughing at some joke between them. Without asking permission, they walked past her and went into her house.

"My condolences," Beck said, stepping over the rubble on his way to her. "I know you love the roses. And—most sorrowfully—my men will be fulfilling a requisition order from your house."

"A requisition?"

The soldiers came out of the house; one carried the oil painting that had been over the mantel and the other had the overstuffed chair from the salon.

"That was my grandmère's favorite chair," Vianne said quietly.

"I'm sorry," Beck said. "I was unable to stop this."

"What in the world . . ."

Vianne didn't know whether to be relieved or concerned when Isabelle yanked her bike over the pile of stone and leaned it against the tree. Already there was no barrier between her property and the road anymore.

Isabelle looked beautiful, even with her face pink from the exertion of riding her bicycle and shiny with perspiration. Glossy blond waves framed her face. Her faded red dress clung to her body in all the right places.

The soldiers stopped to stare at her, the rolled-up Aubusson rug from the living room slung between them.

Beck removed his military cap. He said something to the soldiers who were carrying the rolled-up carpet, and they hurried toward the lorry.

"You've torn down our wall?" Isabelle said.

"The Sturmbannführer wants to be able to see all houses from the road. Somebody is distributing anti-German propaganda. We will find and arrest him."

"You think harmless pieces of paper are worth all of this?" Isabelle asked.

"They are far from harmless, Mademoiselle. They encourage terrorism."

"Terrorism must be avoided," Isabelle said, crossing her arms.

Vianne couldn't look away from Isabelle. There was something going on. Her sister seemed to be drawing her emotions back, going still, like a cat preparing to pounce. "Herr Captain," Isabelle said after a while.

"*Oui*, M'mselle?"

Soldiers walked past them, carrying out the breakfast table.

Isabelle let them pass and then walked to the captain. "My papa is ill."

"He is?" Vianne said. "Why don't I know this? What's wrong with him?"

Isabelle ignored Vianne. "He has asked that I come to Paris to nurse him. But . . ."

"He wants *you* to nurse him?" Vianne said, incredulous.

Beck said, "You need a travel pass to leave, M'mselle. You know this."

"I know this." Isabelle seemed to barely breathe. "I . . . thought perhaps you would procure one for me. You are a family man. Certainly you understand how important it is to answer a father's call?"

Strangely, as Isabelle spoke, the captain turned slightly to look at Vianne, as if she were the one who mattered.

"I could get you a pass, *oui*," the captain said. "For a family emergency such as this."

"I am grateful," Isabelle said.

Vianne was stunned. Did Beck not see how her sister was manipulating him—and why had he looked at Vianne when making his decision?

As soon as Isabelle got what she wanted, she returned to her bicycle. She took hold of the handlebars and walked it toward the barn. The rubber wheels bumped and thumped on the uneven ground.

Vianne rushed after her. "Papa's ill?" she said when she caught up with her sister.

"Papa's fine."

"You lied? Why?"

Isabelle's pause was slight but perceptible. "I suppose there is no reason to lie. It's all out in the open now. I have been sneaking out on Friday mornings to meet Henri and now he has asked me to go to Paris with him. He has a lovely little *pied-à-terre* in the Montmarte, apparently."

"Are you mad?"

"I'm in love, I think. A little. Maybe."

"You are going to cross Nazi-occupied France to spend a few nights in Paris in the bed of a man whom you might love. A little."

"I know," Isabelle said. "It's so romantic."

"You must be feverish. Perhaps you have a brain sickness of some kind." She put her hands on her hips and made a huff of disapproval.

"If love is a disease, I suppose I'm infected."

"Good God." Vianne crossed her arms. "Is there anything I can say to stop this foolishness?"

Isabelle looked at her. "You believe me? You believe I would cross Nazi-occupied France on a lark?"

"This is not like running away to see the circus, Isabelle."

"But . . . you believe this of me?"

"Of course." Vianne shrugged. "So foolish."

Isabelle looked oddly crestfallen. "Just stay away from Beck while I'm gone. Don't trust him."

"Isn't that just like you? You're worried enough to warn me, but not worried enough to stay with me. What *you* want is what really matters. Sophie and I can rot for all you care."

"That's not true."

"Isn't it? Go to Paris. Have your fun but don't for one minute forget that you are abandoning your niece and me." Vianne crossed her arms and glanced back at the man in her yard who was supervising the looting of her house. "With him."

FOURTEEN

April 27, 1995
The Oregon Coast

I am trussed up like a chicken for roasting. I know these modern seat belts are a good thing, but they make me feel claustrophobic. I belong to a generation that didn't expect to be protected from every danger.

I remember what it used to be like, back in the days when one was required to make smart choices. We knew the risks and took them anyway. I remember driving too fast in my old Chevrolet, my foot pressed hard on the gas, smoking a cigarette and listening to Price sing "Lawdy, Miss Clawdy" through small black speakers while children rolled around in the backseat like bowling pins.

My son is afraid that I will make a break for it, I suppose, and it is a reasonable fear. In the past month, my entire life has been turned upside down. There is a SOLD sign in my front yard and I am leaving home.

"It's a pretty driveway, don't you think?" my son says. It's what he does; he fills space with words, and he chooses them carefully. It is what makes him a good surgeon. Precision.

"Yes."

He turns into the parking lot. Like the driveway, it is lined in flowering trees. Tiny white blossoms drop to the ground like bits of lace on a dressmaker's floor, stark against the black asphalt.

I fumble with my seat belt as we park. My hands do not obey my will these days. It frustrates me so much that I curse out loud.

"I'll do that," my son says, reaching sideways to unhook my seat belt.

He is out of the automobile and at my door before I have even re-trieved my handbag.

The door opens. He takes me by the hand and helps me out of the car. In the short distance between the parking lot and the entrance, I have to stop twice to catch my breath.

"The trees are so pretty this time of year," he says as we walk together across the parking lot.

"Yes." They are flowering plum trees, gorgeous and pink, but I think suddenly of chestnut trees in bloom along the Champs Élysées.

My son tightens his hold on my hand. It is a reminder that he under-stands the pain of leaving a home that has been my sanctuary for nearly fifty years. But now it is time to look ahead, not behind.

To the Ocean Crest Retirement Community and Nursing Home.

To be fair, it doesn't look like a bad place, a little industrial maybe, with its rigidly upright windows and perfectly maintained patch of grass out front and the American flag flying above the door. It is a long, low build-ing. Built in the seventies, I'd guess, back when just about everything was ugly. There are two wings that reach out from a central courtyard, where I imagine old people sit in wheelchairs with their faces turned to the sun, waiting. Thank God, I am not housed in the east side of the building—the nursing home wing. Not yet anyway. I can still manage my own life, thank you very much, and my own apartment.

Julien opens the door for me, and I go inside. The first thing I see is a large reception area decorated to look like the hospitality desk of a seaside hotel, complete with a fishing net full of shells hung on the wall. I imagine that at Christmas they hang ornaments from the netting and stockings from the edge of the desk. There are probably sparkly HO-HO-HO signs tacked up to the wall on the day after Thanksgiving.

"Come on, Mom."

Oh, right. Mustn't dawdle.

The place smells of what? Tapioca pudding and chicken noodle soup. Soft foods.

Somehow I keep going. If there's one thing I never do, it's stop.

"Here we are," my son says, opening the door to room 317A.

It's nice, honestly. A small, one-bedroom apartment. The kitchen is tucked into the corner by the door and from it one can look out over a Formica counter and see a dining table with four chairs and the living room, where a coffee table and sofa and two chairs are gathered around a gas fireplace.

The TV in the corner is brand new, with a built-in VCR player. Someone—my son, probably, has stacked a bunch of my favorite movies in the bookcase. *Jean de Florette, Breathless, Gone with the Wind.*

I see my things: an afghan I knitted thrown over the sofa's back; my books in the bookcase. In the bedroom, which is of a fine size, the nightstand on my side of the bed is lined with prescription pill containers, a little jungle of plastic orange cylinders. My side of the bed. It's funny, but some things don't change after the death of a spouse, and that's one of them. The left side of the bed is mine even though I am alone in it. At the foot of the bed is my trunk, just as I have requested.

"You could still change your mind," he says quietly. "Come home with me."

"We've talked about this, Julien. Your life is too busy. You needn't worry about me 24/7."

"Do you think I will worry less when you are here?"

I look at him, loving this child of mine and knowing my death will devastate him. I don't want him to watch me die by degrees. I don't want that for his daughters, either. I know what it is like; some images, once seen, can never be forgotten. I want them to remember me as I am, not as I will be when the cancer has had its way.

He leads me into the small living room and gets me settled on the couch. While I wait, he pours us some wine and then sits beside me.

I am thinking of how it will feel when he leaves, and I am sure the same thought occupies his mind. With a sigh, he reaches into his briefcase and pulls out a stack of envelopes. The sigh is in place of words, a breath of transition. In it, I hear that moment where I go from one life to another. In this new, pared-down version of my life, I am to be cared for by my son instead of vice versa. It's not really comfortable for either of us. "I've paid this month's bills. These are things I don't know what to do with. Junk, mostly, I think."

I take the stack of letters from him and shuffle through them. A "personalized" letter from the Special Olympics committee . . . a free estimate awning offer . . . a notice from my dentist that it has been six months since my last appointment.

A letter from Paris.

There are red markings on it, as if the post office has shuffled it around from place to place, or delivered it incorrectly.

"Mom?" Julien says. He is so observant. He misses nothing. "What is that?"

When he reaches for the envelope, I mean to hold on to it, keep it from him, but my fingers don't obey my will. My heartbeat is going all which-a-way.

Julien opens the envelope, extracts an ecru card. An invitation. "It's in French," he says. "Something about the Croix de Guerre. So it's about World War Two? Is this for Dad?"

Of course. Men always think war is about them.

"And there's something handwritten in the corner. What is it?"

Guerre. The word expands around me, unfolds its black crow wings, becoming so big I cannot look away. Against my will, I take up the invitation. It is to a *passeurs'* reunion in Paris.

They want me to attend.

How can I possibly go without remembering all of it—the terrible things I have done, the secret I kept, the man I killed . . . and the one I should have?

"Mom? What's a *passeur*?"

I can hardly find enough voice to say, "It's someone who helped people in the war."

FIFTEEN

Asking yourself a question, that's how resistance begins.
And then ask that very question to someone else.

—REMCO CAMPERT

May 1941
France

On the Monday Isabelle left for Paris, Vianne kept busy. She washed clothes and hung them out to dry; she weeded her garden and gathered a few early-ripening vegetables. At the end of a long day, she treated herself to a bath and washed her hair. She was drying it with a towel when she heard a knock at the door. Startled by an unexpected guest, she buttoned her bodice as she went to the door. Water dripped onto her shoulders.

When she opened the door, she found Captain Beck standing there, dressed in his field uniform, dust peppering his face. "Herr Captain," she said, pushing the wet hair away from her face.

"Madame," he said. "A colleague and I went fishing today. I have brought you what we caught."

"Fresh fish? How lovely. I will fry it up for you."

"For us, Madame. You and me and Sophie."

Vianne couldn't look away from either Beck or the fish in his hands. She knew without a doubt that Isabelle wouldn't accept this gift. Just as she knew that her friends and neighbors would claim to turn it down. Food. From the enemy. It was a matter of pride to turn it down. Everyone knew that.

"I have neither stolen nor demanded it. No Frenchman has more of a right to it than I. There can be no dishonor in your taking it."

He was right. This was a fish from local waters. He had not confiscated it. Even as she reached for the fish, she felt the weight of rationalization settle heavily upon her.

"You rarely do us the honor of eating with us."

"It is different now," he said. "With your sister away."

Vianne backed into the house to allow him entry. As always, he removed his hat as soon as he stepped inside, and clomped across the wooden floor to his room. Vianne didn't notice until she heard the click-shut of his door that she was still standing there, holding a dead fish wrapped in a recent edition of the *Pariser Zeitung*, the German newspaper printed in Paris.

She returned to the kitchen. When she laid the paper-wrapped fish out on the butcher block, she saw that he'd already cleaned the fish, even going so far as to shave off the scales. She lit the gas stove and put a cast-iron pan over the heat, adding a precious spoonful of oil to the pan. While cubes of potato browned and onion carmelized, she seasoned the fish with salt and pepper and set it aside. In no time, tantalizing aromas filled the house, and Sophie came running into the kitchen, skidding to a stop in the empty space where the breakfast table used to be.

"Fish," she said with reverence.

Vianne used her spoon to create a well within the vegetables and put the fish in the middle to fry. Tiny bits of grease popped up; the skin sizzled and turned crisp. At the very end, she placed a few preserved lemons in the pan, watching them melt over everything.

"Go tell Captain Beck that supper is ready."

"He is eating with us? Tante Isabelle would have something to say about that. Before she left, she told me to never look him in the eye and to try not to be in the same room with him."

Vianne sighed. The ghost of her sister lingered. "He brought us the fish, Sophie, and he lives here."

"*Oui*, Maman. I know that. Still, she said—"

"Go call the captain for supper. Isabelle is gone, and with her, her extreme worries. Now, go."

Vianne returned to the stove. Moments later, she carried out a heavy ceramic tray bearing the fried fish surrounded by the pan-roasted vegetables and preserved lemons, all of it enhanced with fresh parsley. The tangy, lemony sauce in the bottom of the pan, swimming with crusty brown bits, could have benefited from butter, but still it smelled heavenly. She carried it into the dining room and found Sophie already seated, with Captain Beck beside her.

In Antoine's chair.

Vianne missed a step.

Beck rose politely and moved quickly to pull out her chair. She paused only slightly as he took the platter from her.

"This looks most becoming," he said in a hearty voice. Once again, his French was not quite right.

Vianne sat down and scooted in to her place at the table. Before she could think of what to say, Beck was pouring her wine.

"A lovely '37 Montrachet," he said.

Vianne knew what Isabelle would say to that.

Beck sat across from her. Sophie sat to her left. She was talking about something that had happened at school today. When she paused, Beck said something about fishing and Sophie laughed, and Vianne felt Isabelle's absence as keenly as she'd previously felt her presence.

Stay away from Beck.

Vianne heard the warning as clearly as if it had been spoken aloud beside her. She knew that in this one thing her sister was right. Vianne couldn't forget the list, after all, and the firings, or the sight of Beck seated at his desk with crates of food at his feet and a painting of the Führer behind him.

". . . my wife quite despaired of my skill with a net after that . . ." he was saying, smiling.

Sophie laughed. "My papa fell into the river one time when we were fishing, remember, Maman? He said the fish was so big it pulled him in, right, Maman?"

Vianne blinked slowly. It took her a moment to notice that the conversation had circled back to include her.

It felt . . . odd to say the least. In all their past meals with Beck at the table, conversation had been rare. Who could speak surrounded by Isabelle's obvious anger?

It is different now, with your sister away.

Vianne understood what he meant. The tension in the house—at this table—was gone now.

What other changes would her absence bring?

Stay away from Beck.

How was Vianne to do that? And when was the last time she'd eaten a meal this good . . . or heard Sophie laugh?

⁂

The Gare de Lyon was full of German soldiers when Isabelle disembarked from the train carriage. She wrestled her bicycle out with her; it wasn't easy with her valise banging into her thighs the whole time and impatient Parisians shoving at her. She had dreamed of coming back here for months.

In her dreams, Paris was Paris, untouched by the war.

But on this Monday afternoon, after a long day's travel, she saw the truth. The occupation might have left the buildings in place, and there was no evidence outside the Gare de Lyon of bombings, but there was a darkness here, even in the full light of day, a hush of loss and despair as she rode her bicycle down the boulevard.

Her beloved city was like a once-beautiful courtesan grown old and thin, weary, abandoned by her lovers. In less than a year, this magnificent city had been stripped of its essence by the endless clatter of German jackboots on the streets and disfigured by swastikas that flew from every monument.

The only cars she saw were black Mercedes-Benzes with miniature swastika flags flapping from prongs on the fenders, and Wehrmacht lorries, and now and then a gray panzer tank. All up and down the boulevard, windows were blacked out and shutters were drawn. At every other corner, it seemed, her way was barricaded. Signs in bold, black lettering offered directions in German, and the clocks had been changed to run two hours ahead—on German time.

She kept her head down as she pedaled past pods of German soldiers and sidewalk cafés hosting uniformed men. As she rounded onto the boulevard de la Bastille, she saw an old woman on a bicycle trying to bypass a barricade. A Nazi stood in her way, berating her in German—a language she obviously didn't understand. The woman turned her bicycle and pedaled away.

It took Isabelle longer to reach the bookshop than it should have, and by the time she coasted to a stop out front, her nerves were taut. She leaned her bicycle against a tree and locked it in place. Clutching her valise in sweaty, gloved hands, she approached the bookshop. In a bistro window, she caught sight of herself: blond hair hacked unevenly along the bottom; face pale with bright red lips (the only cosmetic she still had); she had worn her best ensemble for traveling—a navy and cream plaid jacket with a matching hat and a navy skirt. Her gloves were a bit the worse for wear, but in these times no one noticed a thing like that.

She wanted to look her best to impress her father. Grown-up.

How many times in her life had she agonized over her hair and clothing before coming home to the Paris apartment only to discover that Papa was gone and Vianne was "too busy" to return from the country and that some female friend of her father's would care for Isabelle while she was on holiday? Enough so that by the time she was fourteen she'd stopped coming home on holidays at all; it was better to sit alone in her empty dormitory room than be shuffled among people who didn't know what to do with her.

This was different, though. Henri and Didier—and their mysterious friends in the Free French—needed Isabelle to live in Paris. She would not let them down.

The bookshop's display windows were blacked out and the grates that protected the glass during the day were drawn down and locked in place. She tried the door and found it locked.

On a Monday afternoon at four o'clock? She went to the crevice in the store façade that had always been her father's hiding place and found the rusted skeleton key and let herself in.

The narrow store seemed to hold its breath in the darkness. Not a sound came at her. Not her father turning the pages of a beloved novel or the sound of his pen scratching on paper as he struggled with the poetry that had been his passion when Maman was alive. She closed the door behind her and flicked on the light switch by the door.

Nothing.

She felt her way to the desk and found a candle in an old brass holder. An extended search of the drawers revealed matches, and she lit the candle.

The light, meager as it was, revealed destruction in every corner of the shop. Half of the shelves were empty, many of them broken and hanging on slants, the books a fallen pyramid on the floor beneath the low end. Posters had been ripped down and defaced. It was as if marauders had gone through on a rampage looking for something hidden and carelessly destroyed everything along the way.

Papa.

Isabelle left the bookshop quickly, not even bothering to replace the key. Instead, she dropped it in her jacket pocket and unlocked her bicycle and climbed aboard. She kept to the smaller streets (the few that weren't barricaded) until she came to rue de Grenelle; there, she turned and pedaled for home.

The apartment on the Avenue de La Bourdonnais had been in her father's family for more than a hundred years. The city street was lined on either side by pale, sandstone buildings with black ironwork balconies and slate roofs. Carved stone cherubs decorated the cornices. About six blocks away, the Eiffel Tower rose high into the sky, dominating the view. On the street level were dozens of storefronts with pretty awnings and cafés, with tables set up out front; the high floors were all residential. Usually, Isabelle walked slowly along the sidewalk, window shopping, appreciating the hustle and bustle around her. Not today. The cafés and bistros were empty. Women in worn clothes and tired expressions stood in queues for food.

She stared up at the blacked-out windows as she fished the key from her bag. Opening the door, she pushed her way into the shadowy lobby, hauling her bicycle with her. She locked it to a pipe in the lobby. Ignoring the coffin-sized cage elevator, which no doubt didn't run in these days of limited electricity, she climbed the narrow, steeply pitched stairs that coiled around the elevator shaft and came to the fifth-floor landing, where there were two doors, one on the left side of the building, and theirs, on the right. She unlocked the door and stepped inside. Behind her, she thought she heard the neighbor's door open. When she turned back to say hello to Madame Leclerc, the door clicked quietly shut. Apparently the nosy old woman was watching the comings and goings in apartment 6B.

She entered her apartment and closed the door behind her. "Papa?"

Even though it was midday, the blacked-out windows made it dark inside. "Papa?"

There was no answer.

Truthfully, she was relieved. She carried her valise into the salon. The darkness reminded her of another time, long ago. The apartment had been shadowy and musty; there had been breathing then, and footsteps creaking on wooden floors.

Hush, Isabelle, no talking. Your maman is with the angels now.

She turned on the light switch in the living room. An ornate blown-glass chandelier flickered to life, its sculpted glass branches glittering as if from another world. In the meager light, she looked around the apartment, noticing that several pieces of art were missing from the walls. The room reflected both her mother's unerring sense of style and the collection of antiques from other generations. Two paned windows—covered now—should have revealed a beautiful view of the Eiffel Tower from the balcony.

Isabelle turned off the light. There was no reason to waste precious electricity while she waited. She sat down at the round wooden table beneath the chandelier, its rough surface scarred by a thousand suppers over the years. Her hand ran lovingly over the banged-up wood.

Let me stay, Papa. Please. I'll be no trouble.

How old had she been that time? Eleven? Twelve? She wasn't sure. But she'd been dressed in the blue sailor uniform of the convent school. It all felt a lifetime ago now. And yet here she was, again, ready to beg him to—(*love her*)—let her stay.

Later—how much longer? She wasn't sure how long she'd sat here in the dark, remembering the circumstances of her mother because she had all but forgotten her face in any real way—she heard footsteps and then a key rattling in the lock.

She heard the door open and rose to her feet. The door clicked shut. She heard him shuffling through the entry, past the small kitchen.

She needed to be strong now, determined, but the courage that was as much a part of her as the green of her eyes had always faded in her father's presence and it retreated now. "Papa?" she said into the darkness. She knew he hated surprises.

She heard him go still.

Then a light switch clicked and the chandelier came on. "Isabelle," he said with a sigh. "What are you doing here?"

She knew better than to reveal uncertainty to this man who cared so little for her feelings. She had a job to do now. "I have come to live with you in Paris. Again," she added as an afterthought.

"You left Vianne and Sophie alone with the Nazi?"

"They are safer with me gone, believe me. Sooner or later, I would have lost my temper."

"Lost your temper? What is wrong with you? You will return to Carriveau tomorrow morning." He walked past her to the wooden sideboard that was tucked against the papered wall. He poured himself a glass of brandy, drank it down in three large gulps, and poured another. When he finished the second drink, he turned to her.

"No," she said. The single word galvanized her. Had she ever said it to him before? She said it again for good measure. "No."

"Pardon?"

"I said no, Papa. I will not bend to your will this time. I will not leave. This is my home. My *home*." Her voice weakened on that. "Those are the drapes I watched Maman make on her sewing machine. This is the table she inherited from her great-uncle. On the walls of my bedroom you'll find my initials, drawn in Maman's lipstick when she wasn't looking. In my secret room, my fort, I'll bet my dolls are still lined up along the walls."

"Isabelle—"

"No. You will not turn me away, Papa. You have done that too many times. You are my father. This is my home. We are at war. I'm staying." She bent down for the valise at her feet and picked it up.

In the pale glow of the chandelier, she saw defeat deepen the lines in her father's cheeks. His shoulders slumped. He poured himself another brandy, gulped it greedily. Obviously he could barely stand to look at her without the aid of alcohol.

"There are no parties to attend," he said, "and all your university boys are gone."

"This is really what you think of me," she said. Then she changed the subject. "I stopped by the bookshop."

"The Nazis," he said in response. "They stormed in one day and pulled out everything by Freud, Mann, Trotsky, Tolstoy, Maurois—all of them, they burned—and the music, too. I would rather lock the doors than sell only what I am allowed to. So, I did just that."

"So, how are you making a living? Your poetry?"

He laughed. It was a bitter, slurred sound. "This is hardly a time for gentler pursuits."

"Then, how are you paying for electricity and food?"

Something changed in his face. "I've got a good job at the Hôtel de Crillon."

"In service?" She could hardly credit him serving beer to German brutes.

He glanced away.

Isabelle got a sick feeling in her stomach. "For whom do you work, Papa?"

"The German high command in Paris," he said.

Isabelle recognized that feeling now. It was shame. "After what they did to you in the Great War—"

"Isabelle—"

"I remember the stories Maman told us about how you'd been before the war and how it had broken you. I used to dream that someday you'd remember that you were a father, but all that was a lie, wasn't it? You're just a coward. The minute the Nazis return you race to aid them."

"How dare you judge me and what I've been through? You're eighteen years old."

"Nineteen," she said. "Tell me, Papa, do you get our conquerors coffee or hail them taxis on their way to Maxim's? Do you eat their lunch leftovers?"

He seemed to deflate before her eyes; age. She felt unaccountably regretful for her sharp words even though they were true and deserved. But she couldn't back down now. "So we are agreed? I will move into my old room and live here. We need barely speak if that is your condition."

"There is no food here in the city, Isabelle; not for us Parisians anyway. All over town are signs warning us not to eat rats and these signs are necessary. People are raising guinea pigs for food. You will be more comfortable in the country, where there are gardens."

"I am not looking for comfort. Or safety."

"What are you looking for in Paris, then?"

She realized her mistake. She'd set a trap with her foolish words and stepped right into it. Her father was many things; stupid was not one of them. "I'm here to meet a friend."

"Tell me we are not talking about some boy. Tell me you are smarter than that."

"The country was dull, Papa. You know me."

He sighed, poured another drink from the bottle. She saw the telltale glaze come into his eyes. Soon, she knew, he would stumble away to be alone with whatever it was he thought about. "If you stay, there will be rules."

"Rules?"

"You will be home by curfew. Always and without exception. You will leave me my privacy. I can't stomach being hovered over. You will go to the shops each morning and see what our ration cards will get us. And you will find a job." He paused, looked at her, his eyes narrowed. "And if you get yourself in trouble like your sister did, I will throw you out. Period."

"I am not—"

"I don't care. A job, Isabelle. Find one."

He was still talking when she turned on her heel and walked away. She went into her old bedroom and shut the door. Hard.

She had done it! For once, she'd gotten her way. Who cared that he'd been mean and judgmental? She was here. In her bedroom, in Paris, and staying.

The room was smaller than she remembered. Painted a cheery white, with a twin iron-canopied bed and a faded old rug on the wooden plank floor and a Louis XV armchair that had seen better days. The window—blacked out—overlooked the interior courtyard of the apartment building. As a girl, she'd always known when her neighbors were taking out the trash, because she could hear them clanking out there, slamming down lids. She tossed her valise on the bed and began to unpack.

The clothes she'd taken on exodus—and returned to Paris with—were shabbier for the constant wear and hardly worth hanging in the armoire along with the clothes she'd inherited from her maman—beautiful vintage flapper dresses with flared skirts, silk-fringed evening gowns, woolen suits that had been cut down to fit her, and crepe day dresses. An array of matching hats and shoes made for dancing on ballroom floors or walking through the Rodin Gardens with the right boy on one's arm. Clothes for a world that had vanished. There were no more "right" boys in Paris. There were practically no boys at all. They were all captive in camps in Germany or hiding out somewhere.

When her clothes were returned to hangers in the armoire, she closed the mahogany doors and pushed the armoire sideways just enough to reveal the secret door behind it.

Her fort.

She bent down and opened the door set into the white paneled wall by pushing on the top right corner. It sprang free, creaked open, revealing a storage room about six feet by six feet, with a roof so slanted that even as a ten-year-old girl, she'd had to hunch over to stand in it. Sure enough, her dolls were still in there, some slumped and others standing tall.

Isabelle closed the door on her memories and moved the armoire back in place. She undressed quickly and slipped into a pink silk dressing gown that reminded her of her maman. It still smelled vaguely of rose water—or she pretended it did. As she headed out of the room to brush her teeth, she paused at her father's closed door.

She could hear him writing; his fountain pen scratched on rough paper. Every now and then he cursed and then fell silent. (That was when he was drinking, no doubt.) Then came the thunk of a bottle—or a fist—on the table.

Isabelle readied for bed, setting her hair in curlers and washing her face and brushing her teeth. On her way back to bed, she heard her father curse again—louder this time, maybe drinking—and she ducked into her bedroom and slammed the door behind her.

I can't stomach being hovered over.

Apparently what this really meant was that her father couldn't stand to be in the same room with her.

Funny that she hadn't noticed it last year, when she'd lived with him for those weeks between her expulsion from the finishing school and her exile to the country.

True, they'd never sat down to a meal together then. Or had a conversation meaningful enough to remember. But somehow she hadn't noticed. They'd been together in the bookshop, working side by side. Had she been so pathetically grateful for his presence that his silence escaped her notice?

Well, she noticed it now.

He pounded on her bedroom door so hard she released a little yelp of surprise.

"I'm leaving for work," her father said through the door. "The ration cards are on the counter. I left you one hundred francs. Get what you can."

She heard his footsteps echo down the wooden hall, heavy enough to rattle the walls. Then the door slammed shut.

"Good-bye to you, too," Isabelle mumbled, stung by the tone of his voice.

Then she remembered.

Today was the day.

She threw back the coverlet and climbed out of bed and dressed without bothering to turn on the light. She had already planned her outfit: a drab gray dress and black beret, white gloves, and her last pair of black slingback pumps. Sadly, she had no stockings.

She studied herself in the salon mirror, trying to be critical, but all she saw was an ordinary girl in a dull dress, carrying a black handbag.

She opened her handbag (again) and stared down at the silk hammock-like lined interior. She had slit a tiny opening in the lining and slipped the thick envelope inside of it. Upon opening the handbag, it looked empty. Even if she did get stopped (which she wouldn't—why would she? a nineteen-year-old girl dressed for lunch?) they would see nothing in her handbag except her papers, her ration coupons, and her *carte d'identité, certificate of domicile,* and her *Ausweis.* Exactly what should be there.

At ten o'clock, she left the apartment. Outside, beneath a bright, hot sun, she climbed aboard her blue bicycle and pedaled toward the quay.

When she reached the rue de Rivoli, black cars and green military lorries with fuel tanks strapped onto their sides and men on horseback filled the street. There were Parisians about, walking along the sidewalks, pedaling down the few streets upon which they were allowed to ride, queueing for food in lines that extended down the block. They were noticeable by the look of defeat on their faces and the way they hurried past the Germans without making eye contact. At Maxim's restaurant, beneath the famous red awning, she saw a cluster of high-ranking Nazis waiting to get inside. The rumor was rampant that all of the country's best meats and produce went straight to Maxim's, to be served to the high command.

And then she spotted it: the iron bench near the entrance to the Comédie Française.

Isabelle hit the brakes on her bicycle and came to a bumpy, sudden stop, then stepped off the pedal with one foot. Her ankle gave a little twist when she put her weight on it. For the first time, her excitement turned a little sharp with fear.

Her handbag felt heavy suddenly; noticeably so. Sweat collected in her palms and along the rim of her felt hat.

Snap out of it.

She was a *courier,* not a frightened schoolgirl. What risk there was she accepted.

While she stood there, a woman approached the bench and sat down with her back to Isabelle.

A woman. She hadn't expected her contact to be a woman, but that was strangely comforting.

She took a deep, calming breath and walked her bicycle across the busy crosswalk and past the kiosks, with their scarves and trinkets for sale. When she was directly beside the woman on the bench, she said what she'd been told to say. "Do you think I'll need an umbrella today?"

"I expect it to remain sunny." The woman turned. She had dark hair which she'd coiled away from her face with care and bold, Eastern European features. She was older—maybe thirty—but the look in her eyes was even older.

Isabelle started to open her handbag when the woman said, "No," sharply. Then, "Follow me," she said, rising quickly.

Isabelle remained behind the woman as she made her way across the wide, gravelly expanse of the Cœur Napoléon with the mammoth elegance of the Louvre rising majestically around them. Although it didn't feel like a place that had once been a palace of emperors and kings, not with swastika flags everywhere and German soldiers sitting on benches in the Tuilleries garden. On a side street, the woman ducked into a small café. Isabelle locked her bicycle to a tree out front and followed her inside, taking a seat across from her.

"You have the envelope?"

Isabelle nodded. In her lap, she opened her handbag and withdrew the envelope, which she handed to the woman beneath the table.

A pair of German officers walked into the bistro, took a table not far away.

The woman leaned over and straightened Isabelle's beret. It was a strangely intimate gesture, as if they were sisters or best friends. Leaning close, the woman whispered in her ear, "Have you heard of *les collabos?*"

"No."

"Collaborators. French men and women who are working with the Germans. They are not only in Vichy. Be aware, always. These collaborators love to report us to the Gestapo. And once they know your name, the Gestapo are always watching. Trust no one."

She nodded.

The woman drew back and looked at her. "Not even your father."

"How do you know about my father?"

"We want to meet you."

"You just have."

"*We*," she said quietly. "Stand at the corner of boulevard Saint-Germain and rue de Saint-Simon tomorrow at noon. Do not be late, do not bring your bicycle, and do not be followed."

Isabelle was surprised by how quickly the woman got to her feet. In an instant, she was gone, and Isabelle was at the café table alone, under the watchful eye of the German soldier at the other table. She forced herself to order a *café au lait* (although she knew there would be no milk and the coffee would be chicory). Finishing it quickly, she exited the café.

At the corner, she saw a sign pasted to the window that warned of executions in retaliation for infractions. Beside it, in the cinema window, was a yellow poster that read *INTERDIT AUX JUIFS*—no Jews allowed.

As she unlocked her bicycle, the German soldier appeared beside her. She bumped into him.

He asked solicitously if she was all right. Her answer was an actress's smile and a nod. "*Mais oui. Merci.*" She smoothed her dress and clamped her purse in her armpit and climbed onto the bicycle. She pedaled away from the soldier without looking back.

She had done it. She'd gotten an *Ausweis* and come to Paris and forced her papa to let her stay, and she had delivered her first secret message for the Free French.

SIXTEEN

Vianne had to admit that life at Le Jardin was easier without Isabelle. No more outbursts, no more veiled comments made just within Captain Beck's earshot, no more pushing Vianne to wage useless battles in a war already lost. Still, sometimes without Isabelle, the house was too quiet, and in the silence, Vianne found herself thinking too loudly.

Like now. She'd been awake for hours, just staring at her own bedroom ceiling, waiting for the dawn.

Finally, she got out of bed and went downstairs. She poured herself a cup of bitter made-from-acorns coffee and took it out into the backyard, where she sat on the chair that had been Antoine's favorite, beneath the sprawling branches of the yew tree, listening to the chickens scratching lethargically through the dirt.

Her money was all but gone. They would now have to live on her meager teaching salary.

How was she to do it? And alone . . .

She finished her coffee, as terrible as it was. Carrying the empty cup back into the shadowy, already warming house, she saw the door to Captain Beck's bedroom was open. He had left for the day while she was out back. Good.

She woke Sophie, listened to the story of her latest dream, and made her a breakfast of dry toast and peach jam. Then the two of them headed for town.

Vianne rushed Sophie as much as possible, but Sophie was in a foul mood and complained and dragged her feet. Thus, it was late afternoon by the time they reached the butcher's shop. There was a queue that snaked out the door and down the street. Vianne took her place at the end and glanced nervously at the Germans in the square.

The queue shuffled forward. At the display window, Vianne noticed a new propaganda poster that showed a smiling German soldier offering bread to a group of French children. Beside it was a new sign that read: NO JEWS ALLOWED.

"What does that mean, Maman?" Sophie said, pointing to the sign.

"Hush, Sophie," Vianne said sharply. "We have talked about this. Some things are no longer spoken of."

"But Father Joseph says—"

"Hush," Vianne said impatiently, giving Sophie's hand a tug for emphasis.

The queue moved forward. Vianne stepped to the front and found herself staring at a gray-haired woman with skin the color and texture of oatmeal.

Vianne frowned. "Where is Madame Fournier?" she asked, offering her ration ticket for today's meat. She hoped there was still some to be had.

"No Jews allowed," the woman said. "We have a little smoked pigeon left."

"But this is the Fourniers' shop."

"Not anymore. It's mine now. You want the pigeon or not?"

Vianne took the small tin of smoked pigeon and dropped it in her willow basket. Saying nothing, she led Sophie outside. On the opposite corner, a German sentry stood guard in front of the bank, reminding the French people that the bank had been seized by the Germans.

"Maman," Sophie whined. "It's wrong to—"

"Hush." Vianne grabbed Sophie's hand. As they walked out of town and along the dirt road home, Sophie made her displeasure known. She huffed and sighed and grumbled.

Vianne ignored her.

When they reached the broken gate to Le Jardin, Sophie yanked free and spun to face Vianne. "How can they just take the butcher's shop? Tante Isabelle would do something. You're just afraid!"

"And what should I do? Storm into the square and demand that Madame Fournier get her shop back? And what would they do to me for that? You've seen the posters in town." She lowered her voice. "They're executing French people, Sophie. *Executing* them."

"But—"

"No buts. These are dangerous times, Sophie. You need to understand that."

Sophie's eyes glazed with tears. "I wish Papa were here . . ."

Vianne pulled her daughter into her arms and held her tightly. "Me, too."

They held each other for a long time, and then slowly separated. "We are going to make pickles today, how about that?"

"Oh. Fun."

Vianne couldn't disagree. "Why don't you go pick cucumbers? I'll get the vinegar started."

Vianne watched her daughter run ahead, dodging through the heavily laden apple trees toward the garden. The moment she disappeared, Vianne's worry returned. What would she do without money? The garden was producing well, so there would be fruit and vegetables, but what about the coming winter? How could Sophie stay healthy without meat or milk or cheese? How would they get new shoes? She was shaking as she made her way into the hot, blacked-out house. In the kitchen, she clutched the counter's edge and bowed her head.

"Madame?"

She turned so fast she almost tripped over her own feet.

He was in the living room, sitting on the divan, with an oil lamp lit beside him, reading a book.

"Captain Beck." She said his name quietly. She moved toward him, her shaking hands clasped together. "Your motorcycle is not out front."

"It was such a beautiful day. I decided to walk from town." He rose. She saw that he had recently had a haircut, and that he'd nicked himself shaving this morning. A tiny red cut marred his pale cheek. "You look upset. Perhaps it is because you have not been sleeping well since your sister left."

She looked at him in surprise.

"I hear you walking around in the dark."

"You're awake, too," she said stupidly.

"I often cannot sleep, either. I think of my wife and children. My son is so young. I wonder if he will know me at all."

"I think the same about Antoine," she said, surprising herself with the admission. She knew she shouldn't be so open with this man—the enemy—but just now she was too tired and scared to be strong.

Beck stared down at her, and in his eyes, she saw the loss they shared. Both of them were a long way from the people they loved, and lonelier for it.

"Well. I mean not to intrude on your day, of course, but I have some news for you. With much research, I have discovered that your husband is in an *Oflag* in Germany. A friend of mine is a guard there. Your husband is an officer. Did you know this? No doubt he was valiant on the battlefield."

"You found Antoine? He's alive?"

He held out a crumpled, stained envelope. "Here is a letter he has written to you. And now you may send him care packages, which I believe would cheer him most immeasurably."

"Oh . . . my." She felt her legs weaken.

He grasped her, steadied her, and led her over to the divan. As she slumped to the seat, she felt tears welling in her eyes. "Such a kind thing to do," she whispered, taking the letter from him, pressing it to her chest.

"My friend delivered the letter to me. From now on, my apologies, you will correspond on the postcards only."

He smiled at her and she had the strangest feeling that he knew about the lengthy letters she concocted in her head at night.

"*Merci,*" she said, wishing it weren't such a small word.

"*Au revoir,* Madame," he said, then turned on his heel and left her alone.

The crumpled, dirty letter shook in her grasp; the letters of her name blurred and danced as she opened it.

> *Vianne, my beloved,*
>
> *First, do not worry about me. I am safe and fed well enough. I am unhurt. Truly. No bullet holes in me.*
>
> *In the barracks, I have been lucky enough to claim an upper bunk, and it gives me some privacy in a place of too many men. Through a small window, I can see the*

*moon at night and the spires of Nuremburg. But it
is the moon that makes me think of you.*

 *Our food is enough to sustain us. I have grown
used to pellets of flour and small pieces of potato. When
I get home, I look forward to your cooking. I dream of it—
and you and Sophie—all the time.*

 *Please, my beloved, don't fret. Just stay strong and be there
for me when the time comes for me to leave this cage. You are my
sunlight in the dark and the ground beneath my feet. Because
of you, I can survive. I hope that you can find strength in me,
too, V. That because of me, you will find a way to be strong.*

 *Hold my daughter tightly tonight, and tell her that
somewhere far away, her papa is thinking of her. And tell
her I will return.*

 I love you, Vianne.

*P.S. The Red Cross is delivering packages. If you could
send me my hunting gloves, I would be very happy.*

 The winters here are cold.

Vianne finished the letter and immediately began reading it again.

❧

Exactly a week after her arrival in Paris, Isabelle was to meet the others who shared her passion for a free France, and she was nervous as she walked among the sallow-faced Parisians and well-fed Germans toward an unknown destination. She had dressed carefully this morning in a fitted blue rayon dress with a black belt. She'd set her hair last night and combed it out into precise waves this morning, pinning it back from her face. She wore no makeup; an old convent school blue beret and white gloves completed the outfit.

I am an actress and this is a role, she thought as she walked down the street. *I am a schoolgirl in love sneaking out to meet a boy . . .*

That was the story she'd decided on and dressed for. She was sure that—if questioned—she could make a German believe her.

With all of the barricaded streets, it took her longer than expected to arrive at her destination, but finally she ducked around a barricade and moved onto the boulevard Saint-Germain.

She stood beneath a streetlamp. Behind her, traffic moved slowly up the boulevard; horns honking, motors grumbling, horse hooves clomping, bicycle bells ringing. Even with all that noise, this once lively street felt stripped of its life and color.

A police wagon pulled up alongside of her, and a gendarme stepped out of the vehicle, his cloak folded over his shoulders. He was carrying a white stick.

"Do you think I'll need an umbrella today?"

Isabelle jumped, made a little sound. She'd been so focused on the policeman—he was crossing the street now, heading toward a woman coming out of a café—that she'd forgotten her mission. "I-I expect it to remain sunny," she said.

The man clutched her upper arm (there was no other word for it, really; he had a tight grip) and led her down the suddenly empty street. It was funny how one police wagon could make Parisians disappear. No one stuck around for an arrest—neither to witness it nor to help.

Isabelle tried to see the man beside her, but they were moving too fast. She glimpsed his boots—slashing quickly across the sidewalk beneath them—old leather, torn laces, a hole emerging from scuff marks at the left toe.

"Close your eyes," he said as they crossed a street.

"Why?"

"Do it."

She was not one to follow orders blindly (a quip she might have made under other circumstances), but she wanted so badly to be a part of this that she did as instructed. She closed her eyes and stumbled along beside him, almost tripping over her own feet more than once.

At last they came to a stop. She heard him knock four times on a door. Then there were footsteps and she heard the whoosh of a door opening and the acrid smell of cigarette smoke wafted across her face.

It occurred to her now—just this instant—that she could be in danger.

The man pulled her inside and the door slammed shut behind them.

Isabelle opened her eyes, even though she had not been told to do so. Best that she show her mettle now.

The room didn't come into focus instantly. It was dark, the air thick with cigarette smoke. All of the windows were blacked out. The only light came from two oil lamps, sputtering valiantly against the shadows and smoke.

Three men sat at a wooden table that bore an overflowing ashtray. Two were young, wearing patched coats and ragged pants. Between them sat a pencil-thin old man with a waxed gray moustache, whom she recognized. Standing at the back wall was the woman who had been Isabelle's contact. She was dressed all in black, like a widow, and was smoking a cigarette.

"M'sieur Lévy?" Isabelle asked the older man. "Is that you?"

He pulled the tattered beret from his shiny, bald head and held it in clasped hands. "Isabelle Rossignol."

"You know this woman?" one of the men asked.

"I was a regular patron of her father's bookshop," Lévy said. "Last I heard she was impulsive, undisciplined, and charming. How many schools expelled you, Isabelle?"

"One too many, my father would say. But what good is knowing where to seat an ambassador's second son at a dinner party these days?" Isabelle said. "I am still charming."

"And still outspoken. A rash head and thoughtless words could get everyone in this room killed," he said carefully.

Isabelle understood her mistake instantly. She nodded.

"You are very young," the woman in the back said, exhaling smoke.

"Not anymore," Isabelle said. "I dressed to look younger today. I think it is an asset. Who would suspect a nineteen-year-old girl of anything illegal? And you, of all people, should know that a woman can do anything a man can do."

Monsieur Lévy sat back in his chair and studied her.

"A friend recommends you highly."

Henri.

"He tells us you have been distributing our tracts for months. And Anouk says you were quite steady yesterday."

Isabelle glanced at the woman—Anouk—who nodded in response. "I will do anything to help our cause," Isabelle said. Her chest felt tight with anticipation. It had never occurred to her that she could come all this way and be denied entrance to this network of people whose cause was her own.

At last, Monsieur Lévy said, "You will need false papers. A new identity. We will get that for you, but it will take some time."

Isabelle drew in a sharp breath. She had been accepted! A sense of destiny seemed to fill the room. She would do something that mattered now. She knew it.

"For now, the Nazis are so arrogant, they do not believe that any kind of resistance can succeed against them," Lévy said, "but they will see . . . they will see, and then the danger to all of us will increase. You must tell no one of your association with us. No one. And that includes your family. It is for their safety and your own."

It would be easy for Isabelle to hide her activities. No one cared particularly where she went or what she did. "*Oui*," she said. "So . . . what do I do?"

Anouk pulled away from the wall and crossed the room, stepping over the stack of terrorist papers that were on the floor. Isabelle couldn't see the headline clearly—it was something about the RAF bombing of Hamburg and Berlin. She reached into her pocket and pulled out a small package, about the size of a deck of cards, wrapped in crinkled tan-colored paper and tied up with twine. "You will deliver this to the *tabac* in the old quarter in Amboise; the one directly below the chateau. It must arrive no later than tomorrow, four P.M." She handed Isabelle the package and one half of a torn five-franc note. "Offer him the note. If he shows you another half, give him the package. Leave then. Do not look back. Do not speak to him."

As she took the package and the note, she heard a sharp, short knock on the door behind her. An instant tension tightened the air in the room. Glances were exchanged. Isabelle was reminded keenly that this was dangerous work. It could be a policeman on the other side of the door, or a Nazi.

Three knocks followed.

Monsieur Lévy nodded evenly.

The door opened and in walked a fat man with an egg-shaped head and an age-spotted face. "I found him wandering around," the old man said as he stepped aside to reveal an RAF pilot still in his flight suit.

"*Mon Dieu*," Isabelle whispered. Anouk nodded glumly.

"They are everywhere," Anouk said under her breath. "Falling from the skies." She smiled tightly at the joke. "Evaders, escapees from German prisons, downed airmen."

Isabelle stared at the airman. Everyone knew the penalty for helping British airmen. It was announced on billboards all over town: imprisonment or death.

"Get him some clothes," Lévy said.

The old man turned to the airman and began speaking.

Clearly the airman didn't speak French.

"They are going to get you some clothes," Isabelle said.

The room fell silent. She felt everyone looking at her.

"You speak English?" Anouk said quietly.

"Passably. Two years in a Swiss finishing school."

Another silence fell. Then Lévy said, "Tell the pilot we will put him in hiding until we can find a way out of France for him."

"You can do that?" Isabelle said.

"Not at present," Anouk said. "Don't tell him that, of course. Just tell him we are on his side and he is safe—relatively—and he is to do as he is told."

Isabelle went to the airman. As she neared him, she saw the scratches on his face and the way something had torn the sleeve of his flight suit. She was pretty sure dried blood darkened his hairline, and she thought: *He dropped bombs on Germany.*

"Not all of us are passive," she said to the young man.

"You speak English," he said. "Thank God. My aeroplane crashed four days ago. I've been crouching in dark corners ever since. I didn't know where to go till this man grabbed me and dragged me here. You will help me?"

She nodded.

"How? Can you get me back home?"

"I don't have the answers. Just do as they tell you, and Monsieur?"

"Yes, ma'am?"

"They are risking their lives to help you. You understand that?"

He nodded.

Isabelle turned to face her new colleagues. "He understands and will do as you ask."

"*Merci*, Isabelle," Lévy said. "Where do we contact you after your return from Amboise?"

The moment she heard the question, Isabelle had an answer that surprised her. "The bookshop," she said firmly. "I am going to reopen it."

Lévy gave her a look. "What will your father say about that? I thought he closed it when the Nazis told him what to sell."

"My father works for the Nazis," she said bitterly. "His opinions don't account for much. He asked me to get a job. This will be my job. I will be accessible to all of you at any time. It is the perfect solution."

"It is," Lévy said, although it sounded as if he didn't agree. "Very well then. Anouk will bring you new papers as soon as we can get a *carte d'identité* made. We will need a photograph of you." His gaze narrowed. "And Isabelle, allow me to be an old man for a moment and to remind a young girl who is used to being impulsive that there can be none of that anymore. You know I am friends with your father—or I was until he showed his true colors—and I have heard stories about you for years. It is time for you to grow up and do as you are told. Always. Without exception. It is for your safety as much as ours."

It embarrassed Isabelle that he felt the need to say this to her, and in front of everyone. "Of course."

"And if you get caught," Anouk said, "it will be as a *woman*. You understand? They have special . . . unpleasantries for us."

Isabelle swallowed hard. She had thought—briefly—of imprisonment and execution. This was something she had never even considered. Of course she should have.

"What we all demand of each other—or, hope for, at any rate—is two days."

"Two days?"

"If you are captured and . . . questioned. Try to say nothing for two days. That gives us time to disappear."

"Two days," Isabelle said. "That's not so long."

"You are so young," Anouk said, frowning.

In the past six days, Isabelle had left Paris four times. She'd delivered packages in Amboise, Blois, and Lyon. She'd spent more time in train stations than in her father's apartment—an arrangement that suited them both. As long as she stood in food queues during the day and returned home before the curfew, her father didn't care what she did. Now, though, she was back in Paris and ready to move forward with the next phase of her plan.

"You are not reopening the bookshop."

Isabelle stared at her father. He stood near the blacked-out window. In the pale light, the apartment looked shabbily grand, decorated as it was with ornate antiques collected over the generations. Good paintings in heavy gilt frames graced the walls (some were missing, and black shadows hung on the wall in their place; probably Papa had sold them), and if the blackout shades could be lifted, a breathtaking view of the Eiffel Tower lay just beyond their balcony.

"You told me to get a job," she said stubbornly. The paper-wrapped package in her handbag gave her a new strength with her father. Besides, he was already half drunk. In no time, he'd be sprawled in the bergère in the salon, whimpering in his sleep. When she was a girl, those sad sounds he made in his sleep had made her long to comfort him. No more.

"I meant a *paid* job," he said dryly. He poured himself another snifter of brandy.

"Why don't you just use a soup bowl?" she said.

He ignored that. "I won't have it. That's all. You will not open the bookshop."

"I have already done it. Today. I was there cleaning all afternoon."

He seemed to go still. His bushy gray eyebrows raised into his lined brow. "You cleaned?"

"I cleaned," she said. "I know it surprises you, Papa, but I am not twelve years old." She moved toward him. "I am doing this, Papa. I have decided. It will allow me time to queue up for food and a chance to make some small bit of money. The Germans will buy books from me. I promise you that."

"You'll flirt with them?" he said.

She felt the sting of his judgment. "Says the man who works for them."

He stared at her.

She stared at him.

"Fine," he said at last. "You'll do what you will. But the storeroom in back. That's mine. *Mine,* Isabelle. I will lock it up and take the key and you will respect my wishes by staying out of that room."

"Why?"

"It doesn't matter why."

"Do you have assignations with women there? On the sofa?"

He shook his head. "You are a foolish girl. Thank God your maman did not live to see who you have become."

Isabelle hated how deeply that hurt her. "Or you, Papa," she said. "Or you."

SEVENTEEN

*I*n mid-June of 1941, on the second-to-the-last school day of the term, Vianne was at the blackboard, conjugating a verb, when she heard the now-familiar *putt-putt-putt* of a German motorcycle.

"Soldiers again," Gilles Fournier said bitterly. The boy was always angry lately, and who could blame him? The Nazis had seized his family's butcher shop and given it to a collaborator.

"Stay here," she said to her students, and went out into the hallway. In walked two men—a Gestapo officer in a long black coat and the local gendarme, Paul, who had gained weight since his collaboration with the Nazis. His stomach strained at his belt. How many times had she seen him strolling down rue Victor Hugo, carrying more food than his family could eat, while she stood in a lengthy queue, clutching a ration card that would provide too little?

Vianne moved toward them, her hands clasped tightly at her waist. She felt self-conscious in her threadbare dress, with its frayed collar and cuffs, and although she had carefully drawn a brown seam line up the back of her bare calves, it was obvious that it was a ruse. She had no stockings on, and that made her feel strangely vulnerable to these men. On either side of the hallway, classroom doors opened and teachers stepped out to see what the officers wanted. They made eye contact with one another but no one spoke.

The Gestapo agent walked determinedly toward Monsieur Paretsky's classroom at the end of the building. Fat Paul struggled to keep up, huffing along behind him.

Moments later, Monsieur Paretsky was dragged out of his classroom by the French policeman.

Vianne frowned as they passed her. Old man Paretsky—who had taught her sums a lifetime ago and whose wife tended to the school's flowers—gave her a terrified look. "Paul?" Vianne said sharply. "What is happening?"

The policeman stopped. "He is accused of something."

"I did nothing wrong!" Paretsky cried, trying to pull free of Paul's grasp.

The Gestapo agent noticed the commotion and perked up. He came at Vianne fast, heels clicking on the floor. She felt a shiver of fear at the glint in his eyes. "Madame. What is your reason for stopping us?"

"H-he is a friend of mine."

"Really," he said, drawing length from the word, making it a question. "So you know that he is distributing anti-German propaganda."

"It's a *news*paper," Paretsky said. "I'm just telling the French people the truth. Vianne! Tell them!"

Vianne felt attention turn to her.

"Your name?" the Gestapo demanded, opening a notebook and taking out a pencil.

She wet her lips nervously. "Vianne Mauriac."

He wrote it down. "And you work with M'sieur Paretsky, distributing flyers?"

"No!" she cried out. "He is a *teaching* colleague, sir. I know nothing about anything else."

The Gestapo closed the notebook. "Has no one told you that it is best to ask no questions?"

"I didn't mean to," she said, her throat dry.

He gave a slow smile. It frightened her, disarmed her, that smile; enough so that it took her a minute to register his next words.

"You are terminated, Madame."

Her heart seemed to stop. "E-excuse me?"

"I speak of your employment as a teacher. You are terminated. Go home, Madame, and do not return. These students do not need an example such as you."

⟢

At the end of the day, Vianne walked home with her daughter and even remembered now and then to answer one of Sophie's nonstop questions, but all the while she was thinking: *What now?*

What now?

The stalls and shops were closed this time of day, their bins and cases empty. There were signs everywhere saying NO EGGS, NO BUTTER, NO OIL, NO LEMONS, NO SHOES, NO THREAD, NO PAPER BAGS.

She had been frugal with the money Antoine left for her. More than frugal—miserly—even though it had seemed like so much money in the beginning. She had used it for necessities only—wood, electricity, gas, food. But still it was gone. How would she and Sophie survive without her salary from teaching?

At home, she moved in a daze. She made a pot of cabbage soup and loaded it up with shredded carrots that were soft as noodles. As soon as the meal was finished, she did laundry, and when it was hanging out on the line, she darned socks until night fell. Too early, she shuffled a whiny, complaining Sophie off to bed.

Alone (and feeling it like a knife pressed to her throat), she sat down at the dining table with an official postcard and a fountain pen.

> *Dearest Antoine,*
> *We are out of money and I have lost my job.*
> *What am I to do? Winter is only months away.*

She lifted the pen from the paper. The blue words seemed to expand against the white paper.

Out of money.

What kind of woman was she to even think of sending a letter like this to her prisoner-of-war husband?

She balled up the postcard and threw it into the cold, soot-caked fireplace, where it lay all alone, a white ball on a bed of gray ash.

No.

It couldn't be in the house. What if Sophie found it, read it? She retrieved it from the ashes and carried it out to the backyard, where she threw it into the pergola. The chickens would trample and peck it to death.

Outside, she sat down in Antoine's favorite chair, feeling dazed by the suddenness of her changed circumstances and this new and terrible fear. If only she could do it all over again. She'd spend even less money . . . she'd go without more . . . she'd let them take Monsieur Paretsky without a word.

Behind her, the door creaked open and clicked shut.

Footsteps. Breathing.

She should get up and leave, but she was too tired to move.

Beck came up behind her.

"Would you care for a glass of wine? It's a Chateau Margaux '28. A very good year, apparently."

Wine. She wanted to say yes, please (perhaps she'd never needed a glass more), but she couldn't do it. Neither could she say no, so she said nothing.

She heard the *thunk* of a cork being freed, and then the gurgle of wine being poured. He set a full glass on the table beside her. The sweet, rich scent was intoxicating.

He poured himself a glass and sat down in the chair beside her. "I am leaving," he said after a long silence.

She turned to him.

"Do not look so eager. It is only for a while. A few weeks. I have not been home in two years." He took a drink. "My wife may be sitting in our garden right now, wondering who will return to her. I am not the man who left, alas. I have seen things . . ." He paused. "This war, it is not as I expected. And things change in an absence this long, do you not agree?"

"*Oui*," she said. She had often thought the same thing.

In the silence between them, she heard a frog croak and the leaves fluttering in a jasmine-scented breeze above their heads. A nightingale sang a sad and lonely song.

"You do not seem yourself, Madame," he said. "If you do not mind me saying so."

"I was fired from my teaching position today." It was the first time she'd said the words aloud and they caused hot tears to glaze her eyes. "I . . . drew attention to myself."

"A dangerous thing to do."

"The money my husband left is gone. I am unemployed. And winter will soon be upon us. How am I to survive? To feed Sophie and keep her warm?" She turned to look at him.

Their gazes came together. She wanted to look away but couldn't.

He placed the wineglass in her hand, forced her fingers to coil around it. His touch felt hot against her cold hands, made her shiver. She remembered his office suddenly—and all that food stacked within it. "It is just wine," he said again, and the scent of it, of black cherries and dark rich earth and a hint of lavender, wafted up to her nose, reminding her of the life she'd had before, the nights she and Antoine had sat out here, drinking wine.

She took a sip and gasped; she'd forgotten this simple pleasure.

"You are beautiful, Madame," he said, his voice as sweet and rich as the wine. "Perhaps it has been too long since you heard that."

Vianne got to her feet so fast she knocked into the table and spilled the wine. "You should not say such things, Herr Captain."

"No," he said, rising to his feet. He stood in front of her, his breath scented by red wine and spearmint gum. "I should not."

"Please," she said, unable even to finish the sentence.

"Your daughter will not starve this winter, Madame," he said. Softly, as if it were their secret accord. "That is one thing you can be sure of."

God help Vianne, it relieved her. She mumbled something—she wasn't even sure what—and went back into the house, where she climbed into bed with Sophie, but it was a long time before she slept.

The bookshop had once been a gathering place for poets and writers and novelists and academics. Isabelle's best childhood memories took place in these musty rooms. While Papa had worked in the back room on his printing press, Maman had read Isabelle stories and fables and made up plays for them to act out. They had been happy here, for a time, before Maman took sick and Papa started drinking.

There's my Iz, come sit on Papa's lap while I write your maman a poem.

Or maybe she had imagined that memory, constructed it from the threads of her own need and wrapped it tightly around her shoulders. She didn't know anymore.

Now it was Germans who crowded into the shadowy nooks and crannies.

In the six weeks since Isabelle had reopened the shop, word had apparently spread among the soldiers that a pretty French girl could be found often at the shop's counter.

They arrived in a stream, dressed in their spotless uniforms, their voices loud as they jostled one another. Isabelle flirted with them mercilessly but made sure never to leave the shop until it was empty. And she always left by the back door, wearing a charcoal cloak with the hood drawn up, even in the heat of summer. The soldiers might be jovial and smiling—boys, really, who talked of pretty *fräuleins* back home and bought French classics by "acceptable" authors for their families—but she never forgot that they were the enemy.

"M'mselle, you are so beautiful, and you are ignoring us. How will we survive?" A young German officer reached for her.

She laughed prettily and pirouetted out of his reach. "Now, M'sieur, you know I can show no favorites." She sidled into place behind the sales counter. "I see you are holding a book of poetry. Certainly you have a girl back home who would love to receive such a thoughtful gift from you."

His friends shoved him forward, all of them talking at once.

Isabelle was taking his money when the bell above the front door tinkled gaily.

Isabelle looked up, expecting to see more German soldiers, but it was Anouk. She was dressed, as usual, more for her temperament than the season, in all black. A fitted V-neck black sweater and straight skirt with a black beret and gloves. A Gauloises cigarette hung from her bright red lips, unlit.

She paused in the open doorway, with a rectangle of the empty alley behind her, a flash of red geraniums and greenery.

At the bell, the Germans turned.

Anouk let the door shut behind her. She casually lit her cigarette and inhaled deeply.

With half of the store length between them, and three German soldiers milling about, Isabelle's gaze caught Anouk's. In the weeks that Isabelle had been a courier (she'd gone to Blois, Lyon, and Marseilles, to Amboise and Nice, not to mention at least a dozen drops in Paris recently, all under her new name—Juliette Gervaise—using false papers that Anouk had slipped her one day in a bistro, right under the Germans' noses), Anouk had been her most frequent contact and even with their age difference— which had to be at least a decade, maybe more—they had become friends in the way of women who live parallel lives—wordlessly but no less real for its silence. Isabelle had learned to see past Anouk's dour expression and flat mouth, to ignore her taciturn demeanor. Behind all that, Isabelle thought there was sadness. A lot of it. And anger.

Anouk walked forward with a regal, disdainful air that cut a man down to size before he even spoke. The Germans fell silent, watching her, moving sideways to let her pass. Isabelle heard one of them say "mannish" and another "widow."

Anouk seemed not to notice them at all. At the counter she stopped and took a long drag on her cigarette. The smoke blurred her face, and for a moment, only her cherry-red lips were noticeable. She reached down for her handbag and withdrew a small brown book. The author's name— Baudelaire—was etched into the leather, and although the surface was so scratched and worn and discolored the title was impossible to read, Isabelle knew the volume. *Les Fleurs du mal. The Flowers of Evil.* It was the book they used to signal a meeting.

"I am looking for something else by this author," Anouk said, exhaling smoke.

"I am sorry, Madame. I have no more Baudelaire. Some Verlaine, perhaps? Or Rimbaud?"

"Nothing then." Anouk turned and left the bookshop. It wasn't until the bell tinkled that her spell broke and the soldiers began speaking again.

When no one was looking, Isabelle palmed the small volume of poetry. Inside of it was a message for her to deliver, along with the time it was to be delivered. The place was as usual: the bench in front of the Comédie Française. The message was hidden beneath the end papers, which had been lifted and reglued dozens of times.

Isabelle watched the clock, willing the time to advance. She had her next assignment.

At precisely six P.M., she herded the soldiers out of the bookshop and closed up for the night. Outside, she found the chef and owner of the bistro next door, Monsieur Deparde, smoking a cigarette. The poor man looked as tired as she felt. She wondered sometimes, when she saw him sweating over the fryer or shucking oysters, how he felt about feeding Germans. "*Bonsoir,* M'sieur," she said.

"*Bonsoir,* M'mselle."

"Long day?" she commiserated.

"*Oui.*"

She handed him a small, used copy of fables for his children. "For Jacques and Gigi," she said with a smile.

"One moment." He rushed into the café and returned with a small, grease-stained sack. "*Frites,*" he said.

Isabelle was absurdly grateful. These days she not only ate the enemy's leftovers, she was thankful for them. "*Merci.*"

Leaving her bicycle in the shop, she decided to ignore the crowded, depressingly silent Métro and walk home, enjoying the greasy, salty *frites* on her way. Everywhere she looked, Germans were pouring into cafés and bistros and restaurants, while the ashen-faced Parisians hurried to be home before curfew. Twice along the way, she had a niggling sense that she was being followed, but when she turned, there was no one behind her.

She wasn't sure what brought her to a halt on the corner near the park, but all at once, she knew that something was wrong. Out of place. In front of her, the street was full of Nazi vehicles honking at one another. Somewhere someone screamed.

Isabelle felt the hairs on the back of her neck raise. She glanced back quickly, but no one was behind her. Lately she often felt as if she were being followed. It was her nerves working overtime. The golden dome of the

Invalides shone in the fading rays of the sun. Her heart started pounding. Fear made her perspire. The musky, sour scent of it mingled with the greasy odor of *frites*, and for a moment her stomach tilted uncomfortably.

Everything was fine. No one was following her. She was being foolish.

She turned onto rue de Grenelle.

Something caught her eye, made her stop.

Up ahead she saw a shadow where there shouldn't be a shadow. Movement where it should be still.

Frowning, she crossed the street, picking her way through the slow-moving traffic. On the other side, she moved briskly past the clot of Germans drinking wine in the bistro toward an apartment building on the next corner.

There, hidden in the dense shrubbery beside an ornate set of glossy black doors, she saw a man crouched down behind a tree in a huge copper urn.

She opened the gate and stepped into the yard. She heard the man scramble backward, his boots crunching on the stones beneath him.

Then he stilled.

Isabelle could hear the Germans laughing at the café down the street, yelling out *Sikt! s'il vous plaît* to the poor, overworked waitress.

It was the supper hour. The one hour of the day when all the enemy cared about was entertainment and stuffing their stomachs with food and wine that belonged to the French. She crept over to the potted lemon tree.

The man was squatted down, trying to make himself as small as possible. Dirt smeared his face and one eye was swollen shut, but there was no mistaking him for a Frenchman: he was wearing a British flight suit.

"*Mon Dieu,*" she muttered. "*Anglais?*"

He said nothing.

"RAF?" she asked in English.

His eyes widened. She could see him trying to decide whether to trust her. Very slowly, he nodded.

"How long have you been hiding here?"

After a long moment, he said, "All day."

"You'll get caught," she said. "Sooner or later." Isabelle knew she needed to question him further, but there wasn't time. Every second she stood here with him, the danger to both of them increased. It was amazing that the Brit hadn't been caught already.

She needed either to help him or to walk away before attention was drawn. Certainly walking away was the smart move. "Fifty-seven Avenue de La Bourdonnais," she said quietly, in English. "That's where I am going. In one hour, I will go out for a cigarette. You come to the door then. If you arrive without being seen, I will help you. You understand me?"

"How do I know I can trust you?"

She laughed at that. "This is a foolish thing I am doing. And I *promised* not to be so impetuous. Ah well." She pivoted on her heel and left the garden area, clanging the gate shut behind her. She hurried down the street. All the way home, her heart was pounding and she second-guessed her decision. But there was nothing to do about it now. She didn't look back, not even at her apartment building. There, she stopped and faced the big brass knob in the center of the oak door. She felt dizzy and headachy, she was so scared.

She fumbled with the key in the lock and twisted the knob and surged into the dark, shadowy interior. Inside, the narrow lobby was crowded with bicycles and handcarts. She made her way to the base of the winding stairway and sat on the bottom step, waiting.

She looked at her wristwatch a thousand times, and each time she told herself not to do this, but at the appointed time, she went back outside. Night had fallen. With the blackout shades and unlit streetlamps, the street was as dark as a cave. Cars rumbled past, unseen without their headlamps on; heard and smelled but invisible unless an errant bit of moonlight caught them. She lit her brown cigarette, took a deep drag, and exhaled slowly, trying to calm herself.

"I'm here, miss."

Isabelle stumbled backward and opened the door. "Stay behind me. Eyes down. Not too close."

She led him through the lobby, both of them banging into bicycles, clanging them, and rattling wooden carts. She had never run up the five flights of stairs faster. She pulled him into her apartment and slammed the door shut behind him.

"Take off your clothes," she said.

"Pardon me?"

She flicked on the light switch.

He towered over her; she saw that now. He was broad-shouldered and skinny at the same time, narrow-faced, with a nose that looked like it had been broken a time or two. His hair was so short it looked like fuzz. "Your flight suit. Take it off. Quickly."

What had she been thinking to do this? Her father would come home and find the airman and then turn them both in to the Germans.

Where would she hide his flight suit? And those boots were a dead give-away.

He bent forward and stepped out of his flight suit.

She had never seen a grown man in his undershorts and T-shirt before. She felt her face flush.

"No need to blush, miss," he said, grinning as if this were ordinary.

She yanked his suit into her arms and held out her hand for his identification tags. He handed them over; two small discs worn around his neck. Both contained the same information. Lieutenant Torrance MacLeish. His blood group and religion and number.

"Follow me. Quietly. What's the word . . . on the edges of your toes."

"Tiptoes," he whispered.

She led him to her bedroom. There—slowly, gently—she pushed the armoire out of the way and revealed the secret room.

A row of glassy doll eyes stared back at her.

"That's creepy, miss," he said. "And it's a small space for a big man."

"Get in. Stay quiet. *Any* untoward sound could get us searched. Madame Leclerc next door is curious and could be a collaborator, you understand? Also, my father will be home soon. He works for the German high command."

"Blimey."

She had no idea what that meant, and she was sweating so profusely her clothes were starting to stick to her chest. What had she been thinking to offer this man help?

"What if I have to . . . you know?" he asked.

"Hold it." She pushed him into the room, giving him a pillow and blanket from her bed. "I'll come back when I can. Quiet, *oui?*"

He nodded. "Thank you."

She couldn't help shaking her head. "I'm a fool. A *fool*." She shut the door on him and shoved the armoire back into place, not quite where it went, but good enough for now. She had to get rid of his flight suit and tags before her father came home.

She moved through the apartment on bare feet, as quietly as possible. She had no idea if the people downstairs would notice the sound of the armoire being moved or too many people moving about up here. Better safe than sorry. She jammed the flight suit in an old Samaritaine department store bag and crushed it to her chest.

Leaving the apartment felt dangerous suddenly. So did staying.

She crept past the Leclerc apartment and then rushed down the stairs.

Outside, she drew in a gulping breath.

Now what? She couldn't throw this just anywhere. She didn't want someone else to get in trouble . . .

For the first time, she was grateful for the city's blackout conditions. She slipped into the darkness on the sidewalk and all but disappeared. There were few Parisians out this close to curfew and the Germans were too busy drinking French wine to glance outside.

She drew in a deep breath, trying to calm down. To think. She was probably moments away from curfew—although that was hardly her biggest problem. Papa would be home soon.

The river.

She was only a few blocks away, and there were trees along the quay.

She found a smaller, barricaded side street and made her way to the river, past the row of military lorries parked along the street.

She had never moved so slowly in her life. One step—one breath—at a time. The last fifty feet between her and the banks of the Seine seemed to grow and expand with each step she took, and then again as she descended the stairs to the water, but at last she was there, standing beside the river. She heard boat lines creaking in the darkness, waves slapping their wooden hulls. Once again she thought she heard footsteps behind her. When she stilled, so did they. She waited for someone to come up behind her, for a voice demanding her papers.

Nothing. She was imagining it.

One minute passed. Then another.

She threw the bag into the black water and then hurled the identification tags in after it. The dark, swirling water swallowed the evidence instantly.

Still, she felt shaky as she climbed the steps and crossed the street and headed for home.

At her apartment door, she paused, finger-combing her sweat-dampened hair and pulling the damp cotton blouse from her breasts.

The one light was on. The chandelier. Her father sat hunched over the dining room table with paperwork spread out before him. He appeared haggard and too thin. She wondered suddenly how much he had been eating lately. In the weeks she'd been home, she had not once seen him have a meal. They ate—like they did everything else—separately. She had assumed that he ate German scraps at the high command. Now she wondered.

"You're late," he said harshly.

She noticed the brandy bottle on the table. It was half empty. Yesterday it had been full. How was it that he always found his brandy? "The Germans wouldn't leave." She moved toward the table and put several franc notes down. "Today was a good day. I see your friends at the high command have given you more brandy."

"The Nazis do not give much away," he said.

"Indeed. So you have earned it."

A noise sounded, something crashing to the hardwood floor, maybe. "What was that?" her father said, looking up.

Then came another sound, like a scraping of wood on wood.

"Someone is in this apartment," Papa said.

"Don't be absurd, Papa."

He rose quickly from the table and left the room. Isabelle rushed after him. "Papa—"

"Hush," he hissed.

He moved down the entryway, into the unlit part of the apartment. At the bombé chest near the front door, he picked up a candle in a brass holder and lit it.

"Surely you don't think someone has broken in," she said.

He threw her a harsh, narrow-eyed look. "I will not ask you to be silent again. Now hold your tongue." His breath smelled of brandy and cigarettes.

"But why—"

"Shut up." He turned his back on her and moved down the narrow, slanted-floor hallway toward the bedrooms.

He passed the miniscule coat closet (nothing but coats inside) and followed the candle's quavering path into Vianne's old room. It was empty but for the bed and nightstand and writing desk. Nothing was out of place in here. He got slowly to his knees and looked under the bed.

Satisfied at last that the room was empty, he headed for Isabelle's room.

Could he hear the pounding of her heart?

He checked her room—under the bed, behind the door, behind the floor-to-ceiling damask curtains that framed the blacked-out courtyard window.

Isabelle forced herself not to stare at the armoire. "See?" she said loudly, hoping the airman would hear voices and sit still. "No one is here. Really, Papa, working for the enemy is making you paranoid."

He turned to her. In the corona of candlelight, his face looked haggard and worn. "It wouldn't hurt you to be afraid, you know."

Was that a threat? "Of you, Papa? Or of the Nazis?"

"Are you paying no attention at all, Isabelle? You should be afraid of everyone. Now, get out of my way. I need a drink."

EIGHTEEN

*I*sabelle lay in bed, listening. When she was sure her father was asleep (a drunken sleep, no doubt) she left her bed, went in search of her grand-mère's porcelain chamber pot, and holding it, stood in front of the armoire.

Slowly—a half inch at a time—she moved it away from the wall. Just enough to open the hidden door.

Inside, it was dark and quiet. Only when she listened intently did she hear him breathing. "Monsieur?" she whispered.

"Hello, miss" came at her from the dark.

She lit the oil lamp by her bed and carried it into the space.

He was sitting against the wall with his legs stretched out; in the candlelight, he seemed softer somehow. Younger.

She handed him the chamber pot and saw that color rose on his cheeks as he took it from her.

"Thank you."

She sat down opposite him. "I got rid of your identification tags and flight suit. Your boots will have to be cut down for you to wear. Here's a knife. Tomorrow morning I will get you some of my father's clothes. I don't imagine they'll fit well."

He nodded, saying, "And what is your plan?"

That made her smile nervously. "I'm not sure. You are a pilot?"

"Lieutenant Torrance MacLeish. RAF. My aeroplane went down over Reims."

"And you've been on your own since then? In your flight suit?"

"Fortunately my brother and I played hide-and-seek a lot when we were lads."

"You're not safe here."

"I gathered." He smiled and it changed his face, reminded her that he was really just a young man far from home. "If it makes you feel better, I took three German aeroplanes down with me."

"You need to get back to Britain so you can get back to it."

"I can't agree more. But how? The whole coastline is behind barbed wire and patrolled by dogs. I can't exactly leave France by boat or air."

"I have some . . . friends who are working on this. We will go see them tomorrow."

"You are very brave," he said softly.

"Or foolish," she said, unsure of which was more true. "I have often heard I'm impetuous and unruly. I imagine I will hear it from my friends tomorrow."

"Well, miss, you won't hear anything but brave from me."

❧

The next morning, Isabelle heard her father walk past her room. Moments later, she smelled coffee wafting her way, and then, after that, the front door clicked shut.

She left her room and went into her father's—which was a mess of clothes on the floor and an unmade bed, with an empty brandy bottle lying on its side on his writing desk. She pulled the blackout shade and peered past the empty balcony to the street below, where she saw her father emerge out onto the sidewalk. He had his black briefcase held close to his chest (as if his poetry actually mattered to anyone) and a black hat pulled low on his brow. Hunched like an overworked secretary, he headed for the Métro. When he passed out of her view, she went to the armoire in his room and rummaged through it for old clothes. A shapeless turtleneck sweater with fraying sleeves, old corduroy pants, patched in the seat and bereft of several buttons, and a gray beret.

Isabelle cautiously moved the armoire and opened the door. The secret room smelled of sweat and piss, so much that she had to clamp her hand over her nose and mouth as she gagged.

"Sorry, miss," MacLeish said sheepishly.

"Put these on. Wash up there at the pitcher and meet me in the salon. Put the armoire back. Move quietly. People are downstairs. They may know my father is gone and expect only one person to be walking around up here."

Moments later, he stepped into the kitchen, dressed in her father's cast-offs. He looked like a fairy-tale boy who'd sprouted overnight; the sweater strained across his broad chest and the corduroy pants were too small to button at the waist. He was wearing the beret flat on the crown of his head, as if it were a yarmulke.

This would never work. How would she get him across town in broad daylight?

"I can do this," he said. "I'll follow along behind you. Trust me, miss. I've been walking about in a flight suit. This is easy."

It was too late to back out now. She'd taken him in and hidden him. Now she needed to get him someplace safe. "Walk at least a block behind me. If I stop, you stop."

"If I get pinched, you keep walking. Don't even look back."

Pinched must mean arrested. She went to him, adjusted his beret, set it at a jaunty angle. Her gaze held his. "Where are you from, Lieutenant MacLeish?"

"Ipswich, miss. You'll tell my parents . . . if necessary?"

"It won't be necessary, Lieutenant." She drew in a deep breath. He had reminded her again of the risk that she'd undertaken to help him. The false papers in her handbag—identifying her as Juliette Gervaise of Nice, baptized in Marseille, and a student at the Sorbonne—were the only protection she had if the worst happened. She went to the front door, opened it, and peered out. The landing was empty. She shoved him out, saying, "Go. Stand outside by the milliner's empty shop. Then follow me."

He stumbled out of the apartment, and she closed the door behind him.

One. Two. Three . . .

She counted silently, imagining trouble with every step. When she could stand it no more, she left the apartment and went down the stairs.

All was quiet.

She found him outside, standing where he'd been told to. She lifted her chin and walked past him without a glance.

All the way to the Saint-Germain, she walked briskly, never turning around, never looking back. Several times she heard German soldiers yell out *"Halt!"* and blow their whistles. Twice she heard gunshots, but she neither slowed nor looked.

By the time she reached the red door at the apartment on rue de Saint-Simon, she was sweating and a little light-headed.

She knocked four times in rapid succession.

The door opened.

Anouk appeared in the slit of an opening. Surprise widened her eyes. She opened the door and stepped back. "What are you doing here?"

Behind her, several of the men Isabelle had met before were seated around tables, with maps set out in front of them, the pale blue lines illuminated by candlelight.

Anouk started to shut the door. Isabelle said, "Leave it open."

Tension followed her directive. She saw it sweep the room, change the expressions around her. At the table, Monsieur Lévy began putting the maps away.

Isabelle glanced outside and saw MacLeish coming up the walkway. He stepped into the apartment and she slammed the door shut behind him. No one spoke.

Isabelle had their full attention. "This is Lieutenant Torrance MacLeish of the RAF. Pilot. I found him hiding in the bushes near my apartment last night."

"And you brought him here," Anouk said, lighting a cigarette.

"He needs to get back to Britain," Isabelle said. "I thought—"

"No," Anouk said. "You did not."

Lévy sat back in his chair and pulled a Gauloises from his breast pocket and lit it up, studying the airman. "There are others that we know of in the city, and more who escaped from German prisons. We want to get them out, but the coasts and the airfields are sewn up tight." He took a long drag on the cigarette; the tip glowed and crackled and blackened. "It is a problem we have been working on."

"I know," Isabelle said. She felt the full weight of her responsibility. Had she acted rashly again? Were they disappointed in her? She didn't know. Should she have ignored MacLeish? She was about to ask a question when she heard someone talking in another room.

Frowning, she said, "Who else is here?"

"Others," Lévy answered. "Others are always here. No one of concern to you."

"We need a plan for the airmen, it is true," Anouk said.

"We believe we could get them out of Spain," Lévy said. "If we could get them *into* Spain."

"The Pyrenees," Anouk said.

Isabelle had seen the Pyrenees, so she understood Anouk's comment. The jagged peaks rose impossibly high into the clouds and were usually snow-covered or ringed in fog. Her mother had loved Biarritz, a small coastal town nearby, and twice, in the good days, long ago, the family had vacationed there.

"The border with Spain is guarded by both German and Spanish patrols," Anouk said.

"The whole border?" Isabelle asked.

"Well, no. Of course not. But where they are and where they aren't, who knows?" Lévy said.

"The mountains are smaller near Saint-Jean-de-Luz," Isabelle pointed out.

"*Oui*, but so what? They are still impassable and the few roads are guarded," Anouk said.

"My maman's best friend was a Basque whose father was a goat herder. He crossed the mountains on foot all the time."

"We have had this idea. We even tried it once," Lévy said. "None of the party was heard from again. Getting past the German sentries at Saint-Jean-de-Luz is hard enough for one man, let alone several, and then there is the actual crossing of the mountains on foot. It is nearly impossible."

"Nearly impossible and impossible are not the same thing. If goat herders can cross the mountains, certainly airmen can do it," Isabelle said. As she said it, an idea came to her. "And a woman could move easily across the check-points. Especially a young woman. No one would suspect a pretty girl."

Anouk and Lévy exchanged a look.

"I will do it," Isabelle said. "Or try it, anyway. I'll take this airman. And are there others?"

Monsieur Lévy frowned. Obviously this turn of events surprised him. Cigarette smoke clouded blue-gray between them. "And you have climbed mountains before?"

"I'm in good shape" was her answer.

"If they catch you, they'll imprison you . . . or kill you," he said quietly. "Put your impetuousness aside for a moment and think on that, Isabelle. This is not handing over a piece of paper. You have seen the signs posted all over town? The rewards offered for people who aid the enemy?"

Isabelle nodded earnestly.

Anouk sighed heavily, stabbing out her cigarette in the overflowing ashtray. She gazed at Isabelle a long time, eyes narrowing; then she walked to the open door behind the table. She pushed the door open a little and whistled, gave a trilling little bird call.

Isabelle frowned. She heard something in the other room, a chair pushing back from a table, footsteps.

Gaëtan stepped into the room.

He was dressed shabbily, in corduroy pants that were patched at the knees and ragged at the hem and a little too short, in a sweater that hung on his wiry frame, its collar pulled out of shape. His black hair, longer now, in need of cutting, had been slicked back from his face, which was sharper, al-most wolflike. He looked at her as if they were the only two in the room.

In an instant, it was all undone. The feelings she'd discounted, tried to bury, to ignore, came flooding back. One look at him and she could barely breathe.

"You know Gaët," Anouk said.

Isabelle cleared her throat. She understood that he'd known she was here all along, that he'd chosen to stay away from her. For the first time since she'd joined this underground group, Isabelle felt keenly young. Apart. Had they all known about it? Had they laughed about her naïveté behind her back? "I do."

"So," Lévy said after an uncomfortable pause, "Isabelle has a plan."

Gaëtan didn't smile. "Does she?"

"She wants to lead this airman and others across the Pyrenees on foot and get them into Spain. To the British consulate, I assume."

Gaëtan swore under his breath.

"We need to try *something*," Lévy said.

"Do you truly understand the risk, Isabelle?" Anouk asked, coming forward. "If you succeed, the Nazis will hear of it. They will hunt you down. There is a ten-thousand-franc reward for anyone who leads the Nazis to someone aiding airmen."

Isabelle had always simply reacted in her life. Someone left her behind; she followed. Someone told her she couldn't do something; she did it. Every barrier she turned into a gate.

But this . . .

She let fear give her a little shake and she almost gave in to it. Then she thought about the swastikas that flew from the Eiffel Tower and Vianne living with the enemy and Antoine lost in some prisoner of war camp. And Edith Cavell. Certainly she had been afraid sometimes, too; Isabelle would *not* let fear stand in her way. The airmen were needed in Britain to drop more bombs on Germany.

Isabelle turned to the airman. "Are you a fit man, Lieutenant?" she said in English. "Could you keep up with a girl on a mountain crossing?"

"I could," he said. "Especially one as pretty as you, miss. I wouldn't let you out of my sight."

Isabelle faced her compatriots. "I'll take him to the consulate in San Sebastián. From there, it will be up to the Brits to get him home."

Isabelle saw the conversation that passed in silence around her, concerns and questions unvoiced. A decision reached in silence. Some risks simply had to be taken; everyone in this room knew it.

"It will take weeks to plan. Maybe longer," Lévy said. He turned to Gaëtan. "We will need money immediately. You will speak to your contact?"

Gaëtan nodded. He grabbed a black beret from the sideboard, putting it on.

Isabelle couldn't look away. She was angry at him—she knew that, felt it—but as he came toward her, that anger dried up and blew away like dust beneath the longing that mattered so much more. Their gazes met, held; and then he was past her, reaching for the doorknob, going outside. The door clicked shut behind him.

"So," Anouk said. "The planning. We should begin."

❦

For six hours, Isabelle sat at the table in the apartment on rue de Saint-Simon. They brought in others from the network and gave them tasks: to gather clothes for the pilots and stockpile supplies. They consulted maps and devised routes and began the long, uncertain process of setting up safe houses along the way. At some point, they began to see it as a reality instead of merely a bold and daring idea.

It wasn't until Monsieur Lévy mentioned the curfew that Isabelle pushed back from the table. They tried to talk her into staying the night, but such a choice would make her father suspicious. Instead, she borrowed a heavy black peacoat from Anouk and put it on, grateful for the way it camouflaged her.

The boulevard Saint-Germain was eerily quiet, shutters closed tightly and blacked out, streetlamps dark.

She kept close to the buildings, grateful that the worn-down heels of her white oxfords didn't clatter on the sidewalk. She crept past barricades and around groups of German soldiers patrolling the streets.

She was almost home when she heard an engine growling. A German lorry shambled up the street behind her, its blue-painted headlights turned off.

She pressed flat against the rough stone wall behind her and the phantom lorry rolled past, grumbling in the darkness. Then everything was silent again.

A bird whistled, a trilling song. *Familiar.*

Isabelle knew then that she'd been waiting for him, hoping . . .

She straightened slowly, rose to her feet. Beside her, a potted plant released the scent of flowers.

"Isabelle," Gaëtan said.

She could barely make out his features in the dark, but she could smell the pomade in his hair and the rough scent of his laundry soap and the cigarette he'd smoked some time ago. "How did you know I was working with Paul?"

"Who do you think recommended you?"

She frowned. "Henri—"

"And who told Henri about you? I had Didier following you from the beginning, watching over you. I knew you would find your way to us."

He reached out, tucked the hair behind her ears, and the intimacy of the act left her parched with hope. She remembered saying "I love you," and shame and loss twisted her up inside. She didn't want to remember how he'd made her feel, how he'd fed her roasted rabbit by hand and carried her when she was too tired to walk . . . and showed her how much one kiss could matter.

"I'm sorry I hurt you," he said.

"Why did you?"

"It doesn't matter now." He sighed. "I should have stayed in that back room today. It's better not seeing you."

"Not for me."

He smiled. "You have a habit of saying whatever is on your mind, don't you, Isabelle?"

"Always. Why did you leave me?"

He touched her face with a gentleness that made her want to cry; it felt like a good-bye, that touch, and she knew good-bye. "I wanted to forget you."

She wanted to say something more, maybe "kiss me" or "don't go" or "say I matter to you," but it was already too late, the moment—whatever it was—was past. He was stepping away from her, disappearing into the shadows. He said softly, "Be careful, Iz," and before she could answer, she knew he was gone; she felt his absence in her bones.

She waited a moment more, for her heartbeat to slow down and her emotions to stabilize, then she headed for home. She had barely released the lock on her front door when she felt herself being yanked inside. The door slammed shut behind her.

"Where in the hell have you been?"

Her father's alcoholic breath washed over her, its sweetness a cloak over something dark, bitter. As if he'd been chewing aspirin. She tried to pull free but he held her so close it was almost an embrace, his grasp on her wrist tight enough to leave a bruise.

Then, as quickly as he'd grasped her, he let her go. She stumbled back, flailing for the light switch. When she flipped it, nothing happened.

"No more money for electricity," her father said. He lit an oil lamp, held it between them. In the wavering light, he looked to be sculpted of melting wax; his lined face sagged, his eyelids were puffy and a little blue. His paddle nose showed black pores the size of pinheads. Even with all of that, with as . . . tired and old as he suddenly seemed, it was the look in his eyes that made her frown.

Something was wrong.

"Come with me," he said, his voice raspy and sharp, unrecognizable this time of night without a slur. He led her down past the closet and around the corner to her room. Inside, he turned to look at her.

Behind him, in the lamp's glow, she saw the moved armoire and the door to the secret room ajar. The smell of urine was strong. Thank God the airman was gone.

Isabelle shook her head, unable to speak.

He sank to sit on the edge of her bed, bowing his head. "Christ, Isabelle. You are a pain in the ass."

She couldn't move. Or think. She glanced at the bedroom door, wondering if she could make it out of the apartment. "It was nothing, Papa. A boy." *Oui.* "A date. We were kissing, Papa."

"And do all of your dates piss in the closet? You must be very popular, then." He sighed. "Enough of this charade."

"Charade?"

"You found an airman last night and hid him in the closet and today you took him to Monsieur Lévy."

Isabelle could not have heard correctly. "Pardon?"

"Your downed airman—the one who pissed in the closet and left dirty bootprints in the hallway—you took him to Monsieur Lévy."

"I do not know what you are talking about."

"Good for you, Isabelle."

When he fell silent, she couldn't stand the suspense. "Papa?"

"I know you came here as a courier for the underground and that you are working with Paul Lévy's network."

"H-how—"

"Monsieur Lévy is an old friend. In fact, when the Nazis invaded, he came to me and pulled me out of the bottle of brandy that was all I cared about. He put me to work."

Isabelle felt so unsteady, she couldn't stand. It was too intimate to sit by her father, so she sank slowly to the carpet.

"I didn't want you involved in this, Isabelle. That's why I sent you from Paris in the first place. I didn't want to put you at risk with my work. I should have known you'd find your own way to danger."

"And all the other times you sent me away?" She wished instantly that she hadn't asked the question, but the moment she had the thought, it was given voice.

"I am no good as a father. We both know that. At least not since your maman's death."

"How would we know? You never tried."

"I tried. You just don't remember. Anyway, that is all water gone by now. We have bigger concerns."

"*Oui*," she said. Her past felt upended somehow, off balance. She didn't know what to think or feel. Better to change the subject than to dwell on it. "I am . . . planning something. I will be gone for a while."

He looked down at her. "I know. I have spoken to Paul." He was silent for a long moment. "You know that your life changes right now. You will have to live underground—not here with me, not with anyone. You will not be able to spend more than a few nights in any one place. You will trust absolutely no one. And you will not be Isabelle Rossignol at all anymore; you will be Juliette Gervaise. The Nazis and the collaborators will always be searching for you, and if they find you . . ."

Isabelle nodded.

A look passed between them. In it, Isabelle felt a connection that had never existed before.

"You know that prisoners of war receive some mercy. You can expect none."

She nodded.

"Can you do this, Isabelle?"

"I can do it, Papa."

He nodded. "The name you are looking for is Micheline Babineau. Your maman's friend in Urrugne. Her husband was killed in the Great War. I think she would welcome you. And tell Paul I will need photographs immediately."

"Photographs?"

"Of the airmen." At her continued silence, he finally smiled. "Really, Isabelle? Have you not put the pieces together?"

"But—"

"I forge papers, Isabelle. That's why I work at the high command. I began by writing the very tracts you distributed in Carriveau, but . . . it turns out that the poet has a forger's hand. Who do you think gave you the name Juliette Gervaise?"

"B-but . . ."

"You believed I collaborated with the enemy. I can hardly blame you."

In him, suddenly, she saw someone foreign, a broken man where a cruel, careless man had always stood. She dared to rise up, to move toward him, to kneel in front of him. She stared up at him, feeling hot tears glaze her eyes. "Why did you push me and Vianne away?"

"I hope you never know how fragile you are, Isabelle."

"I'm not fragile," she said.

The smile he gave her was barely one at all. "We are all fragile, Isabelle. It's the thing we learn in war."

NINETEEN

WARNING

All males who come to the aid, either directly or indirectly, of the crews of enemy aircraft coming down in parachutes or having made a forced landing, help in their escape, hide them, or come to their aid in any fashion will be shot on the spot.

Women who render the same help will be sent to concentration camps in Germany.

I guess I am lucky to be a woman," Isabelle muttered to herself. How was it that the Germans hadn't noticed by now—October 1941—that France had become a country of women?

Even as she said the words, she recognized the false bravado in them. She wanted to feel brave right now—Edith Cavell risking her life—but here, in this train station patrolled by German soldiers, she was scared.

There was no backing out now, no changing her mind. After months of planning and preparation, she and four airmen were ready to test the escape plan.

On this cool October morning, her life would change. From the moment she boarded this train bound for Saint-Jean-de-Luz, she would no longer be Isabelle Rossignol, the girl in the bookshop who lived on the Avenue de La Bourdonnais.

From now on, she was Juliette Gervaise, code name the Nightingale.

"Come." Anouk linked arms with Isabelle and led her away from the warning sign and toward the ticket counter.

They had gone over these preparations so many times Isabelle knew the plan well. There was only one flaw: All of their attempts to reach Madame Babineau had thus far failed. That one key component—finding a guide—Isabelle would have to do on her own. Off to her left, waiting for her signal, Lieutenant MacLeish stood dressed as a peasant. All he'd kept from his escape kit were two Benzedrine tablets and a tiny compass that looked like a button and was pinned to his collar. He had been given false papers—now he was a Flemish farmworker. He had an identity card and a work permit, but her father couldn't guarantee that the papers would pass close inspection. He had cut off the tops of his flight boots and shaved off his moustache.

Isabelle and Anouk had spent countless hours training him in proper behavior. They'd dressed him in a baggy coat and a worn, stained pair of work trousers. They'd bleached the nicotine stains from the first and second fingers of his right hand and taught him to smoke like a Frenchman, using his thumb and forefinger. He knew he was to look left before crossing the street—not right—and he was never to approach Isabelle unless she approached him first. She had instructed him to play deaf and dumb and to read a newspaper while on the train—the entire trip. He was also to buy his own ticket and sit apart from Isabelle. They all were. When they disembarked in Saint-Jean-de-Luz, the airmen were to walk a good distance behind her.

Anouk turned to Isabelle. *Are you ready?* her gaze asked.

She nodded slowly.

"Cousin Etienne will board the train in Poitiers, Uncle Emile in Ruffec, and Jean-Claude in Bordeaux."

The other airmen. *"Oui."*

Isabelle was to disembark at Saint-Jean-de-Luz with the four airmen—two Brits and two Canadians—and cross the mountains into Spain. Once there, she was to send a telegram. "The Nightingale has sung" meant success.

She kissed each of Anouk's cheeks, murmured *au revoir,* and then walked briskly over to the ticket window. "Saint-Jean-de-Luz," she said, and handed the attendant her money. Taking the ticket, she headed for platform C. Not once did she look back, although she wanted to.

The train whistle sounded.

Isabelle stepped aboard, taking a seat on the left side. More passengers filed in, took seats. Several German soldiers boarded the train, sitting across from her.

MacLeish was the last to board. He stepped into the train and shuffled past her without a glance, his shoulders hunched in an effort to appear smaller. As the doors eased shut, he settled into a seat at the other end of the compartment and immediately opened his newspaper.

The train whistle blew again and the giant wheels began to turn, picking up speed slowly. The compartment banged a little, heaved left and right, and then settled into a steady thrumming movement, the wheels *clackety-clacking* on the iron tracks.

The German soldier across from Isabelle glanced down the compartment. His gaze settled on MacLeish. He tapped his friend in the shoulder and both men started to rise.

Isabelle leaned forward. *"Bonjour,"* she said with a smile.

The soldiers immediately sat back down. *"Bonjour,* M'mselle," they said in unison.

"Your French is quite good," she lied. Beside her, a heavyset woman in peasant clothes made a harrumphing sound of disgust and whispered, "You should be ashamed of yourself" in French.

Isabelle laughed prettily. "Where are you going?" she asked the soldiers. They would be on this carriage for hours. It would be good to keep their attention on her.

"Tours," one said, as the other said, "Onzain."

"Ah. And do you know any card games to pass the time? I have a deck with me."

"Yes. Yes!" the younger one said.

Isabelle reached in her handbag for her playing cards. She was dealing a new hand—and laughing—when the next airman boarded the train and shuffled past the Germans.

Later, when the conductor came through, she offered up her ticket. He took it and moved on.

When he came to the airman, MacLeish did exactly as instructed—he handed over his ticket while he kept reading. The other airman did the same.

Isabelle released her breath in a sigh of relief and leaned back in her seat.

⚜

Isabelle and the four airmen made it to Saint-Jean-de-Luz without incident. Twice they'd walked—separately, of course—past German checkpoints. The soldiers on guard had barely looked at the series of false papers, saying *danke schön* without even looking up. They were not on the lookout for downed airmen and apparently hadn't considered a plan as bold as this.

But now Isabelle and the men were approaching the mountains. In the foothills, she went to a small park along the river and sat on a bench overlooking the water. The airmen arrived as planned, one by one, with MacLeish first. He sat down beside her.

The others took seats within earshot.

"You have your signs?" she asked.

MacLeish withdrew a piece of paper from his shirt pocket. It read: DEAF AND DUMB. WAITING FOR MY MAMAN TO PICK ME UP. The other airmen did the same.

"If a German soldier hassles any of you, you show him your papers and your sign. Do *not* speak."

"And I act stupid, which is easy for me." MacLeish grinned.

Isabelle was too anxious to smile.

She shrugged off her canvas rucksack and handed it to MacLeish. In it were a few essentials—a bottle of wine, three plump pork sausages, two pairs of heavy woolen socks, and several apples. "Sit where you can in Urrugne. Not together, of course. Keep your heads down and pretend to read your books. Don't look up until you hear me say, 'There you are, cousin, we've been looking all over for you.' Understood?"

They all nodded.

"If I am not back by dawn, travel separately to Pau and go to the hotel I told you about. A woman named Eliane will help you."

"Be careful," MacLeish said.

Taking a deep breath, she left them and walked to the main road. A mile or so later, as night began to fall, she crossed a rickety bridge. The road turned to dirt and narrowed into a cart track that climbed up, up, up into the verdant foothills. Moonlight came to her aid, illuminating hundreds of tiny white specks—goats. There were no cottages up this high, just animal sheds.

At last, she saw it: a two-storied, half-timbered house with a red roof that was exactly as her father had described. No wonder they had not been able to reach Madame Babineau. This cottage seemed designed to keep people away—as did the path up to it. Goats bleated at her appearance and bumped into one another nervously. Light shone through the haphazardly blacked-out windows, and smoke puffed cheerily from the chimney, scenting the air.

At her knock, the heavy wooden door opened just enough to reveal a single eye and a mouth nearly hidden by a gray beard.

"Bonsoir," Isabelle said. She waited a moment for the old man to reply in kind, but he said nothing. "I am here to see Madame Babineau."

"Why?" the man demanded.

"Julien Rossignol sent me."

The old man made a clicking sound between his teeth and tongue; then the door opened.

The first thing Isabelle noticed inside was the stew, simmering in a big black pot that hung from a hook in the giant stone-faced fireplace.

A woman was seated at a huge, scarred trestle table in the back of the wide, timber-beamed room. From where Isabelle stood, it looked as if she were dressed in charcoal-colored rags, but when the old man lit an oil lamp, Isabelle saw that the woman was dressed like a man, in rough breeches and a linen shirt with a leather lace-up neckline. Her hair was the color of iron shavings and she was smoking a cigarette.

Still, Isabelle recognized the woman, even though it had been fifteen years. She remembered sitting on the beach at Saint-Jean-de-Luz. Hearing the women laugh. And Madame Babineau saying, *This little beauty will cause you endless trouble, Madeleine, the boys will someday swarm her,* and Maman saying, *She is too smart to toss her life to boys, aren't you, my Isabelle?*

"Your shoes are caked with dirt."

"I've walked here from the train station at Saint-Jean-de-Luz."

"Interesting." The woman used her booted foot to push out the chair across from her. "I am Micheline Babineau. Sit."

"I know who you are," Isabelle said. She added nothing. Information was dangerous these days. It was traded with care.

"Do you?"

"I'm Juliette Gervaise."

"Why do I care?"

Isabelle glanced nervously at the old man, who watched her warily. She didn't like turning her back on him, but she had no choice. She sat down across from the woman.

"You want a cigarette? It's a Gauloises Bleu. They cost me three francs and a goat, but it's worth it." The woman took a long, sensual drag off of her cigarette and exhaled the distinctively scented blue smoke. "Why do I care about you?"

"Julien Rossignol believes I can trust you."

Madame Babineau took another drag on the cigarette and then stubbed it out on the sole of her boot. She dropped the rest of it in her breast pocket.

"He says his wife was close friends with you. You are godmother to his eldest daughter. He is the godfather to your youngest son."

"Was. The Germans killed both of my sons at the front. And my husband in the last war."

"He wrote letters to you recently . . ."

"The *poste* is shit these days. What does he want?"

Here it was. The biggest flaw in this plan. If Madame Babineau was a collaborator, it was all over. Isabelle had imagined this moment a thousand times, planned it down to the pauses. She'd thought of ways to word things to protect herself.

Now she saw the folly of all that, the uselessness. She simply had to dive in.

"I left four downed pilots in Urrugne, waiting for me. I want to take them to the British consulate in Spain. We hope the British can get them back to England so they can fly more missions over Germany and drop more bombs."

In the silence that followed, Isabelle heard the beat of her heart, the tick of the mantel clock, the distant bleating of a goat.

"And?" Madame Babineau said at last, almost too softly to hear.

"A-and I need a Basque guide to help me cross the Pyrenees. Julien thought you could help me."

For the first time, Isabelle knew she had the woman's undivided attention. "Get Eduardo," Madame Babineau said to the old man, who jumped to do her bidding. The door banged shut so hard the ceiling rattled.

The woman retrieved the half-smoked cigarette from her pocket and lit it up, inhaling and exhaling several times in silence as she studied Isabelle.

"What do you—" Isabelle started to ask.

The woman pressed a tobacco-stained finger to her lips.

The door to the farmhouse crashed open and a man burst in. All Isabelle could make out were broad shoulders, burlap, and the smell of alcohol.

He grabbed her by the arm and lifted her out of the chair and threw her up against the rough-hewn wall. She gasped in pain and tried to get free, but he pinned her in place, wedged his knee roughly between her legs.

"Do you know what the Germans do to people like you?" he whispered, his face so close to hers she couldn't focus, couldn't see anything but black eyes and thick black lashes. He smelled of cigarettes and brandy. "Do you know how much they will pay us for you and your pilots?"

Isabelle turned her head to avoid his sour breath.

"Where are these pilots of yours?"

His fingers dug into the flesh of her upper arms.

"Where are they?"

"What pilots?" she gasped.

"The pilots you are helping escape."

"W-what pilots? I don't know what you're talking about."

He growled again and cracked her head against the wall. "You asked for our help to get pilots over the Pyrenees."

"Me, a woman, climb across the Pyrenees? You must be joking. I don't know what you're talking about."

"Are you saying Madame Babineau is lying?"

"I don't know Madame Babineau. I just stopped here to ask for directions. I'm lost."

He smiled, revealing tobacco- and wine-stained teeth. "Clever girl," he said, letting her go. "And not a bit weak in the knees."

Madame Babineau stood. "Good for her."

The man stepped back, giving her space. "I am Eduardo." He turned to the old woman. "The weather is good. Her will is strong. The men may sleep here tonight. Unless they are weaklings, I will take them tomorrow."

"You'll take us?" Isabelle said. "To Spain?"

Eduardo looked to Madame Babineau, who looked at Isabelle. "It would be our great pleasure to help you, Juliette. Now, where are these pilots of yours?"

❧

In the middle of the night, Madame Babineau woke Isabelle and led her into the farmhouse's kitchen, where a fire was already blazing in the hearth. "Coffee?"

Isabelle finger-combed her hair and tied a cotton scarf around her head. "No, *merci*, it is too precious."

The old woman gave her a smile. "No one suspects a woman my age of anything. It makes me good at trading. Here." She offered Isabelle a cracked porcelain mug full of steaming black coffee. *Real* coffee.

Isabelle wrapped her hands around the mug and breathed deeply of the familiar, never-again-to-be-taken-for-granted aroma.

Madame Babineau sat down beside her.

She looked into the woman's dark eyes and saw a compassion that reminded her of her maman. "I am scared," Isabelle admitted. It was the first time she'd said this to anyone.

"As you should be. As we all must be."

"If something goes wrong, will you get word to Julien? He's still in Paris. If we . . . don't make it, tell him the Nightingale didn't fly."

Madame Babineau nodded.

As the women sat there, the airmen came into the room, one by one. It was the middle of the night, and none looked like they had slept well. Still, the hour appointed for their departure was here.

Madame Babineau set out a meal of bread and sweet lavender honey and creamy goat cheese. The men planted themselves on the mismatched chairs and scooted close to the table, talking all at once, devouring the food in an instant.

The door banged open, bringing with it a rush of cold night air. Dried leaves scudded inside, dancing across the floor, plastering themselves like tiny black hands to the stones of the fireplace. The flames within shivered and thinned. The door slammed shut.

Eduardo stood there, looking like a scruffy giant in the low-ceilinged room. He was a typical Basque—with broad shoulders and a face that seemed to have been carved in stone with a dull blade. The coat he wore was thin for the weather and patched in more places than it was whole.

He handed Isabelle a pair of Basque shoes, called espadrilles, with rope soles that were supposedly good in the rough terrain.

"How is the weather for this journey, Eduardo?" Madame Babineau asked.

"Cold is coming. We must not tarry." He swung a ragged rucksack from his shoulder and dropped it on the ground. To the men, he said, "These are espadrilles. They will help you. Find a pair that fits." Isabelle stood beside him, translating for the men.

The men came forward obediently and squatted around the rucksack, pulling out shoes, passing them around.

"None fit me," MacLeish said.

"Do what you can," Madame Babineau said. "Sadly, we aren't a shoe shop."

When the men had exchanged their flight boots for walking shoes, Eduardo had them stand in a line. He studied each man in turn, checking his clothing and his small pack. "Take everything out of your pockets and leave it here. The Spanish will arrest you for anything, and you do not want to escape the Germans only to find yourself in a Spanish prison." He handed them each a goatskin bota bag full of wine and a walking stick that he'd made from knobby, mossy branches. When he was finished, he slapped them on the back hard enough to send most of them stumbling forward.

"Silence," Eduardo said. "Always."

They left the cottage and filed onto the uneven terrain of the goat pasture outside. The sky was lit by a weak blue moon. "Night is our protection," Eduardo said. "Night and speed and quiet." He turned, stopped them with a raised hand. "Juliette will be at the back of the line. I will be at the front. When I walk, you walk. You walk in single file. There is no talking. None. You will be cold—freezing cold on this night—and hungry and soon you will be tired. Keep walking."

Eduardo turned his back on the men and began walking up the hill.

Isabelle felt the cold instantly; it bit into her exposed cheeks and slipped through the seams of her woolen coat. She used her gloved hand to hold the pieces of her collar together and began the long trek up the grassy hillside.

Sometime around three in the morning, the walk became a hike. The terrain steepened, the moon slid behind invisible clouds and blinked out, leaving them in near-total darkness. Isabelle heard the men's breathing become labored in front of her. She knew they were cold; most of them did not have adequate clothing for this freezing air, and few of them had shoes that fit correctly. Twigs snapped beneath their feet, rocks clattered away from them, made a sound like rain on a tin roof as they fell down the steep mountainside. The first pangs of hunger twisted her empty stomach.

It started to rain. A gnashing wind swept up from the valley below, slamming into the party walking single file. It turned the rain into freezing shards that attacked their exposed skin. Isabelle began to shiver uncontrollably, her breath came out in great, heaving gasps, and still she climbed. Up, up, up, past the tree line.

Ahead, someone made a yelping sound and fell hard. Isabelle couldn't see who it was; the night had closed around them. The man in front of her stopped; she ran into his back and he stumbled sideways, fell into a boulder and cursed.

"Don't stop, men," Isabelle said, trying to keep the spirit in her voice.

They climbed until Isabelle gasped with every step, but Eduardo allowed them no respite. He stopped only long enough to make sure they were still behind him and then he was off again, clambering up the rocky hillside like a goat.

Isabelle's legs were on fire, aching painfully, and even with her espadrilles, blisters formed. Every step became an agony and a test of will.

Hours and hours and hours passed. Isabelle grew so breathless she couldn't have formed the words needed to beg for a drink of water, but she knew that Eduardo wouldn't have listened to her anyway. She heard MacLeish in front of her, gasping, cursing every time he slipped, crying out in pain at the blisters she knew were turning his feet into open sores.

She couldn't make out the path at all anymore. She just trudged upward, her eyelids struggling to stay open.

Angling forward against the wind, she pulled her scarf up over her nose and mouth and kept going. Her breath, coming in pants, warmed her scarf. The fabric turned moist and then froze into solid, icy folds.

"Here." Eduardo's booming voice came at her from the darkness. They were so high up the mountain that there were sure to be no German or Spanish patrols. The risk to their lives up here came from the elements.

Isabelle collapsed in a heap, landing hard enough on a piece of rock that she cried out, but she was too tired to care.

MacLeish dropped down beside her, gasping, "Christ Almighty," and pitching forward. She grabbed his arm, steadied him as he started to slide downward.

She heard a cacophony of voices come after it—"thank God . . . bloody well time"—and then she heard bodies hit the ground. They fell downward in a group, as if their legs could hold them no more.

"Not here," Eduardo said. "The goatherder's shack. Over there."

Isabelle staggered to her feet. In the back of the line, she waited, shivering, her arms crossed around her body as if she could hold heat within, but there was no heat. She felt like a shard of ice, brittle and frozen. Her mind fought the stupor that wanted to take over. She had to keep shaking her head to keep her thoughts clear.

She heard a footstep and knew Eduardo was standing beside her in the darkness, their faces pelted by icy rain.

"Are you all right?" he asked.

"I'm frozen solid. And I'm afraid to look at my feet."

"Blisters?"

"The size of dinner plates, I'm pretty sure. I can't tell if the rain is making my shoes wet or if blood is bubbling through the material."

She felt tears sting her eyes and freeze instantly, binding her lashes together.

Eduardo took her hand and led her to the goatherder's shed, where he started a fire. The ice in her hair turned to water and dripped to the floor, puddling at her feet. She watched the men collapse where they stood, thumping back against the rough wooden walls as they pulled their rucksacks into their laps and began searching through them for food. MacLeish waved her over.

Isabelle picked her way through the men and collapsed beside Mac-Leish. In silence, listening to men chewing and belching and sighing around her, she ate the cheese and apples she'd brought with her.

She had no idea when she fell asleep. One minute she was awake, eating what passed for supper on the mountain, and the next thing she knew, Eduardo was waking them again. Gray light pressed against the dirty window of the shack. They'd slept through the day and been wakened in the late afternoon.

Eduardo started a fire, made a pot of ersatz coffee, and handed it out to them. Breakfast was stale bread and hard cheese—good, but not nearly enough to stave off the hunger that was still sharp from yesterday.

Eduardo took off at a brisk walk, climbing the slick, frost-covered shale of the treacherous trail like a billy goat.

Isabelle was the last one out of the shack. She looked up the trail. Gray clouds obscured the peaks and snowflakes hushed the world until there was no earthly sound except their breathing. Men vanished in front of her, becoming small black dots in the whiteness. She plunged into the cold, climbing steadily, following the man in front of her. He was all she could see in the falling snow.

Eduardo's pace was punishing. He climbed up the twisting path without pause, seemingly unaware of the biting, burning cold that turned every breath into a fire that exploded in the lungs. Isabelle panted and kept going, encouraging the men when they started to lag, cajoling them and teasing them and urging them on.

When darkness fell again, she redoubled her efforts to keep morale up. Even though she felt sick to her stomach with fatigue and parched with thirst, she kept going. If any one of them got more than a few feet away from the person in front of him, he could be lost forever in this frozen darkness. To leave the path for a few feet was to die.

She stumbled on through the night.

Someone fell in front of her, made a yelping sound. She rushed forward, found one of the Canadian fliers on his knees, wheezing hard, his moustache frozen. "I'm beat, baby doll," he said, trying to smile.

Isabelle slid down beside him, felt her backside instantly grow cold. "It's Teddy, right?"

"You got me. Look. I'm done for. Just go on ahead."

"You got a wife, Teddy, a girl back home in Canada?"

She couldn't see his face, but she heard the way he sucked in his breath at her question. "You aren't playin' fair, doll."

"There's no fair in life and death, Teddy. What's her name?"

"Alice."

"Get on your feet for Alice, Teddy."

She felt him shift his weight, get his feet back underneath him. She angled her body against him, let him lean against her as he stood. "All right, then," he said, shuddering hard.

She let him go, heard him walk on ahead.

She sighed heavily, shivering at the end of it. Hunger gnawed at her stomach. She swallowed dryly, wishing they could stop just for a minute. Instead, she pointed herself in the direction of the men and kept going. Her mind was muddling again, her thoughts blurring. All she could think of was taking this step, and the next one, and the next one.

Sometime near dawn, the snow turned to rain that turned their woolen coats into sodden weights. Isabelle hardly noticed when they started going down. The only real difference was the men falling, slipping on the wet rocks and tumbling down the rocky, treacherous mountainside. There was no way to stop them; she just had to watch them fall and help them get back on their feet when they came to a breathless, broken stop. The visibility was so bad that they were constantly in fear of losing sight of the man in front and plunging off the path.

At daybreak, Eduardo stopped and pointed to a yawning black cave tucked into the mountainside. The men gathered inside, making huffing sounds as they sat and stretched out their legs. Isabelle heard them opening their packs, burrowing through for the last bits of their food. Somewhere deep inside, an animal scurried around, its claws scratching lightly on the hard-packed dirt floor.

Isabelle followed the men inside; roots hung down from the dripping stone-and-mud interior. Eduardo knelt down and made a small fire, using the moss he'd picked that morning and packed in his waistband. "Eat and sleep," he said when the flames danced up. "Tomorrow we make the final trek." He reached for his goatskin bota, drank deeply, and then left the cave.

The damp wood crackled and popped, sounding like gunfire in the cave, but Isabelle—and the men—were too exhausted even to flinch. Isabelle sat down beside MacLeish and leaned tiredly against him.

"You're a wonder," he said in a hushed voice.

"I've been told I don't make smart decisions. This may be proof of that." She shivered, whether from cold or exhaustion, she didn't know.

"Dumb but brave," he said with a smile.

Isabelle was grateful for the conversation. "That's me."

"I don't think I've thanked you properly . . . for saving me."

"I don't think I've saved you yet, Torrance."

"Call me Torry," he said. "All my mates do."

He said something else—about a girl waiting for him in Ipswich, maybe—but she was too tired to hear what it was.

When she wakened, it was raining.

"Bollocks," one of the men said. "It's pissing out there."

Eduardo stood outside the cave, his strong legs braced widely apart, his face and hair pelted by rain that he seemed not to notice at all. Behind him, there was darkness.

The airmen opened their rucksacks. No one had to be told to eat anymore; they knew the routine. When you were allowed to stop, you drank, you ate, you slept, and in that order. When you were wakened, you ate and drank and got to your feet, no matter how much it hurt to do so.

As they stood, a groan moved from man to man. A few cursed. It was a rainy, moonless night. Utterly dark.

They had made it over the mountain—almost one thousand meters high where they crossed the previous night—and were halfway down the other side, but the weather was worsening.

As Isabelle left the cave, wet branches smacked her in the face. She pushed them away with a gloved hand and kept going. Her walking stick thumped with each step. Rain made the shale as slick as ice and ran in rivulets alongside them. She heard the men grunting in front of her. She trudged forward on blistered, aching feet. The pace set by Eduardo was gruelingly hard. Nothing stopped or slowed the man, and the airmen struggled to keep up.

"Look!" she heard someone say.

In the distance, far away, lights twinkled, a spiderweb pattern of white dots spanned the darkness.

"Spain," Eduardo said.

The sight rejuvenated the group. They continued, their walking sticks thumping, their feet landing solidly as the ground gradually leveled out.

How many hours passed this way? Five? Six? She didn't know. Enough that her legs began to ache and the small of her back was a pit of pain. She was constantly spitting rain and wiping it out of her eyes, and the emptiness in her stomach was a rabid animal. A pale sheen of daylight began to appear at the horizon, a blade of lavender light, then pink, then yellow as she zigzagged down the trail. Her feet hurt so much she gritted her teeth to keep from crying out in pain.

By the fourth nightfall, Isabelle had lost all sense of time and place. She had no idea where they were or how much longer this agony would go on. Her thoughts became a simple plea, tumbling through her mind, keeping pace with her aching steps. *The consulate, the consulate, the consulate.*

"Stop," Eduardo said, holding up his hand.

Isabelle stumbled into MacLeish. His cheeks were bright red with cold and his lips were chapped and his breathing ragged.

Not far away, past a blurry green hillside, she saw a patrol of soldiers in light green uniforms.

Her first thought was, *We are in Spain,* and then Eduardo shoved them both behind a stand of trees.

They hid for a long time and then set off again.

Hours later, she heard a roar of rushing water. As they neared the river, the sound obliterated everything else.

Finally, Eduardo stopped and gathered the men close together. He was standing in a pool of mud, his espadrilles disappearing into the muck. Behind him were gray granite cliffs upon which spindly trees grew in defiance of the laws of gravity. Bushes sprouted like cattle catchers around formidable gray rocks.

"We hide here until nightfall," Eduardo said. "Over that ridge is the Bidassoa River. On the other bank is Spain. We are close—but close is nothing. Between the river and your freedom are patrols with dogs. These patrols will shoot at anything they see moving. Do not move."

Isabelle watched Eduardo walk away from the group. When he was gone, she and the men hunkered down behind giant boulders and inside the lee of fallen trees.

For hours, the rain beat down on them, turned the mud beneath them into a marsh. She shivered and drew her knees into her chest and closed her eyes. Impossibly, she fell into a deep, exhausted sleep that was over much too quickly.

At midnight, Eduardo wakened her.

The first thing Isabelle noticed when she opened her eyes was that the rain had stopped. The sky overhead was studded with stars. She climbed tiredly to her feet and immediately winced in pain. She could only imagine how much the airmen's feet hurt—she was lucky enough to have shoes that fit.

Under cover of night, they set off again, the sound of their footsteps swallowed by the roar of the river.

And then they were there, standing amid the trees at the edge of a giant gorge. Far below, the water crashed and roiled and roared, splashing up along the rock sides.

Eduardo gathered them close. "We can't swim across. The rains have made the river a beast that will swallow us all. Follow me."

They walked along the river for a mile or two, and then Eduardo stopped again. She heard a creaking sound, like a boat line stretched by rising seas, and an occasional clatter.

At first, there was nothing to see. Then the bright white searchlights on the other side flashed across the white-tipped, rushing river, and shone on a rickety suspension bridge that linked this side of the gorge to the opposite shore. There was a Spanish checkpoint not far away, with guards patrolling back and forth.

"Holy Mother o' God," one of the airmen said.

"Fuck me," said another.

Isabelle joined the men in a crouch behind some bushes, where they waited, watching the searchlights crisscross the river.

It was after two in the morning when Eduardo finally nodded. There was no movement on the other side of the gorge at all. If their luck held—or if they had any at all—the sentries were asleep at their posts.

"Let's go," Eduardo whispered, getting the men to their feet. He led them to the start of the bridge—a sagging sling with rope sides and a wooden-slat floor, through which the rushing white river could be seen in strips. Several of the slats were missing. The bridge blew side to side in the wind and made a whining, creaking sound.

Isabelle looked at the men, most of whom were pale as ghosts.

"One step at a time," Eduardo said. "The slats look weak but they'll hold your weight. You have sixty seconds to cross—that's the amount of time between the searchlights. As soon as you get to the other side, drop to your knees and crawl beneath the window of the guardhouse."

"You've done this before, right?" Teddy said, his voice breaking on "before."

"Plenty of times, Teddy," Isabelle lied. "And if a girl can do it, a strapping pilot like you will have no problem at all. Right?"

He nodded. "You bet your arse."

Isabelle watched Eduardo cross. When he was on the other side, she gathered the airmen close. One by one, counting off in sixty-second intervals, she guided them onto the rope bridge and watched them cross, holding her breath and fisting her hands until each man landed on the opposite shore.

Finally it was her turn. She pushed the sodden hood off her head, waiting for the light to scrape past her and keep going. The bridge looked flimsy and unsound. But it had held the men's weight; it would hold hers.

She clutched the rope sides and stepped onto the first plank. The bridge swung around her, dipped right and left. She glanced down and saw strips of raging white waters one hundred feet below. Gritting her teeth, she moved steadily forward, stepping from plank to plank to plank until she was on the other side, where she immediately dropped to her knees. The searchlight passed above her. She scrambled forward and up the embankment and into the bushes on the other side, where the airmen were crouched beside Eduardo.

Eduardo led them to a hidden hillock of land and finally let them sleep.

When the sun rose again, Isabelle blinked dully awake.

"It's not s' bad here," Torry whispered beside her.

Isabelle looked around, bleary-eyed. They were in a gully above a dirt road, hidden by a stand of trees.

Eduardo handed them wine. His smile was as bright as the sun that shone in her eyes. "There," he said, pointing to a young woman on a bicycle not far away. Behind her, a town glinted ivory in the sunlight; it looked like something out of a children's picture book, full of turrets and clock towers and church spires. "Almadora will take you to the consulate in San Sebastián. Welcome to Spain."

Isabelle instantly forgot the struggle it had taken to get here, and the fear that accompanied her every step. "Thank you, Eduardo."

"It won't be so easy next time," he said.

"It wasn't easy this time," she said.

"They didn't expect us. Soon, they will."

He was right, of course. They hadn't had to hide from German patrols or disguise their scents from dogs, and the Spanish sentinels were relaxed.

"But when you come back again, with more pilots, I'll be here," he promised.

She nodded her gratitude and turned to the men around her, who looked as exhausted as she felt. "Come on, men, off we go."

Isabelle and the men staggered down the road toward a young woman who stood beside a rusted old bicycle. After the false introductions were made, Almadora led them down a maze of dirt roads and back alleys; miles passed until they stood outside an elaborate caramel-hued building in Parte Viejo—the old section of San Sebastián. Isabelle could hear the crashing of distant waves against a seawall.

"*Merci,*" Isabelle said to the girl.

"*De nada.*"

Isabelle looked up at the glossy black door. "Come on, men," she said, striding up the stone steps. At the door, she knocked hard, three times, and then rang the bell. When a man in a crisp black suit answered, she said, "I am here to see the British consul."

"Is he expecting you?"

"No."

"Mademoiselle, the consul is a busy—"

"I've brought four RAF pilots with me from Paris."

The man's eyes bulged a bit.

MacLeish stepped forward. "Lieutenant Torrance MacLeish. RAF."

The other men followed suit, standing shoulder to shoulder as they introduced themselves.

The door opened. Within a matter of moments, Isabelle found herself seated on an uncomfortable leather chair, facing a tired-looking man across a large desk. The airmen stood at attention behind her.

"I brought you four downed airmen from Paris," Isabelle said proudly. "We took the train south and then walked across the Pyrenees—"

"You *walked?*"

"Well, perhaps hiked is a more accurate word."

"You *hiked* over the Pyrenees from France and into Spain." He sat back in his chair, all traces of a smile gone.

"I can do it again, too. With the increased RAF bombings, there are going to be more downed airmen. To save them, we will need financial help. Money for clothes and papers and food. And something for the people we enlist to shelter us along the way."

"You'll want to ring up MI9," MacLeish said. "They'll pay whatever Juliette's group needs."

The man shook his head, made a tsking sound. "A *girl* leading pilots across the Pyrenees. Will wonders never cease?"

MacLeish grinned at Isabelle. "A wonder indeed, sir. I told her the very same thing."

TWENTY

*G*etting out of Occupied France was difficult and dangerous. Getting back in—at least for a twenty-year-old girl with a ready smile—was easy.

Only a few days after her arrival in San Sebastián, and after endless meetings and debriefings, Isabelle was on the train bound for Paris again, sitting in one of the wooden banquettes in the third-class carriage—the only seat available on such short notice—watching the Loire Valley pass by. The carriage was freezing cold and packed with loquacious German soldiers and cowed French men and women who kept their heads down and their hands in their laps. She had a piece of hard cheese and an apple in her handbag, but even though she was hungry—starving, really—she didn't open her bag.

She felt conspicuous in her ragged, snagged brown pants and woolen coat. Her cheeks were windburned and scratched and her lips were chapped and dry. But the real changes were within. The pride of what she'd accomplished in the Pyrenees had changed her, matured her. For the first time in her life, she knew exactly what she wanted to do.

She had met with an agent from MI9 and formally set up the escape route. She was their primary contact—they called her the Nightingale. In her handbag, hidden in the lining, were one hundred forty thousand francs. Enough to set up safe houses and buy food and clothing for the airmen and the people who dared to house them along the way. She'd given her word to her contact Ian (code name Tuesday) that other airmen would follow. Sending word to Paul—"The Nightingale has sung"—was perhaps the proudest moment of her life.

It was nearing curfew when she disembarked in Paris. The autumnal city shivered beneath a cold, dark sky. Wind tumbled through the bare trees, clattering the empty flower baskets, ruffling and flapping the awnings.

She went out of her way to walk past her old apartment on Avenue de La Bourdonnais and as she passed it, she felt a wave of . . . longing she supposed. It was as close to a home as she could remember, and she hadn't stepped inside—or seen her father—in months. Not since the inception of the escape route. It wasn't safe for them to be together. Instead, she went to the small, dingy apartment that was her most recent home. A mismatched table and chairs, a mattress on the floor, and a broken stove. The rug smelled of the last tenant's tobacco and the walls were waterstained.

At her front door, she paused, glanced around. The street was quiet, dark. She fitted the skeleton key in the lock and gave a little twist. At the click of sound, she sensed danger. Something was wrong, out of place—a shadow where it shouldn't be, a clanking of metal from the bistro next door, abandoned by its owner months ago.

She turned around slowly, peered out into the dark, quiet street. Unseen lorries were parked here and there and a few sad little cafés cast triangles of light onto the sidewalk; within the glow, soldiers were thin silhouettes, moving back and forth. An air of desertion hung over the once lively neighborhood.

Across the street, a lamp stood unlit, a barely darker slash against the night air around it.

He was there. She knew it, even though she couldn't see him.

She moved down the steps, slowly, her senses alert, taking one cautious step at a time. She was sure she could hear him breathing, not far away. Watching her. She knew instinctively that he'd been waiting for her to return, worrying.

"Gaëtan," she said softly, letting her voice be a lure, casting out, trying to catch him. "You've been following me for months. Why?"

Nothing. Silence blew in the wind around her, biting and cold.

"Come here," she pleaded, tilting her chin.

Still, nothing.

"Now who isn't ready?" she said. It hurt, that silence, but she understood it, too. With all the risks they were taking, love was probably the most dangerous choice of all.

Or maybe she was wrong, and he wasn't here, had never been here, watching her, waiting for her. Maybe she was just a silly girl longing for a man who didn't want her, standing alone in an empty street.

No.

He was there.

❧

That winter was even worse than the year before. An angry God smote Europe with leaden skies and falling snow, day after day after day. The cold was a cruel addendum to a world already bleak and ugly.

Carriveau, like so many small towns in the Occupied Zone, became an island of despair, cut off from its surroundings. The villagers had limited information about what was going on in the world around them, and no one had time to burrow through propagandist papers looking for truth when surviving took so much effort. All they really knew was that the Nazis had become angrier, meaner, since the Americans had joined the war.

On a bleak and freezing predawn morning in early February 1942, when tree limbs snapped and windowpanes looked like cracked pond ice, Vianne woke early and stared at the deeply pitched ceiling of her bedroom. A headache pounded behind her eyes. She felt sweaty and achy. When she drew in a breath, it burned in her lungs and made her cough.

Getting out of bed was not appealing, but neither was starving to death. More and more often this winter, their ration cards were useless; there was simply no food to be had, and no shoes or fabric or leather. Vianne no longer had wood for the stove or money to pay for electricity. With gas so dear, the simple act of bathing became a chore to be endured. She and Sophie slept wrapped together like puppies, beneath a mountain of quilts

and blankets. In the past few months, Vianne had begun to burn everything made of wood and to sell her valuables.

Now she was wearing almost every piece of clothing she owned—
flannel pants, underwear she'd knitted herself, an old woolen sweater, a
neck scarf, and still she shivered when she left the bed. When her feet hit
the floor, she winced at the pain from her chilblains. She grabbed a wool
skirt and put it on over her pants. She'd lost so much weight this winter
that she had to pin the waist in place. Coughing, she went downstairs. Her
breath preceded her in white puffs that disappeared almost instantly. She
limped past the guest room door.

The captain was gone, and had been for weeks. As much as Vianne
hated to admit it, his absences were worse than his appearances these
days. At least when he was there, there was food to eat and a fire in the
hearth. He refused to let the home be cold. Vianne ate as little of the food
he provided as she could—she told herself it was her duty to be hungry—
but what mother could let her child suffer? Was Vianne really supposed to
let Sophie starve to prove her loyalty to France?

In the darkness, she added another pair of holey socks to the two pairs
already on her feet. Then she wrapped herself in a blanket and put on the
mittens she'd recently knit from an old baby blanket of Sophie's.

In the frost-limned kitchen, she lit an oil lamp and carried it outside,
moving slowly, breathing hard as she climbed the slick, icy hillside to the
barn. Twice she slipped and fell on the frozen grass.

The barn's metal door handle felt burningly cold, even through her
heavy mittens. She had to use all of her weight to slide the door open.
Inside, she set down the lantern. The idea of moving the car was almost
more than she could stand in her weakened state.

She took a deep painful breath, steeled herself, and went to the car. She
put it in neutral, then bent down to the bumper and pushed with all of her
strength. The car rolled forward slowly, as if in judgment.

When the trapdoor was revealed, she retrieved the oil lamp and
climbed slowly down the ladder. In the long, dark months since her firing
and the end of her money, she had sold off her family's treasures one by
one: a painting to feed the rabbits and chickens through the winter, a

Limoges tea set for a sack of flour, silver salt and pepper shakers for a stringy pair of hens.

Opening her maman's jewelry box, she stared down into the velvet-lined interior. Not long ago there had been lots of paste jewelry in here, as well as a few good pieces. Earrings, a filigree silver bracelet, a brooch made of rubies and hammered metal. Only the pearls were left.

Vianne removed one mitten and reached down for the pearls, scooping them into her palm. They shone in the light, as lustrous as a young woman's skin.

They were the last link to her mother—and to their family's heritage.

Now Sophie would not wear them on her wedding day or hand them down to her own daughters.

"But she will eat this winter," Vianne said. She wasn't sure if it was grief that serrated her voice, or sadness, or relief. She was lucky to have something to sell.

She gazed down at the pearls, felt their weight in her palm, and the way they drew warmth from her body for themselves. For a split second, she saw them glow. Then, grimly, she put the mitten over her hand and climbed back up the ladder.

❦

Three more weeks passed in desolate cold with no sign of Beck. On a frozen late February morning, Vianne woke with a pounding headache and a fever. Coughing, she climbed out of bed and shivered, slowly lifting a blanket from the bed. She wrapped it around herself but it didn't help. She shivered uncontrollably, even though she wore pants and two sweaters and three pairs of socks. The wind howled outside, clattering against the shutters, rattling the ice-sheened glass beneath the blackout shade.

She moved slowly through her morning routine, trying not to breathe too deeply lest a cough come up from her chest. On chilblained feet that radiated pain with every step, she made Sophie a meager breakfast of watery corn mush. Then the two of them went out into the falling snow.

In silence, they trudged to town. Snow fell relentlessly, whitening the road in front of them, coating the trees.

The church sat on a small, jutting bit of land at the edge of town, bordered on one side by the river and backed by the limestone walls of the old abbey.

"Maman, are you all right?"

Vianne had hunched forward again. She squeezed her daughter's hand, feeling nothing but mitten on mitten. The breath stuttered in her lungs, burned. "I'm fine."

"You should have eaten breakfast."

"I wasn't hungry," Vianne said.

"Ha," Sophie said, trudging forward through the heavy snow.

Vianne led Sophie into the chapel. Inside, it was warm enough that they no longer saw their breath. The nave arched gracefully upward, shaped like hands held together in prayer, held in place by graceful wooden beams. Stained-glass windows glittered with bits of color. Most of the pews were filled, but no one was talking, not on a day this cold, in a winter this bad.

The church bells pealed and a clanging echoed in the nave, and the giant doors slammed shut, extinguishing what little natural light could make it through the snow.

Father Joseph, a kindly old priest who had presided over this church for the whole of Vianne's life, stepped up to the pulpit. "We will pray today for our men who are gone. We will pray that this war does not last much longer . . . and we will pray for the strength to resist our enemy and stay true to who we are."

This was not the sermon Vianne wanted to hear. She had come to church—braved the cold—to be comforted by Father's sermon on this Sunday, to be inspired by words like "honor" and "duty" and "loyalty." But today, those ideals felt far, far away. How could you hold on to ideals when you were sick and cold and starving? How could she look at her neighbors when she was taking food from the enemy, even as small an amount as it was? Others were hungrier.

She was so deep in thought that it took her a moment to realize the service had ended. Vianne stood, feeling a wave of dizziness at the motion. She clutched the pew for support.

"Maman?"

"I'm fine."

In the aisle to their left, the parishioners—mostly women—filed past. Each looked as weak and thin and washed out as she felt, wrapped in layers of wool and newsprint.

Sophie took Vianne's hand and led her toward the wide-open double doors. At the threshold, Vianne paused, shivering and coughing. She didn't want to go out into the cold white world again.

She stepped over the threshold (where Antoine had carried her after their wedding . . . no, that was the threshold of Le Jardin; she was confused) and out into the snowstorm. Vianne held the heavy-knit scarf around her head, clutching it closed at her throat. Bending forward, angling into the wind, she trudged through the wet, heavy snow.

By the time she reached the broken gate in her yard, she was breathing heavily and coughing hard. She stepped around the snow-covered motorcycle with the machine-gun-mounted sidecar and went into the orchard of bare branches. He was back, she thought dully; now Sophie would eat. . . . She was almost to the front door when she felt herself start to fall.

"Maman!"

She heard Sophie's voice, heard the fear in it and thought, *I'm scaring her,* and she regretted it, but her legs were too weak to carry her, and she was tired . . . so tired . . .

From far away, she heard the door crack open, heard her daughter scream, "Herr Captain!" and then she heard boot heels striking wood.

She hit the ground hard, cracked her head on the snow-covered step, and lay there. She thought, *I'll rest for a bit, then I'll get up and make Sophie lunch . . . but what is there to eat?*

The next thing she knew, she was floating, no, maybe flying. She couldn't open her eyes—she was so tired and her head hurt—but she could feel herself moving, being rocked. *Antoine, is that you? Are you holding me?*

"Open the door," someone said, and there was a crack of wood on wood, and then, "I'm going to take off her coat. Go get Madame de Champlain, Sophie."

Vianne felt herself being laid on something soft. A bed.

She wet her chapped, dry lips and tried to open her eyes. It took considerable effort, and two tries. When she finally managed it, her vision was blurry.

Captain Beck was sitting beside her on her bed, in her bedroom. He was holding her hand and leaning forward, his face close to hers.

"Madame?"

She felt his warm breath on her face.

"Vianne!" Rachel said, coming into the room at a run.

Captain Beck got to his feet instantly. "She fainted in the snow, Madame, and cracked her head on the step. I carried her up here."

"I'm grateful," Rachel said, nodding. "I'll take care of her now, Herr Captain."

Beck stood there. "She doesn't eat," he said stiffly. "All the food goes to Sophie. I have watched this."

"That's motherhood in war, Herr Captain. Now . . . if you'll excuse me . . ." She stepped past him and sat down on the bed beside Vianne. He stood there another moment, looking flustered, and then he left the room. "So, you are giving her everything," Rachel said softly, stroking Vianne's damp hair.

"What else can I do?" Vianne said.

"Not die," Rachel said. "Sophie needs you."

Vianne sighed heavily and closed her eyes. She fell into a deep sleep in which she dreamed she was lying on a softness that was acres and acres of black field, sprawled out from her on all sides. She could hear people calling out to her from the darkness, hear them walking toward her, but she had no desire to move; she just slept and slept and slept. When she woke, it was to find herself on her own divan in her living room, with a fire roaring in the grate not far away.

She sat up slowly, feeling weak and unsteady. "Sophie?"

The guest room door opened, and Captain Beck appeared. He was dressed in flannel pajamas and a woolen cardigan and his jackboots. He said, "*Bonsoir,* Madame," and smiled. "It is good to have you back."

She was wearing her flannel pants and two sweaters and socks and a knit hat. Who had dressed her? "How long did I sleep?"

"Just a day."

He walked past her and went into the kitchen. Moments later he returned with a cup of steaming *café au lait* and a wedge of blue cheese and a piece of ham and a chunk of bread. Saying nothing, he set the food down on the table beside her.

She looked at it, her stomach grumbling painfully. Then she looked up at the captain.

"You hit your head and could have died."

Vianne touched her forehead, felt the bump that was tender.

"What happens to Sophie if you die?" he asked. "Have you considered this?"

"You were gone so long. There wasn't enough food for both of us."

"Eat," he said, gazing down at her.

She didn't want to look away. Her relief at his return shamed her. When she finally did, when she dragged her gaze sideways, she saw the food.

She reached out and took the plate in her hands, bringing it toward her. The salty, smoky scent of the ham, combined with the slightly stinky aroma of the cheese, intoxicated her, overwhelmed her better intentions, seduced her so thoroughly that there was no choice to be made.

In early March of 1942, spring still felt far away. Last night the Allies had bombed the hell out of the Renault factory in Boulogne-Billancourt, killing hundreds in the suburb on the outskirts of Paris. It had made the Parisians—Isabelle included—jumpy and irritable. The Americans had entered the war with a vengeance; air raids were a fact of life now.

On this cold and rainy evening, Isabelle pedaled her bicycle down a muddy, rutted country road in a heavy fog. Rain plastered her hair to her face and blurred her vision. In the mist, sounds were amplified; the cry of a pheasant disturbed by the sucking sound of her wheels in mud, the near-constant drone of aeroplanes overhead, the lowing of cattle in a field she couldn't see. A woolen hood was her only protection.

As if being drawn in charcoal on vellum by an uncertain hand, the demarcation line slowly came into view. She saw coils of barbed wire stretched out on either side of a black-and-white checkpoint gate. Beside it, a German sentry sat in a chair, his rifle rested across his lap. At Isabelle's approach, he stood and pointed the gun at her.

"Halt!"

She slowed the bike; the wheels stuck in the mud and she nearly flew from her seat. She dismounted, stepped down into the muck. Five hundred franc notes were sewn into the lining of her coat, as well as a set of false identity papers for an airman hiding in a safe house nearby.

She smiled at the German, walked her bicycle toward him, thumping through muddy potholes.

"Documents," he said.

She handed him her forged Juliette papers.

He glanced down at them, barely interested. She could tell that he was unhappy to be manning such a quiet border in the rain. "Pass," he said, sounding bored.

She repocketed her papers and climbed back onto her bicycle, pedaling away as quickly as she could on the wet road.

An hour and a half later, she reached the outskirts of the small town of Brantôme. Here, in the Free Zone, there were no German soldiers, although lately the French police had proven to be as dangerous as the Nazis, so she didn't let her guard down.

For centuries, the town of Brantôme had been considered a sacred place that could both heal the body and enlighten the soul. After the Black Death and the Hundred Years' War ravaged the countryside, the Benedictine monks built an immense limestone abbey, backed by soaring gray cliffs on one side and the wide Dronne River on the other.

Across the street from the caves at the end of town was one of the newest safe houses: a secret room tucked into an abandoned mill built on a triangle of land between the caves and the river. The ancient wooden mill turned rhythmically, its buckets and wheel furred with moss. The windows were boarded up and anti-German graffiti covered the stone walls.

Isabelle paused in the street, glancing both ways to make sure that no one was watching her. No one was. She locked her bicycle to a tree at the end of town and then crossed the street and bent down to the cellar door, opening it quietly. All of the doors to the mill house were boarded up, nailed shut; this was the only way inside.

She climbed down into the black, musty cellar and reached for the oil lamp she kept on a shelf there. Lighting it, she followed the secret passageway that had once allowed the Benedictine monks to escape from the so-called barbarians. Narrow, steeply pitched stairs led to the kitchen. Opening the door, she slipped into the dusty, cobwebby room and kept going upstairs to the secret ten-by-ten room built behind one of the old storerooms.

"She's here! Perk up, Perkins."

In the small room, lit only by a single candle, two men got to their feet, stood at attention. Both were dressed as French peasants in ill-fitting clothes.

"Captain Ed Perkins, miss," the bigger of the two men said. "And this here lout is Ian Trufford or some such name. He's Welsh. I'm a Yank. We're both damned happy to see you. We've been goin' half mad in this small space."

"Only half mad?" she asked. Water dripped from her hooded cloak and made a puddle around her feet. She wanted nothing more than to crawl into her sleeping bag and go to sleep, but she had business to conduct first. "Perkins, you say."

"Yes, miss."

"From?"

"Bend, Oregon, miss. My pa's a plumber and my ma makes the best apple pie in four counties."

"What's the weather like in Bend this time of year?"

"What's this? Middle o' March? Cold, I guess. Not snowing anymore, maybe, but no sunshine yet."

She bent her neck from side to side, massaging the pain in her shoulders. All this pedaling and lying and sleeping on the floor took a toll.

She interrogated the two men until she was certain they were who they said they were—two downed airmen who'd been waiting weeks for their chance to get out of France. When she was finally convinced, she opened her rucksack and brought out supper, such as it was. The three of them sat on a ragged, mouse-eaten carpet on the floor with the candle set in the middle. She brought out a baguette and a wedge of Camembert and a bottle of wine, which they passed around.

The Yank—Perkins—talked almost constantly, while the Welshman chewed in silence, saying no thank you to the offer of wine.

"You must have a husband somewhere who is worried about you," Perkins said as she closed her rucksack. She smiled. Already this had become a common question, especially from the men her age.

"And you must have a wife who is waiting for word," she said. It was what she always said. A pointed reminder.

"Nah," Perkins said. "Not me. A lug like me don't have girls lining up. And now . . ."

She frowned. "Now what?"

"I know it's not exactly heroic to think about, but I could walk out of this boarded-up house in this town I can't fucking pronounce and get shot by some guy I got nothing against. I could die trying to bike across your hills—"

"Mountains."

"I could get shot walking into Spain by the Spanish *or* the Nazis. Hell, I could probably freeze to death in your damned hills."

"Mountains," she said again, her gaze steady on his. "That's not going to happen."

Ian made a sighing sound. "There, you see, Perkins. This slip of a girl is going to save us." The Welshman gave her a tired smile. "I'm glad you're here, miss. This lad's been sending me 'round the bend with his chatter."

"You might as well let him talk, Ian. By this time tomorrow, it'll take all you have inside to keep breathing."

"The hills?" Perkins asked, his eyes wide.

"*Oui*," she said, smiling. "The hills."

Americans. They didn't listen.

⁂

In late May, spring brought life and color and warmth back to the Loire Valley. Vianne found peace in her garden. Today, as she pulled weeds and planted vegetables, a caravan of lorries and soldiers and Mercedes-Benzes rolled past Le Jardin. In the five months since the Americans had joined the war, the Nazis had lost all pretense of politeness. They were always busy now, marching and rallying and gathering at the munitions dump. The Gestapo and the SS were everywhere, looking for saboteurs and resisters. It took nothing to be called a terrorist—just a whispered accusation. The roar of aeroplanes overhead was nearly constant, as were bombings.

How often this spring had someone sidled up to Vianne while she was in a queue for food or walking through town or waiting at the *poste* and asked her about the latest BBC broadcast?

I have no radio. They are not allowed was always her response, and it was true. Still, every time she was asked such a question she felt a shiver of fear. They had learned a new word: *les collabos.* The collaborators. French men and women who did the Nazis' dirty work, who spied on friends and neighbors and reported back to the enemy, relaying every infraction, real or imagined. On their word, people had begun to be arrested for little things, and many who were taken to the Kommandant's office were never seen again.

"Madame Mauriac!" Sarah ran through the broken gate and into the yard. She looked frail and too thin, her skin so pale the blood vessels showed through. "You need to help my maman."

Vianne sat back on her heels and pushed the straw hat back on her head. "What's wrong? Did she hear from Marc?"

"I don't know what's wrong, Madame. Maman won't talk. When I told her Ari was hungry and needed changing, she shrugged and said, 'What does it matter?' She's in the backyard, just staring at her sewing."

Vianne got to her feet and peeled off her gardening gloves, tucking them into the pocket of her denim overalls. "I'll check on her. Get Sophie and we'll all walk over."

While Sarah was in the house, Vianne washed her hands and face at the outdoor pump and put away her hat. In its place, she tied a bandana around her head. As soon as the girls were with her, Vianne put her gardening tools in the shed and the three of them headed next door.

When Vianne opened the door, she found three-year-old Ari asleep on the rug. She scooped him into her arms, kissed his cheek, and turned to the girls. "Why don't you go play in Sarah's room?" She lifted the blackout shade, saw Rachel sitting alone in the backyard.

"Is my maman okay?" Sarah asked.

Vianne nodded distractedly. "Run along now." As soon as the girls were in the next room, she took Ari into Rachel's room and put him in his crib. She didn't bother covering him, not on a day this warm.

Outside, Rachel was in her favorite wooden chair, seated beneath the chestnut tree. At her feet was her sewing basket. She wore a brown khaki twill jumpsuit and a paisley turban. She was smoking a small brown hand-rolled cigarette. There was a bottle of brandy beside her and an empty café glass.

"Rach?"

"Sarah went for reinforcements, I see."

Vianne moved in to stand beside Rachel. She laid a hand on her friend's shoulder. She could feel Rachel trembling. "Is it Marc?"

Rachel shook her head.

"Thank God."

Rachel reached sideways for the brandy bottle, pouring herself a glass. She drank deeply, emptied the glass, then set it down. "They have passed a new statute," she said at last. Slowly, she unfurled her left hand to reveal wrinkled bits of yellow cloth that had been cut into the shape of a star. Written on each one was the word JUIF in black. "We are to wear these," Rachel said. "We have to stitch them onto our clothes—the three pieces of outerwear we are allowed—and wear them at all times in public. I had to *buy* them with my ration cards. Maybe I shouldn't have registered. If we don't wear them, we're subject to 'severe sanctions.' Whatever that means."

Vianne sat down in the chair beside her. "But . . ."

"You've seen the posters in town, how they show us Jews as vermin to be swept away and money grubbers who want to own everything? I can handle it, but . . . what about Sarah? She'll feel so ashamed . . . it's hard enough to be eleven without this, Vianne."

"Don't do it."

"It is immediate arrest if you are caught not wearing it. And they know about me. I've registered. And there's . . . Beck. He knows I am Jewish."

In the silence that followed, Vianne knew they were both thinking of the arrests that were taking place around Carriveau, of the people who were "disappearing."

"You could go to the Free Zone," Vianne said softly. "It's only four miles away."

"A Jew can't get an *Ausweis*, and if I got caught . . ."

Vianne nodded. It was true; running was perilous, especially with children. If Rachel were caught crossing the frontier without an *Ausweis*, she would be arrested. Or executed.

"I'm afraid," Rachel said.

Vianne reached over and held her friend's hand. They stared at each other. Vianne tried to come up with something to say, a bit of hope to offer, but there was nothing.

"It's going to get worse."

Vianne was thinking the same thing.

"Maman?"

Sarah came into the backyard, holding Sophie's hand. The girls looked frightened and confused. They knew how wrong things were these days and both had learned a new kind of fear. It broke Vianne's heart to see how changed these girls had already been by the war. Only three years ago, they'd been ordinary children who laughed and played and defied their mothers for fun. Now they moved forward cautiously, as if bombs could be buried beneath their feet. Both were thin, their puberty held at bay by poor nutrition. Sarah's dark hair was still long, but she'd begun to yank it out in her sleep so there were balding patches here and there, and Sophie never went anywhere without Bébé. The poor pink stuffed animal was beginning to spew stuffing around the house.

"Here," Rachel said. "Come here."

The girls shuffled forward, holding hands so tightly they appeared fused together. And in a way they were, as were Rachel and Vianne, joined by a friendship so strong it was maybe all they had left to believe in. Sarah sat in the chair by Rachel, and Sophie finally let her friend go. She came over to stand by Vianne.

Rachel looked at Vianne. In that single glance, sorrow flowed between them. How could they have to say things like this to their children?

"These yellow stars," Rachel said, opening her fist, revealing the ugly little flower of ragged fabric, with its black marking. "We have to wear them on our clothes at all times now."

Sarah frowned. "But . . . why?"

"We're Jews," Rachel said. "And we're proud of that. You have to remember how proud we are of it, even if people—"

"Nazis," Vianne said more sharply than intended.

"Nazis," Rachel added, "want to make us feel . . . bad about it."

"Will people make fun of me?" Sarah asked, her eyes widening.

"I will wear one, too," Sophie said.

Sarah looked pathetically hopeful at that.

Rachel reached out for her daughter's hand and held it. "No, baby. This is one thing you and your best friend can't do together."

Vianne saw Sarah's fear and embarrassment and confusion. She was trying her best to be a good girl, to smile and be strong even as tears glazed her eyes. "*Oui*," she said at last.

It was the saddest sound Vianne had heard in nearly three years of sorrow.

TWENTY-ONE

When summer came to the Loire Valley, it was as hot as the winter had been cold. Vianne longed to open her bedroom window to let air in, but not a breeze stirred on this hot late June night. She pushed the damp hair from her face and slumped in her chair by the bed.

Sophie made a whimpering sound. In it, Vianne heard a muddled, drawn-out "Maman," and she dipped her rag into the bowl of water she'd placed on the only remaining nightstand. The water was as warm as everything else in this upstairs room. She twisted the rag over the bowl, watched the excess water fall back into the bowl. Then she placed the wet rag on her daughter's forehead.

Sophie muttered something incomprehensible and started to thrash.

Vianne held her down, whispering love words in her ear, feeling heat against her lips. "Sophie," she said, the name a prayer with no beginning, no end. "I'm here." She said it over and over until Sophie calmed again.

The fever was getting worse. For days now Sophie had been ailing, feeling achy and out of sorts. At first Vianne had thought it was an excuse to avoid the responsibilities they shared. Gardening, laundry, canning, sewing. Vianne was constantly trying to do more, get more done. Even now, in the middle of the summer, she worried about the coming winter.

This morning had shown Vianne the truth, however (and made her feel like a terrible mother for not seeing it from the start): Sophie was sick, very sick. She had been plagued by fever all day, and her temperature was rising. She hadn't been able to keep anything down, not even the water her body needed so desperately.

"How about some lemonade?" she said.

No answer.

Vianne leaned over and kissed Sophie's hot cheek.

Dropping the rag back into the bowl full of water, she went downstairs. On the dining room table, a box waited to be filled—her most recent care package to Antoine. She'd started it yesterday and would have finished and mailed it off if not for Sophie's turn for the worse.

She was almost at the kitchen when she heard her daughter's scream.

Vianne ran back up the stairs.

"Maman," Sophie croaked, coughing. It was a terrible, rattling sound. She thrashed in the bed, yanking at the blankets, trying to shove them away. Vianne tried to calm her daughter, but Sophie was a wildcat, twisting and screaming and coughing.

If only she had some of Dr. Collis Browne's Chlorodyne. It worked magic on a cough, but of course there was none left.

"It's all right, Soph. Maman is here," Vianne said soothingly, but her words had no effect.

Beck appeared beside her. She knew she should have been angry that he was here—*here*, in her bedroom—but she was too tired and scared to lie to herself. "I don't know how to help her. There are no aspirin or antibiotics to be had at any price in town."

"Not even for pearls?"

She looked at him in surprise. "You know I sold my maman's pearls?"

"I live with you." He paused. "I make it my business to know what you are doing."

She didn't know what to say to that.

He looked down at Sophie. "She coughed all night. I could hear it."

Sophie had gone still, frighteningly so. "She'll get better."

He reached into his pocket and pulled out a small bottle of antibiotics. "Here."

She looked up at him. Was she overstating it to think that he was saving her daughter's life? Or did he *want* her to think that? She could rationalize what it meant to take food from him—after all, he needed to eat and it was her job to cook for him.

This was a favor, pure and simple, and there would be a price for it.

"Take it," he said gently.

She took the bottle from him. For a second, they were both holding it. She felt his fingers against hers.

Their gazes locked, and something passed between them, a question was asked and answered.

"Thank you," she said.

"You are most welcome."

"Sir, the Nightingale is here."

The British consul nodded. "Send her in."

Isabelle entered the dark, mahogany-lined office at the end of the elaborate hallway. Before she even reached the desk, the man behind it stood. "Good to see you again."

She sank into the uncomfortable leather chair and took the glass of brandy he offered. This latest crossing of the Pyrenees had been difficult, even in the perfect July weather. One of the American airmen had had difficulty following "a girl's" orders and had gone off on his own. They'd gotten word that he'd been arrested by the Spaniards. "Yanks," she said, shaking her head. There was no more that needed to be said. She and her contact, Ian—code name Tuesday—had worked together from the beginning of the Nightingale escape route. With help from Paul's network, they had set up a complex series of safe houses across France and a group of partisans ready to give their lives to help the downed airmen get home. French men and women scanned the skies at night, watching for aeroplanes in trouble and parachutes floating downward. They combed the streets, peering into shadows, looking through barns, seeking Allied soldiers in hiding. Once back in England, the pilots couldn't fly missions again—not with their knowledge of the network—instead, they prepared their colleagues for the worst: taught them evasion techniques, told them how to find help, and supplied them with franc notes and compasses and photographs ready-made for false papers.

Isabelle sipped the brandy. Experience had taught her to be cautious with alcohol after the crossing. She was usually more dehydrated than she realized, especially in the heat of summer.

Ian pushed an envelope toward her. She took it, counted the franc notes inside, and slid the money into a pocket in her coat. "That's eighty-seven airmen you've brought us in the past eight months, Isabelle," he said, taking his seat. Only in this room, one-on-one, did he use her real name. In all official correspondence with MI9, she was the Nightingale. To the other employees of the consulate and in Britain, she was Juliette Gervaise. "I think you should slow down."

"Slow down?"

"The Germans are looking for the Nightingale, Isabelle."

"That's old news, Ian."

"They're trying to infiltrate your escape route. Nazis are out there, pretending to be downed airmen. If you pick up one of them . . ."

"We're careful, Ian. You know that. I interrogate every man myself. And the network in Paris is tireless."

"They're looking for the Nightingale. If they find you . . ."

"They won't." She got to her feet.

He stood, too, and faced her. "Be careful, Isabelle."

"Always."

He came around the desk and took her by the arm and led her out of the building.

She took a little time to enjoy the seaside beauty of San Sebastián, to walk along the path above the crashing white surf below and enjoy buildings that didn't bear swastikas, but such moments of brushing up to ordinary life were a luxury she couldn't indulge for long. She sent Paul a message via courier that read:

> *Dear Uncle,*
>   *I hope this note finds you well.*
>   *I am at our favorite place by the sea.*

Our friends have arrived safely.
Tomorrow I shall visit Grandmère in Paris at three o'clock.
Love always,
Juliette

She returned to Paris via a circuitous route; she stopped at each of the safe houses—in Carriveau and Brantôme and Pau and Poitiers—and paid her helpers. The feeding and clothing of airmen in hiding was no small undertaking, and since every man, woman, and child (mostly women) who maintained the escape route did so at the risk of their lives, the network strived to make it not ruinous financially, too.

She never walked through the streets of Carriveau (hidden beneath a cloak and hood) without thinking about her sister. Lately, she had begun to miss Vianne and Sophie. Memories of their nights playing Belote or checkers by the fire, Vianne teaching Isabelle to knit (or trying to), and Sophie's laughter had taken on a warm patina. She imagined sometimes that Vianne had offered Isabelle a possibility she hadn't seen at the time: a home.

But it was too late for that now. Isabelle couldn't risk putting Vianne in danger by showing up at Le Jardin. Surely Beck would ask what she'd been doing in Paris for so long. Maybe he would wonder enough to check.

In Paris, she exited the train amid a crowd of drab-eyed, dark-clothed people who looked like they belonged in an Edvard Munch painting. As she passed the glittering gold dome of the Invalides, a light fog moved through the streets, plucking color from the trees. Most of the cafés were closed, their chairs and tables stacked beneath tattered awnings. Across the street was the apartment she'd called home for the past month, a dark, squalid lonely little attic tucked above an abandoned charcuterie. The walls still smelled vaguely of pork and spices.

She heard someone yell, *"Halt!"* Whistles shrieked; people screamed. Several Wehrmacht soldiers, accompanied by French policemen, encircled a small group of people, who immediately dropped to their knees and raised their arms. She saw yellow stars on their chests.

Isabelle slowed.

Anouk appeared beside her, linking her arm through Isabelle's. *"Bonjour,"* she said in a voice so animated it alerted Isabelle to the fact that they were being watched. Or at least Anouk worried that they were.

"You are like a character in one of those American comics the way you appear and disappear. The Shadow, perhaps."

Anouk smiled. "And how was your latest holiday in the mountains?"

"Unremarkable."

Anouk leaned close. "We hear word of something being planned. The Germans are recruiting women for clerical work on Sunday night. Double pay. All very secretive."

Isabelle slipped the envelope full of franc notes from her pocket and handed it to Anouk, who dropped it into her open handbag. "Night work? And clerical?"

"Paul has gotten you a position," Anouk said. "You start at nine. When you are finished, go to your father's apartment. He will be waiting for you."

"*Oui.*"

"It might be dangerous."

Isabelle shrugged. "What isn't?"

That night, Isabelle walked across town to the prefecture of police. There was a hum in the pavement beneath her feet, the sound of vehicles moving somewhere close by. A lot of them.

"You, there!"

Isabelle stopped. Smiled.

A German walked up to her, his rifle at the ready. His gaze dropped to her chest, looking for a yellow star.

"I am to work tonight," she said, indicating the prefecture of police building in front of her. Although the windows were blacked out, the place was busy. There were German Wehrmacht officers and French gendarmes milling about, going in and out of the building, which was an oddity at this late hour. In the courtyard was a long row of buses parked end to end. The drivers stood together in a huddle, smoking and talking.

The policeman cocked his head. "Go."

Isabelle clutched the collar of her drab brown coat. Although it was warm out, she didn't want to draw attention to herself tonight. One of the best ways to disappear in plain sight was to dress like a wren—brown, brown, and more brown. She had covered her blond hair with a black scarf, tied in a turban style with a big knot in front, and had used no cosmetics, not even lipstick.

She kept her head down as she walked through a throng of men in French police uniforms. Just inside the building, she stopped.

It was a huge space with staircases on either side and office doors spaced every few feet, but tonight it looked like a sweatshop, with hundreds of women seated at desks pressed close together. Telephones rang nonstop and French police officers moved in a rush.

"You are here to help with the sorting?" asked a bored French gendarme at the desk nearest the door.

"*Oui.*"

"I'll find you a place to work. Come with me." He led her around the perimeter of the room.

Desks were spaced so closely together that Isabelle had to turn sideways to make her way down the narrow aisle to the empty desk he'd indicated. When she sat down and scooted close, she was elbow-to-elbow with the women on either side of her. The surface of her desk was covered with card boxes.

She opened the first box and saw the stack of cards within. She pulled out the first one and stared at it.

STERNHOLZ, ISSAC
12 avenue Rast
4th arrondissement
Sabotier (clog maker)

It went on to list his wife and children.

"You are to separate the foreign-born Jews," said the gendarme, who she hadn't noticed had followed her.

"Pardon?" she said, taking out another card. This one was for "Berr, Simone."

"That box there. The empty one. Separate the Jews born in France from those born elsewhere. We are only interested in foreign-born Jews. Men, women, and children."

"Why?"

"They're Jews. Who cares? Now get to work."

Isabelle turned back around in her seat. She had hundreds of cards in front of her, and there were at least a hundred women in this room. The sheer scale of this operation was impossible to comprehend. What could it possibly mean?

"How long have you been here?" she asked the woman beside her.

"Days," the woman said, opening another box. "My children weren't hungry last night for the first time in months."

"What are we doing?"

The woman shrugged. "I've heard them saying something about Operation Spring Wind."

"What does it mean?"

"I don't want to know."

Isabelle flipped through the cards in the box. One near the end stopped her.

LÉVY, PAUL
61 rue Blandine, Apt. C
7th arrondissement
Professor of literature

She got to her feet so fast she bumped into the woman beside her, who cursed at the interruption. The cards on her desk slid to the floor in a cascade. Isabelle immediately knelt down and gathered them up, daring to stick Monsieur Lévy's card up her sleeve.

The moment she stood, someone grabbed her by the arm and dragged her down the narrow aisle. She bumped into women all down the row.

In the empty space by the wall, she was twisted around and shoved back so hard she slammed into the wall.

"What is the meaning of this?" snarled the French policeman, his grip on her arm tight enough to leave a bruise.

Could he feel the index card beneath her sleeve?

"I'm sorry. So sorry. I need to work, but I'm sick, you see. The flu." She coughed as loudly as she could.

Isabelle walked past him and left the building. Outside, she kept coughing until she got to the corner. There, she started to run.

"What could it mean?"

Isabelle peered past the blackout shade in the apartment, staring down at the avenue. Papa sat at the dining room table, nervously drumming his ink-stained fingers on the wood. It felt good to be here again—with him—after months away, but she was too agitated to relax and enjoy the homey feel of the place.

"You must be mistaken, Isabelle," Papa said, on his second brandy since her return. "You said there had to be tens of thousands of cards. That would be all the Jewish people in Paris. Surely—"

"Question what it means, Papa, but not the facts," she answered. "The Germans are collecting the names and addresses of every foreign-born Jewish person in Paris. Men, women, and children."

"But why? Paul Lévy is of Polish descent, it's true, but he has lived here for decades. He fought for France in the Great War—his brother died for France. The Vichy government has assured us that veterans are protected from the Nazis."

"Vianne was asked for a list of names," Isabelle said. "She was asked to write down every Jewish, communist, and Freemason teacher at her school. Afterward they were all fired."

"They can hardly fire them twice." He finished his drink and poured another. "And it is the French police gathering names. If it were the Germans, it would be different."

Isabelle had no answer to that. They had been having this same conversation for at least three hours.

Now it was edging past two in the morning, and neither of them could come up with a credible reason why the Vichy government and the French police were collecting the names and addresses of every foreign-born Jewish person living in Paris.

She saw a flash of silver outside. Lifting the shade a little higher, she stared down at the dark street.

A row of buses rolled down the avenue, their painted headlamps off, looking like a slow-moving centipede that stretched for blocks.

She had seen buses outside of the prefecture of police, dozens of them parked in the courtyard. "Papa . . ." Before she could finish, she heard footsteps coming up the stairs outside of the apartment.

A pamphlet of some kind slid into the apartment through the slit beneath the door.

Papa left the table and bent to pick it up. He brought it to the table and set it down next to the candle.

Isabelle stood behind him.

Papa looked up at her.

"It's a warning. It says the police are going to round up all foreign-born Jews and deport them to camps in Germany."

"We are talking when we need to be acting," Isabelle said. "We need to hide our friends in the building."

"It's so little," Papa said. His hand was shaking. It made her wonder again—sharply—what he'd seen in the Great War, what he knew that she did not.

"It's what we can do," Isabelle said. "We can make some of them safe. At least for tonight. We'll know more tomorrow."

"Safe. And where would that be, Isabelle? If the French police are doing this, we are lost."

Isabelle had no answer for that.

Saying no more, they left the apartment.

Stealth was difficult in a building as old as this one, and her father, moving in front of her, had never been light on his feet. Brandy made him even more unsteady as he led her down the narrow, twisting staircase to the apartment directly below theirs. He stumbled twice, cursing his imbalance. He knocked on the door.

He waited to the count of ten and knocked again. Harder this time.

Very slowly, the door opened, just a crack at first, and then all the way. "Oh, Julien, it is you," said Ruth Friedman. She was wearing a man's coat over a floor-length nightgown, with her bare feet sticking out beneath. Her hair was in rollers and covered with a scarf.

"You've seen the pamphlet?"

"I got one. It is true?" she whispered.

"I don't know," her father said. "There are buses out front and lorries have been rumbling past all night. Isabelle was at the prefecture of police tonight, and they were collecting the names and addresses of all foreign-born Jewish people. We think you should bring the children to our place for now. We have a hiding place."

"But . . . my husband is a prisoner of war. The Vichy government promises us that we will be protected."

"I am not sure we can trust the Vichy government, Madame," Isabelle said to the woman. "Please. Just hide for now."

Ruth stood there a moment, her eyes widening. The yellow star on her overcoat was a stark reminder of the way the world had changed. Isabelle saw when the woman decided. She turned on her heel and walked out of the room. Less than a minute later, she guided her two daughters toward the door. "What do we bring?"

"Nothing," Isabelle said. She herded the Friedmans up the stairs. When they reached the safety of the apartment, her father led them to the secret room in the back bedroom and closed the door on them.

"I'll get the Vizniaks," Isabelle said. "Don't put the armoire in place yet."

"They're on the third floor, Isabelle. You'll never—"

"Lock the front door behind me. Don't open it unless you hear my voice."

"Isabelle, no—"

She was already gone, running down the stairs, barely touching the banister in her haste. When she was nearly to the third-floor landing, she heard voices below.

They were coming up the stairs.

She was too late. She crouched where she was, hidden by the elevator.

Two French policemen stepped onto the landing. The younger of the two knocked twice on the Vizniaks' door, waited a second or two, and then kicked it open. Inside, a woman wailed.

Isabelle crept closer, listening.

". . . are Madame Vizniak?" the policeman on the left said. "Your husband is Emile and your children, Anton and Hélène?"

Isabelle peered around the corner.

Madame Vizniak was a beautiful woman, with skin the color of fresh cream and luxurious hair that never looked as messy as it did now. She was wearing a lacy silk negligee that must have cost a fortune when it was purchased. Her young son and daughter, whom she had pulled in close, were wide-eyed.

"Pack up your things. Just the necessaries. You are being relocated," said the older policeman as he flipped through a list of names.

"But . . . my husband is in prison near Pithiviers. How will he find us?"

"After the war, you will come back."

"Oh." Madame Vizniak frowned, ran a hand through her tangled hair.

"Your children are French-born citizens," the policeman said. "You may leave them here. They're not on my list."

Isabelle couldn't remain hidden. She got to her feet and descended the stairs to the landing. "I'll take them for you, Lily," she said, trying to sound calm.

"No!" the children wailed in unison, clinging to their mother.

The French policemen turned to her. "What is your name?" one of them asked Isabelle.

She froze. Which name should she give? "Rossignol," she said at last, although without the corresponding papers, it was a dangerous choice. Still, Gervaise might make them wonder why she was in this building at almost three in the morning, putting her nose in her neighbor's business.

The policeman consulted his list and then waved her away. "Go. You are no concern to me tonight."

Isabelle looked past them to Lily Vizniak. "I'll take the children, Madame."

Lily seemed not to comprehend. "You think I'll leave them behind?"

"I think—"

"Enough," the older policeman yelled, thumping his rifle butt on the floor. "You," he said to Isabelle. "Get out. This doesn't concern you."

"Madame, please," Isabelle pleaded. "I'll make sure they are safe."

"Safe?" Lily frowned. "But we are safe with the French police. We've been assured. And a mother can't leave her children. Someday you'll understand." She turned her attention to her children. "Pack a few things."

The French policeman at Isabelle's side touched her arm gently. When she turned, he said, "Go." She saw the warning in his eyes but couldn't tell if he wanted to scare her or protect her. "Now."

Isabelle had no choice. If she stayed, if she demanded answers, sooner or later her name would be passed up to the prefecture of police—maybe even to the Germans. With what she and the network were doing with the escape route, and what her father was doing with false papers, she didn't dare draw attention. Not even for something as slight as demanding to know where a neighbor was being taken.

Silently, keeping her gaze on the floor (she didn't trust herself to look at them), she eased past the policemen and headed for the stairs.

TWENTY-TWO

*A*fter she returned from the Vizniaks' apartment, Isabelle lit an oil lamp and went into the salon, where she found her father asleep at the dining room table, his head resting on the hard wood as if he'd passed out. Beside him was a half-empty brandy bottle that had been full not long ago. She took the bottle and put it on the sideboard, hoping that out of reach would equal out of mind in the morning.

She almost reached out for him, almost stroked the gray hair that obscured his face, a small, oval-shaped bald spot revealed by repose. She wanted to be able to touch him that way, in comfort, in love, in companionship.

Instead, she went into the kitchen, where she made a pot of bitter, dark, made-from-acorns coffee and found a small loaf of the tasteless gray bread that was all the Parisians could get anymore. She broke off a piece (what would Madame Dufour say about that? Eating while walking), and chewed it slowly.

"That coffee smells like shit," her father said, bleary-eyed, lifting his head as she came into the room.

She handed him her cup. "It tastes worse."

Isabelle poured another cup of coffee for herself and sat down beside him. The lamplight accentuated the road-map look of his face, deepening the pits and wrinkles, making the flesh beneath his eyes look wax-like and swollen.

She waited for him to say something, but he just stared at her. Beneath his pointed gaze, she finished her coffee (she needed it to swallow the dry, terrible bread) and pushed the empty cup away. Isabelle stayed there until he fell asleep again and then she went into her own room. But there was no way she could sleep. She lay there for hours, wondering and worrying. Finally, she couldn't stand it anymore. She got out of bed and went into the salon.

"I'm going out to see," she announced.

"Don't," he said, still seated at the table.

"I won't do anything stupid."

She returned to her bedroom and changed into a summer-weight blue skirt and short-sleeved white blouse. She put a faded blue silk scarf around her messy hair, tied it beneath her chin, and left the apartment.

On the third floor, she saw that the door to the Vizniak apartment was open. She peered inside.

The room had been looted. Only the biggest pieces of furniture remained and the drawers of the black bombé chest were open. Clothes and inexpensive knickknacks were scattered across the floor. Rectangular black marks on the wall revealed missing artwork.

She closed the door behind her. In the lobby, she paused just long enough to compose herself and then opened the door.

Buses rolled down the street, one after another. Through the dirty bus windows, she saw dozens of children's faces, with their noses pressed to the glass, and their mothers seated beside them. The sidewalks were curiously empty.

Isabelle saw a French policeman standing at the corner and she went to him. "Where are they going?"

"Vélodrome d'Hiver."

"The sporting stadium? Why?"

"You don't belong here. Go or I'll put you on a bus and you'll end up with them."

"Maybe I'll do that. Maybe—"

The policeman leaned close, whispered, "*Go.*" He grabbed her arm and dragged her to the side of the road. "Our orders are to shoot anyone who tries to escape. You hear me?"

"You'd *shoot* them? Women and children?"

The young policeman looked miserable. "Go."

Isabelle knew she should stay. That was the smart thing to do. But she could walk to the Vél d'Hiv almost as quickly as these buses could drive there. It was only a few blocks away. Maybe then she would know what was happening.

For the first time in months, the barricades on the side streets of Paris were unmanned. She ducked around one and ran down the street, toward the river, past closed-up shops and empty cafés. Only a few blocks away, she came to a breathless stop across the street from the stadium. An endless stream of buses jammed with people drew up alongside the huge building and disgorged passengers. Then the doors wheezed shut and the buses drove off again; others drove up to take their place. She saw a sea of yellow stars.

There were thousands of men, women, and children, looking confused and despairing, being herded into the stadium. Most were wearing layers of clothing—too much for the July heat. Police patrolled the perimeter like American cowboys herding cattle, blowing whistles, shouting orders, forcing the Jewish people forward, into the stadium or onto other buses.

Families.

She saw a policeman shove a woman with his baton so hard she stumbled to her knees. She staggered upright, reaching blindly to the little boy beside her, protecting him with her body as she limped toward the stadium entrance.

She saw a young French policeman and fought through the crowd to get to him.

"What's happening?" she asked.

"That's not your concern, M'mselle. Go."

Isabelle looked back at the large cycling stadium. All she saw were people, bodies crammed together, families trying to hold on to each other in the melee. The police shouted at them, shoved them forward toward the stadium, yanked children and mothers to their feet when they fell. She could hear children crying. A pregnant woman was on her knees, rocking back and forth, clutching her distended belly.

"But . . . there are too many of them in there . . ." Isabelle said.

"They'll be deported soon."

"Where?"

He shrugged. "I know nothing about it."

"You must know something."

"Work camps," he mumbled. "In Germany. That's all I know."

"But . . . they're women and children."

He shrugged again.

Isabelle couldn't comprehend it. How could the French gendarmes be doing this to *Parisians*? To women and children? "Children can hardly work, M'sieur. You must have thousands of children in there, and pregnant women. How—"

"Do I look like the mastermind of this? I just do what I'm told. They tell me to arrest the foreign-born Jews in Paris, so I do it. They want the crowd separated—single men to Drancy, families to the Vél d'Hiv. *Voilà!* It's done. Point rifles at them and be prepared to shoot. The government wants all of France's foreign Jews sent east to work camps, and we're starting here."

All of France? Isabelle felt the air rush out of her lungs. Operation Spring Wind. "You mean this isn't just happening in Paris?"

"No. This is just the start."

Vianne had stood in queues all day, in the oppressive summer heat, and for what—a half a pound of dry cheese and a loaf of terrible bread?

"Can we have some strawberry jam today, Maman? It hides the taste of the bread."

As they left the shop, Vianne kept Sophie close to her, tucked against her hip as if she were a much younger child. "Maybe just a little, but we can't go overboard. Remember how terrible the winter was? Another will be coming."

Vianne saw a group of soldiers coming their way, rifles glinting in the sunshine. They marched past, and tanks followed them, grumbling over the cobblestoned street.

"There is a lot going on out here today," Sophie said.

Vianne had been thinking the same thing. The road was full of French police; gendarmes were coming into town in droves.

It was a relief to step into Rachel's quiet, well-tended yard. She looked forward to her visits with Rachel so much. It was really the only time she felt like herself anymore.

At Vianne's knock, Rachel peered out suspiciously, saw who was at the door, and smiled, opening the door wide, letting sunshine stream into the bare house. "Vianne! Sophie! Come in, come in."

"Sophie!" Sarah yelled.

The two girls hugged each other as if they'd been apart for weeks instead of days. It had taken a toll on both of them to be separated while Sophie was sick. Sarah took Sophie by the hand and led her out into the front yard, where they sat beneath an apple tree.

Rachel left the door open so that they could hear them. Vianne uncoiled the floral scarf from around her head and stuffed it into the pocket of her skirt. "I brought you something."

"No, Vianne. We have talked about this," Rachel said. She was wearing a pair of overalls that she'd made from an old shower curtain. Her summer cardigan—once white and now grayed from too many washings and too much wear—hung from the chair back. From here, Vianne could see two points of the yellow star sewn onto the sweater.

Vianne went to the counter in the kitchen and opened the silverware drawer. There was almost nothing left in it—in the two years of the occupation, they had all lost count of the times the Germans had gone door to door "requisitioning" what they needed. How often had Germans broken into the homes at night, taking whatever they wanted? All of it ended up on trains headed east.

Now most of the drawers and closets and trunks in town were empty. All Rachel had left were a few forks and spoons, and a single bread knife. Vianne took the knife over to the table. Withdrawing the bread and cheese from her basket, she carefully cut both in half and returned her portion to the basket. When she looked up again, Rachel had tears in her eyes. "I want to tell you not to give us that. You need it."

"You need it, too."

"I should just rip the damned star off. Then at least I would be allowed to queue up for food when there was still some to be had." There were constantly new restrictions in place for Jewish people: they could no longer own bicycles and were banned from all public places except between three and four P.M., when they were allowed to shop. By then, there was nothing left.

Before Vianne could answer, she heard a motorcycle out on the road. She recognized the sound of it and went to stand in the open doorway.

Rachel squeezed in beside her. "What is he doing here?"

"I'll see," Vianne said.

"I'm coming with you."

Vianne walked through the orchard, past a hummingbird hovering at the roses, to the gate. Opening it, she stepped through, onto the roadside, let Rachel in behind her. Behind them, the gate made a little click, like the snapping of a bone.

"Mesdames," Beck said, doffing his military cap, wedging it under his armpit. "I am sorry to disturb your ladies' time, but I have come to tell you something, Madame Mauriac." He put the slightest emphasis on *you*. It made it sound as if they shared secrets.

"Oh? And what is it, Herr Captain?" Vianne asked.

He glanced left to right and then leaned slightly toward Vianne. "Madame de Champlain should not be at home tomorrow morning," he said quietly.

Vianne thought perhaps he'd translated his intention poorly. "Pardon?"

"Madame de Champlain should not be at home tomorrow," he repeated.

"My husband and I own this house," Rachel said. "Why should I leave?"

"It will not matter, this ownership of the house. Not tomorrow."

"My children—" Rachel started.

Beck finally looked at Rachel. "Your children are of no concern to us. They were born in France. They are not on the list."

List.

A word that was feared now. Vianne said quietly, "What are you telling us?"

"I am telling you that if she is here tomorrow, she will not be here the day after."

"But—"

"If she were my friend, I would find a way to hide her for a day."

"Only for a day?" Vianne asked, studying him closely.

"That is all I came to say, Mesdames, and I should not have done it. I would be . . . punished if word got out. Please, if you are questioned about this later, do not mention my visit." He clicked his heels together, pivoted, and walked away.

Rachel looked at Vianne. They had heard rumors of roundups in Paris—women and children being deported—but no one believed it. How could they? The claims were crazy, impossible—tens of thousands of people taken from their homes in the middle of the night by the French police. And all at once? It couldn't be true. "Do you trust him?"

Vianne considered the question. She surprised herself by saying, "Yes."

"So what do I do?"

"Take the children to the Free Zone. Tonight." Vianne couldn't believe she was thinking it, let alone saying it.

"Last week Madame Durant tried to cross the frontier and she was shot and her children deported."

Vianne would say the same thing in Rachel's place. It was one thing for a woman to run by herself; it was another thing to risk your children's lives. But what if they were risking their lives by staying here?

"You're right. It's too dangerous. But I think you should do as Beck advises. Hide. It is only for a day. Then perhaps we'll know more."

"Where?"

"Isabelle prepared for this and I thought she was a fool." She sighed. "There's a cellar in the barn."

"You know that if you are caught hiding me—"

"*Oui,*" Vianne said sharply. She didn't want to hear it said aloud. *Punishable by death.* "I know."

Vianne slipped a sleeping draught into Sophie's lemonade and put the child to bed early. (Not the sort of thing that made one feel like a good mother, but neither was it all right to take Sophie with them tonight or let her waken alone. Bad choices. That was all there were anymore.) While waiting for her daughter to fall asleep, Vianne paced. She heard every clatter of wind against the shutters, every creaky settling of the timbers of the old house. At just past six o'clock, she dressed in her old gardening overalls and went downstairs.

She found Beck sitting on her divan, an oil lamp lit beside him. He was holding a small, framed portrait of his family. His wife—Hilda, Vianne knew—and his children, Gisela and Wilhelm.

At her arrival, he looked up but didn't stand.

Vianne didn't know quite what to do. She wanted him to be invisible right now, tucked behind the closed door of his room, someone she could completely discount. And yet he had risked his career to help Rachel. How could she ignore that?

"Bad things are happening, Madame. Impossible things. I trained to be a soldier, to fight for my country and make my family proud. It was an honorable choice. What will be thought of us upon our return? What will be thought of me?"

She sat down beside him. "I worry about what Antoine will think of me, too. I should not have given you that list of names. I should have been more frugal with my money. I should have worked harder to keep my job. Perhaps I should have listened to Isabelle more."

"You should not blame yourself. I'm sure your husband would agree. We men are perhaps too quick to reach for our guns."

He turned slightly, his gaze taking in her attire.

She was dressed in her overalls and a black sweater. A black scarf covered her hair. She looked like a housewife version of a spy.

"It is dangerous for her to run," he said.

"And to stay, apparently."

"And there it is," he said. "A terrible dilemma."

"Which is more dangerous, I wonder?" Vianne asked.

She expected no answer and was surprised when he said, "Staying, I think."

Vianne nodded.

"You should not go," he said.

"I can't let her go alone."

Beck considered that. Finally he nodded. "You know the land of Monsieur Frette, where the cows are raised?"

"*Oui.* But—"

"There is a cattle trail behind the barn. It leads to the least manned of the checkpoints. It is a long walk, but one should make the checkpoint before curfew. If someone were wondering about that. Not that I know anyone who is."

"My father, Julien Rossignol, lives in Paris at 57 Avenue de La Bourdonnais. If I . . . didn't come home one day . . ."

"I would see that your daughter made it to Paris."

He rose, taking the picture with him. "I am to bed, Madame."

She stood beside him. "I am afraid to trust you."

"I would be more afraid not to."

They were closer now, ringed together by the meager light.

"Are you a good man, Herr Captain?"

"I used to think so, Madame."

"Thank you," she said.

"Do not thank me yet, Madame."

He left her alone with the light and returned to his room, closing the door firmly behind him.

Vianne sat back down, waiting. At seven thirty, she retrieved the heavy black shawl that hung from a hook by the kitchen door.

Be brave, she thought. *Just this once.*

She covered her head and shoulders with the shawl and went outside.

Rachel and her children were waiting for her behind the barn. A wheelbarrow was beside them; in it Ari lay wrapped in blankets, asleep. Tucked around him were a few possessions Rachel had chosen to take with her. "You have false papers?" Vianne asked.

Rachel nodded. "I don't know how good they are, and they cost me my wedding ring." She looked at Vianne. They communicated everything without speaking aloud.

Are you sure you want to come with us?

I'm sure.

"Why do we have to leave?" Sarah said, looking frightened.

Rachel put a hand on Sarah's head and gazed down at her. "I need you to be strong for me, Sarah. Remember our talk?"

Sarah nodded slowly. "For Ari and Papa."

They crossed the dirt road and pushed their way through the field of hay toward the copse of trees in the distance. Once in the spindly forest, Vianne felt safer, protected somewhat. By the time they arrived at the Frette property, night had fallen. They found the cattle trail that led into a deeper wood, where thick, ropey roots veined the dry ground, causing Rachel to have to push the wheelbarrow hard to keep it moving. Time and again, it thumped up over some root and clattered back down. Ari whimpered in his sleep and greedily sucked his thumb. Vianne could feel the sweat running down her back.

"I have been in need of exercise," Rachel said, breathing heavily.

"And I love a good walk through the woods," Vianne answered. "What about you, M'mselle Sarah, what do you find lovely about our adventure?"

"I'm not wearing that stupid star," Sarah said. "How come Sophie isn't with us? She loves the woods. Remember the scavenger hunts we used to have? She found everything first."

Through a break in the trees up ahead, Vianne saw a flashing light, and then the black-and-white markings of the border crossing.

The gate was illuminated by lights so bright only the enemy would dare use them—or be able to afford to. A German guard stood by, his rifle glinting silver in the unnatural light. There was a small line of people waiting to pass through. Approval would only be granted if the paperwork was in order. If Rachel's false papers didn't work, she and the children would be arrested.

It was real suddenly. Vianne came to a stop. She would have to watch it all from here.

"I'll write if I can," Rachel said.

Vianne's throat tightened. Even if the best happened, she might not hear from her friend for years. Or ever. In this new world, there was no certain way to keep in touch with those you loved.

"Don't give me that look," Rachel said. "We will be together again in no time, drinking champagne and dancing to that jazz music you love."

Vianne wiped the tears from her eyes. "You know I won't be seen with you in public when you start dancing."

Sarah tugged at her sleeve. "T-tell Sophie I said good-bye."

Vianne knelt down and hugged Sarah. She could have held on forever; instead she let go.

She started to reach for Rachel, but her friend backed away. "If I hug you I'll cry and I can't cry."

Vianne's arms dropped heavily to her side.

Rachel reached down for the wheelbarrow. She and her children left the protection of the trees and joined the queue of people at the checkpoint. A man on a bicycle pedaled through and kept going, and then an old woman pushing a flower cart was waved on. Rachel was almost to the front of the queue when a whistle shrieked and someone yelled in German. The guard turned his machine gun on the crowd and opened fire.

Tiny red bursts peppered the dark.

Ra-ta-ta-tat.

A woman screamed as the man beside her crumpled to the ground. The queue instantly dispersed; people ran in all directions.

It happened so fast Vianne couldn't react. She saw Rachel and Sarah running toward her, back to the trees; Sarah in front, Rachel in back with the wheelbarrow.

"Here!" Vianne cried out, her voice lost in the splatter of gunfire.

Sarah dropped to her knees in the grass.

"Sarah!" Rachel cried.

Vianne swooped forward and pulled Sarah into her arms. She carried her into the woods and laid her on the ground, unbuttoning her coat.

The girl's chest was riddled with bullet holes. Blood bubbled up, spilled over, oozing.

Vianne wrenched off her shawl and pressed it to the wounds.

"How is she?" Rachel asked, coming to a breathless stop beside her. "Is that *blood?*" Rachel crumpled to the grass beside her daughter. In the wheelbarrow, Ari started to scream.

Lights flashed at the checkpoint, soldiers gathered together. Dogs started barking.

"We have to go, Rachel," Vianne said. "Now." She clambered to her feet in the blood-slick grass and took Ari out of the wheelbarrow, shoving him at Rachel, who seemed not to understand. Vianne threw everything out of the wheelbarrow and, as carefully as she could, placed Sarah in the rusted metal, with Ari's blanket behind her head. Clutching the handles in her bloody hands, she lifted the back wheels and began pushing. "Come on," she said to Rachel. "We can save her."

Rachel nodded numbly.

Vianne shoved the wheelbarrow forward, over the ropey roots and dirt. Her heart was pounding and fear was a sour taste in her mouth, but she didn't stop or look back. She knew that Rachel was behind her—Ari was screaming—and if anyone else was following them, she didn't want to know.

As they neared Le Jardin, Vianne struggled to push the heavy wheelbarrow through the gully alongside the road and up the hill to the barn. When she finally stopped, the wheelbarrow thumped down to the ground and Sarah moaned in pain.

Rachel put Ari down. Then she lifted Sarah out of the wheelbarrow and gently placed her on the grass. Ari wailed and held his arms out to be held.

Rachel knelt beside Sarah and saw the terrible devastation of Sarah's chest. She looked up at Vianne, gave her a look of such pain and loss that Vianne couldn't breathe. Then Rachel looked down again, and placed a hand on her daughter's pale cheek.

Sarah lifted her head. "Did we make it across the frontier?" Blood bubbled up from her colorless lips, slid down her chin.

"We did," Rachel said. "We did. We are all safe now."

"I was brave," Sarah said, "wasn't I?"

"*Oui*," Rachel said brokenly. "So brave."

"I'm cold," Sarah murmured. She shivered.

Sarah drew in a shuddering breath, exhaled slowly.

"We are going to go have some candy now. And a macaron. I love you, Sarah. And Papa loves you. You are our star." Rachel's voice broke. She was crying now. "Our heart. You know that?"

"Tell Sophie I . . ." Sarah's eyelids fluttered shut. She drew a last, shuddering breath and went still. Her lips parted, but no breath slipped past them.

Vianne knelt down beside Sarah. She felt for a pulse and found none. The silence turned sour, thick; all Vianne could think about was the sound of this child's laughter and how empty the world would be without it. She knew about death, about the grief that ripped you apart and left you broken forever. She couldn't imagine how Rachel was still breathing. If this was any other time, Vianne would sit down beside Rachel, take her hand, and let her cry. Or hold her. Or talk. Or say nothing. Whatever Rachel needed, Vianne would have moved Heaven and Earth to provide; but she couldn't do that now. It was another terrible blow in all of this: They couldn't even take time to grieve.

Vianne needed to be strong for Rachel. "We need to bury her," Vianne said as gently as she could.

"She hates the dark."

"My maman will be with her," Vianne said. "And yours. You and Ari need to go into the cellar. Hide. I'll take care of Sarah."

"How?"

Vianne knew Rachel wasn't asking how to hide in the barn; she was asking how to live after a loss like this, how to pick up one child and let the other go, how to keep breathing after you whisper "good-bye." "I can't leave her."

"You have to. For Ari." Vianne got slowly to her feet, waiting.

Rachel drew in a breath as clattery as broken glass and leaned forward to kiss Sarah's cheek. "I will always love you," she whispered.

At last, Rachel rose. She reached down for Ari, took him in her arms, held him so tightly he started to cry again.

Vianne reached for Rachel's hand and led her friend into the barn and to the cellar. "I will come get you as soon as it's safe."

"Safe," Rachel said dully, staring back through the open barn door.

Vianne moved the car and opened the trapdoor. "There's a lantern down there. And food."

Holding Ari, Rachel climbed down the ladder and disappeared into the darkness. Vianne shut the door on them and replaced the car and then went to the lilac bush her mother had planted thirty years ago. It had spread tall and wide along the wall. Beneath it, almost lost amid the summer greenery, were three small white crosses. Two for the miscarriages she'd suffered and one for the son who'd lived less than a week.

Rachel had stood here beside her as each of her boys was buried. Now Vianne was here to bury her best friend's daughter. Her daughter's best friend. What kind of benevolent God would allow such a thing?

TWENTY-THREE

*I*n the last few moments before dawn, Vianne sat near the mound of fresh-turned earth. She wanted to pray, but her faith felt far away, the remnant of another woman's life.

Slowly, she got to her feet.

As the sky turned lavender and pink—ironically beautiful—she went to her backyard, where the chickens clucked and flapped their wings at her unexpected arrival. She stripped off her bloody clothes, left them in a heap on the ground, and washed up at the pump. Then she took a linen nightdress from the clothesline, put it on, and went inside.

She was bone tired and soul weary, but there was no way she could rest. She lit an oil lamp and sat on the divan. She closed her eyes and tried to imagine Antoine beside her. What would she say to him now? *I don't know the right thing to do anymore. I want to protect Sophie and keep her safe, but what good is safety if she has to grow up in a world where people disappear without a trace because they pray to a different God? If I am arrested . . .*

The door to the guest room opened. She heard Beck coming toward her. He was dressed in his uniform and freshly shaved, and she knew instinctively that he'd been waiting for her to return. Worrying about her.

"You're returned," he said.

She was sure he saw some spatter of blood or dirt somewhere on her, at her temple or on the back of her hand. There was an almost imperceptible pause; she knew he was waiting for her to look at him, to communicate what had happened, but she just sat there. If she opened her mouth she might start screaming. Or if she looked at him she might cry, might demand to know how it was that children could be shot in the dark for nothing.

"Maman?" Sophie said, coming into the room. "You were not in bed when I woke up," she said. "I got scared."

She clasped her hands in her lap. "I am sorry, Sophie."

"Well," Beck said. "I must leave. Good-bye."

As soon as the door closed behind him, Sophie came closer. She looked a little bleary-eyed. Tired. "You're scaring me, Maman. Is something wrong?"

Vianne closed her eyes. She would have to give her daughter this terrible news, and then what? She would hold her daughter and stroke her head and let her cry and she would have to be strong. She was so tired of being strong. "Come, Sophie," she said, rising. "Let's sleep a little longer if we can."

That afternoon, in town, Vianne expected to see soldiers gathering, rifles drawn, police wagons parked in the town square, dogs straining on leashes, black-clad SS officers; something to indicate trouble.

But there was nothing out of the ordinary.

She and Sophie remained in Carriveau all day, standing in queues Vianne knew were a waste of time, walking down one street after another. At first, Sophie talked incessantly. Vianne barely noticed. How could she concentrate on normal conversation with Rachel and Ari hiding in her cellar and Sarah gone?

"Can we leave now, Maman?" Sophie said at nearly three o'clock. "There's nothing more to be had. We're wasting our time."

Beck must have made a mistake. Or perhaps he was simply being overly cautious.

Certainly they would not round up and arrest Jewish people at this hour. Everyone knew that arrests were never made during mealtimes. The Nazis were much too punctual and organized for that—and they loved their French food and wine.

"*Oui*, Sophie. We can go home."

They headed out of town. Vianne remained on alert, but if anything, the road was less crowded than usual. The airfield was quiet.

"Can Sarah come over?" Sophie asked as Vianne eased the broken gate open.

Sarah.

Vianne glanced down at Sophie.

"You look sad," her daughter said.

"I am sad," Vianne said quietly.

"Are you thinking of Papa?"

Vianne drew in a deep breath and released it. Then she said gently, "Come with me," and led Sophie to a spot beneath the apple tree, where they sat together.

"You are scaring me, Maman."

Vianne knew she was handling it badly already, but she had no idea how to do this. Sophie was too old for lies and too young for the truth. Vianne couldn't tell her that Sarah had been shot trying to cross the border. Her daughter might say the wrong thing to the wrong person.

"Maman?"

Vianne cupped Sophie's thin face in her hands. "Sarah died last night," she said gently.

"Died? She wasn't sick."

Vianne steeled herself. "It happens that way sometimes. God takes you unexpectedly. She's gone to Heaven. To be with her grandmère, and yours."

Sophie pulled away, got to her feet, backed away. "Do you think I'm stupid?"

"Wh-what do you mean?"

"She's Jewish."

Vianne hated what she saw in her daughter's eyes right now. There was nothing young in her gaze—no innocence, no naïveté, no hope. Not even grief. Just anger.

A better mother would shape that anger into loss and then, at last, into the kind of memory of love one can sustain, but Vianne was too empty to be a good mother right now. She could think of no words that weren't a lie or useless.

She ripped away the lacy trim at the end of her sleeve. "You see that bit of red yarn in the tree branch over our heads?"

Sophie looked up. The yarn had lost a bit of color, faded, but still it showed up against the brown branches and green leaves and unripened apples. She nodded.

"I put that there to remember your papa. Why don't you tie one for Sarah and we'll think of her every time we are outside."

"But Papa is not dead!" Sophie said. "Are you lying to—"

"No. No. We remember the missing as much as the lost, don't we?"

Sophie took the thready coil of lace in her hand. Looking a little unsteady on her feet, she tied the strand onto the same branch.

Vianne ached for Sophie to come back, turn to her, reach out for a hug, but her daughter just stood there, staring at the scrap of lace, her eyes bright with tears. "It won't always be like this" was all Vianne could think of to say.

"I don't believe you."

Sophie looked at her at last. "I'm taking a nap."

Vianne could only nod. Ordinarily she would have been undone by this tension with her daughter, overwhelmed by a sense of having failed. Now, she just sighed and got to her feet. She wiped the grass from her skirt and headed up to the barn. Inside, she rolled the Renault forward and opened the cellar door. "Rach? It's me."

"Thank God" came a whispery voice from the darkness. Rachel climbed up the creaking ladder and emerged into the dusty light, holding Ari.

"What happened?" Rachel asked tiredly.

"Nothing."

"Nothing?"

"I went to town. Everything seems normal. Maybe Beck was being overly cautious, but I think you should spend one more night down there."

Rachel's face was drawn, tired-looking. "I'll need diapers. And a quick bath. Ari and I both smell." The toddler started to cry. She pushed the damp curls away from her sweat-dampened forehead and murmured to him in a soft, lilting voice.

They left the barn and headed for Rachel's house next door.

They were nearly to the front door when a French police car pulled up out front. Paul got out of the car and strode into the yard, carrying his rifle. "Are you Rachel de Champlain?" he asked.

Rachel frowned. "You know I am."

"You are being deported. Come with me."

Rachel tightened her hold on Ari. "Don't take my son—"

"He is not on the list," Paul said.

Vianne grabbed the man's sleeve. "You can't do this, Paul. She is French!"

"She's a Jew." He pointed his rifle at Rachel. "Move."

Rachel started to say something, but Paul silenced her; he grabbed her by the arm, yanked her out to the road, and forced her into the backseat of his automobile.

Vianne meant to stay where she was—safe—intended to, but the next thing she knew she was running alongside the automobile, banging on the bonnet, begging to be let inside. Paul slammed on the brakes, let her climb into the backseat, and then he stomped on the gas.

"Go," Rachel said as they passed Le Jardin. "This is no place for you."

"This is no place for anyone," Vianne said.

Even a week ago, she might have let Rachel go alone. She might have turned away—with regret, probably, and guilt, certainly—but she would have thought that protecting Sophie was more important than anything else.

Last night had changed her. She still felt fragile and frightened, maybe more so, but she was angry now, too.

In town, there were barricades on a dozen streets. Police wagons were everywhere, disgorging people with yellow stars on their chests, herding them toward the train station, where cattle cars waited. There were hundreds of people; they must have come from all the communes in the area.

Paul parked and opened the car doors. Vianne and Rachel and Ari stepped into the crowd of Jewish women and children and old men making their way to the platform.

A train waited, puffing black smoke into the already hot air. Two German soldiers were standing on the platform. One of them was Beck. He was holding a whip. A *whip*.

But it was French police who were in charge of the roundup; they were forcing people into lines and shoving them onto the cattle cars. Men went into one cattle car; women and children in the other.

Up ahead, a woman holding a baby tried to run. A gendarme shot her in the back. She pitched to the ground, dead; the baby rolled to the boots of the gendarme holding a smoking gun.

Rachel stopped, turned to Vianne. "Take my son," she whispered.

The crowd jostled them.

"Take him. Save him," Rachel pleaded.

Vianne didn't hesitate. She knew now that no one could be neutral— not anymore—and as afraid as she was of risking Sophie's life, she was suddenly more afraid of letting her daughter grow up in a world where good people did nothing to stop evil, where a good woman could turn her back on a friend in need. She reached for the toddler, took him in her arms.

"You!" A gendarme stabbed Rachel in the shoulder with the butt of his rifle so hard she stumbled. "Move!"

She looked at Vianne, and the universe of their friendship was in her eyes—the secrets they'd shared, the promises they'd made and kept, the dreams for their children that bound them as neatly as sisters.

"Get out of here," Rachel cried hoarsely. "Go."

Vianne backed away. Before she knew it, she had turned and begun shoving her way through the crowd, away from the platform and the sol- diers and the dogs, away from the smell of fear and the crack of whips and the sound of women wailing and babies crying. She didn't allow herself to slow until she reached the end of the platform. There, holding Ari closely, she turned around.

Rachel stood in the black, yawning entrance of a cattle car, her face and hands still smeared with her daughter's blood. She scanned the crowd, saw Vianne, and raised her bloody hand in the air, and then she was gone, shoved back by the women stumbling in around her. The door to the cattle car clanged shut.

❧

Vianne collapsed onto the divan. Ari was crying uncontrollably and his diaper was wet and he smelled of urine. She should get up, take care of him, do something, but she couldn't move. She felt weighed down by loss, suffocated by it.

Sophie came into the living room. "Why do you have Ari?" she said in a quiet, frightened voice. "Where's Madame de Champlain?"

"She is gone," Vianne said. She hadn't the strength to fabricate a lie, and what was the good of one anyway?

There was no way to protect her daughter from all of the evil around them.

No way.

Sophie would grow up knowing too much. Knowing fear and loss and probably hatred.

"Rachel was born in Romania," Vianne said tightly. "That—along with being Jewish—was her crime. The Vichy government doesn't care that she has lived in France for twenty-five years and married a Frenchman and that he fought for France. So they deported her."

"Where will they take her?"

"I don't know."

"Will she come back after the war?"

Yes. No. I hope so. What answer would a good mother give?

"I hope so."

"And Ari?" Sophie asked.

"He will stay with us. He wasn't on the list. I guess our government believes children can raise themselves."

"But Maman, what do we—"

"Do? What do we *do*? I have no idea." She sighed. "For now, you watch the baby. I'll go next door and get his crib and clothes."

Vianne was almost to the door when Sophie said, "What about Captain Beck?"

Vianne stopped dead. She remembered seeing him on the platform with a whip in his hand; a whip he cracked to herd women and children onto a cattle car. "*Oui,*" she said. "What about Captain Beck?"

❧

Vianne washed her blood-soaked clothes and hung them to dry in the back-yard, trying not to notice how red the soapy water was when she splashed it across the grass. She made Sophie and Ari supper (What had she made? She couldn't remember.) and put them to bed, but once the house was quiet and dark, she couldn't suppress her emotions. She was angry—howlingly so—and devastated.

She couldn't stand how dark and ugly her thoughts were, how bottomless her anger and grief. She ripped the pretty lace from her collar and stumbled outside, remembering when Rachel had given her this blouse. Three years ago.

It's what everyone's wearing in Paris.

The apple trees spread their arms above her. It took her two tries to tie the scrap of fabric to the knobby wooden branch between Antoine's and Sarah's, and when she'd done it, she stepped back.

Sarah.

Rachel.

Antoine.

The scraps of color blurred; that was when she realized she was crying.

"Please God," she began to pray, looking up at the bits of fabric and lace and yarn, tied around the knobby branch, interspersed with unripe apples. What good were prayers now, when her loved ones were gone?

She heard a motorcycle come up the road and park outside Le Jardin.

Moments later: "Madame?"

She spun to face him. "Where's your whip, Herr Captain?"

"You were there?"

"How does it feel to whip a Frenchwoman?"

"You can't think I would do that, Madame. It sickens me."

"And yet there you were."

"As were you. This war has put us all where we do not want to be."

"Less so for you Germans."

"I tried to help her," he said.

At that, Vianne felt the rage go out of her; her grief returned. He *had* tried to save Rachel. If only they had listened to him and kept her hidden longer. She swayed. Beck reached out and steadied her.

"You said to hide her in the morning. She was in that terrible cellar all day. By afternoon, I thought . . . everything seemed normal."

"Von Richter adjusted the timetable. There was a problem with the trains."

The trains.

Rachel waving good-bye.

Vianne looked up at him. "Where are they taking her?"

It was the first substantive question she'd ever asked him.

"To a work camp in Germany."

"I hid her all day," Vianne said again, as if it mattered now.

"The Wehrmacht aren't in control anymore. It's the Gestapo and the SS. They're more . . . brutes than soldiers."

"Why were you there?"

"I was following orders. Where are her children?"

"Your Germans shot Sarah in the back at the frontier checkpoint."

"*Mein Gott,*" he muttered.

"I have her son. Why wasn't Ari on the list?"

"He was born in France and is under fourteen. They are not deporting French Jews." He looked at her. "Yet."

Vianne caught her breath. "Will they come for Ari?"

"I believe that soon they will deport all Jews, regardless of age or place of birth. And when they do, it will become dangerous to have *any* Jew in your home."

"Children, deported. Alone." The horror of it was unbelievable, even after what she'd already seen. "I promised Rachel I'd keep him safe. Will you turn me in?" she asked.

"I am not a monster, Vianne."

It was the first time he'd ever used her Christian name.

He moved closer. "I want to protect you," he said.

It was the worst thing he could have said. She had felt lonely for years, but now she truly *was* alone.

He touched her upper arm, almost a caress, and she felt it in every part of her body, like an electrical charge. Unable to help herself, she looked at him.

He was close to her, just a kiss away. All she had to do was give him the slightest encouragement—a breath, a nod, a touch—and he would close the gap between them. For a moment, she forgot who she was and what had happened today; she longed to be soothed, to forget. She leaned the smallest bit forward, enough to smell his breath, feel it on her lips, and then she remembered—all at once, in a whoosh of anger—and she pushed him away so he stumbled.

She scrubbed her lips, as if they'd touched his.

"We can't," she said.

"Of course not."

But when he looked at her—and she looked at him—they both knew that there was something worse than kissing the wrong person.

It was wanting to.

TWENTY-FOUR

*S*ummer ended. Hot golden days gave way to washed-out skies and falling rain. Isabelle was so focused on the escape route that she hardly noticed the change in weather.

On a chilly October afternoon, she stepped out of the train carriage in a crowd of passengers, holding a bouquet of autumn flowers.

As she walked up the boulevard, German motorcars clogged the street, honking loudly. Soldiers strode confidently among the cowed, drab Parisians. Swastika flags flapped in the wintry wind. She hurried down the Métro steps.

The tunnel was crowded with people and papered in Nazi propaganda that demonized the Brits and Jews and made the Führer the answer to every question.

Suddenly, the air raid sirens howled. The electricity snapped off, plunging everyone into darkness. She heard people muttering and babies crying and old men coughing. From far away, she could hear the thump and grumble of explosions. It was probably Boulogne-Billancourt—again—and why not? Renault was making lorries for the Germans.

When the all clear finally sounded, no one moved until moments later, when the electricity and lights came back on.

Isabelle was almost to the train when a whistle blared.

She froze. Nazi soldiers, accompanied by French collaborators, moved through the tunnel, talking to one another, pointing at people, pulling them out to the perimeter, forcing them to their knees.

A rifle appeared in front of her.

"Papers," the German said.

Isabelle clutched the flowers in one hand and fumbled nervously with her purse with the other. She had a message for Anouk wrapped within the bouquet. It was not unexpected, of course, this search. Since the Allied successes in North Africa had begun, the Germans stopped people constantly, demanding papers. In the streets, the shops, the train stations, the churches. There was no safety anywhere. She handed over her false *carte d'identité.* "I am meeting a friend of my mother's for lunch."

The Frenchman sidled up to the German and perused the papers. He shook his head and the German handed Isabelle her papers and said, "Go."

Isabelle smiled quickly, nodded a thank-you, and hurried for the train, slipping into an open carriage just as the doors slid shut.

By the time she exited in the sixteenth arrondissement, her calm had returned. A wet fog clung to the streets, obscuring the buildings and the barges moving slowly on the Seine. Sounds were amplified by the haze, turned strange. Somewhere, a ball was bouncing (probably boys playing in the street). One of the barges honked its horn and the noise lingered.

At the avenue, she turned the corner and went to a bistro—one of the few with its lights on. A nasty wind ruffled the awning. She passed the empty tables and went to the outside counter, where she ordered a *café au lait* (without coffee or milk, of course).

"Juliette? Is that you?"

Isabelle saw Anouk and smiled. "Gabrielle. How lovely to see you." Isabelle handed Anouk the flowers.

Anouk ordered a coffee. While they stood there, sipping coffee in the icy weather, Anouk said, "I spoke with my uncle Henri yesterday. He misses you."

"Is he unwell?"

"No. No. Quite the opposite. He is planning a party for next Tuesday night. He asked me to extend an invitation."

"Shall I take him a gift for you?"

"No, but a letter would be nice. Here, I have it ready for you."

Isabelle took the letter and slipped it into the lining of her purse.

Anouk looked at her. Smoky shadows circled her eyes. New lines had begun to crease her cheeks and brow. This life in the shadows had begun to take a toll on her.

"Are you all right, my friend?" Isabelle asked.

Anouk's smile was tired but true. "*Oui.*" She paused. "I saw Gaëtan last night. He will be at the meeting in Carriveau."

"Why tell me?"

"Isabelle, you are the most transparent person I have ever met. Every thought and feeling you have reveals itself in your eyes. Are you unaware how often you have mentioned him to me?"

"Really? I thought I had hidden it."

"It's nice, actually. It reminds me of what we are fighting for. Simple things: a girl and a boy and their future." She kissed Isabelle's cheeks. Then she whispered, "He mentions you as well."

Luckily for Isabelle, it was raining in Carriveau on this late October day.

No one paid attention to people in weather like this, not even the Germans. She flipped her hood up and held her coat shut at her throat; even so, rain pelted her face and slid in cold streaks down her neck as she hauled her bicycle off the train and walked it across the platform.

On the outskirts of town, she climbed aboard. Choosing a lesser-used alley, she pedaled into Carriveau, bypassing the square. On a rainy autumn day like this, there were few people out and about; only women and children standing in food queues, their coats and hats dripping rainwater. The Germans were mostly inside.

By the time she reached the Hôtel Bellevue, she was exhausted. She dismounted, locked her bicycle to a streetlamp, and went inside.

A bell jangled overhead, announcing her arrival to the German soldiers who were seated in the lobby, drinking their afternoon coffees.

"M'mselle," one of the officers said, reaching for a flaky, golden *pain au chocolat.* "You are soaking wet."

"These French do not know enough to get out of the rain."

They laughed at that.

She kept smiling and walked past them. At the hotel's front desk, she rang the bell.

Henri came out of the back room, holding a tray of coffees. He saw her and nodded.

"One moment, Madame," Henri said, gliding past her, carrying the tray to a table where two SS agents sat like spiders in their black uniforms.

When Henri returned to the front desk, he said, "Madame Gervaise, welcome back. It is good to see you again. Your room is ready, of course. If you'll follow me . . ."

She nodded and followed Henri down the narrow hallway and up the stairs to the second floor. There, he pressed a skeleton key into a lock, gave it a twist, and opened the door to reveal a small bedroom with a single bed, a nightstand, and a lamp. He led her inside, kicked the door shut with his foot, and took her in his arms.

"Isabelle," he said, pulling her close. "It is good to see you." He released her and stepped back. "With Romainville . . . I worried."

Isabelle lowered her wet hood. "*Oui.*" In the past two months, the Nazis had cracked down on what they called saboteurs and resisters. They had finally begun to see the role women were playing in this war and had imprisoned more than two hundred French women in Romainville.

She unbuttoned her coat and draped it over the end of the bed. Reaching into the lining, she pulled out an envelope and handed it to Henri. "Here you go," she said, giving him money that had come from MI9. His hotel was one of the key safe houses their group maintained. Isabelle loved that they housed Brits and Yanks and resisters right under the Nazis' noses. Tonight she would be a guest in this smallest of rooms.

She pulled out a chair from behind a scarred writing desk and sat down. "The meeting is set for tonight?"

"Eleven P.M. In the abandoned barn on the Angeler farm."

"What's it about?"

"I'm not in the know." He sat down on the end of the bed. She could tell by the look on his face that he was going to get serious and she groaned.

"I hear the Nazis are desperate to find the Nightingale. Word is that they're trying to infiltrate the escape route."

"I know this, Henri." She lifted one eyebrow. "I hope you are not going to tell me that it's dangerous."

"You are going too often, Isabelle. How many trips have you made?"

"Twenty-four."

Henri shook his head. "No wonder they are desperate to find you. We hear word of another escape route, running through Marseille and Perpignan, that is having success, too. There is going to be trouble, Isabelle."

She was surprised by how much his concern moved her and how nice it was to hear her own name. It felt good to be Isabelle Rossignol again, even if only for a few moments, and to sit with someone who knew her. So much of her life was spent hiding and on the run, in safe houses with strangers.

Still, she saw no reason to talk about this. The escape route was invaluable and worth the risk they were taking. "You are keeping an eye on my sister, *oui?*"

"*Oui.*"

"The Nazi still billets there?"

Henri's gaze slid away from hers.

"What is it?"

"Vianne was fired from her teaching post some time ago."

"Why? Her students love her. She's an excellent teacher."

"The rumor is that she questioned a Gestapo officer."

"That doesn't sound like Vianne. So she has no income. What is she living on?"

Henri looked uncomfortable. "There is gossip."

"Gossip?"

"About her and the Nazi."

❦

All summer long, Vianne hid Rachel's son in Le Jardin. She made sure never to venture out with him, not even to garden. Without papers, she couldn't pretend he was anyone other than Ariel de Champlain. She had to let Sophie stay at home with the child, and so each journey to town was a nerve-wracking event that couldn't be over soon enough. She told everyone she could think of—shopkeepers, nuns, villagers—that Rachel had been deported with both her children.

It was all she could think of to do.

Today, after a long, slogging day standing in line only to be told there was nothing left, Vianne left town feeling defeated. There were rumors of more deportations, more roundups, happening all over France. Thousands of French Jews were being held at internment camps.

At home, she hung her wet cloak on an exterior hook by the front door. She had no real hope that it would dry out before tomorrow, but at least it wouldn't drip all over her floor. She stepped out of her muddy rubber boots by the door and went into the house. As usual, Sophie was standing by the door, waiting for her.

"I'm fine," Vianne said.

Sophie nodded solemnly. "So are we."

"Will you give Ari a bath while I make supper?"

Sophie scooped Ari into her arms and left the room.

Vianne uncoiled the scarf from her hair and hung it up. Then she set her basket in the sink to dry out and went down to the pantry, where she chose a sausage and some undersized, softening potatoes and onions.

Back in the kitchen, she lit the stove and preheated her black cast-iron skillet. Adding a drop of the precious oil, she browned the sausage.

Vianne stared down at the meat, breaking it up with her wooden spoon, watching it turn from pink to gray to a nice, crusty brown. When it was crispy, she added cubed potatoes and diced onions and garlic. The garlic popped and browned and released its scent into the air.

"That smells delicious."

"Herr Captain," she said quietly. "I didn't hear your motorcycle."

"M'mselle Sophie let me in."

She turned down the flame on the stove and covered the pan, then faced him. By tacit agreement, they both pretended that the night in the orchard had never happened. Neither had mentioned it, and yet it was in the air between them always.

Things had changed that night, subtly. He ate supper with them most nights now; mostly food that he brought home—never large amounts, just a ham slice or a bag of flour or a few sausages. He spoke openly of his wife and children, and she talked about Antoine. All their words were designed to reinforce a wall that had already been breached. He repeatedly offered— most kindly—to mail Vianne's care packages to Antoine, which she filled with whatever small items she could spare—old winter gloves that were too big, cigarettes Beck left behind, a precious jar of jam.

Vianne made sure never to be alone with Beck. That was the biggest change. She didn't go out to the backyard at night or stay up after Sophie went to bed. She didn't trust herself to be alone with him.

"I have brought you a gift," he said.

He held out a set of papers. A birth certificate for a baby born in June of 1939 to Etienne and Aimée Mauriac. A boy named Daniel Antoine Mauriac.

Vianne looked at Beck. Had she told him that she and Antoine had wanted to name a son Daniel? She must have, although she didn't remember it.

"It is unsafe to house Jewish children now. Or it will be very soon."

"You have taken such a risk for him. For us," she said.

"For you," he said quietly. "And they are false papers, Madame. Remember that. To go along with the story that you adopted him from a relative."

"I will never tell them they came from you."

"It is not myself I worry about, Madame. Ari must become Daniel immediately. Completely. And you must be extremely careful. The Gestapo and the SS are . . . brutes. The Allied victories in Africa are hitting us hard. And this final solution for the Jews . . . it is an evil impossible to comprehend. I . . ." He paused, gazed down at her. "I want to protect you."

"You have," she said, looking up at him.

He started to move toward her, and she to him, even as she knew it was a mistake.

Sophie came running into the kitchen. "Ari is hungry, Maman. He keeps complaining."

Beck came to a stop. Reaching past her—brushing her arm with his hand—he picked up a fork on the counter. Taking it, he speared one perfect bite of sausage, a crispy brown cube of potato, a chunk of carmelized onion.

As he ate it, he stared down at her. He was so close now she could feel his breath on her cheek. "You are a most amazing cook, Madame."

"*Merci,*" she said in a tight voice.

He stepped back. "I regret I cannot stay for supper, Madame. I must away."

Vianne tore her gaze away from him and smiled at Sophie. "Set the table for three," she said.

❦

Later, while supper simmered on the stove, Vianne gathered the children together on their bed. "Sophie, Ari, come here. I need to speak with you."

"What is it, Maman?" Sophie asked, looking worried already.

"They are deporting French-born Jews." She paused. "Children, too."

Sophie drew in a sharp breath and looked at three-year-old Ari, who bounced happily on the bed. He was too young to learn a new identity. She could tell him his name was Daniel Mauriac from now until forever and he wouldn't understand why. If he believed in his mother's return, and waited for that, sooner or later he would make a mistake that would get him deported, maybe one that would get them all killed. She couldn't risk that. She would have to break his heart to protect them all.

Forgive me, Rachel.

She and Sophie exchanged a pained look. They both knew what had to be done, but how could one mother do this to another woman's child?

"Ari," she said quietly, taking his face in her hands. "Your maman is with the angels in Heaven. She won't be coming back."

He stopped bouncing. "What?"

"She's gone forever," Vianne said again, feeling her own tears rise and fall. She would say it over and over until he believed it. "I am your maman now. And you will be called Daniel."

He frowned, chewing noisily on the inside of his mouth, splaying his fingers as if he were counting. "You said she was coming back."

Vianne hated to say it. "She's not. She's gone. Like the sick baby rabbit we lost last month, remember?" They had buried it in the yard with great ceremony.

"Gone like the bunny?" Tears filled his brown eyes, spilled over. His mouth trembled. Vianne took him in her arms and held him and rubbed his back. But she couldn't soothe him enough, nor could she let him go. At last, she eased back enough to look at him. "Do you understand . . . Daniel?"

"You'll be my brother," Sophie said, her voice unsteady. "Truly."

Vianne felt her heart break, but she knew there was no other way to keep Rachel's son safe. She prayed that he was young enough to forget he was ever Ari, and the sadness of that prayer was overwhelming. "Say it," she said evenly. "Tell me your name."

"Daniel," he said, obviously confused, trying to please.

Vianne made him say it a dozen times that night, while they ate their supper of sausage and potatoes and later, when they washed the dishes and dressed for bed. She prayed that this ruse would be enough to save him, that his papers would pass inspection. Never again would she call him Ari or even think of him as Ari. Tomorrow, she would cut his hair as short as possible. Then she would go to town and tell everyone (that gossip Hélène Ruelle would be first) of the child she'd adopted from a dead cousin in Nice.

God help them all.

TWENTY-FIVE

*I*sabelle crept through the empty streets of Carriveau dressed in black, her golden hair covered. It was after curfew. A meager moon occasionally cast light on the uneven cobblestones; more often, it was obscured by clouds.

She listened for footsteps and lorry motors and froze when she heard either. At the end of town, she climbed over a rose-covered wall, heedless of the thorns, and dropped into a wet, black field of hay. She was halfway to the rendezvous point when three aeroplanes roared overhead, so low in the sky the trees shivered and the ground shook. Machine guns fired at one another, bursts of sound and light.

The smaller aeroplane banked and swerved. She saw the insignia of America on the underside of its wing as it banked left and climbed. Moments later, she heard the whistling of a bomb—the inhuman, piercing wail—and then something exploded.

The airfield. They were bombing it.

The aeroplanes roared overhead again. There was another round of gunfire and the American aeroplane was hit. Smoke roiled out. A screaming sound filled the night; the aeroplane plummeted toward the ground, twirled, its wings catching the moonlight, reflecting it.

It crashed hard enough to rattle Isabelle's bones and shake the ground beneath her feet; steel hitting dirt, rivets popping from metal, roots being torn up. The broken aeroplane skidded through the forest, breaking trees as if they were matchsticks. The smell of smoke was overwhelming, and then in a giant *whoosh,* the aeroplane burst into flames.

In the sky, a parachute appeared, swinging back and forth, the man suspended beneath it looking as small as a comma.

Isabelle cut through the swath of burning trees. Smoke stung her eyes. Where was he?

A glimpse of white caught her eye and she ran toward it.

The limp parachute lay across the scrubby ground, the airman attached to it.

Isabelle heard the sound of voices—they weren't far away—and the crunching of footsteps. She hoped to God it was her colleagues, coming for the meeting, but there was no way to know. The Nazis would be busy at the airfield, but not for long.

She skidded to her knees, unhooked the airman's parachute, gathered it up, and ran with it as far as she dared, burying it as best she could beneath a pile of dead leaves. Then she ran back to the pilot and grabbed him by the wrists and dragged him deeper into the woods.

"You'll have to stay quiet. Do you understand me? I'll come back, but you need to lie still and be quiet."

"You . . . betcha," he said, his voice barely a whisper.

Isabelle covered him with leaves and branches, but when she stood back, she saw her footprints in the mud, each one oozing with black water now, and the rutted drag marks she'd made hauling him over here. Black smoke rolled past her, engulfed her. The fire was getting closer, burning brighter. "*Merde,*" she muttered.

There were voices. People yelling.

She tried to rub her hands clean but the mud just smeared and smeared, marking her.

Three shapes came out of the woods, moving toward her.

"Isabelle," a man said. "Is that you?"

A torchlight flicked on, revealing Henri and Didier. And Gaëtan.

"You found the pilot?" Henri asked.

Isabelle nodded. "He's wounded."

Dogs barked in the distance. The Nazis were coming.

Didier glanced behind them. "We haven't much time."

"We'll never make it to town," Henri said.

Isabelle made a split-second decision. "I know somewhere close we can hide him."

❧

"This is not a good idea," Gaëtan said.

"Hurry," Isabelle said harshly. They were in the barn at Le Jardin now, with the door shut behind them. The airman lay slumped on the dirty floor, unconscious, his blood smearing across Didier's coat and gloves. "Push the car forward."

Henri and Didier pushed the Renault forward and then lifted the cellar door. It creaked in protest and fell forward and banged into the car's fender.

Isabelle lit an oil lamp and held it in one hand as she felt her way down the wobbly ladder. Some of the provisions she'd left had been used.

She lifted the lamp. "Bring him down."

The men exchanged a worried look.

"I don't know about this," Henri said.

"What choice do we have?" Isabelle snapped. "Now bring him down."

Gaëtan and Henri carried the unconscious airman down into the dark, dank cellar and laid him on the mattress, which made a rustling, whispery sound beneath his weight.

Henri gave her a worried look. Then he climbed out of the cellar and stood above them. "Come on, Gaëtan."

Gaëtan looked at Isabelle. "We'll have to move the car back into place. You won't be able to get out of here until we come for you. If something happened to us, no one would know you were here." She could tell he wanted to touch her, and she ached for it. But they stood where they were, their arms at their sides. "The Nazis will be relentless in their search for this airman. If you're caught . . ."

She tilted her chin, trying to hide how scared she was. "Don't let me be caught."

"You think I don't want to keep you safe?"

"I know you do," she said quietly.

Before he could answer, Henri said, "Come on, Gaëtan," from above. "We need to find a doctor and figure out how to get them out of here to-morrow."

Gaëtan stepped back. The whole world seemed to lie in that small space between them. "When we come back, we'll knock three times and whistle, so don't shoot us."

"I'll try not to," she said.

He paused. "Isabelle . . ."

She waited, but he had no more to say, just her name, spoken with the kind of regret that had become common. With a sigh, he turned and climbed up the ladder.

Moments later, the trapdoor banged shut. She heard the boards over-head groan as the Renault was rolled back into place.

And then, silence.

Isabelle started to panic. It was the locked bedroom again; Madame Doom slamming the door, clicking the lock, telling her to shut up and quit asking for things.

She couldn't get out of here, not even in an emergency.

Stop it. Be calm. You know what needs to be done. She went over to the shelv-ing, pushed her father's shotgun aside, and retrieved the box of medical supplies. A quick inventory revealed scissors, a needle and thread, alcohol, bandages, chloroform, Benzedrine tablets, and adhesive tape.

She knelt beside the airman and set the lamp down on the floor beside her. Blood soaked the chest of his flight suit, and it took great effort to peel the fabric away. When she did, she saw the giant, gaping hole in his chest and knew there was nothing she could do.

She sat beside him, holding his hand until he took one last, troubled breath; then his breathing stopped. His mouth slowly gaped open.

She gently eased the dog tags from around his neck. They would need to be hidden. She looked down at them. "Lieutenant Keith Johnson," she said.

Isabelle blew out the lamp and sat in the dark with a dead man.

The next morning, Vianne dressed in denim overalls and a flannel shirt of Antoine's that she had cut down to fit her. She was so thin these days that still the shirt overwhelmed her slim frame. She would have to take it in again. Her latest care package to Antoine sat on the kitchen counter, ready to be mailed.

Sophie had had a restless night, so Vianne let her sleep. She went downstairs to make coffee and almost ran into Captain Beck, who was pacing the living room. "Oh. Herr Captain. I am sorry."

He seemed not to hear her. She had never seen him look so agitated. His usually pomaded hair was untended; a lock kept falling in his face and he cursed repeatedly as he brushed it away. He was wearing his gun, which he never did in the house.

He strode past her, his hands fisted at his sides. Anger contorted his handsome face, made him almost unrecognizable. "An aeroplane went down near here last night," he said, facing her at last. "An American aeroplane. The one they call a Mustang."

"I thought you wanted their aeroplanes to go down. Isn't that why you shoot at them?"

"We searched all night and didn't find a pilot. Someone is hiding him."

"*Hiding* him? Oh, I doubt that. Most likely he died."

"Then there would be a body, Madame. We found a parachute but no body."

"But who would be so foolish?" Vianne said. "Don't you . . . execute people for that?"

"Swiftly."

Vianne had never heard him speak in such a way. It made her draw back, and remember the whip he'd held on the day Rachel and the others were deported.

"Forgive my manner, Madame. But we have shown you all our best behaviors, and this is what we get from many of you French. Lies and betrayal and sabotage."

Vianne's mouth dropped open in shock.

He looked at her, saw how she was staring at him, and he tried to smile. "Forgive me again. I don't mean you, of course. The Kommandant is blaming me for this failure to find the airman. I am charged with doing better today." He went to the front door, opened it. "If I do not . . ."

Through the open door, she saw a glimpse of gray-green in her yard. Soldiers. "Good day, Madame."

Vianne followed him as far as the front step.

"Lock and close all the doors, Madame. This pilot may be desperate. You wouldn't want him to break into your home."

Vianne nodded numbly.

Beck joined his entourage of soldiers and took the lead. Their dogs barked loudly, strained forward, sniffing at the ground along the base of the broken wall.

Vianne glanced up the hill and saw that the barn door was partially open. "Herr Captain!" she called out.

The captain stopped; so did his men. The snarling dogs strained at their leashes.

And then she thought of Rachel. This is where Rachel would come if she'd escaped.

"N-nothing, Herr Captain," Vianne called out.

He nodded brusquely and led his men up the road.

Vianne slipped into the boots by the door. As soon as the soldiers were out of sight, she hurried up the hill toward the barn. In her haste, she slipped twice in the wet grass and nearly fell. Righting herself at the last minute, she took a deep breath and opened the barn door all the way.

She noticed right away that the car had been moved.

"I'm coming, Rachel!" she said. She put the car in neutral and rolled it forward until the cellar door was revealed. Squatting down, she felt for the flat metal handle and lifted the hatch door. When it was high, she let it bang against the car fender.

She got a lantern, lit it, and peered down into the dark cellar. "Rach?"

"Go away, Vianne. NOW."

"Isabelle?" Vianne descended the ladder, saying, "Isabelle, what are—" She dropped to the ground and turned, the lantern in her hand swinging light.

Her smile faded. Isabelle's dress was covered in blood, her blond hair was a mess—full of leaves and twigs—and her face was so scratched it looked like she'd gone running in a blackberry patch.

But that wasn't the worst of it.

"The pilot," Vianne whispered, staring at the man lying on the misshapen mattress. It scared her so much she backed into the shelving. Something clanged to the ground and rolled. "The one they're looking for."

"You shouldn't have come down here."

"I am the one who shouldn't be here? You *fool.* Do you know what they'll do to us if they find him here? How could you bring this danger to my house?"

"I'm sorry. Just close the cellar door and put the car back in place. Tomorrow when you wake up, we'll be gone."

"You're *sorry,*" Vianne said. Anger swept through her. How dare her sister do this thing, put Sophie and her at risk? And now there was Ari here, who still didn't understand that he needed to be Daniel. "You'll get us all killed." Vianne backed away, reached for the ladder. She had to put as much distance as she could between herself and this airman . . . and her reckless, selfish sister. "Be gone by tomorrow morning, Isabelle. And don't come back."

Isabelle had the nerve to look wounded. "But—"

"Don't," Vianne snapped. "I'm done making excuses for you. I was mean to you as a girl, Maman died, Papa is a drunk, Madame Dumas treated you badly. All of it is the truth, and I have longed to be a better sister to you, but that stops here. You are as thoughtless and reckless as always, only now you will get people killed. I can't let you endanger Sophie. Do not come back. You are not welcome here. If you return, I will turn you in myself." On that, Vianne clambered up the ladder and slammed the cellar door shut behind her.

⁂

Vianne had to keep busy or she would fall into a full-blown panic. She woke the children and fed them a light breakfast and got started on her chores.

After harvesting the last of the autumn's vegetables, she pickled cucumbers and zucchini and canned some pumpkin puree. All the while, she was thinking about Isabelle and the airman in the barn.

What should be done? The question haunted her all day, reasserting itself constantly. Every choice was dangerous. Obviously she should just keep quiet about the airman in the barn. Silence was always safest.

But what if Beck and the Gestapo and the SS and their dogs went into the barn on their own? If Beck found the airman in a barn on the property where he was billeted, the Kommandant would not be pleased. Beck would be humiliated.

The Kommandant is blaming me for this failure to find the airman.

Humiliated men could be dangerous.

Maybe she should tell Beck. He was a good man. He had tried to save Rachel. He had gotten Ari papers. He mailed Vianne's care packages to her husband.

Perhaps Beck could be convinced to take the airman and leave Isabelle out of it. The airman would be sent to a prisoner of war camp; that was not so bad.

She was still grappling with these questions long after supper had ended and she'd put the children to bed. She didn't even try to go to sleep. How could she sleep with her family at such risk? The thought of that made her anger with Isabelle swell again. At ten o'clock, she heard footsteps out front and a sharp *rap-rap* on the door.

She put down her darning and got to her feet. Smoothing the hair back from her face, she went to the door and opened it. Her hands were trembling so badly she fisted them at her sides. "Herr Captain," she said. "You are late. Shall I make you something to eat?"

He muttered, "No, thank you," and pushed past her, rougher than he'd ever been before. He went into his room and came back with a bottle of brandy. Pouring himself a huge draught in a chipped café glass, he downed the liquid and poured himself another.

"Herr Captain?"

"We didn't find the pilot," he said, downing the second drink, pouring a third.

"Oh."

"These Gestapo." He looked at her. "They'll kill me," he said quietly.

"No, surely."

"They do not like to be disappointed." He drank the third glass of brandy and slammed the glass down on the table, almost breaking it.

"I have looked everywhere," he said. "Every nook and cranny of this godforsaken town. I've looked in cellars and basements and chicken pens. In thickets of thorns and under piles of garbage. And what do I have to show for my efforts? A parachute with blood on it and no pilot."

"S-surely you haven't looked everywhere," she said to console him. "Shall I get you something to eat? I saved you some supper."

He stopped suddenly. She saw his gaze narrow, heard him say, "It is not possible, but . . ." He grabbed a torchlight and strode to the closet in the kitchen and yanked the door open.

"What are you d-doing?"

"I am searching your house."

"Surely you don't think . . ."

She stood there, her heart thumping as he searched from room to room and yanked the coats out of the closet and pulled the divan away from the wall.

"Are you satisfied?"

"Satisfied, Madame? We lost fourteen pilots this week, and God knows how many aeroplane crew. A Mercedes-Benz factory was blown up two days ago and all the workers were killed. My uncle works in that building. Worked, I suppose."

"I'm sorry," she said.

Vianne drew in a deep breath, thinking it was over, and then she saw that he was going outside.

Did she make a sound? She was afraid that she did. She surged after him, wanting to grab his sleeve, but she was too late. He was outside now, following the beam of his torchlight, the kitchen door standing open behind him.

She ran after him.

He was at the dovecote, yanking the door open.

"Herr Captain." She slowed, tried to calm her breathing as she rubbed her damp palms down her pant legs. "You will not find anything or anyone here, Herr Captain. You must know that."

"Are you a liar, Madame?" He was not angry. He was afraid.

"No. You know I am not. Wolfgang," she said, using his Christian name for the first time. "Surely your superiors will not blame you."

"This is the problem with you French," he said. "You fail to see the truth when it sits down beside you." He pushed past her and walked up the hill, toward the barn.

He would find Isabelle and the airman . . .

And if he did?

Prison for all of them. Maybe worse.

He would never believe that she didn't know about it. She had already shown too much to go back to innocence. And it was too late now to rely on his honor in saving Isabelle. Vianne had lied to him.

He opened the barn door and stood there, his hands on his hips, looking around. He put down his torchlight and lit an oil lamp. Setting it down, he checked every inch of the barn, each stall and the hayloft.

"Y-you see?" Vianne said. "Now come back to the house. Perhaps you'd like another brandy."

He looked down. There were faint tire tracks in the dust. "You said once that Madame de Champlain hid in a cellar."

No. Vianne meant to say something, but when she opened her mouth, nothing came out.

He opened the Renault's door, put the car in neutral, and pushed it forward, rolling it far enough to reveal the cellar door.

"Captain, please . . ."

He bent down in front of her. His fingers moved along the floor, searching the creases for the edges of the hatch.

If he opened that door, it was over. He would shoot Isabelle, or take her into custody and send her to prison. And Vianne and the children would be arrested. There would be no talking to him, no convincing him.

Beck unholstered his gun, cocked it.

Vianne looked desperately for a weapon, saw a shovel leaned against the wall.

He lifted the hatch and yelled something. As the door banged open, he stood up, taking aim. Vianne grabbed the shovel and swung it at him with all of her strength. The metal scoop made a sickening *thunk* as it hit him in the back of the head and sliced deeply into his skull. Blood spurted down the back of his uniform.

At the same time, two shots rang out; one from Beck's gun and one from the cellar.

Beck staggered sideways and turned. There was a hole the size of an onion in his chest, spurting blood. A flap of hair and scalp hung over one eye. "Madame," he said, crumpling to his knees. His pistol clattered to the floor. The torchlight rolled across the uneven boards, clattering.

Vianne threw the shovel aside and knelt down beside Beck, who lay sprawled face-first in a pool of his blood. Using all of her weight, she rolled him over. He was pale already, chalkily so. Blood clotted his hair, streaked from his nostrils, bubbled at every breath he took.

"I'm sorry," Vianne said.

Beck's eyes fluttered open.

Vianne tried to wipe the blood off his face, but it just made more of a mess. Her hands were red with it now. "I had to stop you," she said quietly.

"Tell my family . . ."

Vianne saw the life leave his body, saw his chest stop rising, his heart stop beating.

Behind her, she heard her sister climbing up the ladder. "Vianne!"

Vianne couldn't move.

"Are . . . you all right?" Isabelle asked in a breathless, wheezing voice. She looked pale and a little shaky.

"I killed him. He's dead," Vianne said.

"No, you didn't. I shot him in the chest," Isabelle said.

"I hit him in the head with a shovel. A *shovel*."

Isabelle moved toward her. "Vianne—"

"Don't," Vianne said sharply. "I don't want to hear some excuse from you. Do you know what you've done? A Nazi. Dead in my barn."

Before Isabelle could answer, there was a loud whistle, and then a mule-drawn wagon entered the barn.

Vianne lurched for Beck's weapon, staggered to her feet on the blood-slicked floorboards, and pointed the gun at the strangers.

"Vianne, don't shoot," Isabelle said. "They're friends."

Vianne looked at the ragged-looking men in the wagon; then at her sister, who was dressed all in black and looked milky pale, with shadows under her eyes. "Of course they are." She moved sideways but kept the gun trained on the men crowded onto the front of the rickety wagon. Behind them, in the bed of the wagon, lay a pine coffin.

She recognized Henri—the man who ran the hotel in town, with whom Isabelle had run off to Paris. The communist with whom Isabelle thought she might be in love a little. "Of course," Vianne said. "Your lover."

Henri jumped down from the wagon and closed the barn door. "What in the fuck happened?"

"Vianne hit him with a shovel and I shot him," Isabelle said. "There's some sisterly dispute on who killed him, but he's dead. Captain Beck. The soldier who billets here."

Henri exchanged a look with one of the strangers—a scrappy, sharp-faced young man with hair that was too long. "That's a problem," the man said.

"Can you get rid of the body?" Isabelle asked. She was pressing a hand to her chest, as if her heart was beating too fast. "And the airman's, too—he didn't make it."

A big, shaggy man in a patched coat and pants that were too small jumped down from the wagon. "Disposing of the bodies is the easy part."

Who were these people?

Isabelle nodded. "They'll come looking for Beck. My sister can't stand up to questioning. We'll need to put her and Sophie in hiding."

That did it. They were talking about Vianne as if she weren't even here. "Running would only prove my guilt."

"You can't stay," Isabelle said. "It isn't safe."

"By all means, Isabelle, worry about me *now*, after you've put me and the children at risk and forced me to kill a decent man."

"Vianne, please—"

Vianne felt something in her harden. It seemed that every time she thought she'd hit rock bottom in this war, something worse came along. Now she was a murderess and it was Isabelle's fault. The last thing she was going to do now was follow her sister's advice and leave Le Jardin. "I will say that Beck left to look for the airman and never returned. What do I, an ordinary French housewife, know of such things? He was here and then he was gone. *C'est la vie.*"

"It's as good an answer as any," Henri said.

"This is my fault," Isabelle said, approaching Vianne. She saw her sister's regret for this, and her guilt, but Vianne didn't care. She was too scared for the children to worry about Isabelle's feelings.

"Yes it is, but you made it mine, too. We killed a good man, Isabelle."

Isabelle swayed a little, unsteady. "V. They'll come for you."

Vianne started to say "And whose fault is that?," but when she looked at Isabelle, the words caught in her throat.

She saw blood oozing out from between Isabelle's fingers. For a split second, the world slowed down, tilted, became nothing but noise—the men talking behind her, the mule stomping his hoof on the wooden floor, her own labored breathing. Isabelle crumpled to the floor, unconscious.

Before Vianne could even cry out, a hand clamped over her mouth, arms yanked her back. The next thing she knew she was being dragged away from her sister. She wrestled to be free but the man holding her was too strong.

She saw Henri drop to his knees beside Isabelle and rip open her coat and blouse to reveal a bullet hole just below her collarbone. Henri tore off his shirt and pressed it to the wound.

Vianne elbowed her captor hard enough to make him *ooph*. She wrenched free and rushed to Isabelle's side, slipping in the blood, almost falling. "There's a medical kit in the cellar."

The dark-haired man—who suddenly looked as shaky as Vianne felt—leaped down the cellar stairs and returned quickly, carrying the supplies.

Vianne's hands were shaking as she reached for the bottle of alcohol and washed her hands as best she could.

She took a deep breath and took over the job of pressing Henri's shirt against the wound, which she felt pulsing beneath her.

Twice she had to draw back, wring blood out of the shirt, and start again, but finally, the bleeding stopped. Gently, she rolled Isabelle into her arms and saw the exit wound.

Thank God.

She carefully laid Isabelle back down. "This is going to hurt," she whispered. "But you're strong, aren't you, Isabelle?"

She doused the wound with alcohol. Isabelle shuddered at the contact, but she didn't waken or cry out.

"That's good," Vianne said. The sound of her own voice calmed her, reminded her that she was a mother and mothers took care of their families. "Unconscious is good." She fished the needle from the medical kit, such as it was, and threaded it. She doused the needle in alcohol and then leaned down to the wound. Very carefully, she began stitching the gaping flesh together. It didn't take long—and she hadn't done a good job, but it was the best she could do.

Once she'd stitched the entrance wound, she felt a little confidence, enough to stitch the exit wound and then to bandage it.

At last, she sat back, staring down at her bloody hands and bloodied skirt.

Isabelle looked so pale and frail, not herself at all. Her hair was filthy and matted, her clothes were wet with her own blood—and the airman's—and she looked young.

So young.

Vianne felt a shame so deep it made her sick to her stomach. Had she really told her sister—her *sister*—to go away and not come back?

How often had Isabelle heard that in her life, and from her own family, from people who were supposed to love her?

"I'll take her to the safe house in Brantôme," the black-haired one said.

"Oh, no, you won't," Vianne said. She looked up from her sister, saw that the three men were standing together by the wagon, conspiring. She got to her feet. "She's not going anywhere with you. You're the reason she's here."

"She's the reason we're here," the dark-haired man said. "I'm taking her. Now."

Vianne approached the young man. There was a look in his eyes—an intensity—that ordinarily would have frightened her, but she was beyond fear now, beyond caution. "I know who you are," Vianne said. "She described you to me. You're the one from Tours who left her with a note pinned to her chest as if she were a stray dog. Gaston, right?"

"Gaëtan," he said in a voice that was so soft she had to lean toward him to hear. "And you should know about that. Aren't you the one who couldn't bother to be her sister when she needed one?"

"If you try to take her away from me, I'll kill you."

"You'll kill me," he said, smiling.

She cocked her head toward Beck. "I killed him with a shovel and I *liked* him."

"Enough," Henri said, stepping between them. "She can't stay here, Vianne. Think about it. The Germans are going to come looking for their dead captain. They don't need to find a woman with a gunshot wound and false papers. You understand?"

The big man stepped forward. "We'll bury the captain and the airman. And we'll make sure the motorcycle disappears. Gaëtan, you get her to a safe house in the Free Zone."

Vianne looked from man to man. "But it's after curfew and the border is four miles away and she's wounded. How will . . ."

Halfway through the question, she figured out the answer.

The coffin.

Vianne took a step back. The idea of it was so terrible, she shook her head.

"I'll take care of her," Gaëtan said.

Vianne didn't believe him. Not for a second. "I'm going with you. As far as the border. Then I'll walk back when I see that you've gotten her to the Free Zone."

"You can't do that," Gaëtan said.

She looked up at him. "You'd be surprised what I can do. Now, let's get her out of here."

TWENTY-SIX

May 6, 1995
The Oregon Coast

*T*hat damned invitation is haunting me. I'd swear it has a heartbeat.

For days I have ignored it, but on this bright spring morning, I find myself at the counter, staring down at it. Funny. I don't remember walking over here and yet here I am.

Another woman's hand reaches out. It can't be my hand, not that veiny, big-knuckled monstrosity that trembles. She picks up the envelope, this other woman.

Her hands are shaking even more than usual.

> *Please join us at the AFEES reunion in Paris, on May 7, 1995.*
> *The fiftieth anniversary of the end of the war.*
>
> *For the first time, families and friends of passeurs will come together*
> *in gratitude to honor the extraordinary "Nightingale," also known as*
> *Juliette Gervaise, in the grand ballroom of the*
> *Île de France Hôtel, in Paris. 7:00 P.M.*

Beside me, the phone rings. As I reach for it, the invitation slips from my grasp, falls to the counter. "Hello?"

Someone is talking to me in French. Or am I imagining that?

"Is this a sales call?" I ask, confused.

"No! No. It is about our invitation."

I almost drop the phone in surprise.

"It has been most difficult to track you down, Madame. I am calling about the *passeurs'* reunion tomorrow night. We are gathering to celebrate the people who made the Nightingale escape route so successful. Did you receive the invitation?"

"*Oui,*" I say, clutching the receiver.

"The first one we sent you was returned, I am sorry to say. Please forgive the tardiness of the invitation. But . . . will you be coming?"

"It is not me people want to see. It's Juliette. And she hasn't existed for a long time."

"You couldn't be more wrong, Madame. Seeing you would be meaningful to many people."

I hang up the phone so hard it is like smashing a bug.

But suddenly the idea of going back—going *home*—is in my mind. It's all I can think about.

For years, I kept the memories at bay. I hid them in a dusty attic, far from prying eyes. I told my husband, my children, myself, that there was nothing for me in France. I thought I could come to America and make this new life for myself and forget what I had done to survive.

Now I can't forget.

Do I make a decision? A conscious, let's-think-it-out-and-decide-what's-best kind of decision?

No. I make a phone call to my travel agent and book a flight to Paris, through New York. Then I pack a bag. It's small, just a rolling carry-on, the sort of suitcase that a businesswoman would take on a two-day trip. In it, I pack some nylons, a few pairs of slacks and some sweaters, the pearl earrings that my husband bought me on our fortieth anniversary, and some other essentials. I have no idea what I will need, and I'm not really thinking straight anyway. Then I wait. Impatiently.

At the last minute, after I have called a taxi, I call my son and get his message machine. A bit of luck, that. I don't know if I would have the courage to tell him the truth straight up.

"Hello, Julien," I say as brightly as I can. "I am going to Paris for the weekend. My flight leaves at one ten and I'll call you when I arrive to let you know I'm all right. Give my love to the girls." I pause, knowing how he will feel when he gets this message, how it will upset him. That's because I have let him think I am weak, all these years; he watched me lean on his father and defer to his decision making. He heard me say, "If that's what you think, dear," a million times. He watched me stand on the sidelines of his life instead of showing him the field of my own. This is my fault. It's no wonder he loves a version of me that is incomplete. "I should have told you the truth."

When I hang up, I see the taxi pull up out front. And I go.

TWENTY-SEVEN

October 1942
France

Vianne sat with Gaëtan in the front of the wagon, with the coffin thumping in the wooden bed behind them. The trail through the woods was hard to find in the dark; they were constantly starting and stopping and turning. At some point, it started to rain. The only words they'd exchanged in the last hour and a half were directions.

"There," Vianne said later, as they reached the end of the woods. A light shone up ahead, straining through the trees, turning them into black slashes against a blinding white.

The border.

"Whoa," Gaëtan said, pulling back on the reins.

Vianne couldn't help thinking about the last time she'd been here.

"How will you cross? It's after curfew," she said, clasping her hands together to still their trembling.

"I will be Laurence Olivier. A man overcome by grief, taking his beloved sister home to be buried."

"What if they check her breathing?"

"Then someone at the border will die," he said quietly.

Vianne heard what he didn't say as clearly as the words he chose. She was so surprised that she couldn't think how to respond. He was saying he would die to protect Isabelle. He turned to her, gazed at her. *Gazed*, not looked. Again she saw the predator intensity in those gray eyes, but there was more there, too. He was waiting—patiently—for what she would say. It mattered to him, somehow.

"My father came home changed from the Great War," she said quietly, surprising herself with the admission. This was not something she talked about. "Angry. Mean. He started drinking too much. While Maman was alive, he was different . . ." She shrugged. "After her death, there was no pretense anymore. He sent Isabelle and me away to live with a stranger. We were both just girls, and heartbroken. The difference between us was that I accepted the rejection. I closed him out of my life and found someone else to love me. But Isabelle . . . she doesn't know how to concede defeat. She hurled herself at the cold wall of our father's disinterest for years, trying desperately to gain his love."

"Why are you telling me this?"

"Isabelle seems unbreakable. She has a steel exterior, but it protects a candyfloss heart. Don't hurt her, that's what I'm saying. If you don't love her—"

"I do."

Vianne studied him. "Does she know?"

"I hope not."

Vianne would not have understood that answer a year ago. She wouldn't have understood how dark a side love could have, how hiding it was the kindest thing you could do sometimes. "I don't know why it's so easy for me to forget how much I love her. We start fighting, and . . ."

"Sisters."

Vianne sighed. "I suppose, although I haven't been much of one to her."

"You'll get another chance."

"Do you believe that?"

His silence was answer enough. At last, he said, "Take care of yourself, Vianne. She'll need a place to come home to when all of this is over."

"If it's ever over."

"*Oui.*"

Vianne got down from the wagon; her boots sunk deep into wet, muddy grass. "I'm not sure she thinks of me as a safe place to come home to," she said.

"You'll need to be brave," Gaëtan said. "When the Nazis come looking for their man. You know our real names. That's dangerous for all of us. You included."

"I'll be brave," she said. "You just tell my sister that she needs to start being afraid."

For the first time, Gaëtan smiled and Vianne understood how this scrawny, sharp-featured man in his beggar's clothes had swept Isabelle off her feet. He had the kind of smile that inhabited every part of his face—his eyes, his cheeks; there was even a dimple. *I wear my heart on my sleeve,* that smile said, and no woman could be unmoved by such transparency. "*Oui,*" he said. "Because it is so easy to tell your sister anything."

Fire.

It's all around her, leaping, dancing. A bonfire. She can see it in quivering strands of red that come and go. A flame licks her face, burns deep.

It's everywhere and then . . . it's gone.

The world is icy, white, sheer and cracked. She shivers with the cold, watches her fingers turn blue and crackle and break apart. They fall away like chalk, dusting her frozen feet.

"Isabelle."

Birdsong. A nightingale. She hears it singing a sad song. Nightingales mean loss, don't they? Love that leaves or doesn't last or never existed in the first place. There's a poem about that, she thinks. An ode.

No, not a bird.

A man. The king of the fire maybe. A prince in hiding in the frozen woods. A wolf.

She looks for footprints in the snow.

"Isabelle. Wake up."

She heard his voice in her imagination. Gaëtan.

He wasn't really here. She was alone—she was always alone—and this was too strange to be anything but a dream. She was hot and cold and achy and worn out.

She remembered something—a loud noise. Vianne's voice: *Don't come back.*

"I'm here."

She felt him sit beside her. The mattress shifted to accommodate his imaginary weight.

Something cool and damp pressed to her forehead and it felt so good that she was momentarily distracted. And then she felt his lips graze hers and linger there; he said something she couldn't quite hear and then he drew back. She felt the end of the kiss as deeply as she'd felt the start of it.

It felt so . . . real.

She wanted to say "Don't leave me," but she couldn't do it, not again. She was so tired of begging people to love her.

Besides, he wasn't really here, so what would be the point of saying anything?

She closed her eyes and rolled away from the man who wasn't there.

***

Vianne sat on Beck's bed.

Ridiculous that she thought of it that way, but there it was. She sat in this room that had become his, hoping that it wouldn't always be his in her mind. In her hand was the small portrait of his family.

You would love Hilda. Here, she sent you this strudel, Madame. For putting up with a lout such as myself.

Vianne swallowed hard. She didn't cry for him again. She refused to, but God, she wanted to cry for herself, for what she had done, for who she had become. She wanted to cry for the man she'd killed and the sister who might not live. It had been an easy choice, killing Beck to save Isabelle. So why had Vianne been so quick to turn on Isabelle before? *You are not welcome here.* How could she have said that to her own sister? What if those were among the last words ever spoken between them?

As she sat, staring at the portrait *(tell my family)*, she waited for a knock at the door. It had been forty-eight hours since Beck's murder. The Nazis should be here any minute.

It wasn't a question of if, but when. They would bang on her door and push their way inside. She had spent hours trying to figure out what to do. Should she go to the Kommandant's office and report Beck missing?

(No, foolish. What French person would report such a thing?)

Or should she wait until they came to her?

(Never a good thing.)

Or should she try to run?

That only made her remember Sarah and the moonlit night that would forever make her think of bloody streaks on a child's face and brought her right back to the beginning again.

"Maman?" Sophie said, standing in the open doorway, the toddler on her hip.

"You need to eat something," Sophie said. She was taller, almost Vianne's height. When had that happened? And she was thin. Vianne remembered when her daughter had had apple-like cheeks and eyes that sparkled with mischief. Now she was like all of them, stretched as thin as jerky and aged beyond her years.

"They're going to come to the door soon," Vianne said. She'd said it so often in the past two days that her words surprised no one. "You remember what to do?"

Sophie nodded solemnly. She knew how important this was, even if she didn't know what had become of the captain. Interestingly, she hadn't asked.

Vianne said, "If they take me away—"

"They won't," Sophie said.

"And if they do?" Vianne said.

"We wait for you to return for three days and then we go to Mother Marie-Therese at the convent."

Someone pounded on the door. Vianne lurched to her feet so fast she stumbled sideways and hit her hip into the corner of the table, dropping the portrait. The glass on it cracked. "Upstairs, Sophie. Now."

Sophie's eyes bulged, but she knew better than to speak. She tightened her hold on the toddler and ran upstairs. When Vianne heard the bedroom door slam shut, she smoothed her worn skirt. She had dressed carefully in a gray wool cardigan and an often-mended black skirt. A respectable look. Her hair had been curled and carefully styled into waves that softened her thin face.

The pounding returned. She allowed herself one indrawn, calming breath as she crossed the room. Her breathing was almost steady as she opened the door.

Two German Schutzstaffel—SS—soldiers stood there, wearing side-arms. The shorter of the two pushed past Vianne, shoving her out of his way as he entered the house. He strode from room to room, pushing things aside, sending what few knickknacks remained crashing to the floor. At Beck's room, he stopped and turned back. "This is Hauptmann Beck's room?"

Vianne nodded.

The taller soldier came at Vianne fast, leaning forward as if there were a harsh wind at his back. He looked down at her from on high, his forehead obscured by a shiny military cap. "Where is he?"

"H-how would I know?"

"Who is upstairs?" the soldier demanded. "I hear something."

It was the first time she'd ever been asked about Ari.

"My . . . children." The lie caught in her voice, came out too soft. She cleared her throat and tried again. "You may go up there, of course, but please don't waken the baby. He's . . . sick with the flu. Or perhaps tuberculosis." This last she added because she knew how frightened the Nazis were of getting sick. She reached down for her handbag, clamped it to her chest as if it offered some protection.

He nodded at the other German, who strode confidently up the stairs. She heard him moving around overhead. The ceiling creaked. Moments later, he came back downstairs and said something in German.

"Come with us," the taller one said. "I'm sure you have nothing to hide."

He grabbed Vianne's arm and dragged her out to the black Citroën parked by the gate. He shoved her into the backseat and slammed the door shut.

Vianne had about five minutes to consider her situation before they stopped again and she was being yanked up the stone steps of the town hall. There were people all around the square, soldiers and locals. The villagers dispersed quickly when the Citroën pulled up.

"It's Vianne Mauriac," she heard someone say, a woman.

The Nazi's hold on her upper arm was bruising, but she made no sound as he pulled her into the town hall and down a set of narrow steps. There, he shoved her through an open door and slammed it shut.

It took her eyes a moment to adjust to the gloom. She was in a small, windowless room with stone walls and a wood floor. A desk sat in the middle of the room, decorated with a plain black lamp that delivered a cone of light onto the scratched wood. Behind the desk—and in front of it—were straight-backed wooden chairs.

She heard the door open behind her and then close. Footsteps followed; she knew someone had come up behind her. She could smell his breath—sausage and cigarettes—and the musky scent of his sweat.

"Madame," he said so close to her ear that she flinched.

Hands clamped around her waist, squeezing tightly. "Do you have any weapons?" he said, his terrible French drawing sibilance from the words. He felt up her sides, slid his spidery fingers across her breasts—giving the smallest of squeezes—and then felt down her legs.

"No weapons. Good." He walked past her and took his seat at the desk. Blue eyes peered out from beneath his shiny black military hat. "Sit."

She did as she was told, folding her hands into her lap.

"I am Sturmbannführer Von Richter. You are Madame Vianne Mauriac?"

She nodded.

"You know why you are here," he said, taking a cigarette from his pocket, lighting it with a match that glowed in the shadows.

"No," she said, her voice unsteady, her hands shaking just a little.

"Hauptmann Beck is missing."

"Missing. Are you certain?"

"When is the last time you saw him, Madame?"

She frowned. "I hardly keep track of his movements, but if pressed . . . I would say two nights ago. He was quite agitated."

"Agitated?"

"It was the downed airman. He was most unhappy that he had not been found. Herr Captain believed someone was hiding him."

"Someone?"

Vianne forced herself not to look away; nor did she tap her foot nervously on the floor or scratch the itch that was making its uncomfortable way across her neck. "He searched all day for the airman. When he came home, he was . . . agitated is the only word I know to use. He drank an entire bottle of brandy and broke a few things in my house in his rage. And then . . ." She paused, letting her frown deepen.

"And then?"

"I'm sure it means nothing at all."

He slammed his palm down on the table so hard the light shuddered. "What?"

"Herr Captain suddenly said, 'I know where he's hiding,' and grabbed his sidearm and left my home, slamming the door shut behind him. I saw him jump on his motorcycle and take off down the road at an unsafe speed, and then . . . nothing. He never returned. I assumed he was busy at the Kommandantur. As I said, his comings and goings are not my concern."

The man drew a long drag on his cigarette. The tip glowed red and then slowly faded to black. Ash rained down on the desk. He studied her from behind a veil of smoke. "A man would not want to leave a woman as beautiful as yourself."

Vianne didn't move.

"Well," he said at last, dropping his cigarette butt to the floor. He stood abruptly and stomped on the still-lit cigarette, grinding on it with his boot heel. "I suspect the young Hauptmann was not as skilled with a gun as he should have been. The Wehrmacht," he said, shaking his head. "Often they are a disappointment. Disciplined but not . . . eager."

He came out from behind the desk and walked toward Vianne. As he neared, she stood. Politeness demanded it. "The Hauptmann's misfortune is my fortune."

"Oh?"

His gaze moved down her throat to the pale skin above her breasts. "I need a new place to billet. The Hôtel Bellevue is unsatisfactory. I believe your house will do nicely."

❧

When Vianne stepped out of the town hall, she felt like a woman who'd just washed ashore. She was unsteady on her feet and trembling slightly, her palms were damp, her forehead itchy. Everywhere she looked in the square were soldiers; these days the black SS uniforms were predominant. She heard someone yell *"Halt!"* and she turned, saw a pair of women in ratty coats with yellow stars on their chests being shoved to their knees by a soldier with a gun. The soldier grabbed one of the two and dragged her to her feet while the older one screamed. It was Madame Fournier, the butcher's wife. Her son, Gilles, yelled, "You can't take my maman!" and started to surge at two French policemen who were nearby.

A gendarme grabbed the boy, yanked hard enough to make him stop. "Don't be a fool."

Vianne didn't think. She saw her former student in trouble and she went to him. He was just a boy, for God's sake. Sophie's age. Vianne had been his teacher since before he could read. "What are you doing?" she demanded to know, realizing a second too late that she should have tempered her voice.

The policeman turned to look at her. Paul. He was even fatter than the last time she'd seen him. His face had puffed out enough to make his eyes as small and slitted as sewing needles. "Stay out of this, Madame," Paul said.

"Madame Mauriac," Gilles cried, "they're taking my maman to the train! I want to go with her!"

Vianne looked at Gilles's mother, Madame Fournier, the butcher's wife, and saw defeat in her eyes.

"Come with me, Gilles," Vianne said without really thinking.

"*Merci,*" Madame Fournier whispered.

Paul yanked Gilles close again. "Enough. The boy is making a scene. He is coming with us."

"No!" Vianne said. "Paul, please, we are all French." She hoped the use of his name would remind him that before all of this they'd been a community. She'd taught his daughters. "The boy is a French citizen. He was born here!"

"We don't care where he was born, Madame. He's on my list. He goes." His eyes narrowed. "Do you want to lodge a complaint?"

Madame Fournier was crying now, clutching her son's hand. The other policeman blew his whistle and prodded Gilles forward with the barrel of his gun.

Gilles and his mother stumbled into the crowd of others being herded toward the train station.

We don't care where he was born, Madame.

Beck had been right. Being French would no longer protect Ari.

She clamped her handbag tightly beneath her armpit and headed for home. As usual, the road had turned to mud and ruined her shoes by the time she reached the gate at Le Jardin.

Both of the children were waiting in the living room. Relief loosened her shoulders. She smiled tiredly as she set down her handbag.

"You're all right?" Sophie said.

Ari immediately moved toward her, grinning, opening his arms for a hug, saying, "Maman," with a grin to prove that he understood the rules of their new game.

She pulled the three-year-old into her arms and held him tightly. To Sophie, she said, "I was questioned and released. That is the good news."

"And the bad news?"

Vianne looked at her daughter, defeated. Sophie was growing up in a world where boys in her class were put in train carriages like cattle at the point of a gun and perhaps never seen again. "Another German is going to billet here."

"Will he be like Herr Captain Beck?"

Vianne thought of the feral gleam in Von Richter's ice-blue eyes and the way he had "searched" her.

"No," she said softly. "I don't expect he will be. You are not to speak to him unless you must. Don't look at him. Just stay as invisible as you can. And Sophie, they're deporting French-born Jews now—children, too— putting them on trains and sending them away to work camps." Vianne tightened her hold on Rachel's son. "He is Daniel now. Your brother. *Always.* Even when we are alone. The story is that we adopted him from a relative in Nice. We can never make a mistake or they'll take him—and us—away. You understand? I don't want anyone to ever even *look* at his papers."

"I'm scared, Maman," she said quietly.

"As am I, Sophie" was all Vianne could say. They were in this together now, taking this terrible risk. Before she could say more, there was a knock on the door and Sturmbannführer Von Richter walked into her home, standing as straight as a bayonet blade, his face impassive beneath the glossy black military hat. Silver iron crosses hung from various places on his black uniform—his stand-up collar, his chest. A swastika pin decorated his left breast pocket. "Madame Mauriac," he said. "I see you walked home in the rain."

"*Mais oui*," she answered, smoothing the damp, frizzy hair from her face.

"You should have asked my men for a ride. A beautiful woman such as yourself should not slog through the mud like a heifer to the trough."

"*Oui, merci*, I will be so bold as to ask them next time."

He strode forward without removing his hat. He looked around, studying everything. She was sure that he noticed the marks on the walls where paintings had once hung and the empty mantel and the discoloration in the floor where rugs had lain for decades. All gone now. "Yes. This will do." He looked at the children. "And who have we here?" he asked in terrible French.

"My son," Vianne said, standing beside him, moving in close enough to touch them both. She didn't say "Daniel" in case Ari corrected her. "And my daughter, Sophie."

"I do not remember Hauptmann Beck mentioning two children."

"And why would he, Herr Sturmbannführer. It is hardly noteworthy."

"Well," he said, nodding crisply to Sophie. "You, girl, go get my bags." To Vianne, he said, "Show me the rooms. I will choose the one I want."

TWENTY-EIGHT

*I*sabelle woke in a pitch-black room. In pain.

"You're awake, aren't you?" said a voice beside her.

She recognized Gaëtan's voice. How often in the past two years had she imagined lying in bed with him? "Gaëtan," she said, and with his name came the memories.

The barn. Beck.

She sat up so fast her head spun and dizziness hit her hard. "Vianne," she said.

"Your sister is fine." He lit the oil lamp and left it on the overturned apple crate by the bed. The butterscotch glow embraced them, created a small oval world in the blackness. She touched the spot of pain in her shoulder, wincing.

"The bastard shot me," she said, surprised to realize that such a thing could be forgotten. She remembered hiding the airman and getting caught by Vianne . . . She remembered being in the cellar with the dead flier . . .

"And you shot him."

She remembered Beck flinging the hatch door open and pointing his pistol at her. She remembered two gunshots . . . and climbing out of the cellar, staggering, feeling dizzy. Had she known she'd been shot?

Vianne holding a shovel covered in gore. Beside her, Beck in a pool of blood.

Vianne pale as chalk, trembling. *I killed him.*

After that her memories were jumbled except for Vianne's anger. *You are not welcome here. If you return, I'll turn you in myself.*

Isabelle lay back down slowly. The pain of that memory was worse than her injury. For once, Vianne had been right to cast Isabelle out. What had she been thinking to hide the airman on her sister's property, with a German Wehrmacht captain billeted there? No wonder people didn't trust her. "How long have I been here?"

"Four days. Your wound is much improved. Your sister stitched it up nicely. Your fever broke yesterday."

"And . . . Vianne? She is not fine, of course. So how is she?"

"We protected her as best we could. She refused to go into hiding. So Henri and Didier buried both bodies and cleaned the barn and tore the motorcycle down to parts."

"She'll be questioned," Isabelle said. "And killing that man will haunt her. Hating doesn't come easy for her."

"It will before this war is over."

Isabelle felt her stomach tighten in shame and regret. "I love her, you know. Or I want to. How come I forget that the minute we disagree about something?"

"She said something very similar at the frontier."

Isabelle started to roll over and gasped at the pain in her shoulder. Taking a deep breath, she steeled herself and eased slowly onto her side. She'd misjudged how close he was to her, how small the bed. They were lying like lovers; she on her side looking up at him; he on his back staring at the ceiling. "Vianne went to the border?"

"You were in a coffin in the back of the wagon. She wanted to make sure we crossed safely." She heard a smile in his voice, or imagined she did. "She threatened to kill me if I didn't take good care of you."

"My *sister* said that?" she said, not quite believing it. But she hardly believed that Gaëtan was the kind of man who would lie to reunite sisters. In profile, his features were razor sharp, even by lamplight. He refused to look at her, and he was as close to the edge of the bed as he could be.

"She was afraid you'd die. We both were."

He said it so softly she barely could hear. "It feels like old times," she said cautiously, afraid to say the wrong thing. More afraid to say nothing at all. Who knew how many chances there would be in such uncertain times? "You and me alone in the dark. Remember?"

"I remember."

"Tours already feels like a lifetime ago," she went on. "I was just a girl."

He said nothing.

"Look at me, Gaëtan."

"Go to sleep, Isabelle."

"You know I will keep asking until you can't stand it."

He sighed and rolled onto his side.

"I think about you," she said.

"Don't." His voice was rough.

"You kissed me," she said. "It wasn't a dream."

"You can't remember that."

Isabelle felt something strange at his words, a breathless little flutter in her chest. "You want me as much as I want you," she said.

He shook his head in denial, but it was the silence she heard; the acceleration of his breathing.

"You think I'm too young and too innocent and too impetuous. Too everything. I get it. People have always said that about me. I'm immature."

"That's not it."

"But you're wrong. Maybe you weren't wrong two years ago. I *did* say I love you, which must have sounded insane." She drew in a breath. "But it's not insane now, Gaëtan. Maybe it's the only sane thing in all of this. Love, I mean. We've seen buildings blown up in front of us and our friends are getting arrested and deported. God knows if we'll ever see them again. I could die, Gaëtan," she said quietly. "I'm not saying that in some schoolgirl-try-to-get-the-boy-to-kiss-me kind of way. It's true and you know it. Either one of us could die tomorrow. And you know what I would regret?"

"What?"

"Us."

"There can't be an us, Iz. Not now. That's what I've been trying to tell you from the beginning."

"If I promise to let it go, will you answer one question truthfully?"

"Just one?"

"One. And then I'll go to sleep. I promise."

He nodded.

"If we weren't here—hiding in a safe house—if the world weren't ripping itself apart, if this was just an ordinary day in an ordinary world, would you want there to be an us, Gaëtan?"

She saw how his face crumpled, how pain exposed his love.

"It doesn't matter, don't you see that?"

"It's the only thing that matters, Gaëtan." She saw love in his eyes. What did words matter after that?

She was wiser than she'd been before. Now she knew how fragile life and love were. Maybe she would love him for only this day, or maybe for only the next week, or maybe until she was an old, old woman. Maybe he would be the love of her life . . . or her love for the duration of this war . . . or maybe he would only be her first love. All she really knew was that in this terrible, frightening world, she had stumbled into something unexpected.

And she would not let it go again.

"I knew it," she said to herself, smiling. His breath skimmed against her lips, as intimate as any kiss. She leaned over him, her gaze on him, steady, honest, and turned off the lamp.

In the dark, she snuggled against him, burrowed deeper under the blankets. At first he lay stiffly against her, as if he were afraid even to touch her, but gradually, he relaxed. He rolled onto his back and started to snore. Sometime—she didn't know when—she closed her eyes and reached out, placing a hand in the hollow of his stomach, feeling it rise and fall with his breathing. It was like resting her hand on the ocean in summer, when the tide was coming in.

Touching him, she fell asleep.

❧

The nightmares wouldn't let her go. In some distant part of her brain she heard her own whimpering, heard Sophie say, "Maman, you're taking all the blankets," but none of it wakened her. In her nightmare, she was in a chair, being interrogated. *The boy, Daniel. He's a Jew. Give him to me,* Von Richter said, shoving his gun in her face . . . then his face changed, melted a little, and he turned into Beck, who was holding the photograph of his wife and shaking his head, but the side of his face was missing . . . and then Isabelle lying on the floor, bleeding, saying, *I'm sorry Vianne,* and Vianne was yelling. *You're not welcome here . . .*

Vianne woke with a start, breathing hard. The same nightmares had plagued her for six days; she consistently woke feeling exhausted and worried. It was November now, and there had been no word about Isabelle at all. She eased out from beneath the blankets. The floor was cold, but not as cold as it would be in a few weeks. She reached for the shawl she'd left on the foot of the bed and wrapped it around her shoulders.

Von Richter had claimed the upstairs bedroom. Vianne had abandoned the floor to him, choosing to move with her children into the smaller downstairs bedroom, where they slept together on the double bed.

Beck's room. No wonder she dreamed of him in here. The air held on to his scent, reminded her that the man she'd known no longer lived, that she had killed him. She longed to do penance for this sin, but what could she do? She had killed a man—a decent man, in spite of it all. It didn't matter to her that he was the enemy or even that she'd done it to save her sister. She knew she had made the right choice. It wasn't right or wrong that haunted her. It was the act itself. *Murder.*

She left the bedroom and closed the door behind her, shutting it with a quiet click.

Von Richter sat on the divan, reading a novel, drinking a cup of real coffee. The aroma made her almost sick with longing. The Nazi had billeted here for several days already, and each of those mornings had smelled of rich, bitter roasted coffee—and Von Richter made sure she smelled it, and wanted it. But she couldn't have so much as a sip; he made sure of that, too. Yesterday morning he had dumped an entire pot into the sink, smiling at her as he did so.

He was a man who had stumbled into a little bit of power and seized it with both hands. She'd known that within the first few hours of his arrival, when he'd chosen the best room and gathered up the warmest blankets for his bed, when he'd taken all of the pillows left in the house and all of the candles, leaving Vianne a single oil lamp for her use.

"Herr Sturmbannführer," she said, smoothing her shapeless dress and worn cardigan.

He didn't look up from the German newspaper that held his attention. "More coffee."

She took his empty cup and went to the kitchen, returning quickly with another cup.

"The Allies are wasting their time in North Africa," he said, taking the cup from her, putting it on the table beside him.

"*Oui*, Herr Sturmbannführer."

His hand snaked out and coiled around her wrist tight enough to leave a bruise. "I am having men over for supper tonight. You will cook. And keep that boy away from me. His crying sounds like a dying pig."

He let go.

"*Oui*, Herr Sturmbannführer."

She got out of his way quickly, hurrying into the bedroom and closing the door behind her. She bent and wakened Daniel, feeling his soft breathing against the crook of her neck.

"Maman," he mumbled around his thumb, which he was furiously sucking. "Sophie is snoring too loud."

Vianne smiled and reached over to tousle Sophie's hair. Amazingly, even though it was wartime and they were terrified and starving, somehow a girl her age could still manage to sleep through anything. "You sound like a water buffalo, Sophie," Vianne teased.

"Very funny," Sophie muttered, sitting up. She glanced at the closed door. "Is Herr Doryphore still here?"

"Sophie!" Vianne admonished, glancing worriedly at the closed door.

"He can't hear us," Sophie said.

"Still," Vianne said quietly, "I cannot imagine why you would compare our guest to a bug that eats potatoes." She tried not to smile.

Daniel hugged Vianne and gave her a sloppy kiss.

As she patted his back and held him close, nuzzling the downy softness of his cheek, she heard a car engine start up.

Thank God.

"He is leaving," she murmured to the boy, nuzzling his cheek. "Come

along, Sophie." She carried Daniel into the living room, which still smelled
of freshly brewed coffee and men's cologne, and began her day.

❧

People had called Isabelle impetuous for as long as she could remember.
And then rash and, most lately, reckless. In the past year, she had grown
up enough to see the truth of it. From earliest memory, she had acted first
and thought about consequences later. Perhaps it was because she'd felt
alone for so long. No one had ever been her sounding board, her best
friend. She hadn't had someone with whom to strategize or work through
her problems.

Beyond that, she had never had great impulse control. Maybe because
she'd never had anything to lose.

Now, she knew what it meant to be afraid, to want something—or
someone—so much it made your heart ache.

The old Isabelle would simply have told Gaëtan she loved him and let
the cards fall as they would.

The new Isabelle wanted to walk away without even trying. She didn't
know if she had the strength to be rejected again.

And yet.

They were at war. Time was the one luxury no one had anymore. Tomorrow felt as ephemeral as a kiss in the dark.

She stood in the small, pitched-roof cupboard they used as a water
closet in the safe house. Gaëtan had carried up buckets of hot water for her
bath, and she had luxuriated in the copper tub until the water cooled. The
mirror on the wall was cracked and hung askew. It made her reflection appear disjointed, with one side of her face slightly lower than the other.

"How can you be afraid?" she said to her reflection. She had hiked the
Pyrenees in the falling snow and swum the rushing cold waters of the Bidassoa River beneath the glare of a Spanish searchlight; she'd once asked a
Gestapo agent to carry a suitcase full of false identity papers across a German checkpoint "because he looked so strong and she was so very tired
from traveling," but she had never been as nervous as she was right now.
She knew suddenly that a woman could change her whole life and uproot
her existence with one choice.

Taking a deep breath, she wrapped herself in a tattered towel and returned to the safe house's main room. She paused at the door just long enough to calm her racing heart (a failed attempt) and then she opened the door.

Gaëtan stood by the blacked-out window in his torn and tattered clothes, still stained with her blood. She smiled nervously and reached for the end of the towel she'd tucked in at her chest.

He went so still it seemed he'd stopped breathing, even as her breathing sped up. "Don't do it, Iz." His eyes narrowed—before, she would have said it was anger, but now she knew better.

She unwrapped the towel, let it fall to the floor. The bandage on her gunshot wound was all she wore now.

"What do you want from me?" he said.

"You know."

"You're an innocent. It's war. I'm a criminal. How many reasons do you need to stay away from me?"

They were arguments for another world. "If times were different, I'd make you chase me," she said, taking a step forward. "I would have made you jump through hoops to get me naked. But we don't have time, do we?"

At the quiet admission, she felt a wave of sadness. This had been the truth between them from the beginning; they had no time. They couldn't court and fall in love and get married and have babies. They might not even have tomorrow. She hated that her first time would be bathed in sorrow, steeped in a sense of having already lost what they'd just found, but that was the world now.

One thing she knew for sure: She wanted him to be the first man in her bed. She wanted to remember him for as long as forever was. "The nuns always said I would come to a bad end. I think they meant you."

He came toward her, cupped her face in his hands. "You terrify me, Isabelle."

"Kiss me" was all she could say.

At the first touch of his lips, everything changed, or Isabelle changed. A shudder of desire moved through her, stopped her breath. She felt lost within his arms and found, broken apart, and remade. The words "I love you" burned in her, desperate to be given voice. But even more, she wanted to *hear* the words, to be told, just once, that she was loved.

"You're going to be sorry you did this," he said.

How could he say that? "Never. Will you be sorry?"

"I already am," he said quietly. Then he kissed her again.

TWENTY-NINE

*T*he next week was one of almost unbearable bliss for Isabelle. There were long conversations by candlelight, and holding hands, and stroking skin; nights of awaking into an aching desire and making love and falling into sleep again.

On this day, as on each of the others, Isabelle woke still tired, and slightly in pain. The wound in her shoulder had begun healing enough that it itched and ached. She felt Gaëtan beside her, his body warm and solid. She knew he was awake; maybe it was his breathing, or the way his foot rubbed absently against hers, or the quiet. She just knew. In the past days, she'd become a student of him. Nothing he did was too small or insignificant for her to notice. She'd repeatedly thought *remember this* over the smallest of details.

She had read countless romantic novels in her life and she had dreamed of love forever; even so, she'd never known that a plain old double mattress could become a world unto itself, an oasis. She turned onto her side and reached past Gaëtan to light the lamp. In the pale glow of it, she settled close to him, an arm draped across his chest. A tiny silver scar cut through his messy hairline. She reached out to touch it, traced it with her fingertip.

"My brother threw a rock at me. I was too slow to duck," he said.

"Georges," he said fondly; the tenor of his voice reminded Isabelle that Gaëtan's brother was a prisoner of war.

He had a whole life she knew almost nothing about. A mother who was a seamstress and a father who raised pigs . . . he lived in the woods somewhere, in a house with no running water and only a single room for all of them. He answered her questions about all of it, but volunteered almost nothing. He said he preferred to hear her stories about the adventures that had gotten her kicked out of so many schools. *It's better than stories of poor people just trying to get by,* he said.

But beneath all their words, the stories traded back and forth, she felt their time eroding. They couldn't stay here long. Already, they'd overstayed. She was fit enough to travel. Not to cross the Pyrenees, perhaps, but certainly she didn't need to lie abed.

How could she leave him? They might never see each other again.

That was the crux of her fear.

"I get it, you know," Gaëtan said.

She didn't know what he meant, but she heard the hollowness in his voice and knew it wasn't good. The sadness that came with being in his bed—matched equally with joy—expanded.

"Get what?" she asked, but she didn't want to hear.

"That every time we kiss, it's good-bye."

She closed her eyes.

"The war is out there, Iz. I need to get back to it."

She knew and agreed, though it caused a constriction in her chest. "I know" was all she could say, afraid that any deeper exploration would hurt more than she could bear.

"There is a group gathering at Urrugne," she said. "I should be there by nightfall on Wednesday, if we're lucky."

"We are not lucky," he said. "You must know that by now."

"You are wrong, Gaëtan. Now that you've met me, you'll never be able to forget me. That's something." She leaned over for a kiss.

He said something softly, quietly, against her lips; maybe it was "it's not enough." She didn't care. She didn't want to hear.

In November, the people of Carriveau began to hunker down into winter survival mode again. They knew now what they hadn't known last winter: Life could get worse. War was being waged all over the world; in Africa, in the Soviet Union, in Japan, on an island somewhere called Guadalcanal. With the Germans fighting on so many fronts, food had become even more scarce, as had wood and gas and electricity and everyday supplies.

This Friday morning was particularly cold and gray. Not a good day for venturing out, but Vianne had decided that today was The Day. It had taken some time to work up the courage to leave the house with Daniel, but she knew that it had to be done. His hair was cut so short he was almost bald and she'd dressed him in oversized clothes to make him look smaller. Anything to disguise him.

She forced herself to show good posture as she walked through town, with a child on each side of her—Sophie and Daniel.

Daniel.

At the *boulangerie*, she took her place at the back of the queue. She waited breathlessly for someone to ask about the boy beside her, but the women in line were too tired and hungry and downtrodden even to look up. When it was finally Vianne's turn at the counter, Yvette looked up. She had been a beautiful woman only two years ago, with flowing copper-colored hair and eyes as black as coal. Now, three years into the war, she looked aged and tired. "Vianne Mauriac. I have not seen you with your daughter for a while. *Bonjour*, Sophie, you have grown so tall." She peered over the counter. "And who is this good-looking young man?"

"Daniel," he said proudly.

Vianne placed a trembling hand on his shorn head. "I adopted him from Antoine's cousin in Nice. She . . . died."

Yvette pushed the frizzy hair out of her eyes, pulled a strand of it out of her mouth as she stared down at the toddler. She had three sons of her own, one not much older than Daniel.

Vianne's heart hammered in her chest.

Yvette stepped back from the counter. She went to the small door that separated the shop from the bakery. "Herr Lieutenant," she said. "Could you come out here?"

Vianne tightened her grip on her willow basket handle, working it as if it were piano keys.

A portly German ambled out of the back room, his arms overflowing with freshly baked baguettes. He saw Vianne and stopped. "Madame," he said, his apple cheeks bulging at the fullness of his mouth.

Vianne could barely nod.

Yvette said to the soldier, "There's no more bread today, Herr Lieutenant. If I make more I will save the best for you and your men. This poor woman couldn't even get a day-old baguette."

The man's eyes narrowed appreciatively. He moved toward Vianne, his flat feet thumping on the stone floor. Wordlessly, he dropped a half-eaten baguette into her basket. Then he nodded and left the shop, a little bell tinkling at his exit.

When they were alone, Yvette moved in close to Vianne, so close she had to fight the urge to step back. "I heard you have an SS officer in your house now. What happened to the handsome captain?"

"He disappeared," Vianne said evenly. "No one knows."

"No one? Why did they bring you in for questioning? Everyone saw you go in."

"I am just a housewife. What could I possibly know of such things?"

Yvette stared at her a moment longer, assessing Vianne in the silence. Then she stepped back. "You are a good friend, Vianne Mauriac," she said quietly.

Vianne nodded briefly and herded the children to the door. The days of stopping to talk to friends on the street were gone. Now it was dangerous enough to simply make eye contact; friendly conversation had gone the way of butter and coffee and pork.

Outside, Vianne paused on the cracked stone step, through which a lush patch of frosted weeds pushed up. She was wearing a winter coat she had made from a tapestried bedspread. She had copied a pattern she'd seen in a magazine: double breasted, knee length, with a wide lapel and buttons she'd taken from one of her mother's favorite Harris tweed jackets. It was warm enough for today, but soon she would need layers of newsprint between her sweater and her coat.

Vianne retied the scarf around her head and knotted it more tightly beneath her chin as the icy wind hit her full in the face. Leaves skittered across the stone aisle, cartwheeled across her booted feet.

She held tightly to Daniel's mittened hand and stepped out into the street. She knew instantly that something was wrong. There were German soldiers and French gendarmes everywhere—in cars, on motorcycles, marching up the icy street, gathered in pods at the cafés.

Whatever was happening out here, it couldn't be good, and it was always best to stay away from the soldiers—especially since the Allied victories in North Africa.

"Come on, Sophie and Daniel. Let's go home."

She tried to turn right at the corner but found the street barricaded. All up and down the street doors were locked and shutters were closed. The bistros were empty. There was a terrible sense of danger in the air.

The next street she tried was barricaded, too. A pair of Nazi soldiers stood guard at it, their rifles pointed at her. Behind them, German soldiers marched up the street toward them, goose-stepping in formation.

Vianne took the children's hands and picked up their pace, but one street after another was barricaded and guarded. It became clear that there was a plan in place. Lorries and buses were thundering up the cobblestoned streets toward the town square.

Vianne came to the square and stopped, breathing hard, pulling the children in close to her sides.

Pandemonium. There were buses lined up in a row, disgorging passengers—all of whom wore a yellow star. Women and children were being forced, pushed, herded into the square. Nazis stood on the perimeter, a terrible, frightening patrol edge, while French policemen pulled people out of the buses, yanked jewelry from women's necks, shoved them at gunpoint.

"Maman!" Sophie cried.

Vianne clamped a hand over her daughter's mouth.

To her left, a young woman was shoved to the ground and then hauled back up by her hair and dragged through the crowd.

"Vianne?"

She swung around, saw Hélène Ruelle carrying a small leather suitcase and holding a little boy's hand. An older boy stood close to her side. A yellow, tattered star identified them.

"Take my sons," Hélène said desperately to Vianne.

"Here?" Vianne said, glancing around.

"No, Maman," the older boy said. "Papa told me to take care of you. I am not leaving you. If you let go of my hand, I'll just follow you. Better we stay together."

Behind them another whistle shrieked.

Hélène shoved the younger boy into Vianne, pushed him hard against Daniel. "He is Jean Georges, like his uncle. Four years old this June. My husband's people are in Burgundy."

"I have no papers for him . . . they'll kill me if I take him."

"You!" a Nazi shouted at Hélène. He came up behind her, grabbed her by the hair, almost yanking her off her feet. She slammed into her older son, who strove to keep her upright.

And then Hélène and her son were gone, lost in the crowd. The boy was beside her, wailing, "Maman!" and sobbing.

"We need to leave," Vianne said to Sophie. "*Now.*" She clutched Jean Georges's hand so tightly he cried harder. Every time he yelled, "Maman!" she flinched and prayed for him to be quiet. They hurried up one street and down the other, dodging the barricades and bypassing the soldiers who were breaking down doors and herding Jewish people into the square. Twice they were stopped and allowed to pass because they had no stars on their clothing. On the muddy road, she had to slow down, but she didn't stop, even when both boys started crying.

At Le Jardin, Vianne finally stopped.

Von Richter's black Citroën was parked out front.

"Oh *no*," Sophie said.

Vianne looked down at her terrified daughter and saw her own fear replicated in the beloved eyes, and all at once she knew what she needed to do. "We have to try to save him or we are as bad as they are," she said. And there it was. She hated to bring her daughter into this, but what choice was there? "I have to save this boy."

"How?"

"I don't know yet," Vianne admitted.

"But Von Richter—"

As if drawn by his own name, the Nazi appeared at the front door, looking fussily precise in his uniform. "Ah, Madame Mauriac," he said, his gaze narrowing as he approached her. "There you are."

Vianne struggled for calm. "We have been to town for shopping."

"Not a good day for that. Jews are being collected for deportation." He walked toward her, his boots tamping down the wet grass. Beside him, the apple tree was barren of leaves; bits of fabric fluttered from the empty branches. Red. Pink. White. A new one for Beck—in black.

"And who is this fine-looking youngster?" Von Richter said, touching the child's tear-streaked cheek with one black-gloved finger.

"A f-friend's boy. His mother died of tuberculosis this week."

Von Richter lurched backward, as if she'd said bubonic plague. "I don't want that child in the house. Is that understood? You will take him to the orphanage this instant."

The orphanage. Mother Marie-Therese.

She nodded. "Of course, Herr Sturmbannführer."

He made a flicking gesture with his hand as if to say, *Go, now.* He started to walk away. Then he stopped and turned back to face Vianne. "I want you home this evening for supper."

"I am always home, Herr Sturmbannführer."

"We leave tomorrow, and I want you to feed me and my men a good meal before we go."

"Leave?" she asked, feeling a spike of hope.

"We are occupying the rest of France tomorrow. No more Free Zone. It's about damn time. Letting you French govern yourselves was a joke. Good day, Madame."

Vianne remained where she was, standing still, holding the child's hand. Above the sound of Jean Georges's crying, she heard the gate squeak open and slam shut. Then a car engine started up.

When he was gone, Sophie said, "Will Mother Marie-Therese hide him?"

"I hope so. Take Daniel into the house and lock the door. Don't open it for anyone but me. I'll be back as soon as I can."

Sophie looked old for her age suddenly, wise beyond her years. "Good for you, Maman."

"We shall see" was all the hope she had left.

When her children were safely in the house, with the door locked, she said to the boy beside her, "Come, Jean Georges, we are going for a walk."

"To my maman?"

She couldn't look at him. "Come."

As Vianne and the boy walked back to town, an intermittent rain began. Jean Georges alternately cried and complained, but Vianne was so nervous she barely heard him.

How could she ask Mother Superior to take this risk?

How could she not?

They walked past the church to the convent hidden behind it. The Order of the Sisters of St. Joseph had begun in 1650 with six like-minded women who simply wanted to serve the poor in their community. They had grown to thousands of members throughout France until religious communities were forbidden by the state during the French revolution. Some of the original six sisters had become martyrs for their beliefs— guillotined for their faith.

Vianne went to the abbey's front door and lifted the heavy iron knocker, letting it fall against the oak door, clattering hard.

"Why are we here?" Jean Georges whined. "Is my maman here?"

"Shhh."

A nun answered, her sweet, plump face bracketed by the white wimple and black hood of her habit. "Ah, Vianne," she said, smiling.

"Sister Agatha, I would like to speak to Mother Superior, if that's possible."

The nun stepped back, her habit swishing on the stone floor. "I will see. You two take a seat in the garden?"

Vianne nodded. "*Merci.*" She and Jean Georges made their way through the cold cloisters. At the end of one arched corridor, they turned left and went into the garden. It was good sized, and square, with frosted brown grass and a marble lion's head fountain and several stone benches placed here and there. Vianne took a seat on one of the cold benches out of the rain, and pulled the boy up beside her.

She didn't have long to wait.

"Vianne," Mother said, coming forward, her habit dragging on the grass, her fingers closed around the large crucifix that hung from a chain around her neck. "How good it is to see you. It's been too long. And who is this young man?"

The boy looked up. "Is my maman here?"

Vianne met Mother Superior's even gaze with one of her own. "His name is Jean Georges Ruelle, Mother. I would speak to you alone if we could."

Mother clapped her hands and a young nun appeared to take the boy away. When they were alone, Mother Superior sat down beside Vianne.

Vianne couldn't corral her thoughts and so a silence fell between them.

"I am sorry about your friend, Rachel."

"And so many others," Vianne said.

Mother nodded. "We have heard terrible rumors coming from Radio London about what is happening in the camps."

"Perhaps our Holy Father—"

"He is silent on this matter," Mother said, her voice heavy with disappointment.

Vianne took a deep breath. "Hélène Ruelle and her elder son were deported today. Jean Georges is alone. His mother . . . left him with me."

"Left him with you?" Mother paused. "It is dangerous to have a Jewish child in your home, Vianne."

"I want to protect him," she said quietly.

Mother looked at her. She was silent so long that Vianne's fear began to put down roots, grow. "And how would you accomplish this?" she asked at last.

"Hide him."

"Where?"

Vianne looked at Mother, saying nothing.

Mother's face drained of color. "Here?"

"An orphanage. What better place?"

Mother Superior stood and then sat. Then she stood again, her hands moved to the cross, held it. Slowly, she sat down again. Her shoulders sagged and then straightened when her decision was made. "A child in our care needs papers. Baptismal certificates—I can . . . get those, of course, but identity papers . . ."

"I will get them," Vianne said, although she had no idea if it was possible.

"You know that it is illegal to hide Jews now. The punishment is deportation if you're lucky, and lately, I believe no one is lucky in France."

Vianne nodded.

Then Mother Superior said, "I will take the boy. And I . . . could make room for more than one Jewish child."

"More?"

"Of course there are more, Vianne. I will speak to a man I know in Girot. He works for the Œuvre de Secours aux Enfants—the Help the Children Fund. I expect he will know many families and children in hiding. I will tell him to expect you."

"M-me?"

"You are the leader of this now, and if we are risking our lives for one child, we may as well try to save more." Mother got abruptly to her feet. She hooked her arm through Vianne's, and the two women strolled the perimeter of the small garden. "No one here can know the truth. The children will have to be coached and have paperwork that passes inspection. And you would need a position here—perhaps as a teacher, *oui*, as a part-time teacher. That would allow us to pay you a small stipend and would answer questions about why you are here with the children."

"*Oui*," Vianne said, feeling shaky.

"Don't look so afraid, Vianne. You are doing the right thing."

She had no doubt that this was true, and still she was terrified. "This is what they have done to us. We are afraid of our own shadows." She looked at Mother. "How will I do it? Go to scared, hungry women and ask them to give me their children?"

"You will ask them if they've seen their friends being herded onto trains and taken away. You will ask them what they would risk to keep their child off of that train. Then you will let each mother decide."

"It is an unimaginable choice. I'm not sure I could do it, just hand Sophie and Daniel over to a stranger."

Mother leaned close. "I hear one of their awful storm troopers is billeted at your house. You realize this puts you—and Sophie—at terrible risk."

"Of course. But how can I let her believe it's all right to do nothing in times such as these?"

Mother stopped. Releasing Vianne, she laid a soft palm against her cheek and smiled tenderly. "Be careful, Vianne. I have already been to your mother's funeral. I do not want to attend yours."

THIRTY

On an ice-cold mid-November day, Isabelle and Gaëtan left Brantôme and boarded a train to Bayonne. The carriage was overflowing with solemn German soldiers—more so than usual—and when they disembarked, they found more soldiers crowding the platform.

Isabelle held Gaëtan's hand as they made their way through the gray-green uniforms. Two young lovers on their way to the beach town. "My maman used to love going to the beach. Did I ever tell you that?" Isabelle asked as they passed near two SS officers.

"You rich kids see all the good stuff."

She smiled. "We were hardly rich, Gaëtan," she said when they were outside the train station.

"Well you weren't poor," he said. "I know poor." He paused, let that settle between them, and then he said, "I could be rich someday.

"Someday," he said again with a sigh, and she knew what he was thinking. It was what they were always thinking: Will there be a France in our future? Gaëtan slowed.

Isabelle saw what had captured his attention.

"Keep moving," he said.

A roadblock had been set up ahead of them. Troops were everywhere, carrying rifles.

"What's going on?" Isabelle asked.

"They've seen us," Gaëtan said. He tightened his hold on her hand. They strolled toward the swarm of German soldiers.

A burly, square-headed sentry blocked their way and demanded to see their passes and papers.

Isabelle offered her Juliette papers. Gaëtan offered his own false documents, but the soldier was more interested in the goings-on behind him. He barely glanced at the documents and handed them back.

Isabelle gave him her most innocent smile. "What's happening today?"

"No more Free Zone," the soldier said, waving them through.

"No more Free Zone? But—"

"We are taking over all of France," he said roughly. "No more pretense that your ridiculous Vichy government is in charge anywhere. Go."

Gaëtan pulled her forward, through the amassing troops.

For hours, as they walked, they were honked at by German lorries and automobiles in a hurry to get past them.

It wasn't until they reached the quaint seaside town of Saint-Jean-de-Luz that they were able to escape the gathering Nazis. They walked along the empty seawall, perched high above the pounding surf of the Atlantic Ocean. Below them, a curl of yellow sand held the mighty, angry ocean at bay. In the distance, a lush green peninsula was dotted with houses built in the Basque tradition, with white sides and red doors and bright red tile roofs. The sky overhead was a faded, washed-out blue, with clouds stretched as taut as clotheslines. There were no other people out today, neither on the beach nor walking along the ancient seawall.

For the first time in hours, Isabelle could breathe. "What does it mean, no Free Zone?"

"It is not good, that's for sure. It will make your work more dangerous."

"I've been moving through Occupied territory already."

She tightened her hold on his hand and led him off the seawall. They stepped down the uneven steps and made their way to the road.

"We used to vacation out here when I was little," she said. "Before my maman died. At least that's what I've heard. I barely remember."

She wanted it to be the start of a conversation, but her words fell into the new silence between them and went unanswered. In the quiet, Isabelle felt the suffocating weight of missing him, even though he was holding her hand. Why hadn't she asked him more questions in their days together, gotten to know everything about him? Now there was no time left and they both knew it. They walked in a heavy silence.

In the haze of early evening, Gaëtan got his first glimpse of the Pyrenees.

The jagged, snow-dusted mountains rose into the leaden sky, their snow-tipped peaks ringed in clouds. "*Merde.* You crossed those mountains how many times?"

"Twenty-seven."

"You're a wonder," he said.

"I am," she said with a smile.

They continued up, through the dark, empty streets of Urrugne, climbing with every step, moving past the closed-up shops and bistros full of old men. Beyond town lay the dirt path that led into the foothills. At last they came to the cottage tucked into the dark foothills, its chimney puffing smoke.

"Are you okay?" he asked, noticing that she had slowed her step.

"I will miss you," she said quietly. "How long can you stay?"

"I have to leave in the morning."

She wanted to release the hold on his hand, but it was difficult. She had this terrible, irrational fear that if she let go of him she would never touch him again and the thought of that was paralyzing. Still, she had a job to do. She let go of him and knocked three times sharply in rapid succession.

Madame opened the door. Dressed in man's clothing, smoking a Gauloises, she said, "Juliette! Come, come." She stepped back, welcoming Isabelle and Gaëtan into the main room, where four airmen stood around the dining table. A fire burned in the hearth, and above the flames a black cast-iron pot bubbled and hissed and popped. Isabelle could smell the stew's ingredients—goat meat; wine; bacon; thick, rich stock; mushrooms and sage. The aroma was heavenly and reminded her that she hadn't eaten all day.

Madame gathered the men together and introduced them—there were three RAF pilots and an American flier. The three Brits had been there for days, waiting for the American, who had arrived yesterday. Eduardo would be leading them over the mountains in the morning.

"It's good to meet you," one of them said, shaking Isabelle's hand as if she were a water pump. "You're just as beautiful as we've been told."

The men started talking all at once. Gaëtan moved easily into their midst, as if he belonged with them. Isabelle stood beside Madame Babineau and handed her the envelope of money that should have been delivered almost two weeks earlier. "I'm sorry about the delay."

"You had a good excuse. How are you feeling?"

Isabelle moved her shoulder, testing it. "Better. In another week, I'll be ready to make the crossing again."

Madame handed Isabelle the Gauloises. Isabelle took a long drag and exhaled, studying the men who were now in her charge. "How are they?"

"See the tall, thin one—nose like a Roman emperor?"

Isabelle couldn't help smiling. "I see him."

"He claims to be a lord or duke or something. Sarah in Pau said he was trouble. Wouldn't follow a girl's orders."

Isabelle made a note of that. It wasn't a rarity, of course, fliers who didn't want to take orders from women—or girls or dames or broads—but it was always a trial.

She handed Isabelle a crumpled, dirt-stained letter. "One of them gave me this to give to you."

She opened it quickly, scanned the contents. She recognized Henri's sloppy handwriting:

> J—*your friend survived her German holiday, but she has guests.*
> *Do not stop by. Will watch out for her.*

Vianne was fine—she had been released after questioning—but another soldier, or soldiers, was billeted there. She crumpled the paper and tossed it in the fire. She didn't know whether to be relieved or more worried. Instinctively, her gaze sought out Gaëtan, who was watching her as he spoke to an airman.

"I see the way you're watching him, you know."

"Lord big nose?"

Madame Babineau barked out a laugh. "I am old but not blind. The young handsome one with the hungry eyes. He keeps looking at you, too."

"He'll be leaving tomorrow morning."

"Ah."

Isabelle turned to the woman who had become her friend in the past two years. "I'm afraid to let him go, which is crazy with all the dangerous things I do."

The look in Madame's dark eyes was both knowing and compassionate. "I would tell you to be careful if these were ordinary times. I would point out that he is young and engaged in a dangerous business and young men in danger can be fickle." She sighed. "But we are cautious about too much these days, and why add love to the list?"

"Love," Isabelle said quietly.

"I will add this, though, since I am a mother and we can't help ourselves: A broken heart hurts as badly in wartime as in peace. Say good-bye to your young man well."

Isabelle waited for the house to go quiet—or as quiet as a room could be with men sleeping on the floor, snoring, rolling over. Moving cautiously, she eased out of her blankets and picked her way through the main room and went outside.

Stars flickered overhead, the sky immense in this dark landscape. Moonlight illuminated the goats, turned them into silver-white dots on the hillside.

She stood at the wooden fence, staring out. She didn't have long to wait.

Gaëtan came up behind her, put his arms around her. She leaned back into him. "I feel safe in your arms," she said.

When he didn't respond, she knew something was wrong. Her heart sank. She turned slowly, looked up at him. "What is it?"

"Isabelle." The way he said it frightened her. She thought, *No, don't tell me. Whatever it is, don't tell me.* In the silence, noises became noticeable—the bleating of goats, the beating of her heart, the tumbling of a rock down a distant hillside.

"That meeting. The one we were going to in Carriveau when you found the airman?"

"*Oui?*" she said. She had studied him so carefully in the past few days, watched every nuance of emotion cross his face, and she knew whatever he was going to say, it wouldn't be good.

"I'm leaving Paul's group. Fighting . . . a different way."

"Different how?"

"With guns," he said quietly. "And bombs. Anything we can find. I'm joining a group of guerrilla partisans who live in the woods. My job is explosives." He smiled. "And stealing bomb parts."

"Your past should help you there." Her teasing fell flat.

His smile faded. "I can't just deliver papers anymore, Iz. I need to do more. And . . . I won't see you for a while, I think."

She nodded, but even as she moved her head in agreement, she thought: *How? How will I walk away and leave him now?* and she understood what he had been afraid of from the start.

The look he gave her was as intimate as a kiss. In it, she saw her own fear reflected. They might never see each other again. "Make love to me, Gaëtan," she said.

Like it's the last time.

❧

Vianne stood outside the Hôtel Bellevue in the pouring rain. The windows of the hotel were fogged; through the haze she could see a crowd of gray-green field uniforms.

Come on, Vianne, you're in it now.

She squared her shoulders and opened the door. A bell tinkled gaily overhead, and the men in the room stopped what they were doing and turned to look at her. Wehrmacht, SS, Gestapo. She felt like a lamb going to slaughter.

At the desk, Henri looked up. Seeing her, he came out from behind the front desk and moved swiftly through the crowd toward her.

He took her by the arm, hissing, "Smile." She tried to comply. She wasn't sure whether she succeeded.

He led her to the front desk, where he let go of her arm. He was saying something—laughing as if at some joke—as he took his place by the heavy black phone and cash register. "Your father, correct?" he said loudly. "A room for two nights?"

She nodded numbly.

"Here, let me show you the room we have available," he said at last.

She followed him out of the lobby and into the narrow hallway. They went past a small table set with fresh fruit (only the Germans could afford such an extravagance) and a water closet that was empty. At the end of the corridor, he led her up a narrow set of stairs and into a room so small there was only a single bed and a blacked-out window.

He closed the door behind them. "You shouldn't be here. I sent you word that Isabelle was fine."

"*Oui, merci.*" She took a deep breath. "I need identity papers. You were the only person I could think of who might be able to help me."

He frowned. "That's a dangerous request, Madame. For whom?"

"A Jewish child in hiding."

"Hiding where?"

"I don't think you want to know that, do you?"

"No. No. Is it a safe place?"

She shrugged, her answer obvious in the silence. Who knew what was safe anymore?

"I hear Sturmbannführer Von Richter is billeted with you. He was here first. He's a dangerous man. Vindictive and cruel. If he caught you—"

"What can we do, Henri, just stand by and watch?"

"You remind me of your sister," he said.

"Believe me, I am not a brave woman."

Henri was quiet for a long while. Then he said, "I'll work on getting you the blank papers. You'll have to learn to forge them yourself. I am too busy to add to my duties. Practice by studying your own."

"Thank you." She paused, looking at him, remembering the note he had delivered to her all those months ago—and the assumptions Vianne had made about her sister at the time. She knew now that Isabelle had been doing dangerous work from the beginning. Important work. Isabelle had shielded Vianne from this knowledge to protect her, even though it meant looking like a fool. She had traded on the fact that Vianne would easily believe the worst of her.

Vianne was ashamed of herself for believing the lie so easily. "Don't tell Isabelle I am doing this. I want to protect her."

Henri nodded.

"Au revoir," Vianne said.

On her way out, she heard him say, "Your sister would be proud of you." Vianne neither slowed nor responded. Ignoring the German soldiers' catcalling, she made her way out of the hotel and headed for home.

Now all of France was occupied by the Germans, but it made little difference in Vianne's daily life. She still spent all day in one queue or another. Her biggest problem was Daniel. It still seemed smart to hide him from the villagers, even though her lie about an adoption seemed unquestioned when she'd told it (and she'd told it to everyone she could find, but people were too busy surviving to care, or maybe they guessed the truth and applauded it, who knew).

She left the children at home now, hidden away behind locked doors. It meant that she was always jittery in town, nervous. Today, when she had gotten all that there was to be had for her rations, she rewrapped the woolen scarf around her throat and left the butcher's shop.

As she braved the cold on rue Victor Hugo, she was so miserable and distracted by worry, it took her a moment to realize that Henri was walking beside her.

He glanced around the street, up and down, but in the wind and cold, no one was about. Shutters clattered and awnings shook. The bistro tables were empty.

He handed her a baguette. "The filling is unusual. My maman's recipe."

She understood. There were papers inside. She nodded.

"Bread with special filling is difficult to obtain these days. Eat it wisely."

"And what if I need more . . . bread?"

"More?"

"So many hungry children."

He stopped, turned to her, gave her a perfunctory kiss on each cheek. "Come see me again, Madame."

She whispered in his ear. "Tell my sister I asked about her. We parted badly."

He smiled. "I am constantly arguing with my brother, even in war. In the end, we're brothers."

Vianne nodded, hoping it was true. She placed the baguette in her basket, covering it with the scrap of linen, tucking it alongside the blancmange powder and oatmeal that had been available today. As she watched him walk away, the basket seemed to grow heavier. Tightening her grip, she headed down the street.

She was almost out of the town square when she heard it.

"Madame Mauriac. What a surprise."

His voice was like oil pooling at her feet, slippery and clinging. She wet her lips and held her shoulders back, trying to look both confident and unconcerned. He had returned last evening, triumphant, crowing about how easy it had been to take over all of France. She had fed dinner to him and his men, pouring them endless glasses of wine—at the end of the meal, he had tossed the leftovers to the chickens. Vianne and the children had gone to bed hungry.

He was in his uniform, heavily decorated with swastikas and iron crosses, smoking a cigarette, blowing the smoke slightly to the left of her face. "You are done with your shopping for the day?"

"Such as it is, Herr Sturmbannführer. There was very little to be had today, even with our ration cards."

"Perhaps if your men hadn't been such cowards, you women wouldn't be so hungry."

She gritted her teeth in what she hoped passed for a smile.

He studied her face, which she knew was chalky pale. "Are you all right, Madame?"

"Fine, Herr Sturmbannführer."

"Allow me to carry your basket. I will escort you home."

She gripped the basket. "No, really, it's not necessary—"

He reached a black-gloved hand toward her. She had no choice but to place the twisted willow handle in his hand.

He took the basket from her and began walking. She fell into step beside him, feeling conspicuous walking with an SS officer through the streets of Carriveau.

As they walked, Von Richter made conversation. He talked about the Allies' certain defeat in North Africa, he talked about the cowardice of the French and the greediness of the Jews, he talked about the Final Solution as if it were a recipe to be exchanged among friends.

She could hardly make out his words over the roar in her head. When she dared to glance at the basket, she saw the baguette peeking out from beneath the red-and-white linen that covered it.

"You are breathing like a racehorse, Madame. Are you unwell?"

Yes. That was it.

She forced a cough, clamped a hand over her mouth. "I am sorry, Herr Sturmbannführer. I was hoping not to bother you with it, but sadly, I fear I caught the flu from that boy the other day."

He stopped. "Have I not asked you to keep your germs away from me?" He shoved the basket at her so hard it hit her in the chest. She grabbed hold of it desperately, afraid it would fall and the baguette would break open and spill false papers at his feet.

"I-I am so sorry. It was thoughtless of me."

"I will not be home for supper," he said, turning on his heel.

Vianne stood there a few moments—just long enough to be polite, in case he turned around—and then she hurried for home.

Well past midnight that night, when Von Richter had been abed for hours, Vianne crept from her bedroom and went to the empty kitchen. She carried a chair back to her bedroom, quietly shutting the door behind her. She brought the chair to the nightstand, tucked it in close, and sat down. By the light of a single candle, she withdrew the blank identity papers from her girdle.

She took out her own identity papers and studied them in minute detail. Then she took out the family Bible and opened it. On every blank space she could find, she practiced forging signatures. At first she was so nervous that her penmanship was unsteady, but the more she practiced, the calmer she felt. When her hands and breathing had stead-ied, she forged a new birth certificate for Jean Georges, naming him Emile Duvall.

But new papers weren't enough. What would happen when the war was over and Hélène Ruelle returned? If Vianne weren't here (with the risk she was taking, she had to consider this terrible possibility), Hélène would have no idea where to look for her son or what name he'd been given.

She would need to create a *fiche*, a file card that had all of the informa-tion she had on him—who he really was, who his parents were, any known relatives. Everything she could think of.

She ripped out three pages from the Bible and made a list on each page.

On the first, in dark ink over the prayers, she wrote:

Ari de Champlain 1
Jean Georges Ruelle 2

On the second sheet, she wrote:

1. Daniel Mauriac
2. Emile Duvall

And on the third, she wrote:

1. Carriveau. Mauriac
2. Abbaye de la Trinité

She carefully rolled each page into a small cylinder. Tomorrow she would hide them in three different places. One in a dirty jar in the shed, which she would fill with nails; one in an old paint can in the barn; and one she would bury in a box in the chicken coop. The *fiche* cards she would leave with Mother at the Abbey.

The cards and lists, when put together, would identify the children after the war and make it possible to get them back to their families. It was dangerous, of course, writing down any of this, but if she didn't keep a record—and the worst happened to her—how would the hidden children ever be reunited with their parents?

For a long time, Vianne stared down at her work, so long that the children sleeping in her bed began to move around and mumble and the candle flame began to sputter. She leaned over and laid a hand on Daniel's warm back to comfort him. Then she climbed into bed with her children. It was a long time before she fell asleep.

THIRTY-ONE

May 6, 1995
Portland, Oregon

I am running away from home," I say to the young woman sitting next
to me. She has hair the color of cotton candy and more tattoos than a
Hell's Angel biker, but she is alone like me, in this airport full of busy
people. Her name, I have learned, is Felicia. In the past two hours—since
the announcement that our flight is delayed—we have become traveling
companions. It was a natural thing, our coming together. She saw me picking at the horrible French fries Americans love, and I saw her watching
me. She was hungry, that was obvious. Naturally, I called her over and
offered to buy her a meal. Once a mother, always a mother.

"Or maybe I'm finally going home after years of running away. It's hard
to know the truth sometimes."

"I'm running away," she says, slurping on the shoebox-sized soft drink I
bought her. "If Paris isn't far enough, my next stop is Antarctica."

I see past the hardware on her face and the defiance in her tattoos, and
I feel a strange connection to her, a compatriotism. We are runaways together. "I'm sick," I say, surprising myself with the admission.

"Sick, like the shingles? My aunt had that. It was gross."

"No, sick like cancer."

"Oh." Slurp. Slurp. "So why are you going to Paris? Don't you need,
like, chemo?"

I start to answer her (no, no treatments for me, I'm done with all that) when her question settles in. *Why are you going to Paris?* And I fall silent.

"I get it. You're dying." She shakes her big cup so that the slushy ice rattles inside. "Done with trying. Lost hope and all that."

"What the *hell?*"

I am so deep in thought—in the unexpected starkness of her statement (*you're dying*) that it takes me a moment to realize that it is Julien who has just spoken. I look up at my son. He is wearing the navy blue silk sport coat I gave him for Christmas this year and trendy, dark-washed jeans. His hair is tousled and he is holding a black leather weekender bag slung over one shoulder. He does not look happy. "Paris, Mom?"

"Air France flight 605 will begin boarding in five minutes."

"That's us," Felicia says.

I know what my son is thinking. As a boy, he begged me to take him to Paris. He wanted to see the places I mentioned in bedtime stories—he wanted to know how it felt to walk along the Seine at night or to shop for art in the Place Des Vosges, or to sit in the Tuilleries Garden, eating a butterfly macaron from Ladurée. I said no to every request, saying simply, *I am an American now, my place is here.*

"We'd like to begin boarding anyone traveling with children under two years of age or anyone who needs a little extra time and our first-class passengers . . ."

I stand, lifting the extendable handle on my rolling bag. "That's me."

Julien stands directly in front of me as if to block my access to the gate. "You're going to Paris, all of a sudden, by yourself?"

"It was a last-minute decision. What the hell, and all that." I give him the best smile I can muster under the circumstances. I have hurt his feelings, which was never my intent.

"It's that invitation," he says. "And the truth you never told me."

Why had I said that on the phone? "You make it sound so dramatic," I say, waving my gnarled hand. "It's not. And now, I must board. I'll call you—"

"No need. I'm coming with you."

I see the surgeon in him suddenly, the man who is used to staring past blood and bone to find what is broken.

Felicia hefts her camo backpack over one shoulder and tosses her empty cup in the wastebasket, where it bounces against the opening and thunks inside. "So much for running away, dude."

I don't know which I feel more—relief or disappointment. "Are you sitting by me?"

"On such short notice? No."

I clutch the handle of my rolling suitcase and walk toward the nice-looking young woman in the blue-and-white uniform. She takes my boarding pass, tells me to have a nice flight, and I nod absently and keep moving.

The jetway draws me forward. I feel a little claustrophobic suddenly. I can hardly catch my breath, I can't yank my suitcase's black wheels into the plane, over the metallic hump.

"I'm here, Mom," Julien says quietly, taking my suitcase, lifting it easily over the obstruction. The sound of his voice reminds me that I am a mother and mothers don't have the luxury of falling apart in front of their children, even when they are afraid, even when their children are adults.

A stewardess takes one look at me and makes that *here's an old one who needs help* face. Living where I do now, in that shoebox filled with the Q-tips that old people become, I've come to recognize it. Usually it irks me, makes me straighten my back and push aside the youngster who is sure that I cannot cope in the world on my own, but just now I'm tired and scared and a little help doesn't seem like a bad thing. I let her help me to my window seat in the second row of the plane. I have splurged on a first-class ticket. Why not? I don't see much reason to save my money anymore.

"Thank you," I say to the stewardess as I sit down. My son is the next one onto the plane. When he smiles at the stewardess, I hear a little sigh, and I think *of course*. Women have swooned over Julien since before his voice changed.

"Are you two traveling together?" she says, and I know she is giving him points for being a good son.

Julien gives her one of his ice-melting smiles. "Yes, but we couldn't get seats together. I'm three rows behind her." He offers her his boarding pass.

"Oh, I'm sure I can solve this for you," she says as Julien stows my suitcase and his weekender in the bin above my seat.

I stare out the window, expecting to see the tarmac busy with men and women in orange vests waving their arms and unloading suitcases, but what I see is water squiggling down the Plexiglas surface, and woven within the silvered lines is my reflection; my own eyes stare back at me.

"Thank you so much," I hear Julien say, and then he is sitting down beside me, clamping his seat belt shut, pulling the strap taut across his waist.

"So," he says after a long enough pause that people have shuffled past us in a steady stream and the pretty stewardess (who has combed her hair and freshened her makeup) has offered us champagne. "The invitation."

I sigh. "The invitation." Yes. That's the start of it. Or the end, depending on your point of view. "It's a reunion. In Paris."

"I don't understand," he says.

"You were never meant to."

He reaches for my hand. It is so sure and comforting, that healer's touch of his.

In his face, I see the whole of my life. I see a baby who came to me long after I'd given up . . . and a hint of the beauty I once had. I see . . . my life in his eyes.

"I know there's something you want to tell me and whatever it is, it's hard for you. Just start at the beginning."

I can't help smiling at that. He is such an American, this son of mine. He thinks one's life can be distilled to a narrative that has a beginning and an end. He knows nothing about the kind of sacrifice that, once made, can never be either fully forgotten or fully borne. And how could he? I have protected him from all of that.

Still. I am here, on a plane heading home, and I have an opportunity to make a different choice than the one I made when my pain was fresh and a future predicated on the past seemed impossible.

"Later," I say, and I mean it this time. I will tell him the story of my war, and my sister's. Not all of it, of course, not the worst parts, but some. Enough that he will know a truer version of me. "Not here, though. I'm exhausted." I lean back into the big first-class chair and close my eyes.

How can I start at the beginning, when all I can think about is the end?

THIRTY-TWO

If you're going through hell, keep going.
—WINSTON CHURCHILL

May 1944
France

*I*n the eighteen months since the Nazis had occupied all of France, life had become even more dangerous, if that were possible. French political prisoners had been interned in Drancy and imprisoned in Fresnes—and hundreds of thousands of French Jews had been deported to concentration camps in Germany. The orphanages of Neuilly-sur-Seine and Montreuil had been emptied and their children sent to the camps, and the children who'd been held at the Vel d'Hiv—more than four thousand of them—had been separated from their parents and sent to concentration camps alone. Allied forces were bombing day and night. Arrests were made constantly; people were hauled out of their homes and their shops for the slightest infraction, for a rumor of resistance, and imprisoned or deported. Innocent hostages were shot in retaliation for things they knew nothing about and every man between eighteen and fifty was supposed to go to forced-labor camps in Germany. No one felt secure. There were no yellow stars on clothing anymore. No one made eye contact or spoke to strangers. Electricity had been shut off.

Isabelle stood on a busy Paris street corner, ready to cross, but before her ratty, wooden-soled shoe hit the cobblestones, a whistle shrieked. She backed into the shade of a flowering chestnut tree.

These days, Paris was a woman screaming. Noise, noise, noise. Whistles blaring, shotguns firing, lorries rumbling, soldiers shouting. The tide of the war had shifted. The Allies had landed in Italy, and the Nazis had failed to drive them back. Losses had spurred the Nazis to greater and greater aggression. In March they had massacred more than three hundred Italians in Rome as retaliation for partisan bombing that killed twenty-eight Germans. At last, Charles de Gaulle had taken control of all Free France forces, and something big was being planned for this week.

A column of German soldiers marched up the boulevard Saint-Germain on their way to the Champs Élysées; they were led by an officer astride a white stallion.

As soon as they passed, Isabelle crossed the street and merged into the crowd of German soldiers gathered on the other sidewalk. She kept her gaze downward and her gloved hands coiled around her handbag. Her clothing was as worn and ragged as that of most Parisians, and the clatter of wooden soles rang out. No one had leather anymore. She bypassed long queues of housewives and hollow-faced children standing outside of *boulangeries* and *boucheries*. Rations had been cut again and again and again in the past two years; people in Paris were surviving on eight hundred calories a day. There was not a dog or cat or rat to be seen on the streets. This week, one could buy tapioca and string beans. Nothing else. At the boulevard de la Gare, there were piles of furniture and art and jewelry—everything of value taken from the people who'd been deported. Their belongings were sorted and crated and sent to Germany.

She ducked into Les Deux Magots in the Saint-Germain and took a seat in the back; on the red moleskin bench, she waited impatiently, watched over by the statues of Chinese mandarins. A woman who might be Simone de Beauvoir sat at a table near the front of the café. She was bent over a piece of paper, writing furiously. Isabelle sank into the comfortable seat; she was bone weary. In the past month alone, she'd crossed the Pyrenees three times and visited each of the safe houses, paying her *passeurs*. Every step was dangerous now that there was no Free Zone.

"Juliette."

She looked up and saw her father. He had aged in the last few years—they all had. Deprivation and hunger and despair and fear had left their marks on him—in skin that was the color and texture of beach sand and deeply lined.

He was so thin that his head now seemed too big for his body.

He slid into the booth across from her, put his wrinkled hands on the pitted mahogany table.

She reached forward, clasped her hands around his wrists. When she drew her hands back, she had palmed the pencil-sized coil of false identity papers he'd had up his sleeve. She tucked them expertly in her girdle and smiled at the waiter who had just appeared.

"Coffee," Papa said in a tired voice.

Isabelle shook her head.

The waiter returned, deposited a cup of barley coffee, and disappeared again.

"They had a meeting today," her father said. "High-ranking Nazis. The SS was there. I heard the word 'Nightingale.'"

"We're careful," she said quietly. "And you are taking more risk than I am, stealing the blank identity papers."

"I am an old man. They don't even see me. You should take a break, maybe. Let someone else do your mountain trips."

She gave him a pointed look. Did people say things like this to men? Women were integral to the Resistance. Why couldn't men see that?

He sighed, seeing the answer in her affronted look. "Do you need a place to stay?"

Isabelle appreciated the offer. It reminded her of how far they'd come. They still weren't close, but they were working together, and that was something. He no longer pushed her away, and now—here, an invitation. It gave her hope that someday, when the war was over, they could actually *talk*. "I can't. It would put you at risk." She hadn't been to the apartment in more than eighteen months. Neither had she been to Carriveau or seen Vianne in all that time. Rarely had Isabelle spent three nights in the same place. Her life was a series of hidden rooms and dusty mattresses and suspicious strangers.

"Have you heard anything about your sister?"

"I have friends looking out for her. I hear she is taking no chances, keeping her head down and her daughter safe. She will be fine," she said, hearing how hope softened that last sentence.

"You miss her," he said.

Isabelle found herself thinking of the past suddenly, wishing she could just let it go. Yes, she missed her sister, but she had missed Vianne for years, for all of her life.

"Well." He stood up abruptly.

She noticed his hands. "Your hands are shaking."

"I quit drinking. It seemed like a bad time to be a drunk."

"I don't know about that," she said, smiling up at him. "Drunk seems like a good idea these days."

"Be careful, Juliette."

Her smile faded. Every time she saw anyone these days, it was hard to say good-bye. You never knew if you'd see them again. "You, too."

Midnight.

Isabelle crouched in the darkness behind a crumbling stone wall. She was deep in the woods and dressed in peasant clothes—denim overalls that had seen better days, wooden-soled boots, and a lightweight blouse made from an old shower curtain. Downwind, she could smell the smoke of nearby bonfires but she couldn't see even a glimmer of firelight.

Behind her, a twig snapped.

She crouched lower, barely breathed.

A whistle sounded. It was the lilting song of the nightingale. Or close to it. She whistled back.

She heard footsteps; breathing. And then, "Iz?"

She rose and turned around. A thin beam of light swept past her and then snapped off. She stepped over a fallen log and into Gaëtan's arms.

"I missed you," he said after a kiss, drawing back with a reluctance she could feel. They had not seen each other for more than eight months. Every time she heard of a train derailing or a German-occupied hotel being blown up or a skirmish with partisans, she worried.

He took her hand and led her through a forest so dark she couldn't see the man beside her or the trail beneath their feet. Gaëtan never turned on his torchlight. He knew these woods intimately, having lived here for well over a year.

At the end of the woods, they came to a huge, grassy field where people stood in rows. They held torchlights, which they swept forward and back like beacons, illuminating the flat area between the trees.

She heard an aeroplane engine overhead, felt the whoosh of air on her cheeks, and smelled exhaust. It swooped in above them, flying low enough to make the trees shudder. She heard a loud mechanical *scree* and the banging of metal on metal and then a parachute appeared, falling, a huge box swinging beneath it.

"Weapons drop," Gaëtan said. Tugging her hand, he led her into the trees again and up a hill, to the encampment deep in the forest. In its center, a bonfire glowed bright orange, its light hidden by the thick fringe of trees. Several men stood around the fire, smoking cigarettes and talking. Most had come here to avoid the STO—compulsory deportation to forced-labor camps in Germany. Once here, they had taken up arms and become partisans who fought a guerrilla war with Germany, in secret, under cover of night. The Maquis. They bombed trains and blew up munitions dumps and flooded canals and did whatever else they could to disrupt the flow of goods and men from France to Germany. They got their supplies—and their information—from the Allies. Their lives were always at risk; when found by the enemy, reprisals were swift and often brutal. Burning, cattle prods, blinding. Each Maquis fighter carried a cyanide pill in his pocket.

The men looked unwashed, starving, haggard. Most wore brown corduroy pants and black berets, all of which were frayed and patched and faded.

For all that Isabelle believed in their cause, she wouldn't want to be alone up here.

"Come," Gaëtan said. He led her past the bonfire to a small, dirty-looking tent with a canvas flap that was open to reveal a single sleeping bag and a pile of clothes and a pair of muddy boots. As usual, it smelled of dirty socks and sweat.

Isabelle ducked her head and crouched low as she made her way inside.

Gaëtan sat down beside her and closed the flap. He didn't light a lamp (the men would see their silhouettes within and start catcalling). "Isabelle," he said. "I've missed you."

She leaned forward, let herself be taken in his arms and kissed. When it ended—too soon—she took a deep breath. "I have a message for your group from London. Paul received it at five P.M. tonight. 'Long sobs of autumn violins.'"

She heard him draw in a breath. Obviously the words, which they'd received over the radio from the BBC, were a code.

"Is it important?" she asked.

His hands moved to her face, held her gently, and drew her in for another kiss. This one was full of sadness. Another good-bye.

"Important enough that I have to leave right now."

All she could do was nod. "There's never any time," she whispered. Every moment they'd ever had together had been stolen somehow, or wrested. They met, they ducked into shadowy corners or dirty tents or back rooms, and they made love in the dark, but they didn't get to lie together afterward like lovers and talk. He was always leaving her, or she was leaving him. Each time he held her, she thought—this will be it, the last time I see him. And she waited for him to say he loved her.

She told herself that it was war. That he did love her, but he was afraid of that love, afraid he would lose her, and it would hurt more somehow if he'd declared himself. On good days, she even believed it.

"How dangerous is it, this thing you're going off to do?"

Again, the silence.

"I'll find you," he said quietly. "Maybe I'll come to Paris for a night and we'll sneak into the cinema and boo at the newsreels and walk through the Rodin Gardens."

"Like lovers," she said, trying to smile. It was what they always said to each other, this dream shared of a life that seemed impossible to remember and unlikely to reoccur.

He touched her face with a gentleness that brought tears to her eyes. "Like lovers."

❧

In the past eighteen months, as the war had escalated and Nazi aggression mounted, Vianne had found and hidden thirteen children at the orphanage. At first she had canvassed the nearby countryside, following leads given to her by the OSE. In time, Mother had connected with the American Jewish Joint Distribution Committee—an umbrella group for Jewish charities in the United States that funded the struggle to save Jewish children—and they had brought Vianne into contact with more children in need. Mothers sometimes showed up on her doorstep, crying, desperate, begging her for help. Vianne never turned anyone away, but she was always terrified.

Now, on a warm June day in 1944, a week after the Allies had landed more than one hundred and fifty thousand troops in Normandy, Vianne stood in her classroom at the orphanage, staring out at the children who sat slumped and tired at their desks. Of course they were tired.

In the past year, the bombing had rarely stopped. Air raids were so constant that Vianne no longer bothered to take her children into the cellar pantry when the alarm sounded at night. She just lay in bed with them, holding them tightly until either all clear sounded or the bombing stopped.

It never stopped for long.

Vianne clapped her hands together and called for attention. Perhaps a game would lift their spirits.

"Is it another air raid, Madame?" asked Emile. He was six years old now and never mentioned his maman anymore. When asked, he said that she "died because she got sick," and that was all there was to it. He had no memory at all of being Jean Georges Ruelle.

Just as Daniel had no memory of who he used to be.

"No. No air raid," she said. "Actually, I was thinking that it's awfully hot in here." She tugged at her loose collar.

"That's because of the blackout windows, Madame," said Claudine (formerly Bernadette). "Mother says she feels like a smoked ham in her woolen habit."

The children laughed at that.

"It's better than the winter cold," Sophie said, and to this there was a round of nodding agreement.

"I was thinking," Vianne said, "that today would be a good day to—"

Before she could finish her thought, she heard the clatter of a motorcycle outside; moments later, footsteps—jackboots—thundered down the stone corridor.

Everyone went still.

The door to her classroom opened.

Von Richter walked into the room. As he approached Vianne, he removed his hat and tucked it beneath his armpit. "Madame," he said. "Will you step into the corridor with me?"

Vianne nodded. "One moment, children," she said. "Read quietly while I am gone."

Von Richter took her by the arm—a painful, punishing grip—and led her into the stone courtyard outside her classroom. The sound of falling water from the mossy fountain gurgled nearby.

"I am here to ask about an acquaintance of yours. Henri Navarre."

Vianne prayed she didn't flinch. "Who, Herr Sturmbannführer?"

"Henri Navarre."

"Ah. *Oui.* The hotelier." She fisted her hands to still them.

"You are his friend?"

Vianne shook her head. "No, Herr Sturmbannführer. I know of him, merely. It is a small town."

Von Richter gave her an assessing look. "If you are lying to me about something so simple, I will perhaps wonder what else you are lying to me about."

"Herr Sturmbannführer, no—"

"You have been seen with him." His breath smelled of beer and bacon, and his eyes were narrowed.

He'll kill me, she thought for the first time. She'd been careful for so long, never antagonizing him or defying him, never making eye contact if she could help it. But in the last few weeks he had become volatile, impossible to predict.

"It is a small town, but—"

"He has been arrested for aiding the enemy, Madame."

"Oh," she said.

"I will speak to you more about this, Madame. In a small room with no windows. And believe me, I will get the truth out of you. I will find out if you are working with him."

"Me?"

He tightened his hold so much she thought her bones might crack. "If I find that you knew anything about this, I will question your children . . . intensely . . . and then I will send you all to Fresnes Prison."

"Don't hurt them, I beg you."

It was the first time she'd ever begged him for anything, and at the desperation in her voice, he went perfectly still. His breathing accelerated. And there it was, as plain as the blue of his eyes: arousal. For more than a year and a half, she had conducted herself with scrupulous care in his presence, dressing and acting like a little wren, never drawing his attention, never saying anything beyond yes or no, Herr Sturmbannführer. Now, in an instant, all of that was undone. She had revealed her weakness, and he had seen it. He knew how to hurt her now.

❧

Hours later, Vianne was in a windowless room in the bowels of the town hall. She sat stiffly upright in her chair, her hands clamped around the armrests so tightly that her knuckles were white.

She had been here for a long time, alone, trying to decide what the best answers would be. How much did they know? What would they believe? Had Henri named her?

No. If they knew that she had forged documents and hidden Jewish children, she would already have been arrested.

Behind her, the door creaked open and then clicked shut.

"Madame Mauriac."

She got to her feet.

Von Richter circled her slowly, his gaze intimate on her body. She was wearing a faded, often-repaired dress and no stockings, and Oxfords with wooden soles. Her hair, unwashed for two days, was covered by a gingham turban with a knot above her forehead. Her lipstick had run out long ago and so her lips were pale.

He came to a stop in front of her, too close, his hands clasped behind his back.

It took courage to tilt her chin upward, and when she did—when she looked in his ice-blue eyes—she knew she was in trouble.

"You were seen with Henri Navarre, walking in the square. He is sus-
pected of working with the Maquis du Limousin, those cowards who live
like animals in the woods and aided the enemy in Normandy." At the same
time as the Allied landing at Normandy, the Maquis had wreaked havoc
across the country, cutting train lines, setting bombs, flooding canals. The
Nazis were desperate to find and punish the partisans.

"I am barely acquainted with him, Herr Sturmbannführer; I know nothing of men who aid the enemy."

"Are you making a fool of me, Madame?"

She shook her head.

He wanted to hit her. She could see it in his blue eyes: an ugly, sick
desire. It had been planted when she'd begged him for something and now
she had no idea how to eradicate it.

He reached out and grazed a finger along her jaw. She flinched. "Are
you truly so innocent?"

"Herr Sturmbannführer, you have lived in my home for eighteen
months. You see me every day. I feed my children and work in my garden
and teach at the orphanage. I am hardly aiding the Allies."

His fingertips caressed her mouth, forcing her lips to part slightly. "If I
find out that you are lying to me, I will hurt you, Madame. And I will enjoy it." He let his hand fall away. "But if you tell the truth—now—I will
spare you. And your children."

She shivered at the thought of his finding out that he had been living
all this time with a Jewish child. It would make a fool of him.

"I would never lie to you, Herr Sturmbannführer. You must know that."

"Here's what I know," he said, leaning closer, whispering in her ear, "I
hope you are lying to me, Madame."

He drew back.

"You are scared," he said, smiling.

"I have nothing to be afraid of," she said, unable to get much volume in
her voice.

"We shall see if that is true. For now, Madame, go home. And pray I do
not discover that you have lied to me."

That same day, Isabelle walked up the cobblestoned street in the hilltop town of Urrugne. She could hear the echo of footsteps behind her. On the journey here from Paris, her two latest "songs"—Major Foley and Sergeant Smythe—had followed her instructions perfectly and had made it past the various checkpoints. She hadn't looked back in quite some time, but she had no doubt that they were there walking as instructed—with at least one hundred yards between them.

At the top of the hill, she saw a man seated on a bench in front of the closed *poste*. He held a sign that read: DEAF AND DUMB. WAITING FOR MY MAMAN TO PICK ME UP. Amazingly, the simple ruse still worked to fool the Nazis.

Isabelle went to him. "I have an umbrella," she said in her heavily accented English.

"It looks like rain," he said.

She nodded. "Walk at least fifty yards behind me."

She kept walking up the hill, alone.

By the time she reached Madame Babineau's property it was nearing nightfall. At the bend in the road, she paused, waiting for her airmen to catch up.

The man who'd been seated on the bench was the first to arrive. "Hello, ma'am," he said, pulling off his borrowed beret. "Major Tom Dowd, ma'am. And I'm to say best wishes from Sarah in Pau, ma'am. She was a first-rate hostess."

Isabelle smiled tiredly. They were so . . . larger than life, these Yanks, with their ready smiles and booming voices. And their gratitude. Not at all like the Brits, who thanked her with clipped words and cool voices and firm handshakes. She'd lost track of the times an American had hugged her so tightly she'd come off her feet. "I'm Juliette," she said to the major.

Major Jack Foley was next to arrive. He gave her a big smile and said, "Those are some mountains."

"You said a mouthful there," Dowd said, thrusting his hand out. "Dowd. Chicago."

"Foley. Boston. Nice to meet you."

Sergeant Smythe brought up the rear. He arrived a few minutes later. "Hello, gentlemen," he said stiffly. "That was a hike."

"Just wait," Isabelle said with a laugh.

She led them to the cottage and knocked three times on the front door.

Madame Babineau opened the door a little, saw Isabelle through the crack, and grinned, stepping back to allow them entrance. As always, a cast-iron cauldron hung above the flames in the soot-blackened fireplace. The table was set for their arrival, with glasses of warm milk and empty soup bowls.

Isabelle glanced around. "Eduardo?"

"In the barn, with two more airmen. We are having trouble getting supplies. It's all this damned bombing. Half of town is rubble." She placed a hand on Isabelle's cheek. "You look tired, Isabelle. Are you well?"

The touch was so comforting that Isabelle couldn't help leaning into it for just a moment. She wanted to tell her friend her troubles, unburden herself for a moment, but that was another luxury lost in this war. Troubles were carried alone. Isabelle didn't tell Madame Babineau that the Gestapo had broadened their search for the Nightingale or that she worried for her father and sister and niece. What was the point? They all had family to worry about. Such were ordinary anxieties, fixed points on the map of this war.

Isabelle reached out for the old woman's hands. There were so many terrible aspects to what their lives now were, but there was this, too: friendships forged in fire that had proven to be as strong as iron. After so many solitary years, spent tucked away in convents and forgotten in boarding schools, Isabelle never took for granted the fact that now she had friends, people whom she cared about and who cared about her.

"I am fine, my friend."

"And that handsome man of yours?"

"Still bombing depots and derailing trains. I saw him just before the invasion at Normandy. I could tell something big was up. I know he's in the thick of it. I'm worried—"

Isabelle heard the distant purr of an engine. She turned to Madame. "Are you expecting anyone?"

"No one ever drives up here."

The airmen heard it, too. They paused in their conversation. Smythe looked up. Foley drew a knife out of his waistband.

Outside, the goats started bleating. A shadow moved across the window.

Before Isabelle could yell out a warning the door smacked open and light poured into the room, along with several SS agents. "Put your hands over your heads!"

Isabelle was hit hard in the back of the head by a rifle butt. She gasped and stumbled forward.

Her legs gave out beneath her and she fell hard, cracking her head on the stone floor.

The last thing she heard before she lost consciousness was "You are all under arrest."

THIRTY-THREE

*I*sabelle woke tied to a wooden chair at her wrists and ankles; the ropes bit into her flesh and were so tight she couldn't move. Her fingers were numb. A single lightbulb hung from the ceiling above her, a cone of light in the darkness. The room smelled of mold and piss and water seeping through cracks in the stone.

Somewhere in front of her, a match flared.

She heard the scratch of sound, smelled the sulfur, and tried to lift her head, but the movement hurt so much she made an involuntary sound.

"*Gut*," someone said. "It hurts."

Gestapo.

He pulled a chair from the darkness and sat down, facing her. "Pain," he said simply. "Or no pain. The choice is yours."

"In that case, no pain."

He hit her hard. Blood filled her mouth, sharp and metallic tasting. She felt it dribble down her chin.

Two days, she thought. *Only two days.*

She had to last under questioning for forty-eight hours without naming names. If she could do that, just not crack, her father and Gaëtan and Henri and Didier and Paul and Anouk would have time to protect themselves. They would know soon that she had been arrested, if they didn't already know. Eduardo would get the word out and then he would go into hiding. That was their plan.

"Name?" he said, withdrawing a small notebook and a pencil from his breast pocket.

She felt blood dripping down her chin, onto her lap. "Juliette Gervaise. But you know that. You have my papers."

"We have papers that name you as Juliette Gervaise, true."

"So why ask me?"

"Who are you, really?"

"I'm really Juliette."

"Born where?" he asked lazily, studying his well-tended fingernails.

"Nice."

"And what were you doing in Urrugne?"

"I was in Urrugne?" she said.

He straightened at that, his gaze returned to hers with interest. "How old are you?"

"Twenty-two, or nearly, I think. Birthdays don't mean much anymore."

"You look younger."

"I feel older."

He slowly got to his feet, towered over her. "You work for the Nightingale. I want his name."

They didn't know who she was.

"I know nothing about birds."

The blow came out of the blue, stunning in its impact. Her head whipped sideways, cracked hard against the chair back.

"Tell me about the Nightingale."

"I told you—"

This time he hit her with an iron ruler across the cheek, so hard she felt her skin break open and blood spill.

He smiled and said again, "The Nightingale."

She spat as hard as she could, but it came out as a dribbling blob of blood that landed in her lap. She shook her head to clear her vision and wished immediately that she hadn't.

He was coming toward her again, methodically slapping the red-dripping ruler into his open palm. "I'm Rittmeister Schmidt, Kommandant of the Gestapo in Amboise. And you are?"

He is going to kill me, Isabelle thought. She struggled against her restraints, breathing hard. She tasted her own blood. "Juliette," she whispered, desperate now that he believe her.

She couldn't last two days.

This was the risk everyone had warned her about, the terrible truth of what she'd been doing. How had it seemed like an adventure? She would get herself—and everyone she cared about—killed.

"We have most of your compatriots. There is no sense in you dying to protect dead men."

Was it true?

No. If it were true, she would be dead, too.

"Juliette Gervaise," she said again.

He backhanded her with the ruler so hard the chair toppled sideways and crashed to the floor. Her head cracked on the stone at the same time he kicked her in the stomach with the toe of his boot. The pain was like nothing she'd ever known. She heard him say, "Now, Madamoiselle, name the Nightingale," and she couldn't have answered if she wanted to.

He kicked her again, with all his weight behind the blow.

❧

Consciousness brought pain.

Everything hurt. Her head, her face, her body. It took effort—and courage—to lift her head. She was still bound at the ankles and wrists. The ropes chafed against her torn, bloodied skin, cut into her bruised flesh.

Where am I?

Darkness surrounded her, and not an ordinary darkness, not an unlit room. This was something else; an impenetrable, inky blackness that pressed against her battered face. She sensed a wall was mere inches from her face. She tried to make the smallest move of her foot to reach forward, and pain roared to life again, biting deep into the rope cuts on her ankles.

She was in a box.

And she was cold. She could feel her breath and knew it would be visible. Her nostril hairs were frozen. She shivered hard, uncontrollably.

She screamed in terror; the sound of her scream echoed back at her and was lost.

Freezing.

Isabelle shuddered with cold, whimpering. She could feel her breath now, pluming in front of her face, turning to frost on her lips. Her eyelashes were frozen.

Think, Isabelle. Don't give up.

She moved her body a little, fighting through the cold and pain.

She was seated, still bound at the ankles and wrists.

Naked.

She closed her eyes, sickened by the image of him undressing her, touching her when she was unconscious.

In the fetid darkness, she became aware of a thrumming noise. At first, she thought it was her blood, pulsing in pain, or her heart, pounding a desperate beat to stay alive, but it wasn't that.

It was a motor, and nearby, humming. She recognized the sound, but what was it?

She shuddered again, trying to wiggle her fingers and toes to combat the dead feeling that had overtaken her extremities. Before there was pain in her feet, and then a tingling, and now . . . nothing. She moved the only thing she could—her head—and it thunked against something hard. She was naked, tied to a chair inside a . . .

Frozen. Dark. Humming. Small . . .

A refrigerator.

She panicked, tried frantically to wrest free, to topple her prison, but all her effort did was wind her. Defeat her. She couldn't move. Not anything except her fingers and toes, which were too frozen to cooperate. *Not like this, please.*

She would freeze to death. Or be asphyxiated.

Her own breathing echoed back at her, surrounded her, a shudder of breath all around it. She started to cry and her tears froze, turning to icicles on her cheeks. She thought of all the people she loved—Vianne, Sophie, Gaëtan, her father. Why hadn't she told them she loved them every day when she had the chance? And now she would die without ever saying a word to Vianne.

Vianne, she thought. Only that. The name. Part prayer, part regret, part good-bye.

&

A dead body hung from every streetlamp in the town square.

Vianne came to a stop, unable to believe what she was seeing. Across the way, an old woman stood beneath one of the bodies. The air was full of the whining creak of ropes pulled taut. Vianne moved cautiously through the square, taking care to keep away from the streetlamps—

Blue-faced, swollen, slack bodies.

There had to be ten dead men here—Frenchmen, she could tell. Maquisards by the look of them—the rough guerrilla partisans of the woods. They wore brown pants and black berets and tricolor armbands.

Vianne went to the old woman, took her by the shoulders. "You should not be here," she said.

"My son," the woman croaked. "He can't stay here—"

"Come," Vianne said, less gently this time. She maneuvered the old woman out of the square. On rue La Grande, the woman pulled free and walked away, mumbling to herself, crying.

Vianne passed three more dead bodies on her way to the *boucherie.* Carriveau seemed to be holding its breath. The Allies had bombed the area repeatedly in the last few months, and several of the town's buildings had been reduced to rubble. Something always seemed to be falling down or crumbling.

The air smelled of death and the town was silent; danger lurked in every shadow, around every corner.

In the queue at the butcher shop, Vianne heard women talking, their voices lowered.

"Retaliation . . ."

"Worse in Tulle . . ."

"Did you hear about Oradour-sur-Glane?"

Even with all of that, with all of the arrests and deportations and executions, Vianne couldn't believe the newest rumors. Yesterday morning the Nazis had marched into the small village of Oradour-sur-Glane—not far from Carriveau—and herded everyone at gunpoint into the town's church, supposedly to check their papers.

"Everyone in town," whispered the woman to whom Vianne had spoken. "Men. Women. Children. The Nazis shot them all, then they slammed the doors shut, locked them all in, and burned the church to the ground." Her eyes welled with tears. "It's true."

"It can't be," Vianne said.

"My Dedee saw them shoot a pregnant woman in the belly."

"She *saw* this?" Vianne asked.

The old woman nodded. "Dedee hid out for hours behind a rabbit hutch and saw the town in flames. She said she'll never forget the screaming. Not everyone was dead when they set the fire."

It was supposedly in retaliation for a Sturmbannführer who'd been captured by the Maquis.

Would the same thing happen here? The next time the war went badly, would the Gestapo or SS round up the villagers of Carriveau and trap them in the town hall and open fire?

She took the small tin of oil that this week's ration card had allowed her and walked out of the shop, flipping up her hood to shield her face.

Someone grabbed her by the arm and pulled her hard to the left. She stumbled sideways, lost her footing, and almost fell.

He pulled her into a dark alley and revealed himself.

"Papa!" Vianne said, too stunned by his appearance to say more.

She saw what the war had done to him, how it had etched lines in his forehead and placed puffy bags of flesh beneath his tired-looking eyes, how it had leached the color from his skin and turned his hair white. He was terribly thin; age spots dotted his sagging cheeks. She was reminded of his return from the Great War, when he'd looked this bad.

"Is there somewhere quiet we can talk?" he said. "I'd rather not meet your German."

"He's not *my* German, but *oui*."

She could hardly blame him for not wanting to meet Von Richter. "The house next to mine is vacant. To the east. The Germans thought it too small to bother with. We can meet there."

"In twenty minutes," he said.

Vianne pulled her hood back up over her scarf-covered hair and stepped out of the alleyway. As she left town and walked along the muddy road toward home, she tried to imagine why her father was here. She knew—or supposed—that Isabelle was living with him in Paris, although even that was conjecture. For all she knew, her sister and her father lived separate lives in the same city. She hadn't heard from Isabelle since that terrible night in the barn, although Henri had reported that she was well.

She hurried past the airfield, barely noticing the aeroplanes that were crumpled and still smoking from a recent bombing raid.

At Rachel's gate, she paused and glanced up and down the road. No one had followed or seemed to be watching her. She slipped inside the yard and hurried to the abandoned cottage. The front door had been broken long ago and now hung askew. She let herself inside.

The interior was shadowy and limned in dust. Almost all of the furniture had been requisitioned or stolen by looters, and missing pictures left black squares on the walls; only an old loveseat with dirty cushions and a broken leg remained in the living room. Vianne sat down, perched nervously, her foot tapping on the rush-covered floor.

She chewed on her thumbnail, unable to be still, and then she heard footsteps. She went to the window, lifting the blackout shade.

Her father was at the door. Only he wasn't her father, not this stooped old man.

She let him into the house. When he looked at her, the lines in his face deepened; the folds of his skin looked like pockets of melting wax. He ran a hand through his thinning hair. The long white strands rearranged themselves into spikes, giving him a strangely electrified look.

He moved toward her slowly, limping just a little. It brought her whole life back in an instant, that shuffling, awkward way he had of moving. Her maman saying, *Forgive him, Vianne, he isn't himself anymore and he can't forgive himself . . . it's up to us to do it.*

"Vianne." He said her name softly, his rough voice lingering over it. Again, she was reminded subtly of Before, when he had been himself. It was a long-forgotten thought. In the After years, she had relegated all thoughts of him to the closet; in time, she'd forgotten. Now she remembered. It scared her to feel this way. He had hurt her so many times.

"Papa."

He went to the loveseat and sat down. The cushions sagged tiredly beneath his meager weight. "I was a terrible father to you girls."

It was so surprising—and true—that Vianne had no idea what to say.

He sighed. "It's too late now to fix all that."

She joined him at the loveseat, sat down beside him. "It's never too late," she said cautiously. Was it true? Could she forgive him?

Yes. The answer came instantly, as unexpected as his appearance here.

He turned to her. "I have so much to say and no time to say it."

"Stay here," she said. "I'll care for you and—"

"Isabelle has been arrested and charged with aiding the enemy. She's imprisoned in Girot."

Vianne drew in a sharp breath. The regret she felt was immense, as was the guilt. What had her last words to her sister been? *Don't come back.* "What can we do?"

"We?" he said. "It is a lovely question, but not one to be asked. You must do nothing. You stay here in Carriveau and stay out of trouble, as you have been. Keep my granddaughter safe. Await your husband."

It was all Vianne could do not to say, *I'm different now, Papa. I am helping to hide Jewish children.* She wanted to see herself reflected in his gaze, wanted just once to make him proud of her.

Do it. Tell him.

How could she? He looked so old sitting there, old and broken and lost. There was only the barest hint of the man he'd been. He didn't need to know that Vianne was risking her life, too, couldn't worry that he would lose both his daughters. Let him think she was as safe as one could be. A coward.

"Isabelle will need you to come home to when this is over. You will tell her that she did the right thing. She will worry about that one day. She will think she should have stayed with you, protected you. She will remember leaving you with the Nazi, risking your lives, and she will agonize over her choice."

Vianne heard the confession that lay beneath. He was telling her his own story in the only way he could, cloaked in Isabelle's. He was saying that he had worried about his choice to join the army in the Great War, that he had agonized over what his fighting had done to his family. He knew how changed he'd been on his return, and instead of pain drawing him closer to his children and wife, it had separated them. He regretted pushing them away, leaving them with Madame Dumas all those years ago.

What a burden such a choice must be. For the first time, she saw her own childhood as an adult, from far away, with the wisdom this war had given her. Battle had broken her father; she had always known that. Her maman had said it repeatedly, but now Vianne understood.

It had *broken* him.

"You girls will be part of the generation that goes on, that remembers," he said. "The memories of what happened will be . . . hard to forget. You will need to stay together. Show Isabelle that she is loved. Sadly, this is a thing I never did. Now it is too late."

"You sound like you're saying good-bye."

She saw the sad, forlorn look in his eyes, and she understood why he was here, what he'd come to say. He was going to sacrifice himself for Isabelle. She didn't know how, but she knew it to be true just the same. It was his way of making up for all the times he'd disappointed them. "Papa," she said. "What are you going to do?"

He laid a hand to her cheek and it was warm and solid and comforting, that father's touch. She hadn't realized—or admitted to herself—how much she'd missed him. And now, just when she glimpsed a different future, a redemption, it dissolved around her. "What would you do to save Sophie?"

"Anything."

Vianne stared at this man who before the war changed him had taught her to love books and writing and to notice a sunset. She hadn't remembered that man in a long time.

"I must go," he said, handing her an envelope. On it was written *Isabelle and Vianne* in his shaky handwriting. "Read it together."

He stood up and turned to leave.

She wasn't ready to lose him. She grabbed for him. A piece of his cuff ripped away in her grasp. She stared down at it: a strip of brown-and-white-checked cotton lay in her palm. A strip of fabric like the others tied to her tree branches. Remembrances for lost and missing loved ones.

"I love you, Papa," she said quietly, realizing how true it was, how true it had always been. Love had turned into loss and she'd pushed it away, but somehow, impossibly, a bit of that love had remained. A girl's love for her father. Immutable. Unbearable but unbreakable.

"How can you?"

She swallowed hard, saw that he had tears in his eyes. "How can I not?"

He gave her a last, lingering look—and a kiss to each cheek—and then he drew back. So softly she almost didn't hear, he said, "I loved you, too," and then left her.

Vianne watched him walk away. When at last he disappeared, she returned home. There, she paused beneath the apple tree full of scraps of fabric. In the years that she had been tying scraps to the branches, the tree had died and the fruit had turned bitter. The other apple trees were hale and healthy, but this one, the tree of her remembrances, was as black and twisted as the bombed-out town behind it.

She tied the brown-checked scrap next to Rachel's.

Then she went into the house.

A fire was lit in the living room; the whole house was warm and smoky. Wasteful. She closed the door behind her, frowning. "Children," she called out.

"They are upstairs in my room. I gave them some chocolates and a game to play."

Von Richter. What was he doing here in the middle of the day?

Had he seen her with her father?

Did he know about Isabelle?

"Your daughter thanked me for the chocolates. She is such a pretty young thing."

Vianne knew better than to show her fear at that. She remained still and silent, trying to calm her racing heart.

"But your *son.*" He put the slightest emphasis on the word. "He looks nothing like you."

"My h-husband, An—"

He struck so fast she didn't even see him move. He grabbed her by the arm, squeezing hard, twisting the soft flesh. She let out a little cry as he shoved her back against the wall. "Are you going to lie to me again?"

He took both of her hands and wrenched them over her head, pinning them to the wall with one gloved hand. "Please," she said, "don't . . ."

She knew instantly that it was a mistake to beg.

"I checked the records. There is only one child born to you and Antoine. A girl, Sophie. You buried others. Who is the boy?"

Vianne was too frightened to think clearly. All she knew for sure was that she couldn't tell the truth or Daniel would be deported. And God knew what they'd do to Vianne . . . to Sophie. "Antoine's cousin died giving birth to Daniel. We adopted the baby just before the war started. You know how difficult official paperwork is these days, but I have his birth certificate and baptismal papers. He's our son now."

"Your nephew, then. Blood but not blood. Who is to say his father isn't a communist? Or Jewish?"

Vianne swallowed convulsively. He didn't suspect the truth. "We're Catholic. You know that."

"What would you do to keep him here with you?"

"Anything," she said.

He unbuttoned her blouse, slowly, letting each button be teased through its fraying hole. When the bodice gaped open, he slid his hand inside, sliding it over her breast, twisting her nipple hard enough that she cried out in pain. "Anything?" he asked.

She swallowed dryly.

"The bedroom, please," she said. "My children."

He stepped back. "After you, Madame."

"You will let me keep Daniel here?"

"Are you *negotiating* with me?"

"I am."

He grabbed her by the hair and yanked hard, pulling her into the bedroom. He kicked the door shut with his booted foot and then shoved her up against the wall. She made an *ooph* as she hit. He pinned her in place and shoved her skirt up and ripped her knitted underpants away.

She turned her head and closed her eyes, hearing his belt unbuckle with a clatter and his buttons release.

"Look at me," he said.

She didn't move, didn't so much as breathe. Neither did she open her eyes.

He hit her again. Still she stayed where she was, her eyes closed tightly.

"If you look at me, Daniel stays."

She turned her head and slowly opened her eyes.

"That's better."

She gritted her teeth as he yanked down his pants and shoved her legs farther apart and violated both her body and her soul. She did not make a single sound.

Nor did she look away.

THIRTY-FOUR

*I*sabelle tried to crawl away from . . . what? Had she just been kicked or burned? Or locked in the refrigerator? She couldn't remember. She dragged her aching, bloody feet backward across the floor, one pain-filled inch at a time. Everything hurt. Her head, her cheek, her jaw, her wrists and ankles.

Someone grabbed her by the hair, yanked her head back. Blunt, dirty fingers forced her mouth open; brandy splashed into her open mouth, gagging her. She spit it back up.

Her hair was thawing. Ice water streamed down her face.

She opened her eyes slowly.

A man stood in front of her, smoking a cigarette. The smell made her sick to her stomach.

How long had she been here?

Think, Isabelle.

She had been moved to this dank, airless cell. Two mornings had dawned with her able to see the sun, right?

Two? Or just one?

Had she given the network enough time to get people hidden? She couldn't think.

The man was talking, asking her questions. His mouth opened, closed, spewed smoke.

She flinched instinctively, curled into a crouch, squatted back. The man behind her kicked her in her spine, hard, and she stilled.

So. Two men. One in front of her and one behind. *Pay attention to the one who is speaking.*

What was he saying?

"Sit."

She wanted to defy him but didn't have the strength. She climbed up onto the chair. The skin around her wrists was torn and bloody, oozing pus. She used her hands to cover her nakedness, but it was useless, she knew. He would pull her legs apart to bind her ankles to the chair legs.

When she was seated, something soft hit her in the face and fell into her lap. Dully, she looked down.

A dress. Not hers.

She clutched it to her bare breasts and looked up.

"Put it on," he said.

Her hands were shaking as she stood and stepped awkwardly into the wrinkled, shapeless blue linen dress that was at least three sizes too large. It took forever to button the sagging bodice.

"The Nightingale," he said, taking a long drag on his cigarette. The tip glowed red-orange and Isabelle instinctively shrank into the chair.

Schmidt. That was his name. "I don't know anything about birds," she said.

"You are Juliette Gervaise," he said.

"I have told you that a hundred times."

"And you know nothing about the Nightingale."

"This is what I've told you."

He nodded sharply and Isabelle immediately heard footsteps, and then the door behind her creaked open.

She thought: *It doesn't hurt, it's just my body. They can't touch my soul.* It had become her mantra.

"We are done with you."

He was smiling at her in a way that made her skin crawl.

"Bring him in."

A man stumbled forward in shackles.

Papa.

She saw horror in his eyes and knew how she looked: split lip and blackened eyes and torn cheek . . . cigarette burns on her forearms, blood matted in her hair. She should stay still, stand where she was, but she couldn't. She limped forward, gritting her teeth at the pain.

There were no bruises on his face, no cuts on his lip, no arm held close to his body in pain.

They hadn't beaten or tortured him, which meant they hadn't interrogated him. "I am the Nightingale," her father said to the man who'd tortured her. "Is that what you need to hear?"

She shook her head, said *no* in a voice so soft no one heard.

"*I* am the Nightingale," she said, standing on burned, bloody feet. She turned to the German who had tortured her.

Schmidt laughed. "You, a girl? The infamous Nightingale?"

Her father said something in English to the German, who clearly didn't understand.

Isabelle understood: They could speak in English.

Isabelle was close enough to her father to touch him, but she didn't. "Don't do this," she begged.

"It's done," he said. The smile he gave her was slow in forming, and when it came, she felt pain constrict her chest. Memories came at her in waves, surging over the breakwater she'd built in the isolated years. Him sweeping her into his arms, twirling her around; picking her up from a fall, dusting her off, whispering, *Not so loud, my little terror, you'll wake your maman* . . .

She drew in short, shallow breaths and wiped her eyes. He was trying to make it up to her, asking for forgiveness and seeking redemption all at once, sacrificing himself for her. It was a glimpse of who he'd once been, the poet her maman had fallen in love with. That man, the one before the war, might have known another way, might have found the perfect words to heal their fractured past. But he wasn't that man anymore. He had lost too much, and in his loss, he'd thrown more away. This was the only way he knew to tell her he loved her. "Not this way," she whispered.

"There is no other. Forgive me," he said softly.

The Gestapo stepped between them. He grabbed her father by the arm and pulled him toward the door.

Isabelle limped after them. "I am the Nightingale!" she called out.

The door slammed in her face. She hobbled to the cell's window, clutching the rough, rusty bars. "I am the Nightingale!" she screamed.

Outside, beneath a yellow morning sun, her father was dragged into the square, where a firing squad stood at the ready, rifles raised.

Her father stumbled forward, lurched across the cobblestoned square, past a fountain. Morning sunlight gave everything a golden, beautiful glow.

"We were supposed to have time," she whispered, feeling tears start. How often had she imagined a new beginning for her and Papa, for all of them? They would come together after the war, Isabelle and Vianne and Papa, learn to laugh and talk and be a family again.

Now it would never happen; she would never get to know her father, never feel the warmth of his hand in hers, never fall asleep on the divan beside him, never be able to say all that needed to be said between them. Those words were lost, turned into ghosts that would drift away, unsaid. They would never be the family maman had promised. "Papa," she said; it was such a big word suddenly, a dream in its entirety.

He turned and faced the firing squad. She watched him stand taller and square his shoulders. He pushed the white strands of hair from his dry eyes. Across the square, their gazes met. She clutched the bars harder, clinging to them for support.

"I love you," he mouthed.

Shots rang out.

⚜

Vianne hurt all over.

She lay in bed, bracketed by her sleeping children, trying not to remember last night's rape in excruciating detail.

Moving slowly, she went to the pump and washed up in cold water, wincing every time she touched an area that was bruised.

She dressed in what was easy—a wrinkled linen button-up dress with a fitted bodice and flared skirt.

All night, she'd lain awake in bed, holding her children close, alternately weeping for what he'd done to her—what he'd taken from her—and fuming that she couldn't stop it.

She wanted to kill him.

She wanted to kill herself.

What would Antoine think of her now?

Truthfully, the biggest part of her wanted to curl up in a ball in some dark corner and never show her face again.

But even that—shame—was a luxury these days. How could she worry about herself when Isabelle was in prison and their father was going to try to save her?

"Sophie," she said when they'd finished their breakfast of dry toast and a poached egg. "I have an errand to run today. You will stay home with Daniel. Lock the door."

"Von Richter—"

"Is gone until tomorrow." She felt her face grow hot. This was the kind of intimacy she shouldn't know. "He told me so last . . . night." Her voice broke on the last word.

Sophie rose. "Maman?"

Vianne dashed tears away. "I'm fine. But I must go. Be good." She kissed both of them good-bye and rushed out before she could start thinking of reasons to stay.

Like Sophie and Daniel.

And Von Richter. He *said* he was leaving for the night, but who knew? He could always have her followed. But if she worried too much about "what ifs" she would never get anything done. In the time she'd been hiding Jewish children, she had learned to go on despite her fear.

She had to help Isabelle—

(*Don't come back.*)

(*I'll turn you in myself.*)

—and Papa if she could.

She boarded the train and sat on a wooden bench in the third-class carriage. Several of the other passengers—mostly women—sat with their heads down, hands clasped in their laps. A tall Hauptsturmführer stood guard by the door, his gun at the ready. A squad of narrow-eyed Milice—the brutal Vichy police—sat in another part of the carriage.

Vianne didn't look at either of the women in the compartment with her. One of them stank of garlic and onions. The smell made Vianne faintly sick in the hot, airless compartment. Fortunately, her destination was not far away, and just after ten o'clock in the morning, she disembarked at the small train station on the outskirts of Girot.

Now what?

The sun rode high overhead, baking the small town into a stupor. Vianne clutched her handbag close, felt perspiration crawl down her back and drip from her temples. Many of the sand-colored buildings had been bombed; piles of rubble were everywhere. A blue Cross of Lorraine had been painted onto the stone sides of an abandoned school.

She encountered few people on the crooked, cobblestoned streets. Now and then a girl on a bicycle or a boy with a wheelbarrow would thump and rattle past her, but for the most part, what she noticed was the silence, an air of desertion.

Then a woman screamed.

Vianne came around the last crooked corner and saw the town square. A dead body was lashed to the fountain in the square. Blood reddened the water that lapped around his ankles. His head had been strapped back with an army belt so that he seemed almost relaxed there, with his mouth slack, his eyes open, sightless. Bullet holes chewed up his chest, left his sweater in tatters; blood darkened his chest and pant legs.

Her father.

<hr />

Isabelle had spent last night huddled in the damp, black corner of her cell. The horror of her father's death replayed itself over and over.

She would be killed soon. Of that she had no doubt.

As the hours passed—time measured in breaths taken and released, in heartbeats—she wrote imaginary letters of good-bye to her father, to Gaëtan, to Vianne. She strung her memories into sentences that she memorized, or tried to, but they all ended with "I'm sorry." When the soldiers came for her, iron keys rattling in ancient locks, worm-eaten doors scraping open across the uneven floor, she wanted to scream and protest, yell *NO*, but she had no voice left.

She was yanked to her feet. A woman built like a panzer tank thrust shoes and socks at her and said something in German. Obviously she didn't speak French.

She gave Isabelle back her Juliette identity papers. They were stained now, and crumpled.

The shoes were too small and pinched her toes but Isabelle was grateful for them. The woman hauled her out of the cell and up the uneven stone steps and out into the blinding sunlight of the square. Several soldiers stood by the opposite buildings, their rifles strapped to their backs, going about their business. She saw her father's bullet-ridden dead body lashed to the fountain and screamed.

Everyone in the square looked up. The soldiers laughed at her, pointed.

"Quiet," the German tank woman hissed.

Isabelle was about to say something when she saw Vianne moving toward her.

Her sister moved forward awkwardly, as if she wasn't quite in control of her body. She wore a tattered dress that Isabelle remembered as once being pretty. Her red-gold hair was dull and lank, tucked behind her ears. Her face was as thin and hollow as a bone china teacup. "I've come to help you," Vianne said quietly.

Isabelle could have cried. More than anything in the world, she wanted to run to her big sister, to drop to her knees and beg for forgiveness and then to hold her in gratitude. To say "I'm sorry" and "I love you" and all the words in between. But she couldn't do any of that. She had to protect Vianne.

"So did he," she said, cocking her head toward her father. "Go away. *Please.* Forget me."

The German woman yanked Isabelle forward. She stumbled along, her feet screaming in pain, not allowing herself to look back. She thought she was being led to a firing squad, but she went past her father's slumped body and out of the square and onto a side street, where a lorry was waiting.

The woman shoved Isabelle into the back of the lorry. She scrambled back to the corner and squatted down, alone. The canvas flaps unfurled, bringing darkness. As the engine roared to life, she rested her chin in the hard and empty valley between her bony knees and closed her eyes.

When she woke, it was to stillness. The truck had stopped moving. Somewhere, a whistle blared.

The flaps of the truck were whisked sideways and light flooded into the back of the truck, so bright Isabelle couldn't see anything but shadow men coming toward her, yelling, "*Schnell, schnell!*"

She was pulled out of the truck and tossed to the cobblestoned street like a sack of trash. There were four empty cattle cars lined up along the platform. The first three were shut tightly. The fourth was open—and crammed with women and children. The noise was overwhelming— screaming, crying, dogs barking, soldiers shouting, whistles blaring, the chugging hum of the waiting train.

The Nazi shoved Isabelle into the crowd, pushing her forward every time she stopped, until the last carriage appeared in front of her.

He picked her up and threw her inside; she stumbled into the crowd, almost fell. Only the other bodies kept her on her feet. They were still coming in, stumbling forward, crying, clutching their children's hands, trying to find a six-inch opening between bodies in which to stand.

Iron bars covered the windows. In the corner, Isabelle saw a single barrel. Their toilet.

Suitcases were piled in the corner on a stack of hay bales.

Limping on feet that ached with every step, Isabelle pushed through the crowd of whimpering, crying women, past their screaming children, to the back of the train carriage. In the corner, she saw a woman standing alone, her arms crossed defiantly across her chest, her coarse gray hair covered by a black scarf.

Madame Babineau's bruised face broke into a brown-toothed smile. Isabelle was so relieved by the sight of her friend that she almost cried.

"Madame Babineau," Isabelle whispered, hugging her friend tightly.

"I think it's time you called me Micheline," her friend said. She was dressed in men's pants that were too long for her and a flannel work shirt. She touched Isabelle's cracked, bruised, bloodied face. "What have they done to you?"

"Their worst," she said, trying to sound like herself.

"I think not." Micheline let that sink in a moment and then cocked her head toward a bucket near her booted feet. This one was filled with a gray water that sloshed over the edges as the wooden floor rattled beneath so many moving bodies. A split wooden ladle lay to one side. "Drink. While it's there," she said.

Isabelle filled the ladle with the fetid-smelling water. Gagging at the taste, she forced herself to swallow. She stood, offered a ladleful to Micheline, who drank it all and wiped her wet lips with the back of her sleeve.

"This is going to be bad," Micheline said.

"I'm sorry I got you into this," Isabelle said.

"You did not get me into anything, Juliette," Micheline said. "I wanted to be a part of it."

The whistle sounded again and the car doors banged shut, plunging them all into darkness. Bolts clanged into place, locking them in. The train lurched forward. People fell into one another, fell down. Babies screamed and children whined. Someone was peeing in the bucket and the smell overlaid the stench of the sweat and fear.

Micheline put an arm around Isabelle and the two women climbed to the top of the hay bales and sat together.

"I am Isabelle Rossignol," she said quietly, hearing her name swallowed by the darkness. If she was going to die on this train, she wanted someone to know who she was.

Micheline sighed. "You are Julien and Madeleine's daughter."

"Did you know from the start?"

"*Oui.* You have your mother's eyes and your father's temperament."

"He was executed," she said. "He admitted to being the Nightingale."

Micheline held her hand. "Of course he did. Someday, when you are a mother, you will understand. I remember thinking your parents were unmatched—quiet, intellectual Julien and your vivacious, steel-spined maman. I thought they had nothing in common, but now I know how often love is like that. It was the war, you know; it broke him like a cigarette. Irreparable. She tried to save him. So hard."

"When she died . . ."

"*Oui.* Instead of fixing himself, he drank and made himself worse, but the man he became was not the man he was," Micheline said. "Some stories don't have happy endings. Even love stories. Maybe especially love stories."

The hours rolled by slowly. Often, the train stopped to take on more women and children or to avoid bombing. The women took turns sitting down and standing up, each helping the others when they could. The water disappeared and the urine barrel overfilled, sloshing over. Whenever the train slowed, Isabelle pushed to the sides of the carriage, peering through the slats, trying to see where they were, but all she saw were more soldiers and dogs and whips . . . more women being herded like cattle into more train cars. Women wrote their names on scraps of paper or cloth and shoved them through cracks in the carriage walls, hoping against hope to be remembered.

By the second day, they were all exhausted and hungry and so thirsty they remained quiet, saving their saliva. The heat and stench in the carriage was unbearable.

Be afraid.

Wasn't that what Gaëtan had said to her? He said the warning had come from Vianne that night in the barn.

Isabelle hadn't fully understood it then. She understood it now. She had thought herself indestructible.

But what would she have done differently?

"Nothing," she whispered into the darkness.

She would do it all again.

And this wasn't the end. She had to remember that. Each day she lived there was a chance for salvation. She couldn't give up. She could *never* give up.

❧

The train stopped. Isabelle sat up, bleary-eyed, her body aching and in pain from the beatings of her interrogation. She heard harsh voices, dogs barking. A whistle blared.

"Wake up, Micheline," Isabelle said, gently jostling the woman beside her.

Micheline edged upright.

The seventy other people in the car—women and children—slowly roused themselves from the stupor of the journey. Those who were seated rose. The women came together instinctively, packed in closer.

Isabelle winced in pain as she stood on torn feet in shoes too small. She held Micheline's cold hand.

The giant carriage doors rumbled open. Sunlight poured in, blinding them all. Isabelle saw SS officers dressed in black, with their snarling, barking dogs. They were shouting orders at the women and children, incomprehensible words with obvious meaning. *Climb down, move on, get into line.*

The women helped one another down. Isabelle held on to Micheline's hand and stepped down onto the platform.

A truncheon hit her in the head so hard she stumbled sideways and dropped to her knees.

"Get up," a woman said. "You must."

Isabelle let herself be helped to her feet. Dizzy, she leaned into the woman. Micheline came up on her other side, put an arm around her waist to steady her.

To Isabelle's left, a whip snaked through the air, hissing, and cracked into the fleshy pink of a woman's cheek. The woman screamed and held the torn skin of her cheek together. Blood poured between her fingers, but she kept moving.

The women formed ragged lines and marched across uneven ground through an open gate that was surrounded by barbed wire. A watchtower loomed above them.

Inside the gates, Isabelle saw hundreds—thousands—of women who looked like ghosts moving through a surreal landscape of gray, their bodies emaciated, their eyes sunken and dead looking in gray faces, their hair shorn. They wore baggy, dirty striped dresses; some were barefooted. Only women and children. No men.

Behind the gates and beneath the watchtower, she saw barracks stretching out in lines.

A corpse of a woman lay in the mud in front of them. Isabelle stepped over the dead woman, too numb to think anything but *keep moving*. The last woman who'd stopped had been hit so hard she didn't get up again.

Soldiers yanked the suitcases from their hands, snatched necklaces, pulled earrings and wedding rings off. When their valuables were all gone, they were led into a room, where they stood crowded together, sweating from the heat, dizzy from thirst. A woman grabbed Isabelle's arms, pulled her aside. Before she could even think, she was being stripped naked— they all were. Rough hands scratched her skin with dirty fingernails. She was shaved everywhere—under her arms, her head, and her pubic hair— with a viciousness that left her bleeding.

"Schnell!"

Isabelle stood with the other shaved, freezing, naked women, her feet aching, her head still ringing from the blows. And then they were being moved again, herded forward toward another building.

She remembered suddenly the stories she'd heard at MI9 and on the BBC, news stories about Jewish people being gassed to death at the concentration camps.

She felt a feeble sense of panic as she shuffled forward with the herd, into a giant room full of showerheads.

Isabelle stood beneath one of the showerheads, naked and trembling. Over the noise of the guards and the prisoners and the dogs, she heard the rattling of an old ventilation system. Something was coming on, clattering through the pipes.

This is it.

The doors of the building banged shut.

Ice-cold water gushed from the showerheads, shocking Isabelle, chilling her to the bone. In no time it was over and they were being herded again. Shivering, trying futilely to cover her nakedness with her trembling hands, she moved into the crowd and stumbled forward with the other women. One by one they were deloused. Then Isabelle was handed a shapeless striped dress and a dirty pair of men's underwear and two left shoes without laces.

Clutching her new possessions to her clammy breasts, she was shoved into a barn-like building with stacks of wooden bunks. She climbed into one of the bunks and lay there with nine other women. Moving slowly, she dressed and then lay back, staring up at the gray wooden underside of the bunk above her. "Micheline?" she whispered.

"I'm here, Isabelle," her friend said from the bunk above.

Isabelle was too tired to say more. Outside, she heard the smacking of leather belts, the hissing of whips, and the screams of women who moved too slowly.

"Welcome to Ravensbrück," said the woman beside her.

Isabelle felt the woman's skeletal hip against her leg.

She closed her eyes, trying to block out the sounds, the smell, the fear, the pain.

Stay alive, she thought.

Stay. Alive.

THIRTY-FIVE

*A*ugust.

Vianne breathed as quietly as she could. In the hot, muggy darkness of this upstairs bedroom—*her* bedroom, the one she'd shared with Antoine—every sound was amplified. She heard the bedsprings ping in protest as Von Richter rolled onto his side. She watched his exhalations, gauging each one. When he started to snore, she inched sideways and peeled the damp sheet away from her naked body.

In the last few months, Vianne had learned about pain and shame and degradation. She knew about survival, too—how to gauge Von Richter's moods and when to stay out of his way and when to be silent. Sometimes, if she did everything just right, he barely saw her. It was only when he'd had a bad day, when he came home already angry, that she was in trouble. Like last night.

He'd come home in a terrible temper, muttering about the fighting in Paris. The Maquis had started fighting in the streets. Vianne had known instantly what he'd want that night.

To inflict pain.

She'd herded her children out of the room quickly, put them to bed in the downstairs bedroom. Then she'd gone upstairs.

That was the worst of it, maybe; that he made her come to him and she did. She took off her clothes so he wouldn't rip them away.

Now, as she dressed she noticed how much it hurt to raise her arms. She paused at the blacked-out window. Beyond it lay fields destroyed by incendiary bombs; trees broken in half, many of them still smoldering, gates and chimneys broken. An apocalyptic landscape. The airfield was a crushed pile of stone and wood surrounded by broken aeroplanes and bombed-out lorries. Since Général de Gaulle had taken over the Free French Army and the Allies had landed in Normandy, the bombing of Europe had become constant.

Was Antoine out there still? Was he somewhere in his prison camp, looking out a slit in the barracks wall or a boarded-up window, looking at this moon that had once shone on a house filled with love? And Isabelle. She'd been gone only two months, but it felt like a lifetime. Vianne worried about her constantly, but there was nothing to be done about worry; it had to be borne.

Downstairs, she lit a candle. The electricity had been off for a long time now. In the water closet, she set the candle down by the sink and stared at herself in the oval mirror. Even in candlelight, she looked pasty and gaunt. Her dull, reddish gold hair hung limp on either side of her face. In the years of deprivation, her nose seemed to have lengthened and her cheekbones had become more prominent. A bruise discolored her temple. Soon, she knew, it would darken. She knew without looking that there would be handprints on her upper arms and an ugly bruise on her left breast.

He was getting meaner. Angrier. The Allied forces had landed in southern France and begun liberating towns. The Germans were losing the war, and Von Richter seemed hell-bent on making Vianne pay for it.

She stripped and washed in tepid water. She scrubbed until her skin was mottled and red, and still she didn't feel clean. She never felt clean.

When she could stand no more, she dried off and redressed in her nightgown, adding a robe over it. Tying it at the waist, she left the bathroom, carrying her candle.

Sophie was in the living room, waiting for her. She sat on the last good piece of furniture in the room—the divan—with her knees drawn together and her hands clasped. The rest of the furniture had been requisitioned or burned.

"What are you doing up so late?"

"I could ask you the same question, but I don't really need to, do I?"

Vianne tightened the belt on her robe. It was a nervous habit, some-thing to do with her hands. "Let's go to bed."

Sophie looked up at her. At almost fourteen, Sophie's face had begun to mature. Her eyes were black against her pale skin, her lashes lush and long. A poor diet had thinned Sophie's hair, but it still hung in ringlets. She pursed her full lips. "Really, Maman? How long must we pretend?" The sadness— and the anger—in those beautiful eyes was heartbreaking. Vianne appar-ently had hidden nothing from this child who'd lost her childhood to war.

What was the right thing for a mother to say to her nearly grown daughter about the ugliness in the world? How could she be honest? How could Vianne expect her daughter to judge her less harshly than she judged herself?

Vianne sat down beside Sophie. She thought about their old life— laughter, kisses, family suppers, Christmas mornings, lost baby teeth, first words.

"I'm not stupid," Sophie said.

"I have never thought you were. Not for a moment." She drew in a breath and let it out. "I only wanted to protect you."

"From the truth?"

"From everything."

"There's no such thing," Sophie said bitterly. "Don't you know that by now? Rachel is gone. Sarah is dead. Grandpère is dead. Tante Isabelle is . . ." Tears filled her eyes. "And Papa . . . when did we last hear from him? A year? Eight months? He's probably dead, too."

"Your father is alive. So is your aunt. I'd feel it if they were gone." She put a hand over her heart. "I'd know it here."

"Your heart? You'd feel it in your *heart*?"

Vianne knew that Sophie was being shaped by this war, roughened by fear and desperation into a sharper, more cynical version of herself, but still it was hard to see in such sharp detail.

"How can you just . . . go to him? I see the bruises."

"That's *my* war," Vianne said quietly, ashamed almost more than she could stand.

"Tante Isabelle would have strangled him in his sleep."

"*Oui*," she agreed. "Isabelle is a strong woman. I am not. I am just . . . a mother trying to keep her children safe."

"You think we want you to save us this way?"

"You're young," she said, her shoulders slumping in defeat. "When you are a mother yourself . . ."

"I won't be a mother," she said.

"I'm sorry to have disappointed you, Sophie."

"I want to kill him," Sophie said after a moment.

"Me, too."

"We could hold a pillow over his head while he sleeps."

"You think I have not dreamed of doing it? But it is too dangerous. Beck already disappeared while living in this house. To have a second officer do the same? They would turn their attention on us, which we don't want."

Sophie nodded glumly.

"I can stand what Von Richter does to me, Sophie. I couldn't stand losing you or Daniel or being sent away from you. Or seeing you hurt."

Sophie didn't look away. "I hate him."

"So do I," Vianne said quietly. "So do I."

⁂

"It is hot out today. I was thinking it would be a good day for swimming," Vianne said with a smile.

The uproar was immediate and unanimous.

Vianne guided the children out of the orphanage classroom, keeping them tucked in close as they walked down the cloisters. They were passing Mother Superior's office when the door opened.

"Madame Mauriac," Mother said, smiling. "Your little gaggle looks happy enough to burst into song."

"Not on a day this hot, Mother." She linked her arm through Mother's. "Come to the pond with us."

"A thoroughly lovely idea on a September day."

"Single file," Vianne said to the children as they reached the main road. The children immediately fell into line. Vianne started them off on a song and they picked it up instantly, singing loudly as they clapped and bounced and skipped.

Did they even notice the bombed-out buildings they passed? The smoking piles of rubble that had once been homes? Or was destruction the ordinary view of their childhoods, unremarkable, unnoticeable?

Daniel—as always—stayed with Vianne, clinging to her hand. He was like that lately, afraid to be apart from her for long. Sometimes it bothered her, even broke her heart. She wondered if there was a part of him, deep down, that remembered all that he had lost—the mother, the father, the sister. She worried that when he slept, curled up against her side, he was Ari, the boy left behind.

Vianne clapped her hands. "Children, you are to cross the street in an orderly fashion. Sophie, you are my leader."

The children crossed the street carefully and then raced up the hill to the wide, seasonal pond that was one of Vianne's favorite places. Antoine had first kissed her at this very spot.

At the water's edge, the students started stripping down. In no time, they were in the water.

She looked down at Daniel. "Do you want to go play in the water with your sister?"

Daniel chewed his lower lip, watching the children splash in the still, blue water. "I don't know . . ."

"You don't have to swim if you don't want to. You could just get your feet wet."

He frowned, his round cheeks bunched in consideration. Then he let go of her hand and walked cautiously toward Sophie.

"He still clings to you," Mother said.

"He has nightmares, too." Vianne was about to say, *Lord knows I do,* when nausea hit. She mumbled, "Excuse me," and ran through the tall grass to a copse of trees, where she bent over and vomited. There was almost nothing in her stomach, but the dry heaves went on and on, leaving her feeling weak and exhausted.

She felt Mother's hand on her back, rubbing her, soothing her.

Vianne straightened. She tried to smile. "I'm sorry. I don't—" She stopped. The truth washed over her. She turned to Mother. "I threw up yesterday morning."

"Oh, no, Vianne. A baby?"

Vianne didn't know whether to laugh or cry or scream at God. She had prayed and prayed for another child to grow in her womb.

But not now.

Not *his*.

❧

Vianne hadn't slept in a week. She felt rickety and tired and terrified. And her morning sickness had gotten even worse.

Now she sat at the edge of the bed, looking down at Daniel. At five, he was outgrowing his pajamas again; skinny wrists and ankles stuck out from the frayed sleeves and pant legs. Unlike Sophie, he never complained about being hungry or reading by candlelight or the terrible gray bread their rations provided. He remembered nothing else.

"Hey, Captain Dan," she said, pushing the damp black curls out of his eyes. He rolled onto his back and grinned up at her, showing off his missing front teeth.

"Maman, I dreamed there was candy."

The door to the bedroom banged open. Sophie appeared, breathing hard. "Come quick, Maman."

"Oh, Sophie, I am—"

"*Now.*"

"Come on, Daniel. She looks serious."

He surged at her exuberantly. He was too big for her to carry, so she hugged him tightly and then withdrew. She retrieved the only clothes that fit him—a pair of canvas pants that had been made from painter's cloth she'd found in the barn and a sweater she'd knitted with precious blue wool. When he was dressed, she took his hand and led him into the living room. The front door was standing open.

Bells were ringing. Church bells. It sounded as if music were playing somewhere. "La Marseillaise"? On a Tuesday at nine in the morning?

Outside, Sophie stood beneath the apple tree. A line of Nazis marched past the house. Moments later came the vehicles. Tanks and lorries and automobiles rumbled past Le Jardin, one after another, churning up dust.

A black Citroën pulled over to the side of the road and parked. Von Richter got out and came to her, his boots dirty, his eyes hidden behind black sunglasses, his mouth drawn into a thin, angry line.

"Madame Mauriac."

"Herr Sturmbannführer."

"We are leaving your sorry, sickly little town."

She didn't speak. If she had, she would have said something that could get her killed.

"This war isn't over," he said, but whether this was for her benefit or his own, she wasn't sure.

His gaze flicked past Sophie and landed on Daniel.

Vianne stood utterly still, her face impassive.

He turned to her. The newest bruise on her cheek made him smile.

"Von Richter!" someone in the entourage yelled. "Leave your French whore behind."

"That's what you were, you know," he said.

She pressed her lips together to keep from speaking.

"I'll forget you." He leaned forward. "I wonder if you can say the same."

He marched into the house and came out again, carrying his leather valise. Without a glance at her, he returned to his automobile. The door slammed shut behind him.

Vianne reached for the gate to steady herself.

"They're leaving," Sophie said.

Vianne's legs gave out. She crumpled to her knees. "He's gone."

Sophie knelt beside Vianne and held her tightly.

Daniel ran barefooted through the patch of dirt between them. "Me, too!" he yelled. "I want a hug!" He threw himself into them so hard they toppled over, fell into the dry grass.

❦

In the month since the Germans had left Carriveau, there was good news everywhere about the Allied victories, but the war hadn't ended. Germany hadn't surrendered. The blackout had been softened to a "dim out," so the windows let in light again—a surprising gift. But still Vianne couldn't re-lax. Without Von Richter on her mind (she would never say his name out loud again, not as long as she lived, but she couldn't stop thinking about him), she was obsessed with worry for Isabelle and Rachel and Antoine. She wrote Antoine a letter almost every day and stood in line to mail them, even though the Red Cross reported that no mail was getting through. They hadn't heard from him in more than a year.

"You're pacing again, Maman," Sophie said. She was seated at the divan, snuggled up with Daniel, a book open between them. On the fireplace mantel were a few of the photographs Vianne had brought in from the cel-lar in the barn. It was one of the few things she could think to do to make Le Jardin a home again.

"Maman?"

Sophie's voice brought Vianne back to herself.

"He's coming home," Sophie said. "And so is Tante Isabelle."

"*Mais oui.*"

"What will we tell Papa?" Sophie asked, and Vianne knew by the look in Sophie's eyes that she'd wanted to ask this for a while.

Vianne placed a hand on her still flat abdomen. There was no sign of the baby yet, but Vianne knew her body well; a life was growing within her. She left the living room and went to the front door, pushing it open. Barefooted, she stepped down on the cracked stone steps, feeling the soft moss on the bottoms of her feet. Taking care not to step on a sharp rock, she walked out to the road and turned toward town. Kept walking.

The cemetery appeared on her right. It had been ruined by a bomb blast two months ago. Aged stone markers lay on their sides, split in pieces. The ground was cracked and broken, with gaping holes here and there; skeletons hung from the tree branches, bones clattering in the breeze.

In the distance, she saw a man coming around the bend in the road.

In years to come, she would ask herself what had drawn her out here on this hot autumn day at exactly this hour, but she knew.

Antoine.

She started to run, heedless of her bare feet. It wasn't until she was al-most in his arms, close enough to reach out, that she stopped suddenly, drew herself up short. He would take one look at her and know that she had been ruined by another man.

"Vianne," he said in a voice she barely recognized. "I escaped."

He was so changed; his face had sharpened and his hair had gone gray. White stubble covered his hollow cheeks and jawline, and he was so terribly thin. His left arm hung at an odd angle, as if it had been broken and badly reset.

He was thinking the same of her. She could see it in his eyes.

His name came out in a whisper of breath. "Antoine." She felt the sting of tears and saw that he was crying, too. She went to him, kissed him, but when he drew back, he looked like a man she'd never seen before.

"I can do better," he said.

She took his hand. More than anything she wanted to feel close to him, connected, but the shame of what she'd endured created a wall between them.

"I thought of you every night," he said as they walked toward home. "I imagined you in our bed, thought of how you looked in that white nightgown . . . I knew you were as alone as I was."

Vianne couldn't find her voice.

"Your letters and packages kept me going," he said.

At the broken gate in front of Le Jardin, he paused.

She saw the house through his eyes. The tilted gate, the fallen wall, the dead apple tree that grew dirty scraps of cloth instead of bright red fruit.

He pushed the gate out of the way. It clattered sideways, still connected to the crumbling post by a single unsteady screw and bolt. It creaked in protest at being touched.

"Wait," she said.

She had to tell him now, before it was too late. The whole town knew Nazis had billeted with Vianne. He would hear gossip, for sure. If a baby was born in eight months, they would suspect.

"It was hard without you," she began, trying to find her way. "Le Jardin is so close to the airfield. The Germans noticed the house on their way into town. Two officers billeted here—"

The front door burst open and Sophie screamed, "Papa!" and came running across the yard.

Antoine dropped awkwardly to one knee and opened his arms and Sophie ran into him.

Vianne felt pain open up and expand. He was home, just as she'd prayed for, but she knew now that it wasn't the same; it couldn't be. He was changed. She was changed. She placed a hand on her flat belly.

"You are so grown up," Antoine said to his daughter. "I left a little girl and came home to a young woman. You'll have to tell me what I missed."

Sophie looked past him to Vianne. "I don't think we should talk about the war. *Any* of it. Ever. It's over."

Sophie wanted Vianne to lie.

Daniel appeared in the doorway, dressed in short pants and a red knit turtleneck that had lost its shape and socks that sagged over his ill-fitting secondhand shoes. Clutching a picture book to his narrow chest, he jumped down from the step and came toward them, frowning.

"And who is this good-looking young man?" Antoine asked.

"I'm Daniel," he said. "Who are you?"

"I'm Sophie's father."

Daniel's eyes widened. He dropped the book and threw himself at Antoine, yelling, "Papa! You're home!"

Antoine scooped the boy into his arms and lifted him up.

"I'll tell you," Vianne said. "But let's go inside now and celebrate."

Vianne had fantasized about her husband's return from war a thousand times. In the beginning, she'd imagined him dropping his suitcase at the sight of her and sweeping her into his big, strong arms.

And then Beck had moved into her home, making her feel things for a man—an enemy—that even now she refused to name. When he'd told her of Antoine's imprisonment, she'd pared down her expectations. She'd imagined her husband thinner, more ragged looking, but still *Antoine* when he returned.

The man at her dinner table was a stranger. He hunched over his food and wrapped his arms around his plate, spooning marrow bone broth into his mouth as if the meal were a timed event. When he realized what he was doing, he flushed guiltily and gave them a mumbled apology.

Daniel talked constantly, while Sophie and Vianne studied the shadow version of Antoine. He jumped at every sound and flinched when he was touched, and the pain in his eyes was impossible to miss.

After supper, he put the children to bed while Vianne did the dishes alone. She was happy to let him go, which only increased her guilt. He was her husband, the love of her life, and yet, when he touched her, it was all she could do not to turn away. Now, standing at the window in her bedroom, she felt nervous as she awaited him.

He came up behind her. She felt his strong sure hands on her shoulders, heard him breathing behind her. She longed to lean back, rest her body against his with the familiarity that came from years together, but she couldn't. His hands caressed her shoulders, ran down her arms, and then settled on her hips. He gently turned her to face him.

He eased the collar of her robe sideways and kissed her shoulder. "You're so thin," he said, his voice hoarse with passion and something else, something new between them—loss, maybe, an acknowledgment that change had occurred in their absence.

"I've gained weight since the winter," she said.

"Yeah," he said. "Me, too."

"How did you escape?"

"When they started losing the war, it got . . . bad. They beat me so badly I lost the use of my left arm. I decided then I'd rather get shot running to you than be tortured to death. Once you're ready to die, the plan gets easy."

Now was the time to tell him the truth. He might understand that rape was torture and that she'd been a prisoner, too. It wasn't her fault, what had happened to her. She believed that, but she didn't think fault mattered in a thing like this.

He took her face in his hands and forced her to lift her chin.

Their kiss was sad, an apology almost, a reminder of what they'd once shared. She trembled as he undressed her. She saw the red marks that crisscrossed his back and torso, and the jagged, angry, puckering scars that ran the length of his left arm.

She knew Antoine wouldn't hit her or hurt her. And still she was afraid.

"What is it, Vianne?" he said, drawing back.

She glanced at the bed, their bed, and all she could think about was *him*. Von Richter. "W-while you were gone . . ."

"Do we need to talk about it?"

She wanted to confess it all, to cry in his arms and be comforted and told that it would be all right. But what about Antoine? He'd been through hell, too. She could see it in him. There were red, slashing scars on his chest that looked like whip marks.

He loved her. She saw that, too, felt it.

But he was a man. If she told him she'd been raped—and that another man's baby grew in her belly—it would eat at him. In time, he would wonder if she could have stopped Von Richter. Maybe someday he'd wonder if she'd enjoyed it.

And there it was. She could tell him about Beck, even that she'd killed him, but she could never tell Antoine she'd been raped. This child in her belly would be born early. Children were born a month early all the time.

She couldn't help wondering if this secret would destroy them either way.

"I could tell you all of it," she said quietly. Her tears were tears of shame and loss and love. Love most of all. "I could tell you about the German officers who billeted here and how hard life was and how we barely survived and how Sarah died in front of me and how strong Rachel was when they put her on the cattle car and how I promised to keep Ari safe. I could tell you how my father died and Isabelle was arrested and deported . . . but I think you know it all." *God forgive me.* "And maybe there's no point talking about any of it. Maybe . . ." She traced a red welt that ran like a lightning bolt down his left bicep. "Maybe it's best to just forget the past and go on."

He kissed her. When he drew back, his lips remained against hers. "I love you, Vianne."

She closed her eyes and returned his kiss, waiting for her body to come alive at his touch, but when she slid beneath him and felt their bodies come together as they'd done so many times before, she felt nothing at all.

"I love you, too, Antoine." She tried not to cry as she said it.

❧

A cold November night. Antoine had been home for almost two months. There had been no word from Isabelle.

Vianne couldn't sleep. She lay in bed beside her husband, listening to his quiet snore. It had never bothered her before, never kept her awake, but now it did.

No.

That wasn't true.

She turned, lay on her side, and stared at him. In the darkness, with the light of a full moon coming through the window, he was unfamiliar: thin, sharp, gray-haired at thirty-five. She inched out of bed and covered him with the heavy eiderdown that had been her grandmère's.

She put on her robe. Downstairs, she wandered from room to room, looking for—what? Her old life perhaps, or the love for a man she'd lost.

Nothing felt right anymore. They were like strangers. He felt it, too. She knew he did. The war lay between them at night.

She got a quilt from the living room trunk, wrapped it around herself, and went outside.

A full moon hung over the ruined fields. Light fell in crackled patches on the ground below the apple trees. She went to the middle tree, stood beneath it. The dead black branch arched above her, leafless and gnarled. On it were all her scraps of twine and yarn and ribbon.

When she'd tied the remembrances onto this branch, Vianne had naïvely thought that staying alive was all that mattered. The door behind her opened and closed quietly. She felt her husband's presence as she always had.

"Vianne," he said, coming up behind her. He put his arms around her. She wanted to lean back into him but she couldn't do it. She stared at the first ribbon she'd tied to this tree. Antoine's. The color of it was as changed, as weathered, as they were.

It was time. She couldn't wait any longer. Her belly was growing.

She turned, looked up at him. "Antoine" was all she could say.

"I love you, Vianne."

She drew in a deep breath and said, "I'm going to have a baby."

He went still. It was a long moment before he said, "What? When?"

She stared up at him, remembering their other pregnancies, how they'd come together in loss and in joy. "I'm almost two months along, I think. It must have happened . . . that first night you were home."

She saw every nuance of emotion in his eyes: surprise, worry, concern, wonder, and, finally, joy. He grazed her chin, tilted her face up. "I know why you look so afraid, but don't worry, V. We won't lose this one," he said. "Not after all of this. It's a miracle."

Tears stung her eyes. She tried to smile, but her guilt was suffocating.

"You've been through so much."

"We all have."

"So we choose to see miracles."

Was that his way of saying he knew the truth? Had suspicion planted itself? What would he say when the baby was born early? "Wh-what do you mean?"

She saw tears glaze his eyes. "I mean forget the past, V. Now is what matters. We will always love each other. That's the promise we made when we were fourteen. By the pond when I first kissed you, remember?"

"I remember." She was so lucky to have found this man. No wonder she had fallen in love with him. And she would find her way back to him, just as he'd found his way back to her.

"This baby will be our new beginning."

"Kiss me," she whispered. "Make me forget."

"It's not forgetting we need, Vianne," he said, leaning down to kiss her. "It's remembering."

THIRTY-SIX

*In February 1945, snow covered the naked bodies piled outside the camp's newly built crematorium. Putrid black smoke roiled up from the chimneys.

Isabelle stood, shivering, in her place at the morning *Appell*—roll call. It was the kind of cold that ached in the lungs and froze eyelashes and burned fingertips and toes.

She waited for the roll call to end, but no whistle blared.

Snow was still falling. In the prisoners' ranks, some women started to cough. Another one pitched face-first into the mushy, muddy snow and couldn't be raised. A bitter wind blew across the camp.

Finally, an SS officer on horseback rode past the women, eyeing them one by one. He seemed to notice everything—the shorn hair, the flea bites, the blue tips of frostbitten fingers, and the patches that identified them as Jews, or homosexuals, or political prisoners. In the distance, bombs fell, exploded like distant thunder.

When the officer pointed out a woman, she was immediately pulled from the line.

He pointed at Isabelle, and she was yanked nearly off her feet, dragged out of line.

The SS squads surrounded the women who'd been chosen, forced them to form two lines. A whistle blared. *"Schnell! Eins! Zwei! Drei!"*

Isabelle marched forward, her feet aching with cold, her lungs burning. Micheline fell into step beside her.

They had made it a mile or so outside of the gates when a lorry rumbled past them, its back heaped high with naked corpses.

Micheline stumbled. Isabelle reached out, holding her friend upright.

And still they marched.

At last they came to a snowy field blanketed in fog.

The Germans separated the women again. Isabelle was yanked away from Micheline and pushed into a group of other *Nacht und Nebel* political prisoners.

The Germans shoved them together and shouted at them and pointed until Isabelle understood.

The woman beside her screamed when she saw what they'd been chosen for. Road crew.

"Don't," Isabelle said just as a truncheon hit the woman hard enough to send her sprawling.

Isabelle stood as numb as a plow mule as the Nazis slipped rough leather harness straps over her shoulders and tightened them at her waist. She was harnessed to eleven other young women, elbow-to-elbow. Behind them, attached to the harness, was a steel wheel the size of an automobile.

Isabelle tried to take a step, couldn't.

A whip cracked across her back, setting her flesh on fire. She clutched the harness straps and tried again, taking a step forward. They were exhausted. They had no strength and their feet were freezing on the snowy ground, but they had to move or they'd be whipped. Isabelle angled forward, straining to move, to get the stone wheel turning. The straps bit into her chest. One of the women stumbled, fell; the others kept pulling. The leather harness creaked and the wheel turned.

They pulled and pulled and pulled, creating a road from the snow-covered ground behind them. Other women used shovels and wheelbarrows to clear the way.

All the while, the guards sat in pods, gathered around open fires, talking and laughing among themselves.

Step.

Step.

Step.

Isabelle couldn't think of anything else. Not the cold, not her hunger or thirst, not the flea and lice bites that covered her body. And not real life. That was the worst of all. The thing that would get her to miss a step, to draw attention to herself, to be hit or whipped or worse.

Step.

Just think about moving.

Her leg gave out. She crumpled to the snow. The woman beside her reached out. Isabelle grabbed the shaking, blue-white hand, gripped it in her numb fingers, and crawled back to stand. Gritting her teeth, she took another pain-filled step. And then another.

❧

The siren went off at 3:30 A.M., as it did every morning for roll call. Like her nine bunkmates, Isabelle slept in every bit of clothing she had— ill-fitting shoes and underwear; the baggy, striped dress with her prisoner identification number sewn on the sleeve. But none of it provided warmth. She tried to encourage the women around her to hold strong, but she herself was weakening. It had been a terrible winter; all of them were dying, some quickly, of typhus and cruelty, and some slowly of starvation and cold, but all were dying.

Isabelle had had a fever for weeks, but not high enough to send her to the hospital block, and last week she'd been beaten so badly she'd lost consciousness at work—and then she'd been beaten for falling down. Her body, which couldn't have weighed more than eighty pounds, was crawling with lice and covered in open sores.

Ravensbrück had been dangerous from the beginning, but now, in March 1945, it was even more so. Hundreds of women had been killed or gassed or beaten in the last month. The only women who'd been left alive were the *Verfügbaren*—the disposables, who were sick or frail or elderly—and the women of *Nacht und Nebel*, "Night and Fog." Political prisoners, like Isabelle and Micheline. Women of the Resistance. The rumor was that the Nazis were afraid to gas them now that the tide of war had turned.

"You're going to make it."

Isabelle realized she'd been weaving in place, beginning to fall.

Micheline Babineau gave her a tired, encouraging smile. "Don't cry."

"I'm not crying," Isabelle said. They both knew that the women who cried at night were the women who died in the morning. Sadness and loss were drawn in with each breath but never expelled. You couldn't give in. Not for a second.

Isabelle knew this. In the camp, she fought back the only way she knew how—by caring for her fellow prisoners and helping them to stay strong. All they had in this hell was each other. In the evenings, they crouched in their dark bunks, whispering among themselves, singing softly, trying to keep alive some memory of who they'd been. Over the nine months Isabelle had been here, she had found—and lost—too many friends to count.

But Isabelle was tired now, and sick.

Pneumonia, she was pretty sure. And typhus, maybe. She coughed quietly and did her job and tried to draw no attention. The last thing she wanted was to end up in the "tent"—a small brick building with tarp walls, into which the Nazis put any woman with an incurable disease. It was where women went to die.

"Stay alive," Isabelle said softly.

Micheline nodded encouragingly.

They had to stay alive. Now more than ever. Last week, new prisoners had come with news: the Russians were advancing across Germany, smashing and defeating the Nazi army. Auschwitz had been liberated. The Allies were said to be winning one victory after another in the west.

A race for survival was on and everyone knew it. The war was ending. Isabelle had to stay alive long enough to see an Allied victory and a free France.

A whistle blared at the front of the line.

A hush fell over the crowd of prisoners—women, mostly, and a few children. In front of them, a trio of SS officers paced with their dogs.

The camp Kommandant appeared in front of them. He stopped and clasped his hands behind his back. He called out something in German and the SS officers advanced. Isabelle heard the words *"Nacht und Nebel."*

An SS officer pointed at her, and another one pushed through the crowd, knocking women to the ground, stepping on or over them. He grabbed Isabelle's skinny arm and pulled hard. She stumbled along beside him, praying her shoes wouldn't fall off—it was a whipping offense to lose a shoe, and if she did, she'd spend the rest of this winter with a bare, frost-bitten foot.

Not far away, she saw Micheline being dragged off by another officer.

All Isabelle could think was that she needed to keep her shoes on.

An SS officer called out a word Isabelle recognized.

They were being sent to another camp.

She felt a wave of impotent rage. She would never survive a forced march through the snow to another camp.

"No," she muttered. Talking to herself had become a way of life. For months, as she stood in line at work, doing something that repelled and horrified her, she whispered to herself. As she sat on a hole in a row of pit toilets, surrounded by other woman with dysentery, staring at the women sitting across from her, trying not to gag on the stench of their bowel movements, she whispered to herself. In the beginning, it had been stories she told herself about the future, memories she shared with herself about the past.

Now it was just words. Gibberish sometimes, anything to remind herself that she was human and alive.

Her toe caught on something and she pitched to the ground, falling face-first in the dirty snow.

"To your feet," someone yelled. "March."

Isabelle couldn't move, but if she stayed there, they'd whip her again. Or worse.

"On your feet," Micheline said.

"I can't."

"You can. Now. Before they see you've fallen." Micheline helped her to her feet.

Isabelle and Micheline fell into the ragged line of prisoners, walking wearily forward, past the brick-walled perimeter of the camp, beneath the watchful eye of the soldier in the watchtower.

They walked for two days, traveled thirty-five miles, collapsing on the cold ground at night, huddling together for warmth, praying to see the dawn, only to be wakened by whistles and told to march again.

How many died along the way? She wanted to remember their names, but she was so cold and hungry and exhausted her brain barely worked.

Finally, they arrived at their destination, a train station, where they were shoved onto cattle cars that smelled of death and excrement. Black smoke rose into the snow-whitened sky. The trees were bare. There were no birds anymore in the sky, no chirping or screeching or chatter of living things filled this forest.

Isabelle clambered up onto the bales of hay that were stacked along the wall and tried to make herself as small as possible. She pulled her bleeding knees into her chest and wrapped her arms around her ankles to conserve what little warmth she had.

The pain in her chest was excruciating. She covered her mouth just as a cough racked her, bent her forward.

"There you are," Micheline said in the dark, climbing onto the hay bale beside her.

Isabelle let out a sigh of relief, and immediately she was coughing again. She put a hand over her mouth and felt blood spray into her palm. She'd been coughing up blood for weeks now.

Isabelle felt a dry hand on her forehead and she coughed again.

"You're burning up."

The cattle car doors clanged shut. The carriage shuddered and the giant iron wheels began to turn. The car swayed and clattered. Inside, the women banded together and sat down. At least in this weather their urine would freeze in the barrel and not slosh all over.

Isabelle sagged next to her friend and closed her eyes.

From somewhere far away, she heard a high-pitched whistling sound. A bomb falling. The train screeched to a halt and the bomb exploded, near enough that the carriage rattled. The smell of smoke and fire filled the air. The next one could fall on this train and kill them all.

❦

Four days later, when the train finally came to a complete stop (it had slowed dozens of times to avoid being bombed) the doors clattered open to reveal a white landscape broken only by the black greatcoats of the SS officers waiting outside.

Isabelle sat up, surprised to find that she wasn't cold. She felt hot; so hot she was perspiring.

She saw how many of her friends had died overnight, but there was no time to grieve for them, no time to say a prayer or whisper a good-bye. The Nazis on the platform were coming for them, blowing their whistles, yelling.

"*Schnell! Schnell!*"

Isabelle nudged Micheline awake. "Take my hand," Isabelle said.

The two women held hands and climbed gingerly down from the hay bales. Isabelle stepped over a dead body, from which someone had already taken the shoes.

On the other side of the platform, a line of prisoners was forming.

Isabelle limped forward. The woman in front of Isabelle stumbled and fell to her knees.

An SS officer yanked the woman to her feet and shot her in the face.

Isabelle didn't slow down. Alternately freezing cold and burning hot, unsteady on her feet, she plodded forward through the snowy forest until another camp came into view.

"*Schnell!*"

Isabelle followed the women in front of her. They passed through open gates, past a throng of skeletal men and women in gray-striped pajamas who looked at them through a chain-link fence.

"Juliette!"

She heard the name. At first it meant nothing to her, just another sound. Then she remembered.

She'd been Juliette. And Isabelle before that. And the Nightingale. Not just F-5491.

She glanced at the skeletal prisoners lined up behind the chain link.

Someone was waving at her. A woman: gray skin and a hooked, pointed nose and sunken eyes.

Eyes.

Isabelle recognized the tired, knowing gaze fixed on her.

Anouk.

Isabelle stumbled to the chain-link fence.

Anouk met her. Their fingers clasped through the ice-cold metal. "Anouk," she said, hearing the break in her voice. She coughed a little, covered her mouth.

The sadness in Anouk's dark eyes was unbearable. Her friend's gaze cut to a building whose chimney puffed out putrid black smoke. "They're killing us to cover what they've done."

"Henri? Paul? . . . Gaëtan?"

"They were all arrested, Juliette. Henri was hanged in the town square. The rest . . ." She shrugged.

Isabelle heard an SS soldier yell at her. She backed away from the fence. She wanted to say something *real* to Anouk, something that would last, but she couldn't do anything but cough. She covered her mouth and stumbled sideways, got back into line.

She saw her friend mouth "Good-bye," and Isabelle couldn't even respond. She was so, so tired of good-byes.

THIRTY-SEVEN

*E*ven on this blue-skied March day, the apartment on the Avenue de La Bourdonnais felt like a mausoleum. Dust covered every surface and layered the floor. Vianne went to the windows and tore the blackout shades down, letting light into this room for the first time in years.

It looked like no one had been in this apartment for some time. Probably not since that day Papa had left to save Isabelle.

Most of the paintings were still on the walls and the furniture was in place—some of it had been hacked up for firewood and piled in the corner. An empty soup bowl and spoon sat on the dining room table. His volumes of self-published poetry lined the mantel. "It doesn't look like she's been here. We must try the Hôtel Lutetia."

Vianne knew she should pack up her family's things, claim these remnants of a different life, but she couldn't do it now. She didn't want to. Later.

She and Antoine and Sophie left the apartment. On the street outside, all around them were signs of recovery. Parisians were like moles, coming out into the sunshine after years in the dark. But still there were food lines everywhere and rationing and deprivation. The war might have been winding down—the Germans were retreating everywhere—but it wasn't over yet.

They went to the Hôtel Lutetia, which had been home to the Abwehr under the occupation and was now a reception center for people returning from the camps.

Vianne stood in the elegant, crowded lobby. As she looked around, she felt sick to her stomach and grateful that she'd left Daniel with Mother Marie-Therese. The reception area was filled with rail-thin, bald, vacant-eyed people dressed in rags. They looked like walking cadavers. Moving among them were doctors and Red Cross workers and journalists.

A man approached Vianne, stuck a faded black-and-white photograph in her face. "Have you seen her? Last we heard she was at Auschwitz."

The photograph showed a lovely girl standing beside a bicycle, smiling brightly. She couldn't have been more than fifteen years old.

"No," Vianne said. "I'm sorry."

The man was already walking away, looking as dazed as Vianne felt.

Everywhere Vianne looked she saw anxious families, photographs held in their shaking hands, begging for news of their loved ones. The wall to her right was covered with photographs and notes and names and addresses. The living looking for the lost. Antoine moved close to Vianne, put a hand on her shoulder. "We will find her, V."

"Maman?" Sophie said. "Are you all right?"

She looked down at her daughter. "Perhaps we should have left you at home."

"It's too late to protect me," Sophie said. "You must know that."

Vianne hated that truth as much as any. She held on to her daughter's hand and moved resolutely through the crowd, with Antoine beside her. In an area to the left, she saw a gathering of men in dirty striped pajamas who looked like skeletons. How were they still alive?

She didn't even realize that she had stopped again until a woman appeared in front of her.

"Madame?" the woman—a Red Cross worker—said gently.

Vianne tore her gaze from the ragged survivors. "I have people I'm looking for . . . my sister, Isabelle Rossignol. She was arrested for aiding the enemy and deported. And my best friend, Rachel de Champlain, was deported. Her husband, Marc, was a prisoner of war. I . . . don't know what happened to any of them or how to look for them. And . . . I have a list of Jewish children in Carriveau. I need to reunite them with their parents."

The Red Cross worker, a thin, gray-haired woman, took out a piece of paper and wrote down the names Vianne had given her. "I will go to the records desk and check these names. As to the children, come with me." She led the three of them to a room down the hall, where an ancient-looking man with a long beard sat behind a desk piled with papers.

"M'sieur Montand," the Red Cross worker said, "this woman has information on some Jewish children."

The old man looked up at her through bloodshot eyes and made a flicking motion with his long, hair-tufted fingers. "Come in."

The Red Cross worker left the room. The sudden quiet was disconcerting after so much noise and commotion.

Vianne approached the desk. Her hands were damp with perspiration. She rubbed them along the sides of her skirt. "I am Vianne Mauriac. From Carriveau." She opened her handbag and withdrew the list she had compiled last night from the three lists she'd kept throughout the war. She set it on his desk. "These are some hidden Jewish children, M'sieur. They are in the Abbaye de la Trinité orphanage under the care of Mother Superior Marie-Therese. I don't know how to reunite them with their parents. Except for the first name on the list. Ari de Champlain is with me. I am searching for his parents."

"Nineteen children," he said quietly.

"It is not many, I know, but . . ."

He looked up at her as if she were a heroine instead of a scared survivor. "It is nineteen who would have died in the camps along with their parents, Madame."

"Can you reunite them with their families?" she asked softly.

"I will try, Madame. But sadly, most of these children are indeed orphans now. The lists coming from the camps are all the same: mother dead, father dead, no relatives alive in France. And so few children survived." He ran a hand through the thinning gray hair on his head. "I will forward your list to the OSE in Nice. They are trying to reunite families. *Merci,* Madame."

Vianne waited a moment, but the man said no more. She rejoined her husband and daughter and they left the office and stepped back into the crowd of refugees and families and camp survivors.

"What do we do now?" Sophie asked.

"We wait to hear from the Red Cross worker," Vianne said.

Antoine pointed to the wall of photographs and names of the missing. "We should look for her there."

A look passed between them, an acknowledgment of how much it would hurt to stand there, looking through the photographs of the missing. Still, they moved to the sea of pictures and notes and began to look through them, one by one.

They were there for nearly two hours before the Red Cross worker returned.

"Madame?"

Vianne turned.

"I am sorry, Madame. Rachel and Marc de Champlain are listed among the deceased. And there is no record of an Isabelle Rossignol anywhere."

Vianne heard *deceased* and felt an almost unbearable grief. She pushed the emotion aside resolutely. She would think of Rachel later, when she was alone. She would have a glass of champagne outside, beneath the yew tree, and talk to her friend. "What does that mean? No record of Isabelle? I saw them take her away."

"Go home and wait for your sister's return," the Red Cross worker said. She touched Vianne's arm. "Have hope. Not all of the camps have been liberated."

Sophie looked up at her. "Maybe she made herself invisible."

Vianne touched her daughter's face, managed a small, sad smile. "You are so grown-up. It makes me proud and breaks my heart at the same time."

"Come on," Sophie said, tugging on her hand. Vianne allowed her daughter to lead her away. She felt more like the child than the parent as they made their way through the crowded lobby and out onto the brightly lit street.

Hours later, when they were on the train bound for home, seated on a wooden banquette in the third-class carriage, Vianne stared out the window at the bombed-out countryside. Antoine sat sleeping beside her, his head resting against the dirty window.

"How are you feeling?" Sophie asked.

Vianne placed a hand on her swollen abdomen. A tiny flutter—a kick—tapped against her palm. She reached for Sophie's hand.

Sophie tried to pull away; Vianne gently insisted. She placed her daughter's hand on her belly.

Sophie felt the flutter of movement and her eyes widened. She looked up at Vianne. "How can you . . ."

"We are all changed by this war, Soph. Daniel is your brother now that Rachel is . . . gone. Truly your brother. And this baby; he or she is innocent of . . . his or her creation."

"It's hard to forget," she said quietly. "And I'll never forgive."

"But love has to be stronger than hate, or there is no future for us."

Sophie sighed. "I suppose," she said, sounding too adult for a girl of her age.

Vianne placed a hand on top of her daughter's. "We will remind each other, *oui?* On the dark days. We will be strong for each other."

Roll call had been going on for hours. Isabelle dropped to her knees. The minute she hit the ground, she thought *stay alive* and clambered back up.

Guards patrolled the perimeter with their dogs, selecting women for the gas chamber. Word was that another march was coming. This one to Mauthausen, where thousands had already been worked to death: Soviet prisoners of war, Jews, Allied airmen, political prisoners. It was said that none who walked through its gates would ever walk out.

Isabelle coughed. Blood sprayed across her palm. She wiped it on her dirty dress quickly, before the guards could see.

Her throat burned, her head pulsed and ached. She was so focused on her agony that it took her a moment to notice the sound of engines.

"Do you hear that?" Micheline said.

Isabelle felt a commotion moving through the prisoners. It was hard to concentrate when she hurt so badly. Her lungs ached with every breath.

"They're leaving," she heard.

"Isabelle, look!"

At first all she saw was bright blue sky and trees and prisoners. Then she noticed.

"The guards are gone," she said in a hoarse, ragged voice.

The gates clattered open and a stream of American trucks drove through the gates; soldiers sat on the bonnets and hung out the back, their rifles held across their chests.

Americans.

Isabelle's knees gave out. "Mich . . . e . . . line," she whispered, her voice as broken as her spirit. "We . . . made . . . it."

꧁

That spring, the war began to end. General Eisenhower broadcast a demand for the German surrender. Americans crossed the Rhine and went into Germany; the Allies won one battle after another and began to liberate the camps. Hitler was living in a bunker.

And still, Isabelle didn't come home.

Vianne let the letter box clang shut. "It's as if she disappeared."

Antoine said nothing. For weeks they had been searching for Isabelle. Vianne stood in queues for hours to make telephone calls and sent countless letters to agencies and hospitals. Last week they visited more displaced-person camps, but to no avail. There was no record of Isabelle Rossignol anywhere. It was as if she had disappeared from the face of the earth—along with hundreds of thousands of others.

Maybe Isabelle had survived the camps, only to be shot a day before the Allies arrived. Supposedly in one of the camps, a place called Bergen-Belsen, the Allies had found heaps of still-warm bodies at liberation.

Why?

So they wouldn't talk.

"Come with me," Antoine said, taking her by the hand. She no longer stiffened at his touch, or flinched, but she couldn't seem to relax into it, either. In the months since Antoine's return, they were playacting at love and both of them knew it. He said he didn't make love to her because of the baby, and she agreed that it was for the best, but they knew.

"I have a surprise for you," he said, leading her into the backyard.

The sky was a bright cerulean beneath which the yew tree provided a patch of cool brown shade. In the pergola, the few chickens that were left pecked at the dirt, clucking and flapping.

An old bedsheet had been stretched between a branch of the yew tree and an iron hat rack that Antoine must have found in the barn. He led her to one of the chairs set on the stone patio. In the years of his absence, the moss and grass had begun to overtake this part of the yard, so her chair sat unsteadily on the uneven surface. She sat down carefully; she was unwieldy these days. The smile her husband gave her was both dazzling in its joy and startling in its intimacy. "The kids and I have been working on this all day. It's for you."

The kids and I.

Antoine took his place in front of the sagging sheet and lifted his good arm in a sweeping gesture. "Ladies and gentlemen, children and scrawny rabbits and chickens who smell like shit—"

Behind the curtain, Daniel giggled and Sophie shushed him.

"In the rich tradition of Madelaine in Paris, which was Mademoiselle Mauriac's first starring role, I give you the Le Jardin singers." With a flourish, he unsnapped one side of the sheet-curtain and swept it aside to reveal a wooden platform set upon the grass at a not-quite-level slant. On it, Sophie stood beside Daniel. Both wore blankets as capes, with a sprig of apple blossoms at the throat and crowns made of some shiny metal, onto which they had glued pretty rocks and bits of colored glass.

"Hi, Maman!" Daniel said, waving furiously.

"Shhh," Sophie said to him. "Remember?"

Daniel nodded seriously.

They turned carefully—the plank floor teetered beneath them—and held hands, facing Vianne.

Antoine brought a silver harmonica to his mouth and let out a mournful note. It hung in the air for a long time, vibrating in invitation, and then he started to play.

Sophie began to sing in a high, pure voice. *"Frère Jacques, Frère Jacques . . ."*

She squatted down and Daniel popped up, singing, *"Dormez-vous? Dormez-vous?"*

Vianne clamped her hand over her mouth but not before a little laughter slipped out.

Onstage, the song went on. She could see how happy Sophie was to do this once-ordinary thing, this little performance for her parents, and how hard Daniel was concentrating to do his part well.

It felt both profoundly magical and beautifully ordinary. A moment from the life they'd had before.

Vianne felt joy open up inside of her.

We're going to be all right, she thought, looking at Antoine. In the shade cast by the tree her great-grandfather had planted, with their children's voices in the air, she saw her other half, thought again: *We're going to be all right*.

"*. . . ding . . . dang . . . dong . . .*"

When the song ended, Vianne clapped wildly. The children bowed majestically. Daniel tripped on his bedspread cape and tumbled to the grass and came up laughing. Vianne waddled to the stage and smothered her children with kisses and compliments.

"What a lovely idea," she said to Sophie, her eyes shining with love and pride.

"I was concentrating, Maman," Daniel said proudly.

Vianne couldn't let them go. This future she'd glimpsed filled her soul with joy.

"I planned with Papa," Sophie said. "Just like before, Maman."

"I planned it, too," Daniel said, puffing out his little chest.

She laughed. "How *grand* you both were at singing. And—"

"Vianne?" Antoine said from behind her.

She couldn't look away from Daniel's smile. "How long did it take you to learn your part?"

"Maman," Sophie said quietly. "Someone is here."

Vianne turned to look behind her.

Antoine was standing near the back door with two men; both wore threadbare black suits and black berets. One carried a tattered briefcase.

"Sophie, take care of your brother for a minute," Antoine said to the children. "We have something to discuss with these men." He moved in beside Vianne, placing a hand at the small of her back, helping her to her feet, urging her forward. They filed into the house in a silent line.

When the door closed behind them, the men turned to face Vianne.

"I am Nathaniel Lerner," said the older of the two men. He had gray hair and skin the color of tea-stained linen. Age spots discolored large patches of his cheeks.

"And I am Phillipe Horowitz," said the other man. "We are from the OSE."

"Why are you here?" Vianne asked.

"We are here for Ari de Champlain," Phillipe said in a gentle voice. "He has relatives in America—Boston, in fact—and they have contacted us."

Vianne might have collapsed if Antoine had not held her steady.

"We understand you rescued nineteen Jewish children all by yourself. And with German officers billeted in your home. That's impressive, Madame."

"Heroic," Nathaniel added.

Antoine placed his hand on her shoulder and at that, his touch, she realized how long she'd been silent. "Rachel was my best friend," she said quietly. "I tried to help her sneak into the Free Zone before the deportation, but . . ."

"Her daughter was killed," Lerner said.

"How do you know that?"

"It is our job to collect stories and to reunite families," he answered. "We have spoken to several women who were in Auschwitz with Rachel. Sadly, she lived less than a month there. Her husband, Marc, was killed in Stalag 13A. He was not as lucky as your husband."

Vianne said nothing. She knew the men were giving her time and she both appreciated and hated it. She didn't want to accept any of this. "Daniel—*Ari*—was born a week before Marc left for the war. He has no memory of either of his parents. It was the safest way—to let him believe he was my son."

"But he is not your son, Madame." Lerner's voice was gentle but the words were like the lash of a whip.

"I promised Rachel I would keep him safe," she said.

"And you have. But now it is time for Ari to return to his family. To his people."

"He won't understand," she said.

"Perhaps not," Lerner said. "Still."

Vianne looked at Antoine for help. "We love him. He's part of our family. He should stay with us. You want him to stay, don't you, Antoine?"

Her husband nodded solemnly.

She turned to the men. "We could adopt him, raise him as our own. But Jewish, of course. We will tell him who he is and take him to synagogue and—"

"Madame," Lerner said with a sigh.

Phillipe approached Vianne, took her hands in his. "We know you love him and he loves you. We know that Ari is too young to understand and that he will cry and miss you—perhaps for years."

"But you want to take him anyway."

"You look at the heartbreak of one boy. I am here because of the heartbreak of my people. You understand?" His face sagged, his mouth curved into a small frown. "Millions of Jews were killed in this war, Madame. *Millions.*" He let that sink in. "An entire generation is gone. We need to band together now, those few of us who are left; we need to rebuild. One boy with no memory of who he was may seem a small thing to lose, but to us, he is the future. We cannot let you raise him in a religion that is not yours and take him to synagogue when you remember. Ari needs to be who he is, and to be with his people. Surely his mother would want that."

Vianne thought of the people she'd seen at the Hôtel Lutetia, those walking skeletons with their haunted eyes, and the endless wall of photographs.

Millions had been killed.

A generation lost.

How could she keep Ari from his people, his family? She would fight to the death for either of her children, but there was no opponent for her to fight, just loss on both sides.

"Who is taking him?" she said, not caring that her voice cracked on the question.

"His mother's first cousin. She has an eleven-year-old girl and a six-year-old son. They will love Ari as their own."

Vianne couldn't find the strength even to nod, or wipe the tears from her eyes. "Maybe they will send me pictures?"

Phillipe gazed at her. "He will need to forget you, Madame, to start a new life."

How keenly Vianne knew the truth of that. "When will you take him?"

"Now," Lerner said.

Now.

"We cannot change this?" Antoine asked.

"No, M'sieur," Phillipe said. "It is the right thing for Ari to return to his people. He is one of the lucky ones—he still has family living."

Vianne felt Antoine take her hand in his. He led her to the stairs, tugging more than once to keep her moving. She climbed the wooden steps on legs that felt leaden and unresponsive.

In her son's bedroom (no, not her son's) she moved like a sleepwalker, picking up his few clothes and gathering his belongings. A threadbare stuffed monkey whose eyes had been loved off, a piece of petrified wood he'd found by the river last summer, and the quilt Vianne had made from scraps of clothes he'd outgrown. On its back, she'd embroidered "To Our Daniel, love Maman, Papa, and Sophie."

She remembered when he'd first read it and said, "Is Papa coming back?" and she'd nodded and told him that families had a way of finding their way home.

"I don't want to lose him. I can't . . ."

Antoine held her close and let her cry. When she'd finally stilled, he murmured, "You're strong," against her ear. "We have to be. We love him, but he's not ours."

She was so tired of being strong. How many losses could she bear?

"You want me to tell him?" Antoine asked.

She wanted him to do it, wanted it more than anything, but this was a mother's job.

With shaking hands, she stuffed Daniel's—Ari's—belongings into a ragged canvas rucksack, and then walked out of the room, realizing a second too late that she'd left Antoine behind. It took everything she had to keep breathing, keep moving. She opened the door to her bedroom and burrowed through her armoire until she found a small framed photograph of herself and Rachel. It was the only picture she had of Rachel. It had been taken ten or twelve years ago. She wrote their names on the back and then shoved it into the pocket of the rucksack and left the room. Ignoring the men downstairs, she went out to the backyard, where the children—still in capes and crowns—were playing on the makeshift stage.

The three men followed her.

Sophie looked at all of them. "Maman?"

Daniel laughed. How long would she remember exactly that sound? Not long enough. She knew that now. Memories—even the best of them—faded.

"Daniel?" She had to clear her throat and try again. "Daniel? Could you come here?"

"What's wrong, Maman?" Sophie said. "You look like you've been crying."

She moved forward, clutching the rucksack to her side. "Daniel?"

He grinned up at her. "You want us to sing it again, Maman?" he asked, righting the crown as it slipped to one side of his head.

"Can you come here, Daniel?" she asked it twice, just to be sure. She was afraid too much of this was happening in her head.

He padded toward her, yanking his cape sideways so he didn't trip over it.

She knelt in the grass and took his hands in hers. "There's no way to make you understand this." Her voice caught. "In time, I would have told you everything. When you were older. We would have gone to your old house, even. But time's up, Captain Dan."

He frowned. "What do you mean?"

"You know how much we love you," she said.

"*Oui*, Maman," Daniel said.

"We love you, Daniel, and we have from the moment you came into our lives, but you belonged to another family first. You had another maman and another papa, and they loved you, too."

Daniel frowned. "I had another maman?"

Behind her, Sophie said, "Oh, no . . ."

"Her name was Rachel de Champlain, and she loved you with all her heart. And your papa was a brave man named Marc. I wish I could be the one to tell you their stories, but I can't"—she dashed tears from her eyes—"because your maman's cousin loves you, too, and she wants you to come live with them in America, where people have plenty to eat and lots of toys to play with."

Tears filled his eyes. "But *you're* my maman. I don't want to go."

She wanted to say "I don't want you to go," but that would only frighten him more, and her last job as his mother was to make him feel safe. "I know," she said quietly, "but you are going to love it, Captain Dan, and your new family will love and adore you. Maybe they will even have a puppy, like you've always wanted."

He started to cry, and she pulled him into her arms. It took perhaps the greatest courage of her life to let go of him. She stood. The two men immediately appeared at her side.

"Hello, young man," Phillipe said to Daniel, giving him an earnest smile. Daniel wailed.

Vianne took Daniel's hand and led him through the house and into the front yard, past the dead apple tree littered with remembrance ribbons and through the broken gate to the blue Peugeot parked on the side of the road.

Lerner got into the driver's seat while Phillipe waited near the back fender. The engine fired up; smoke puffed out from the rear exhaust.

Phillipe opened the back door. Giving Vianne one last sad look, he slid into the seat, leaving the car door open.

Sophie and Antoine came up beside her, and bent down together to hug Daniel.

"We will always love you, Daniel," Sophie said. "I hope you remember us."

Vianne knew that only she could get Daniel into the automobile. He would trust only her.

Of all the heartbreaking, terrible things she'd done in this war, none hurt as badly as this: She took Daniel by the hand and led him into the automobile that would take him away from her. He climbed into the backseat.

He stared at her through teary, confused eyes. "Maman?"

Sophie said, "Just a minute!" and ran back to the house. She returned a moment later with Bébé and thrust the stuffed rabbit at Daniel.

Vianne bent down to look him in the eye. "You need to go now, Daniel. Trust Maman."

His lower lip trembled. He clutched the toy to his chest. "*Oui*, Maman."

"Be a good boy."

Phillipe leaned over and shut the door.

Daniel launched himself at the window, pressing his palms to the glass. He was crying now, yelling, "Maman! Maman!" They could hear his screams for minutes after the automobile was gone.

Vianne said quietly, "Have a good life, Ari de Champlain."

THIRTY-EIGHT

*I*sabelle stood at attention. She needed to stand up straight for roll call. If she gave in to her dizziness and toppled over, they would whip her, or worse.

No. It wasn't roll call. She was in Paris now, in a hospital room.

She was waiting for something. For someone.

Micheline had gone to speak to the Red Cross workers and journalists gathered in the lobby. Isabelle was supposed to wait here.

The door opened.

"Isabelle," Micheline said in a scolding tone. "You shouldn't be standing."

"I'm afraid I'll die if I lie down," Isabelle said. Or maybe she thought the words.

Like Isabelle, Micheline was as thin as a matchstick, with hip bones that showed like knuckles beneath her shapeless dress. She was almost entirely bald—only tufts of hair grew here and there—and she had no eyebrows. The skin at her neck and along her arms was riddled with oozing, open sores. "Come," Micheline said. She led her out of the room, through the strange crowd of silent, shuffling, rag-dressed returnees and the loud, watery-eyed family members in search of loved ones, past the journalists who asked questions. She steered her gently to a quieter room, where other camp survivors sat slumped in chairs.

Isabelle sat down in a chair and dutifully put her hands in her lap. Her lungs ached and burned with every breath she drew and a headache pounded inside her skull.

"It's time for you to go home," Micheline said.

Isabelle looked up, blank and bleary-eyed.

"Do you want me to travel with you?"

She blinked slowly, trying to think. Her headache was blinding in its intensity. "Where am I going?"

"Carriveau. You're going to see your sister. She's waiting for you."

"She is?"

"Your train leaves in forty minutes. Mine leaves in an hour."

"How do we go back?" Isabelle dared to ask. Her voice was barely above a whisper.

"We are the lucky ones," Micheline said, and Isabelle nodded.

Micheline helped Isabelle stand.

Together they limped to the hospital's back door, where a row of automobiles and Red Cross lorries waited to transport survivors to the train station. As they waited their turn, they stood together, tucked close as they'd done so often in the past year—in *Appell* lines, in cattle cars, in food queues.

A bright-faced young woman in a Red Cross uniform came into the room, carrying a clipboard. "Rossignol?"

Isabelle lifted her hot, sweaty hands and cupped Micheline's wrinkled, grayed face. "I loved you, Micheline Babineau," she said softly and kissed the older woman's dry lips.

"Don't talk about yourself in the past tense."

"But I am past tense. The girl I was . . ."

"She's not gone, Isabelle. She's sick and she's been treated badly, but she can't be gone. She had the heart of a lion."

"Now you're speaking in the past tense." Honestly, Isabelle couldn't remember that girl at all, the one who'd jumped into the Resistance with barely a thought. The girl who'd recklessly brought an airman into her father's apartment and foolishly brought another one into her sister's barn. The girl who had hiked across the Pyrenees and fallen in love during the exodus from Paris.

"We made it," Micheline said.

Isabelle had heard those words often in the past week. *We made it.* When the Americans had arrived to liberate the camp, those three words had been on every prisoner's lips. Isabelle had felt relief then—after all of it, the beatings, the cold, the degradation, the disease, the forced march through the snow, she had survived.

Now, though, she wondered what her life could possibly be. She couldn't go back to who she'd been, but how could she go forward? She gave Micheline a last wave good-bye and climbed into the Red Cross vehicle.

Later, on the train, she pretended not to notice how people stared at her. She tried to sit up straight, but she couldn't do it. She slumped sideways, rested her head against the window.

She closed her eyes and was asleep in no time, dreaming feverishly of a clattering ride in a cattle car, of babies crying and women trying desperately to soothe them . . . and then the doors opened and the dogs were waiting—

Isabelle jolted awake. She was so disoriented it took her a moment to remember that she was safe. She dabbed at her forehead with the end of her sleeve. Her fever was back.

Two hours later, the train rumbled into Carriveau.

I made it. So, why didn't she *feel* anything?

She got to her feet and shuffled painfully from the train. As she stepped down onto the platform, a coughing spasm took over. She bent, hacking and coughing up blood into her hand. When she could breathe again, she straightened, feeling hollowed out and drained. Old.

Her sister stood at the edge of the platform. She was big with pregnancy and dressed in a faded and patched summer dress. Her strawberry blond hair was longer now, past her shoulders and wavy. As she scanned the crowd leaving the train, her gaze went right past Isabelle.

Isabelle raised her bony hand in greeting.

Vianne saw her wave and paled. "Isabelle!" Vianne cried, rushing toward her. She cupped Isabelle's hollow cheeks in her hands.

"Don't get too close. My breath is terrible."

Vianne kissed Isabelle's cracked, swollen, dry lips and whispered, "Welcome home, sister."

"Home," Isabelle repeated the unexpected word. She couldn't bring up any images to go along with it, her thoughts were so jumbled and her head pounded.

Vianne gently put her arms around Isabelle and pulled her close. Isabelle felt her sister's soft skin and the lemony scent of her hair. She felt her sister stroking her back, just as she'd done when she was a little girl, and Isabelle thought, *I made it.*

Home.

"You're burning up," Vianne said when they were back at Le Jardin, and Isabelle was clean and dry and lying in a warm bed.

"*Oui.* I can't seem to get rid of this fever."

"I will get you some aspirin." Vianne started to rise.

"No," Isabelle said. "Don't leave me. Please. Lie with me."

Vianne climbed into the small bed. Afraid that the lightest touch would leave a bruise, she gathered Isabelle close with exquisite care.

"I'm sorry about Beck. Forgive me . . ." Isabelle said, coughing. She'd waited so long to say it, imagined this conversation a thousand times. ". . . for the way I put you and Sophie in danger . . ."

"No, Isabelle," Vianne said softly, "forgive me. I failed you at every turn. Starting when Papa left us with Madame Dumas. And when you ran off to Paris, how could I believe your ridiculous story about an affair? That has haunted me." Vianne leaned toward her. "Can we start over now? Be the sisters Maman wanted us to be?"

Isabelle fought to stay awake. "I'd like that."

"I am so, so proud of what you did in this war, Isabelle."

Isabelle's eyes filled with tears. "What about you, V?"

Vianne looked away. "After Beck, another Nazi billeted here. A bad one."

Did Vianne realize that she touched her belly as she said it? That shame colored her cheeks? Isabelle knew instinctively what her sister had endured. Isabelle had heard countless stories of women being raped by the soldiers billeted with them. "You know what I learned in the camps?"

Vianne looked at her. "What?"

"They couldn't touch my heart. They couldn't change who I was inside. My body . . . they broke that in the first days, but not my heart, V. Whatever he did, it was to your body, and your body will heal." She wanted to say more, maybe add "I love you," but a hacking cough overtook her. When it passed, she lay back, spent, breathing shallow, ragged breaths.

Vianne leaned closer, pressed a cool, wet rag to her fevered forehead.

Isabelle stared at the blood on the quilt, remembering the end days of her mother's life. There had been such blood then, too. She looked at Vianne and saw that her sister was remembering it, too.

⁘

Isabelle woke on a wooden floor. She was freezing and on fire at the same time, shivering and sweating.

She heard nothing, no rats or cockroaches scurrying across the floor, no water bleeding through the wall cracks, turning to fat slugs of ice, no coughing or crying. She sat up slowly, wincing at every movement, no matter how fractional. Everything hurt. Her bones, her skin, her head, her chest; she had no muscles left to hurt, but her joints and ligaments ached.

She heard a loud *ra-ta-ta-tat*. Gunfire. She covered her head and scurried into the corner, crouching low.

No.

She was at Le Jardin, not Ravensbrück.

That sound was rain hitting the roof.

She got slowly to her feet, feeling dizzy. How long had she been here? Four days? Five?

She limped to the nightstand, where a porcelain pitcher sat beside a bowl of tepid water. She washed her hands and splashed water on her face and then dressed in the clothes Vianne had laid out for her—a dress that had belonged to Sophie when she was ten years old and bagged on Isabelle. She began the long, slow journey down the stairs.

The front door was open. Outside, the apple trees were blurred by a falling rain. Isabelle went to the doorway, breathing in the sweet air.

"Isabelle?" Vianne said, coming up beside her. "Let me get you some marrow broth. The doctor says you can drink it."

She nodded absently, letting Vianne pretend that the few tablespoons of broth Isabelle's stomach could hold would make a difference.

She stepped out into the rain. The world was alive with sound—birds cawing, church bells ringing, rain thumping on the roof, splashing in puddles. Traffic clogged the narrow, muddy road; automobiles and lorries and bicyclists, honking and waving, yelling out to one another as people came home. An American lorry rumbled past, full of smiling, fresh-faced soldiers who waved at passersby.

At the sight of them, Isabelle remembered Vianne telling her that Hitler had killed himself and Berlin had been surrounded and would fall soon.

Was that true? Was the war over? She didn't know, couldn't remember. Her mind was such a mess these days.

Isabelle limped out to the road, realizing too late that she was barefoot (she would get beaten for losing her shoes), but she kept going. Shivering, coughing, plastered by rain, she walked past the bombed-out airfield, taken over by Allied troops now.

"Isabelle!"

She turned, coughing hard, spitting blood into her hand. She was trembling now with cold, shivering. Her dress was soaking wet.

"What are you doing out here?" Vianne said. "And where are your shoes? You have typhus and pneumonia and you're out in the rain." Vianne took off her coat and wrapped it around Isabelle's shoulder.

"Is the war over?"

"We talked about this last night, remember?"

Rain blurred Isabelle's vision, fell in streaks down her back. She drew in a wet, shuddering breath and felt tears sting her eyes.

Don't cry. She knew that was important but she didn't remember why.

"Isabelle, you're sick."

"Gaëtan promised to find me after the war was over," she whispered. "I need to get to Paris so he can find me."

"If he came looking for you, he'd come to the house."

Isabelle didn't understand. She shook her head.

"He's been here, remember? After Tours. He brought you home."

My nightingale, I got you home.

"Oh.

"He won't think I'm pretty anymore." Isabelle tried to smile, but she knew it was a failure.

Vianne put an arm around Isabelle and gently turned her around. "We will go and write him a letter."

"I don't know where to send it," Isabelle said, leaning against her sister, shivering with cold and fire.

How did she make it home? She wasn't sure. She vaguely remembered Antoine carrying her up the stairs, kissing her forehead, and Sophie bringing her some hot broth, but she must have fallen asleep at some point because the next thing she knew night had fallen.

Vianne sat sleeping in a chair beneath the window.

Isabelle coughed.

Vianne was on her feet in an instant, fixing the pillows behind Isabelle, propping her up. She dunked a cloth in the water at the bedside, wrung out the excess, and pressed it to Isabelle's forehead. "You want some marrow broth?"

"God, no."

"You're not eating anything."

"I can't keep it down."

Vianne reached for the chair and dragged it close to the bed.

Vianne touched Isabelle's hot, wet cheek and gazed into her sunken eyes. "I have something for you." Vianne got up from her chair and left the room. Moments later, she was back with a yellowed envelope. She handed it to Isabelle. "This is for us. From Papa. He came by here on his way to see you in Girot."

"He did? Did he tell you that he was going to turn himself in to save me?"

Vianne nodded and handed Isabelle the letter.

The letters of her name blurred and elongated on the page. Malnutrition had ruined her eyesight. "Can you read it to me?"

Vianne unsealed the envelope and withdrew the letter and began to read.

> *Isabelle and Vianne,*
>
> *What I do now, I do without misgiving. My regret is not for my death, but for my life. I am sorry I was no father to you.*

I could make excuses—I was ruined by the
war, I drank too much, I couldn't go on without your
maman—but none of that matters.

Isabelle, I remember the first time you ran
away to be with me. You made it all the way to
Paris on your own. Everything about you said,
Love me. And when I saw you on that platform,
needing me, I turned away.

How could I not see that you and Vianne
were a gift, had I only reached out?

Forgive me, my daughters, for all of it,
and know that as I say good-bye, I loved you both
with all of my damaged heart.

Isabelle closed her eyes and lay back into the pillows. All her life she'd waited for those words—his love—and now all she felt was loss. They hadn't loved each other enough in the time they had, and then time ran out. "Hold Sophie and Antoine and your new baby close, Vianne. Love is such a slippery thing."

"Don't do that," Vianne said.

"What?"

"Say good-bye. You'll get strong and healthy and you'll find Gaëtan and you'll get married and be there when this baby of mine is born."

Isabelle sighed and closed her eyes. "What a pretty future that would be."

A week later, Isabelle sat in a chair in the backyard, wrapped in two blankets and an eiderdown comforter. The early May sun blazed down on her and still she was trembling with cold. Sophie sat in the grass at her feet, reading her a story. Her niece tried to use a different voice for each character and sometimes, even as bad as Isabelle felt, as much as her bones felt too heavy for her skin to bear, she found herself smiling, even laughing.

Antoine was somewhere, trying to build a cradle out of whatever scraps of wood Vianne hadn't burned during the war. It was obvious to everyone that Vianne would be going into labor soon; she moved slowly and seemed always to have a hand pressed to the small of her back.

With closed eyes, Isabelle savored the beautiful commonness of the day. In the distance, a church bell pealed. Bells had been ringing constantly in the past week to herald the war's end.

Sophie's voice stopped abruptly in the middle of a sentence.

Isabelle thought she said "keep reading," but she wasn't sure.

She heard her sister say, "Isabelle," in a tone of voice that meant something.

Isabelle looked up. Vianne stood there, flour streaking her pale, freckled face and dusting her apron, her reddish hair bound by a frayed turban. "Someone is here to see you."

"Tell the doctor I'm fine."

"It's not the doctor." Vianne smiled and said, "Gaëtan is here."

Isabelle felt as if her heart might burst through the paper walls of her chest. She tried to stand and fell back to the chair in a heap. Vianne helped her to her feet, but once she was standing, she couldn't move. How could she look at him? She was a bald, eyebrowless skeleton, with some of her teeth gone and most of her fingernails missing. She touched her head, realizing an awkward moment too late that she had no hair to tuck behind her ear.

Vianne kissed her cheek. "You're beautiful," she said.

Isabelle turned slowly, and there he was, standing in the open doorway. She saw how bad he looked—the weight and hair and vibrancy he'd lost—but none of it mattered. He was *here.*

He limped toward her and took her in his arms.

She brought her shaking hands up and put her arms around him. For the first time in days, weeks, a year, her heart was a reliable thing, pumping with life. When he drew back, he stared down at her and the love in his eyes burned away everything bad; it was just them again, Gaëtan and Isabelle, somehow falling in love in a world at war. "You're as beautiful as I remember," he said, and she actually laughed, and then she cried. She wiped her eyes, feeling foolish, but tears kept streaming down her face. She was crying for all of it at last—for the pain and loss and fear and anger, for the war and what it had done to her and to all of them, for the knowledge of evil she could never shake, for the horror of where she'd been and what she'd done to survive.

"Don't cry."

How could she not? They should have had a lifetime to share truths and secrets, to get to know each other. "I love you," she whispered, remembering that time so long ago when she'd said it to him before. She'd been so young and shiny then.

"I love you, too," he said, his voice breaking. "I did from the first minute I saw you. I thought I was protecting you by not telling you. If I'd known . . ."

How fragile life was, how fragile they were.

Love.

It was the beginning and end of everything, the foundation and the ceiling and the air in between. It didn't matter that she was broken and ugly and sick. He loved her and she loved him. All her life she had waited—longed for—people to love her, but now she saw what really mattered. She had known love, been blessed by it.

Papa. Maman. Sophie.

Antoine. Micheline. Anouk. Henri.

Gaëtan.

Vianne.

She looked past Gaëtan to her sister, the other half of her. She remembered Maman telling them that someday they would be best friends, that time would stitch their lives together.

Vianne nodded, crying now, too, her hand on her extended belly.

Don't forget me, Isabelle thought. She wished she had the strength to say it out loud.

THIRTY-NINE

May 7, 1995
Somewhere over France

*T*he lights in the airplane cabin come on suddenly.

I hear the *ding!* of the announcement system. It tells us that we are beginning our descent into Paris.

Julien leans over and adjusts my seat belt, making sure that my seat is in the locked, upright position. That I am safe.

"How does it feel to be landing in Paris again, Mom?"

I don't know what to say.

Hours later, the phone beside me rings.

I am still more than half asleep when I answer it. "Hello?"

"Hey, Mom. Did you sleep?"

"I did."

"It's three o'clock. What time do you want to leave for the reunion?"

"Let's walk around Paris. I can be ready in an hour."

"I'll come by and pick you up."

I ease out of a bed the size of Nebraska and head for the marble-everywhere bathroom. A nice hot shower brings me back to myself and wakens me, but it isn't until I am seated at the vanity, staring at my face magnified in the light-rimmed oval mirror, that it hits me.

I am home.

It doesn't matter that I am an American citizen, that I have spent more of my life in the United States than in France; the truth is that none of that matters. I am home.

I apply makeup carefully. Then I brush the snow-white hair back from my face, creating a chignon at the nape of my neck with hands that won't stop trembling. In the mirror, I see an elegant, ancient woman with velvety, pleated skin, glossy, pale pink lips, and worry in her eyes.

It is the best I can do.

Pushing back from the mirror, I go to the closet and withdraw the winter white slacks and turtleneck that I have brought with me. It occurs to me that perhaps color would have been a better choice. I wasn't thinking when I packed.

I am ready when Julien arrives.

He guides me out into the hallway, helping me as if I am blind and disabled, and I let him lead me through the elegant hotel lobby and out into the magic light of Paris in springtime.

But when he asks the doorman for a taxi, I insist. "We will walk to the reunion."

He frowns. "But it's in the Île de la Cité."

I wince at his pronunciation, but it is my own fault, really.

I see the doorman smile.

"My son loves maps," I say. "And he has never been to Paris before."

The man nods.

"It's a long way, Mom," Julien says, coming up to stand beside me. "And you're . . ."

"Old?" I can't help smiling. "I am also French."

"You're wearing heels."

Again, I say: "I'm French."

Julien turns to the doorman, who lifts his gloved hands and says, "*C'est la vie*, M'sieur."

"All right," Julien says at last. "Let's walk."

I take his arm and for a glorious moment, as we step out onto the bustling sidewalk, arm in arm, I feel like a girl again. Traffic rushes past us, honking and squealing; boys skateboard up the sidewalk, dodging in and out amid the throng of tourists and locals out on this brilliant afternoon. The air is full of chestnut blossoms and smells of baking bread, cinnamon, diesel fuel, car exhaust, and baked stone—smells that will forever remind me of Paris.

To my right, I see one of my mother's favorite *pâtisseries*, and suddenly I remember Maman handing me a butterfly macaron.

"Mom?"

I smile at him. "Come," I say imperiously, leading him into the small shop. There is a long line and I take my place at the end of it.

"I thought you didn't like cookies."

I ignore him and stare at the glass case full of beautifully colored macarons and *pain au chocolat*.

When it is my turn I buy two macarons—one coconut, one raspberry. I reach into the bag and get the coconut macaron, handing it to Julien.

We are outside again, walking, when he takes a bite and stops dead. "Wow," he says after a minute. Then, "Wow," again.

I smile. Everyone remembers their first taste of Paris. This will be his.

When he has licked his fingers and thrown the bag away, he links his arm through mine again.

At a pretty little bistro overlooking the Seine, I say, "Let's have a glass of wine."

It is just past five o'clock. The genteel cocktail hour.

We take a seat outside, beneath a canopy of flowering chestnut trees. Across the street, along the banks of the river, vendors are set up in green kiosks, selling everything from oil paintings to old *Vogue* covers to Eiffel Tower key chains.

We share a greasy, paper-wrapped cone of frites and sip wine. One glass turns into two, and the afternoon begins to give way to the haze of dusk.

I had forgotten how gently time passes in Paris. As lively as the city is, there's a stillness to it, a peace that lures you in. In Paris, with a glass of wine in your hand, you can just *be*.

All along the Seine, streetlamps come on, apartment windows turn golden.

"It's seven," Julien says, and I realize that he has been keeping time all along, waiting. He is so American. No sitting idle, forgetting oneself, not for this young man of mine. He has also been letting me settle myself.

I nod and watch him pay the check. As we stand, a well-dressed couple, both smoking cigarettes, glides in to take our seats.

Julien and I walk arm in arm to the Pont Neuf, the oldest bridge across the Seine. Beyond it is the Île de la Cité, the island that was once the heart of Paris. Notre Dame, with its soaring chalk-colored walls, looks like a giant bird of prey landing, gorgeous wings outstretched. The Seine captures and reflects dots of lamplight along its shores, golden coronas pulled out of shape by the waves.

"Magic," Julien says, and that is precisely true.

We walk slowly, crossing over this graceful bridge that was built more than four hundred years ago. On the other side, we see a street vendor closing up his portable shop.

Julien stops, picks up an antique snow globe. He tilts it and snow flurries and swirls within the glass, obscuring the delicate gilt Eiffel Tower.

I see the tiny white flakes, and I know it's all fake—nothing—but it makes me remember those terrible winters, when we had holes in our shoes and our bodies were wrapped in newsprint and every scrap of clothing we could find.

"Mom? You're shaking."

"We're late," I say. Julien puts down the antique snow globe and we are off again, bypassing the crowd waiting to enter Notre Dame.

The hotel is on a side street behind the cathedral. Next to it is the Hôtel-Dieu, the oldest hospital in Paris.

"I'm afraid," I say, surprising myself with the admission. I can't remember admitting such a thing in years, although it has often been true. Four months ago, when they told me the cancer was back, fear made me cry in the shower until the water ran cold.

"We don't have to go in," he says.

"Yes, we do," I say.

I put one foot in front of the other until I am in the lobby, where a sign directs us to the ballroom on the fourth floor.

When we exit the elevator, I can hear a man speaking through a microphone that amplifies and garbles his voice in equal measure. There is a table out in the hallway, with name tags spread out. It reminds me of that old television show: *Concentration*. Most of the tags are missing, but mine remains.

And there is another name I recognize; the tag is below mine. At the sight of it, my heart gives a little seize, knots up. I reach for my own name tag and pick it up. I peel off the back and stick the name tag to my sunken chest, but all the while, I am looking at the other name. I take the second tag and stare down at it.

"Madame!" says the woman seated behind the table. She stands, looking flustered. "We've been waiting for you. There's a seat—"

"I'm fine. I'll stand in the back of the room."

"Nonsense." She takes my arm. I consider resisting, but haven't the will for it just now. She leads me through a large crowd, seated wall to wall in the ballroom, on folding chairs, and toward a dais behind which three old women are seated. A young man in a rumpled blue sport coat and khaki pants—American, obviously—is standing at a podium. At my entrance, he stops speaking.

The room goes quiet. I feel everyone looking at me.

I sidle past the other old women on the dais and take my place at the empty chair next to the speaker.

The man at the microphone looks at me and says, "Someone very special is with us tonight."

I see Julien at the back of the room, standing against the wall, his arms crossed. He is frowning. No doubt he is wondering why anyone would put me on a dais.

"Would you like to say something?"

I think the man at the podium has asked me this question twice before it registers.

The room is so still I can hear chairs squeaking, feet tapping on carpet, women fanning themselves. I want to say, "no, no, not me," but how can I be so cowardly?

I get slowly to my feet and walk to the podium. While I'm gathering my thoughts, I glance to my right, at the old women seated at the dais and see their names: Almadora, Eliane, and Anouk.

My fingers clutch the wooden edges of the podium. "My sister, Isabelle, was a woman of great passions," I say quietly at first. "Everything she did, she did full speed ahead, no brakes. When she was little, we worried about her constantly. She was always running away from boarding schools and convents and finishing school, sneaking out of windows and onto trains. I thought she was reckless and irresponsible and almost too beautiful to look at. And during the war, she used that against me. She told me that she was running off to Paris to have an affair, and I believed her.

"I *believed* her. All these years later, that still breaks my heart a little. I should have known she wasn't following a man, but her beliefs, that she was doing something important." I close my eyes for a moment and remember: Isabelle, standing with Gaëtan, her arms around him, her eyes on me, shining with tears. With love. And then closing her eyes, saying something none of us could hear, taking her last breath in the arms of the man who loved her.

Then, I saw tragedy in it; now I see beauty.

I remember every nuance of that moment in my backyard, with the branches of the yew tree spread out above our heads and the scent of jasmine in the air.

I look down at the second name tag in my hand.

Sophie Mauriac.

My beautiful baby girl, who grew into a solemn, thoughtful woman, who stayed near me for the whole of her life, always worrying, fluttering around me like a mama hen. Afraid. She was always just a little afraid of the world after all that we had lived through, and I hated that. But she knew how to love, my Sophie, and when cancer came for her, she wasn't afraid. At the end, I was holding her hand, and she closed her eyes and said, "*Tante* . . . there you are."

Now, soon, they will be waiting for me, my sister and my daughter.

I tear my gaze away from the name tag and look out at the audience again. They don't care that I'm teary-eyed. "Isabelle and my father, Julien Rossignol, and their friends ran the Nightingale escape route. Together, they saved over one hundred and seventeen men."

I swallow hard. "Isabelle and I didn't talk much during the war. She stayed away from me to protect me from the danger of what she was doing. So I didn't know everything Isabelle had done until she came back from Ravensbrück."

I wipe my eyes. Now there are no squeaking chairs, no tapping feet. The audience is utterly still, staring up at me. I see Julien in the back, his handsome face a study in confusion. All of this is news to him. For the first time in his life, he understands the gulf between us, rather than the bridge. I am not simply his mother now, an extension of him. I am a woman in whole and he doesn't quite know what to make of me. "The Isabelle who came back from the concentration camp was not the woman who'd survived the bombing at Tours or crossed the Pyrenees. The Isabelle who came home was broken and sick. She was unsure of so many things, but not about what she'd done." I look out at the people seated in front of me. "On the day before she died, she sat in the shade beside me and held my hand and said, 'V, it's enough for me.' I said, 'What's enough?' and she said, 'My life. It's enough.'

"And it was. I know she saved some of the men in this room, but I know that you saved her, too. Isabelle Rossignol died both a hero and a woman in love. She couldn't have made a different choice. And all she wanted was to be remembered. So, I thank you all, for giving her life meaning, for bringing out the very best in her, and for remembering her all these years later."

I let go of the podium and step back.

The audience surges to their feet, clapping wildly. I see how many of the older people are crying and it strikes me suddenly: These are the families of the men she saved. Every man saved came home to create a family: more people who owed their lives to a brave girl and her father and their friends.

After that, I am sucked into a whirlwind of gratitude and memories and photographs. Everyone in the room wants to thank me personally and tell me how much Isabelle and my father meant to them. At some point, Julien settles himself along my side and becomes a bodyguard of sorts. I hear him say, "It looks like we have a lot to talk about," and I nod and keep moving, clinging to his arm. I do my best to be my sister's ambassador, collecting the thanks she deserves.

We are almost through the crowd—it is thinning now, people are making their way to the bar for wine—when I hear someone say, "Hello, Vianne," in a familiar voice.

Even with all the years that have passed, I recognize his eyes. Gaëtan. He is shorter than I remember, a little stooped in the shoulders, and his tanned face is deeply creased by both weather and time. His hair is long, almost to his shoulders, and as white as gardenias, but still I would know him anywhere.

"Vianne," he says. "I wanted you to meet my daughter." He reaches back for a classically beautiful young woman wearing a chic black sheath and vibrant pink neck scarf. She comes toward me, smiling as if we are friends.

"I'm Isabelle," she says.

I lean heavily into Julien's hand. I wonder if Gaëtan knows what this small remembrance would mean to Isabelle.

Of course he does.

He leans close and kisses each of my cheeks, whispering, "I loved her all of my life," as he draws back.

We talk for a few more minutes, about nothing really, and then he leaves.

Suddenly I am tired. Exhausted. I pull free of my son's possessive grip and move past the crowd to the quiet balcony. There, I step out into the night. Notre Dame is lit up, its glow coloring the black waves of the Seine. I can hear the river lapping against stone and boat lines creaking.

Julien comes up beside me.

"So," he says. "Your sister—my aunt—was in a concentration camp in Germany because she helped to create a route to save downed airmen, and this route meant that she hiked across the Pyrenees mountains?"

It is as heroic as he makes it sound.

"Why have I never heard anything about all this—and not just from you? Sophie never said a word. Hell, I didn't even know that people escaped over the mountains or that there was a concentration camp just for women who resisted the Nazis."

"Men tell stories," I say. It is the truest, simplest answer to his question. "Women get on with it. For us it was a shadow war. There were no parades for us when it was over, no medals or mentions in history books. We did what we had to during the war, and when it was over, we picked up the pieces and started our lives over. Your sister was as desperate to forget it as I was. Maybe that was another mistake I made—letting her forget. Maybe we should have talked about it."

"So Isabelle was off saving airmen and Dad was a prisoner of war and you were left alone with Sophie." I know he is seeing me differently already, wondering how much he doesn't know. "What did you do in the war, Mom?"

"I survived," I say quietly. At the admission, I miss my daughter almost more than I can bear, because the truth of it is that *we* survived. Together. Against all odds.

"That couldn't have been easy."

"It wasn't." The admission slips out, surprising me.

And suddenly we are looking at each other, mother and son. He is giving me his surgeon's look that misses nothing—not my newest wrinkles or the way my heart is beating a little too fast or the pulse that pumps in the hollow of my throat.

He touches my cheek, smiling softly. My boy. "You think the past could change how I feel about you? Really, Mom?"

"Mrs. Mauriac?"

I am glad for the interruption. It's a question I don't want to answer.

I turn to see a handsome young man waiting to talk to me. He is American, but not obviously so. A New Yorker, perhaps, with close-cropped graying hair and designer glasses. He is wearing a fitted black blazer and an expensive white shirt, with faded jeans. I step forward, extending my hand. He does the same thing at the same time, and when he does, our eyes meet and I miss a step. It is just that, a missed step, one among many at my age, but Julien is there to catch me. "Mom?"

I stare at the man before me. In him, I can see the boy I loved so deeply and the woman who was my best friend. "Ariel de Champlain," I say, his name a whisper, a prayer.

He takes me in his arms and holds me tightly and the memories return. When he finally pulls back, we are both crying.

"I never forgot you or Sophie," he says. "They told me to, and I tried, but I couldn't. I've been looking for you both for years."

I feel that constriction in my heart again. "Sophie passed away about fifteen years ago."

Ari looks away. Quietly, he says, "I slept with her stuffed animal for years."

"Bébé," I say, remembering.

Ari reaches into his pocket and pulls out the framed photograph of me and Rachel. "My mom gave this to me when I graduated from college."

I stare down at it through tears.

"You and Sophie saved my life," Ari says matter-of-factly.

I hear Julien's intake of breath and know what it means. He has questions now.

"Ari is my best friend's son," I say. "When Rachel was deported to Auschwitz, I hid him in our home, even though a Nazi billeted with us. It was quite . . . frightening."

"Your mother is being modest," Ari says. "She rescued nineteen Jewish children during the war."

I see the incredulity in my son's eyes and it makes me smile. Our children see us so imperfectly.

"I'm a Rossignol," I say quietly. "A Nightingale in my own way."

"A survivor," Ari adds.

"Did Dad know?" Julien asks.

"Your father . . ." I pause, draw in a breath. *Your father.* And there it is, the secret that made me bury it all.

I have spent a lifetime running from it, trying to forget, but now I see what a waste all that was.

Antoine was Julien's father in every way that mattered. It is not biology that determines fatherhood. It is love.

I touch his cheek and gaze up at him. "You brought me back to life, Julien. When I held you, after all that ugliness, I could breathe again. I could love your father again."

I never realized that truth before. Julien brought me back. His birth was a miracle in the midst of despair. He made me and Antoine and Sophie a family again. I named him after the father I learned to love too late, after he was gone. Sophie became the big sister she always wanted to be.

I will tell my son my life story at last. There will be pain in remembering, but there will be joy, too.

"You'll tell me everything?"

"Almost everything," I say with a smile. "A Frenchwoman must have her secrets." And I will . . . I'll keep one secret.

I smile at them, my two boys who should have broken me, but somehow saved me, each in his own way. Because of them, I know now what matters, and it is not what I have lost. It is my memories. Wounds heal. Love lasts.

We remain.

ACKNOWLEDGMENTS

*T*his book was a labor of love, and like a woman in labor, I often felt overwhelmed and desperate in that please-help-me-this-can't-be-what-I-signed-up-for-give-me-drugs kind of way. Yet, miraculously, it all came together in the end.

It literally takes a village of dedicated, tireless, type A–personality people to make a single book live up to its potential and find an audience. In the twenty plus years of my career, my work has been championed by some truly incredible individuals. I would like to take a paragraph or two—at long last and much overdue—to acknowledge a few who made a real difference. Susan Peterson Kennedy, Leona Nevler, Linda Grey, Elisa Wares, Rob Cohen, Chip Gibson, Andrew Martin, Jane Berkey, Meg Ruley, Gina Centrello, Linda Marrow, and Kim Hovey. Thanks to all of you for believing in me before I believed in myself. A special shout-out to Ann Patty, who changed the course of my career and helped me find my voice.

To the folks at St. Martin's and Macmillan. Your support and enthusiasm has had a profound impact on my career and my writing. Thanks to Sally Richardson for your tireless enthusiasm and your enduring friendship. To Jennifer Enderlin, my amazing editor, thank you for pushing me and demanding the very best from me. You rock. Thanks also to Alison Lazarus, Anne Marie Tallberg, Lisa Senz, Dori Weintraub, John Murphy,

Tracey Guest, Martin Quinn, Jeff Capshew, Lisa Tomasello, Elizabeth Catalano, Kathryn Parise, Susan Joseph, Astra Berzinskas, and the always fabulous, absolutely gifted Michael Storrings.

People often say that writing is a lonely profession, and it's true, but it can also be a brilliant party filled with interesting, amazing guests who speak in a shorthand that only a few understand. I have a few very special people who prop me up when I need it, aren't afraid to pour tequila when it's warranted, and help me celebrate the smallest victory. Thanks first and foremost to my longtime agent, Andrea Cirillo. Honestly, I couldn't have done it without you—and more important, I wouldn't have wanted to. To Megan Chance, my first and last reader, the red pen of doom, I thank you from the bottom of my heart. I wouldn't be here at all without our partnership. To Jill Marie Landis, you taught me an invaluable writing lesson this year, and it made *The Nightingale* what it is.

I would also like to thank fellow author Tatiana de Rosnay, whose generosity was an unexpected gift in the writing of this novel. She took time out of her busy schedule to help me make *The Nightingale* as accurate as possible. I am forever and profoundly grateful. Of course, any and all mistakes (and creative licenses) are my responsibility alone.

Thanks also to Dr. Miriam Klein Kassenoff, Director, Holocaust Studies Summer Institute/School of Education, University of Miami Coral Gables. Your help was invaluable.

Last, but certainly not least, to my family: Benjamin, Tucker, Kaylee, Sara, Laurence, Debbie, Kent, Julie, Mackenzie, Laura, Lucas, Logan, Frank, Toni, Jacqui, Dana, Doug, Katie, and Leslie. Storytellers, all. I love you guys.